D0821870

Also by
ALAN MAITLAND

Favourite Winter Stories
from Fireside Al

Favourite Summer Stories
from Front Porch Al

Favourite Christmas Stories
from Fireside Al

Favourite Sea Stories
from Seaside Al

Favourite Scary Stories from

GRAVESIDE AL

SELECTED
AND
INTRODUCED
BY

ALAN MAITLAND

VIKING

VIKING
Published by the Penguin Group
Penguin Books Canada Ltd, 10 Alcorn Avenue, Toronto, Ontario M4V 3B2
Penguin Books Ltd, 27 Wrights Lane, London W8 5TZ, England
Viking Penguin, a division of Penguin Books USA Inc., 375 Hudson Street,
New York, New York 10014, U.S.A.
Penguin Books Australia Ltd, Ringwood, Victoria, Australia
Penguin Books (NZ) Ltd, 182–190 Wairau Road, Auckland 10, New Zealand

Penguin Books Ltd, Registered Offices: Harmondsworth, Middlesex, England

First published 1996
10 9 8 7 6 5 4 3 2 1

Introductions, Notes and Selection Copyright © Alan Maitland, 1996

All rights reserved. Without limiting the rights under copyright reserved
above, no part of this publication may be reproduced, stored in or introduced into a retrieval system, or transmitted in any form or by any means
(electronic, mechanical, photocopying, recording or otherwise), without the
prior written permission of both the copyright owner and the above publisher
of this book.

Printed and bound in the United States of America on acid-free paper ⊖

Canadian Cataloguing in Publication Data

Main entry under title:

Favourite scary stories from Graveside Al

ISBN: 0-670-86863-9

1. Horror stories. I. Maitland, Alan.

PN6071.H727F3 1996   808.83'8738   C96-931025-0

Copyright acknowledgments appear on page 301. The acknowledgments
constitute an extension of this copyright page.

This book is dedicated to them
that craves and seeks terror.
In whispers, in the wind, the sea, the trees, a creaking
step, the fog; the unexplained—the unexplainable!
Have a sip of amontillado to provoke the imagination.
In pace requiescat.

"From ghoulies and ghosties and long-leggety beasties
And things that go bump in the night,
Good Lord, deliver us!"
anonymous,
Cornish prayer

ACKNOWLEDGMENTS

I am indebted to CBC's Mark Starowicz for starting the stories on "As It Happens," and of course to those who continued them. To Barbara Frum who dubbed me Fireside Al. To Jackie Kaiser of Penguin for transferring them from tape to the written page. It's exciting to see them collected in print. To George Jamieson and John Sweet for doing much of the early work, and to John for his help on historical matters. And to the many who have enjoyed the stories over the years on CBC radio. Now you can read them for yourselves. Enjoy!

Graveside Al

INTRODUCTION

What is it that makes scary stories so deliciously enticing, and so addictive? For as long as I can remember, I've had a special affection for the tales that can cause an otherwise rational individual—like myself—to peek under the bed before climbing into it, and jump six feet in the air when something goes thump.

I don't know the reason for the seemingly universal desire to terrify ourselves through fiction. Perhaps it's the comfort in understanding that, in the end, it *is* only a story—that black ink on a white page can do no real harm. But whatever the reason, scary tales are irresistible to me.

I recall as a child being tucked up in bed on stormy nights, hands clutching blankets to my chin, knees pulled up so far towards my head that they were almost on the pillow. The bedtime story always started off normally enough, with a description of a boy just like me—one who had to go to school every day, and who more often than not shared my dislike of spinach. Then, slowly but surely, the tension would mount. I think it was the *anticipation* of fear that was the most enjoyable thing. The certainty that the story would inevitably take a turn for the worse always produced nervous giggles, goosebumps and screams of delight.

The stories in this collection are all but guaranteed to haunt your imagination long after you've finished reading them. In fact, with many spooky stories, I find that the most chilling part comes after I put the book down, and my mind revisits the terrible, blood-curdling events. I was out chopping wood one recent afternoon, the light dusting of snow looking increasingly like a blinding Nova Scotia blizzard, when I found myself thinking of a tale I had reread a week or so earlier, the one about a boy who experiences everything through a veil of snow. The story took on a new power for me, and, as the final sentence reverberated in my mind, I felt a shiver of horror that had nothing to do with the sub-zero temperature. Such is the power of the written word.

Some readers may wonder whether immersing myself in so many scary stories has given me nightmares, or otherwise interfered with my ability to get a restful night's sleep. I am happy to report that despite my intimate relationship with stories that feature ghosts, werewolves, vampires and the like, I am sleeping very soundly these days—just as soundly, in fact, as I did at age nine, when I would drift off into blissful oblivion as the hero of my bedtime story escaped from the cusp of danger and returned to his warm home, his loving family, his chums, and of course his dreaded plate of spinach. So read on, and fear not.

TABLE OF CONTENTS

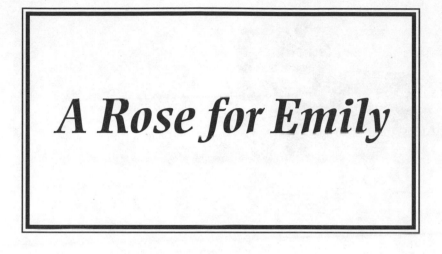

A Rose for Emily

by
WILLIAM FAULKNER
(1897–1962)

Certain localities seem especially well suited to the scary story: the fog-bound, barren moors of Cornwall, for example, or the remote mountainous regions of Germany and Romania with their wealth of folklore. William Faulkner's southern United States is such a place—a secretive land, where rigid protocol and manners can obscure the most awful deeds. "A Rose for Emily" is redolent of faded portraits, family pride, overstuffed furniture, dust and decay, and gossip behind lace curtains—all of which create the palpably oppressive atmosphere in which the townspeople speculate about the secrets hidden within Miss Emily's mansion.

1

When Miss Emily Grierson died, our whole town went to her funeral: the men through a sort of respectful affection for a fallen monument, the women mostly out of curiosity to see the inside of her house, which no one save an old manservant—a combined gardener and cook—had seen in at least ten years.

It was a big, squarish frame house that had once been white, decorated with cupolas and spires and scrolled balconies in the heavily lightsome style of the seventies, set on what had once been our most select street. But garages and cotton gins had encroached and obliterated even the august names of that neighbourhood; only Miss Emily's house was left, lifting its stubborn and coquettish decay above the cotton wagons and the gasoline pumps—an eyesore among eyesores. And now Miss Emily had gone to join the representatives of those august names where they lay in the cedar-bemused cemetery among the ranked and anonymous graves of Union and Confederate soldiers who fell at the battle of Jefferson.

Alive, Miss Emily had been a tradition, a duty, and a care; a sort of hereditary obligation upon the town, dating from that day in 1894 when Colonel Sartoris, the mayor—he who fathered the edict that no Negro woman should appear on the streets without an apron—remitted her taxes, the dispensation dating from the death of her father on into perpetuity. Not that Miss Emily would have accepted charity. Colonel Sartoris invented an involved tale to the effect that Miss Emily's father had loaned money to the town, which the town, as a matter of business, preferred this way of repaying. Only a man of Colonel Sartoris' generation and thought could have invented it, and only a woman could have believed it.

When the next generation, with its more modern ideas, became mayors and aldermen, this arrangement created some little dissatisfaction. On the first of the year they mailed her a tax notice. February came, and there was no reply. They wrote her a formal letter, asking her to call at the sheriff's office at her convenience. A week later the mayor wrote her himself, offering to call or to send his car for her, and received in reply a note on paper of an archaic shape, in a thin, flowing calligraphy in faded ink, to the effect that she no longer went out at all. The tax notice was also enclosed, without comment.

They called a special meeting of the Board of Aldermen. A deputation waited upon her, knocked at the door through which no visitor had passed since she ceased giving china-painting lessons eight or ten years earlier. They were admitted by the old Negro into a dim hall from which a stairway mounted into still more shadow. It smelled of dust and disuse—a close, dank smell. The Negro led them into the parlour. It was furnished in heavy, leather-covered furniture. When the Negro opened the blinds of one window, they could see that the leather was cracked and when they sat down, a faint dust rose sluggishly about their thighs, spinning with slow motes in the single sun-ray. On a tarnished gilt easel before the fireplace stood a crayon portrait of Miss Emily's father.

They rose when she entered—a small, fat woman in black, with a thin gold chain descending to her waist and vanishing into her belt, leaning on an ebony cane with a tarnished gold head. Her skeleton was small and spare; perhaps that was why what would have been merely plumpness in another was obesity in her. She looked bloated, like a body long submerged in motionless water, and of that pallid hue. Her eyes, lost in the fatty ridges of her face, looked like two small pieces of coal pressed into a lump of dough as they moved from one face to another while the visitors stated their errand.

She did not ask them to sit. She just stood in the door and listened quietly until the spokesman came to a stumbling halt. Then they could hear the invisible watch ticking at the end of the gold chain.

Her voice was dry and cold. "I have no taxes in Jefferson. Colonel Sartoris explained it to me. Perhaps one of you can gain access to the city records and satisfy yourselves."

"But we have. We are the city authorities, Miss Emily. Didn't you get a notice from the sheriff, signed by him?"

"I received a paper, yes," Miss Emily said. "Perhaps he considers himself the sheriff… I have no taxes in Jefferson."

"But there is nothing on the books to show that, you see. We must go by the—"

"See Colonel Sartoris. I have no taxes in Jefferson."

"But, Miss Emily—"

"See Colonel Sartoris." (Colonel Sartoris had been dead almost ten years.) "I have no taxes in Jefferson. Tobe!" The Negro appeared. "Show these gentlemen out."

2

So she vanquished them, horse and foot, just as she had vanquished their fathers thirty years before about the smell. That was two years after her father's death and a short time after her sweetheart—the one we believed would marry her—had deserted her. After her father's death she went out very little; after her sweetheart went away, people hardly saw her at all. A few of the ladies had the temerity to call, but were not received, and the only sign of life about the place was the Negro man—a young man then—going in and out with a market basket.

"Just as if a man—any man—could keep a kitchen properly," the ladies said; so they were not surprised when the smell developed. It was another link between the gross, teeming world and the high and mighty Griersons.

A neighbour, a woman, complained to the mayor, Judge Stevens, eighty years old.

"But what will you have me do about it, madam?" he said.

"Why, send her word to stop it," the woman said. "Isn't there a law?"

"I'm sure that won't be necessary," Judge Stevens said. "It's probably just a snake or a rat that nigger of hers killed in the yard. I'll speak to him about it."

The next day he received two more complaints, one from a man who came in diffident deprecation. "We really must do something about it, Judge. I'd be the last one in the world to bother Miss Emily, but we've got to do something." That night, the Board of Aldermen met—three greybeards and one younger man, a member of the rising generation.

"It's simple enough," he said. "Send her word to have her place cleaned up. Give her a certain time to do it in, and if she don't…"

"Dammit, sir," Judge Stevens said, "will you accuse a lady to her face of smelling bad?"

So the next night, after midnight, four men crossed Miss Emily's lawn and slunk about the house like burglars, sniffing along the base of the brickwork and at the cellar openings while one of them performed a regular sowing motion with his hand out of a sack slung from his shoulder. They broke open the cellar door and sprinkled lime there, and in all the out-buildings. As they recrossed the lawn, a window that had been dark was lighted and Miss Emily sat in it, the light behind her, and her upright torso motionless as that of an idol. They crept quietly across the lawn and into the shadow of the locusts that lined the street. After a week or two the smell went away.

That was when people had begun to feel really sorry for her. People in our town, remembering how old lady Wyatt, her great-aunt, had gone completely crazy at last, believed that the Griersons held themselves a little too high for what they really were. None of the young men were quite good enough for Miss Emily and such. We had long thought of them as a tableau, Miss Emily a slender figure in white in the back-ground, her father a spraddled silhouette in the foreground, his back to her and clutching a horsewhip, the two of them framed by the back-flung front door. So when she got to be thirty and was still single, we were not pleased exactly, but vindicated; even with insanity in the family she wouldn't have turned down all of her chances if they had really materialized.

When her father died, it got about that the house was all that was left to her; and in a way, people were glad. At last they could pity Miss Emily. Being left alone, and a pauper, she had become humanized. Now she too would know the old thrill and the old despair of a penny more or less.

The day after his death all the ladies prepared to call at the house and offer condolence and aid, as is our custom. Miss Emily met them at the door, dressed as usual and with no trace of grief on her face. She told them that her father was not dead. She did that for three days, with the ministers calling on her, and the doctors, trying to persuade her to let them dispose of the body. Just as they were about to resort to law and force, she broke down, and they buried her father quickly.

We did not say she was crazy then. We believed she had to do that. We remembered all the young men her father had driven away, and we knew that with nothing left, she would have to cling to that which had robbed her, as people will.

3

She was sick for a long time. When we saw her again, her hair was cut short, making her look like a girl, with a vague resemblance to those angels in coloured church windows—sort of tragic and serene.

The town had just let the contracts for paving the sidewalks, and in the summer after her father's death they began the work. The construction company came with niggers and mules and machinery, and a foreman named Homer Barron, a Yankee—a big, dark, ready man, with a big voice and eyes lighter than his face. The little boys would follow in groups to hear him cuss the niggers, and the niggers singing in time to the rise and fall of picks. Pretty soon he knew everybody in town. Whenever you heard a lot of laughing anywhere about the square, Homer Barron would be in the centre of the group. Presently we began to see him and Miss Emily on Sunday afternoons driving in the yellow-wheeled buggy and the matched team of bays from the livery stable.

At first we were glad that Miss Emily would have an interest, because the ladies all said, "Of course a Grierson would not think seriously of a Northerner, a day labourer." But there were still others, older people, who said that even grief could not cause a real lady to forget *noblesse oblige*—without calling it *noblesse oblige*. They just said, "Poor Emily. Her kinsfolk should come to her." She had some kin in Alabama; but years ago her father had fallen out with them over the estate of old lady Wyatt, the crazy woman, and there was no communication between the two families. They had not even been represented at the funeral.

And as soon as the old people said, "Poor Emily," the whispering began. "Do you suppose it's really so?" they said to one another. "Of course it is. What else could..." This behind their hands; rustling of craned silk and satin behind jalousies closed upon the sun of Sunday afternoon as the thin, swift clop-clop-clop of the matched team passed: "Poor Emily."

She carried her head high enough—even when we believed that she was fallen. It was as if she demanded more than ever the recognition of her dignity as the last Grierson; as if it had wanted that touch of earthiness to reaffirm her imperviousness. Like when she bought the rat poison, the arsenic. That was over a year after they had begun to say "Poor Emily," and while the two female cousins were visiting her.

"I want some poison," she said to the druggist. She was over thirty then, still a slight woman, though thinner than usual, with cold, haughty black eyes in a face the flesh of which was strained across the temples and about the eye-sockets as you imagine a lighthouse-keeper's face ought to look. "I want some poison," she said.

"Yes, Miss Emily. What kind? For rats and such? I'd recom—"

"I want the best you have. I don't care what kind."

The druggist named several. "They'll kill anything up to an elephant. But what you want is—"

"Arsenic," Miss Emily said. "Is that a good one?"

"Is...arsenic? Yes, ma'am. But what you want—"

"I want arsenic."

The druggist looked down at her. She looked back at him, erect, her face like a strained flag. "Why, of course," the druggist said. "If that's what you want. But the law requires you to tell what you are going to use it for."

Miss Emily just stared at him, her head tilted back in order to look him eye for eye, until he looked away and went and got the arsenic and wrapped it up. The Negro delivery boy brought her the package; the druggist didn't come back. When she opened the package at home there was written on the box, under the skull and bones: "For rats."

4

So the next day we all said, "She will kill herself"; and we said it would be the best thing. When she had first begun to be seen with Homer Barron, we had said, "She will marry him." Then we said, "She will persuade him yet," because Homer himself had remarked—he liked men, and it was known that he drank with the younger men in the Elks' Club—that he was not a marrying man. Later we said, "Poor Emily" behind the jalousies as they passed on Sunday afternoon in the glittering buggy, Miss Emily with her head high and Homer Barron with his hat cocked and a cigar in his teeth, reins and whip in a yellow glove.

Then some of the ladies began to say that it was a disgrace to the town and a bad example to the young people. The men did not want to interfere, but at last the ladies forced the Baptist minister—Miss Emily's people were Episcopal—to call upon her. He would never divulge what happened during that interview, but he refused to go back again. The next Sunday they again drove about the streets, and the following day the minister's wife wrote to Miss Emily's relations in Alabama.

So she had blood-king under her roof again and we sat back to watch developments. At first nothing happened. Then we were sure that they were to be married. We learned that Miss Emily had been to the jeweller's and ordered a man's toilet set in silver, with the letters H.B. on each piece. Two days later we learned that she had bought a complete outfit of men's clothing, including a nightshirt, and we said, "They are married." We were really glad. We were glad because the two female cousins were even more Grierson that Miss Emily had ever been.

So we were not surprised when Homer Barron—the streets had been finished some time since—was gone. We were a little disappointed that there was not a public blowing-off, but we believed that he had gone on to prepare for Miss Emily's coming, or to give her a chance to get rid of the cousins. (By that time it was a cabal, and we were all Miss Emily's allies to help circumvent the cousins.) Sure enough, after another week they departed. And, as we had expected all along, within three days Homer Barron was back in town. A neighbour saw the Negro man admit him at the kitchen door at dusk one evening.

And that was the last we saw of Homer Barron. And of Miss Emily for some time. The Negro man went in and out with the market basket, but the front door remained closed. Now and then we would see her at a window for a moment, as the men did that night when they sprinkled the lime, but for almost six months she did not appear on the streets. Then we knew that this was to be expected too; as if that quality of her father which had thwarted her woman's life so many times had been too virulent and too furious to die.

When we next saw Miss Emily, she had grown fat and her hair was turning grey. During the next few years it grew greyer and greyer until it attained an even pepper-and-salt iron-grey, when it ceased turning. Up to the day of her death at seventy-four it was still that vigorous iron-grey, like the hair of an active man.

From that time on her front door remained closed, save for a period of six or seven years, when she was about forty, during which she gave lessons in china-painting. She fitted up a studio in one of the downstairs rooms, where the daughters and granddaughters of Colonel Sartoris' contemporaries were

sent to her with the same regularity and in the same spirit that
they were sent to church on Sundays with a twenty-five-cent
piece for the collection plate. Meanwhile her taxes had been
remitted.

Then the newer generation became the backbone and the
spirit of the town, and the painting pupils grew up and fell
away and did not send their children to her with boxes of
colour and tedious brushes and pictures cut from the ladies'
magazines. The front door closed upon the last one and
remained closed for good. When the town got free postal
delivery, Miss Emily alone refused to let them fasten the metal
numbers above her door and attach a mailbox to it. She would
not listen to them.

Daily, monthly, yearly we watched the Negro grow greyer
and more stooped, going in and out with the market basket.
Each December we sent her a tax notice, which would be
returned by the post office a week later, unclaimed. Now and
then we would see her in one of the downstairs windows—
she had evidently shut up the top floor of the house—like the
carven torso of an idol in a niche, looking or not looking at
us, we could never tell which. Thus she passed from generation to generation—dear, inescapable, impervious, tranquil,
and perverse.

And so she died. Fell ill in the house filled with dust and
shadows, with only a doddering Negro man to wait on her. We
did not even know she was sick; we had long since given up
trying to get any information from the Negro. He talked to no
one, probably not even to her, for his voice had grown harsh
and rusty, as if from disuse.

She died in one of the downstairs rooms, in a heavy walnut
bed with a curtain, her grey head propped on a pillow yellow
and mouldy with age and lack of sunlight.

5

The Negro met the first of the ladies at the front door and let
them in, with their hushed, sibilant voices and their quick,
curious glances, and then he disappeared. He walked right
through the house and out the back and was not seen again.

The two female cousins came at once. They held a funeral on the second day, with the town coming to look at Miss Emily beneath a mass of bought flowers, with the crayon face of her father musing profoundly above the bier and the ladies sibilant and macabre; and the very old men—some in their brushed Confederate uniforms—on the porch and the lawn, talking of Miss Emily as if she had been a contemporary of theirs, believing that they had danced with her and courted her perhaps, confusing time with its mathematical progression, as the old do, to whom all the past is not a diminishing road but, instead, a huge meadow which no winter ever quite touches, divided from them now by the narrow bottleneck of the most recent decade of years.

Already we knew that there was one room in that region above stairs which no one had seen in forty years, and which would have to be forced. They waited until Miss Emily was decently in the ground before they opened it.

The violence of breaking down the door seemed to fill this room with pervading dust. A thin, acrid pall as of the tomb seemed to lie everywhere upon this room decked and furnished as for a bridal: upon the valance curtains of faded rose colour, upon the rose-shaded lights, upon the dressing-table, upon the delicate array of crystal and the man's toilet things backed with tarnished silver, silver so tarnished that the monogram was obscured. Among them lay a collar and tie, as if they had just been removed, which, lifted, left upon the surface a pale crescent in the dust. Upon a chair hung the suit, carefully folded; beneath it the two mute shoes and the discarded socks.

The man himself lay in the bed.

For a long while we just stood there, looking down at the profound and fleshless grin. The body had apparently once lain in the attitude of an embrace, but now the long sleep that outlasts love, that conquers even the grimace of love, had cuckolded him. What was left of him, rotted beneath what was left of the nightshirt, had become inextricable from the bed in which he lay; and upon him and upon the pillow beside him lay that even coating of the patient and biding dust.

Then we noticed that in the second pillow was the indentation of a head. One of us lifted something from it, and leaning forward, that faint and invisible dust dry and acrid in the nostrils, we saw a long strand of iron-grey hair.

Fear and *Which?*

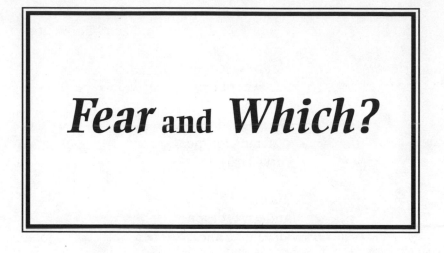

by
WALTER DE LA MARE
(1873–1956)

The scary poem is a rare creature. Walter de la Mare, poet and short-story writer, has a true affinity for that which is not seen but sensed, not heard but suggested. These two short pieces are wonderfully atmospheric, delicate evocations of those things (real or imagined?) that frighten us.

Fear

I know where lurk
The eyes of Fear;
I, I alone,
Where shadowy-clear,
Watching for me,
Lurks Fear.

'Tis ever still
And dark, despite
All singing and
All candlelight,
'Tis ever cold,
And night.

He touches me;
Says quietly,
"Stir not, nor whisper,
I am nigh;
Walk noiseless on,
I am by!"

He drives me
As a dog a sheep;
Like a cold stone
I cannot weep.
He lifts me
Hot from sleep.

In marble hands
To where on high
The jewelled horror
Of his eye
Dares me to struggle
Or cry.

No breast wherein
To chase away
That watchful shape!
Vain, vain to say,
"Haunt not with night
The day!"

Which?

"What did you say?"
"I? Nothing." "No?...
What was that sound?"
            "When?"
            "Then."
"I do not know."
"Whose eyes were those on us?"
                    "Where?"
                    "There."
            "No eyes I saw."
"Speech, footfall, presence—how cold the night may be!"
"Phantom or fantasy, it's all one to *me*."

Kiss Me Again, Stranger

by
DAPHNE DU MAURIER
(1907–1989)

Daphne du Maurier sometimes seems to me like a literary Alfred Hitchcock, effortlessly creating suspense from the very first paragraph (or, rather, using great effort and craft to create the illusion of effortless suspense). It's not surprising that Hitchcock used her work as the basis for a couple of his films. In "Kiss Me Again, Stranger," du Maurier's narrator is an innocent young mechanic who aspires to nothing more than a moderately comfortable existence with his "girl." The sincerity of the narrative voice (with its slang expressions and conversational quality) is perhaps the author's finest achievement here, instilling in the reader an empathy that enables the story to transcend the horror genre.

17

I looked around for a bit, after leaving the army and before settling down, and then I found myself a job up Hampstead way, in a garage it was, at the bottom of Haverstock Hill near Chalk Farm, and it suited me fine. I'd always been one for tinkering with engines, and in R.E.M.E. that was my work and I was trained to it—it had always come easy to me, anything mechanical.

My idea of having a good time was to lie on my back in my greasy overalls under a car's belly, or a lorry's, with a spanner in my hand, working on some old bolt or screw, with the smell of oil about me, and someone starting up an engine, and the other chaps around clattering their tools and whistling. I never minded the smell or the dirt. As my old Mum used to say when I'd be that way as a kid, mucking about with a grease can, "It won't hurt him, it's clean dirt," and so it is, with engines.

The boss at the garage was a good fellow, easygoing, cheerful, and he saw I was keen on my work. He wasn't much of a mechanic himself, so he gave me the repair jobs, which was what I liked.

I didn't live with my old Mum—she was too far off, over Shepperton way, and I saw no point in spending half the day getting to and from my work. I like to be handy, have it on the spot, as it were. So I had a bedroom with a couple called Thompson, only ten minutes' walk away from the garage. Nice people, they were. He was in the shoe business, cobbler I suppose he'd be called, and Mrs. Thompson cooked the meals and kept the house for him over the shop. I used to eat with them, breakfast and supper—we always had a cooked supper—and being the only lodger I was treated as family.

I'm one for routine. I like to get on with my job, and then when the day's work's over settle down to a paper and a smoke and a bit of music on the wireless, variety or something of the sort, and then turn in early. I never had much use for girls, not even when I was doing my time in the army. I was out in the Middle East, too, Port Said and that.

No, I was happy enough living with the Thompsons, carrying on much the same day after day, until that one night, when it happened. Nothing's been the same since. Nor ever will be. I don't know...

The Thompsons had gone to see their married daughter up at Highgate. They asked me if I'd like to go along, but somehow I didn't fancy barging in, so instead of staying home alone after leaving the garage I went down to the picture palace, and taking a look at the poster saw it was cowboy and Indian stuff—there was a picture of a cowboy sticking a knife into the Indian's guts. I like that—proper baby I am for westerns—so I paid my one and twopence and went inside. I handed my slip of paper to the usherette and said, "Back row, please," because I like sitting far back and leaning my head against the board.

Well, then I saw her. They dress the girls up no end in some of these places, velvet tams and all, making them proper guys. They hadn't made a guy out of this one, though. She had copper hair, page-boy style I think they call it, and blue eyes, the kind that look short-sighted but see further than you think, and go dark by night, nearly black, and her mouth was sulky-looking, as if she was fed up, and it would take someone giving her the world to make her smile. She hadn't freckles, nor a milky skin, but warmer than that, more like a peach, and natural too. She was small and slim, and her velvet coat—blue it was—fitted her close, and the cap on the back of her head showed up her copper hair.

I bought a programme—not that I wanted one, but to delay going in through the curtain—and I said to her, "What's the picture like?"

She didn't look at me. She just went on staring into nothing, at the opposite wall. "The knifing's amateur," she said, "but you can always sleep."

I couldn't help laughing. I could see she was serious though. She wasn't trying to have me on or anything.

"That's no advertisement," I said. "What if the manager heard you?"

Then she looked at me. She turned those blue eyes in my direction, still fed-up they were, not interested, but there was something in them I'd not seen before, and I've never seen it since, a kind of laziness like someone waking from a long dream and glad to find you there. Cat's eyes have that glean sometimes, when you stroke them, and they purr and curl themselves into a ball and let you do anything you want. She looked at me this way a moment, and there was a smile lurking somewhere behind her mouth if you gave it a chance, and tearing my slip of paper in half she said, "I'm not paid to advertise. I'm paid to look like this and lure you inside."

She drew aside the curtains and flashed her torch in the darkness. I couldn't see a thing. It was pitch black, like it always is at first until you get used to it and begin to make out the shapes of the other people sitting there, but there were two great heads on the screen and some chap saying to the other, "If you don't come clean I'll put a bullet through you," and somebody broke a pane of glass and a woman screamed.

"Looks all right to me," I said, and began groping for somewhere to sit.

She said, "This isn't the picture, it's the trailer for next week," and she flicked on her torch and showed me a seat in the back row, one away from the gangway.

I sat through the advertisements and the news reel, and then some chap came and played the organ, and the colours of the curtains over the screen went purple and gold and green—

funny, I suppose they think they have to give you your money's worth—and looking around I saw the house was half empty—and I guessed the girl had been right, the big picture wasn't going to be much, and that's why nobody much was there.

Just before the hall went dark again she came sauntering down the aisle. She had a tray of ice-creams, but she didn't even bother to call them out and try and sell them. She could have been walking in her sleep, so when she went up the other aisle I beckoned to her.

"Got a sixpenny one?" I said.

She looked across at me. I might have been something dead under her feet, and then she must have recognized me, because that half smile came back again, and the lazy look in the eye, and she walked round the back of the seats to me.

"Wafer or cornet?" she said.

I didn't want either, to tell the truth. I just wanted to buy something from her and keep her talking.

"Which do you recommend?" I asked.

She shrugged her shoulders. "Cornets last longer," she said, and put one in my hand before I had time to give her my choice.

"How about one for you too?" I said.

"No thanks," she said, "I saw them made."

And she walked off, and the place went dark, and there I was sitting with a great sixpenny cornet in my hand looking a fool. The damn thing slopped all over the edge of the holder, spilling on to my shirt, and I had to ram the frozen stuff into my mouth as quick as I could for fear it would all go on my knees, and I turned sideways, because someone came and sat in the empty seat beside the gangway.

I finished it at last, and cleaned myself up with my pocket handkerchief, and the concentrated on the story flashing across the screen. It was a western all right, carts lumbering over prairies, and a train full of bullion being held to ransom, and the heroine in breeches one moment and full evening dress the next. That's the way a picture should be, not a bit like real life at all; but as I watched the story I began to notice the whiff of scent in the air, and I didn't know what it was or where it came from, but it was there just the same. There was a man to the right of me, and on my left were two empty seats, and it certainly wasn't the people in front, and I couldn't keep turning round and sniffing.

I'm not a great one for liking scent. It's too often cheap and nasty, but this was different. There was nothing stale about it, or stuffy, or strong; it was like the flowers they sell up in the West End in the big flower shops before you get them on the barrows—three bob a bloom sort of touch, rich chaps buy them for actresses and such—and it was so darn good, the smell of it there, in that murky old picture palace full of cigarette smoke, that it nearly drove me mad.

At last I turned right round in my seat, and I spotted where it came from. It came from the girl, the usherette; she was leaning on the back board behind me, her arms folded across it.

"Don't fidget," she said. "You're wasting one and twopence. Watch the screen."

But not out loud, so that anyone could hear. In a whisper, for me alone. I couldn't help laughing to myself. The cheek of it! I knew where the scent came from now, and somehow it made me enjoy the picture more. It was as though she was beside me in one of the empty seats and we were looking at the story together.

When it was over, and the lights went on, I saw I'd sat through the last showing and it was nearly ten. Everyone was clearing off for the night. So I waited for a bit, and then she came down with her torch and started squinting under the seats to see if anybody had dropped a glove or a purse, the way they do and only remember about afterwards when they get home, and she took no more notice of me than if I'd been a rag which no one would bother to pick up.

I stood up in the back row, alone—the house was clear now—and when she came to me she said, "Move over, you're blocking the gangway," and flashed about with her torch, but there was nothing there, only an empty packet of Player's which the cleaners would throw away in the morning. Then she straightened herself and looked me up and down, and taking off the ridiculous cap from the back of her head that suited her so well she fanned herself with it and said, "Sleeping here tonight?" and then went off, whistling under her breath, and disappeared through the curtains.

It was proper maddening. I'd never been taken so much with a girl in my life. I went into the vestibule after her, but she had gone through a door to the back, behind the box-office place, and the commissionaire chap was already getting the doors to and fixing them for the night. I went out and stood in the street and waited. I felt a bit of a fool, because the odds were that she would come out with a bunch of others, the way girls do. There was the one who had sold me my ticket, and I dare say there were other usherettes up in the balcony, and perhaps a cloakroom attendant too, and they'd all be giggling together, and I wouldn't have the nerve to go up to her.

In a few minutes, though, she came swinging out of the place alone. She had a mac on, belted, and her hands in her pockets, and she had no hat. She walked straight up the street, and she didn't look to right or left of her. I followed, scared that she would turn round and see me off, but she went on walking, fast and direct, staring straight in front of her, and as she moved her copper page-boy hair swung with her shoulders.

Presently she hesitated, then crossed over and stood waiting for a bus. There was a queue of four or five people, so she didn't see me join the queue, and when the bus came she climbed on to it, ahead of the others, and I climbed too, without the slightest notion where it was going, and I couldn't have cared less. Up the stairs she went with me after her, and settled herself in the back seat, yawning, and closed her eyes.

I sat myself down beside her, nervous as a kitten, the point being that I never did that sort of thing as a rule and expected a rocket, and when the conductor stumped up and asked for fares I said, "Two sixpennies, please," because I reckoned she would never be going the whole distance and this would be bound to cover her fare and mine too.

He raised his eyebrows—they like to think themselves smart, some of these fellows—and he said, "Look out for the bumps when the driver changes gear. He's only just passed his test." And he went down the stairs chuckling, telling himself he was no end of a wag, no doubt.

The sound of his voice woke the girl, and she looked at me out of her sleepy eyes, and looked too at the tickets in my hand—she must have seen by the colour they were sixpennies—and she smiled, the first real smile I had got out of her that evening, and said without any sort of surprise, "Hullo, stranger."

I took out a cigarette, to put myself at ease, and offered her one, but she wouldn't take it. She just closed her eyes again, to settle herself to sleep. Then, seeing there was no one else to notice up on the top deck, only an Air Force chap in the front slopped over a newspaper, I put out my hand and pulled her head down on my shoulder, and got my arm round her, snug and comfortable, thinking of course she'd throw it off and blast me to hell. She didn't, though. She gave a sort of laugh to herself, and settled down like as if she might have been in an armchair, and she said, "It's not every night I get a free ride and a free pillow. Wake me at the bottom of the hill, before we get to the cemetery."

I didn't know what hill she meant, or what cemetery, but I wasn't going to wake her, not me. I had paid for two sixpennies, and I was darn well going to get value for my money.

So we sat there together, jogging along in the bus, very close and very pleasant, and I thought to myself that it was a lot more fun than sitting at home in the bedsit reading the football news, or spending an evening up Highgate at Mr. and Mrs. Thompson's daughter's place.

Presently I got more daring, and let my head lean against hers, and tightened up my arm a bit, not too obvious-like, but nicely. Anyone coming up the stairs to the top deck would have taken us for a courting couple.

Then, after we had had about fourpenny-worth, I got anxious. The old bus wouldn't be turning round and going back again, when we reached the sixpenny limit; it would pack up for the night, we'd have come to the terminus. And there we'd be, the girl and I, stuck out somewhere at the back of beyond, with no return bus, and I'd got about six bob in my pocket and no more. Six bob would never pay for a taxi, not with a tip and all. Besides, there probably wouldn't be any taxis going.

What a fool I'd been not to come out with more money. It was silly, perhaps, to let it worry me, but I'd acted on impulse right from the start, and if only I'd known how the evening was going to turn out I'd have had my wallet filled. It wasn't often I went out with a girl, and I hate a fellow who can't do the thing in style. Proper slap-up at a Corner House—they're good these days with that help-yourself service—and if she had a fancy for something stronger than coffee or orangeade, well, of course as late as this it wasn't much use, but nearer home I knew where to go. There was a pub where my boss went, and you paid for your gin and kept it there, and could go in and have a drink from your bottle when you felt like it. They have the same sort of racket at the posh nightclubs up West, I'm told, but they make you pay through the nose for it.

Anyway, here I was riding a bus to the Lord knows where, with my girl beside me—I called her "my girl" just as if she really was and we were courting—and bless me if I had the money to take her home. I began to fidget about, from sheer nerves, and I fumbled in one pocket after another, in case by a piece of luck I should come across a half-crown, or even a ten bob note I had forgotten all about, and I suppose I disturbed her with all this, because she suddenly pulled my ear and said, "Stop rocking the boat."

Well, I mean to say... It just got me. I can't explain why. She held my ear a moment before she pulled it, like as though she were feeling the skin and liked it, and then she just gave it a lazy tug. It's the kind of thing anyone would do to a child, and the way she said it, as if she had known me for years and we were out picnicking together, "Stop rocking the boat." Chummy, matey, yet better than either.

"Look here," I said, "I'm awfully sorry, I've been and done a darn silly thing. I took tickets to the terminus because I wanted to sit beside you, and when we get there we'll be turned out of the bus, and it will be miles from anywhere, and I've only got six bob in my pocket."

"You've got legs, haven't you?" she said.

"What d'you mean, I've got legs?"

"They're meant to walk on. Mine were," she answered.

Then I knew it didn't matter, and she wasn't angry either, and the evening was going to be all right. I cheered up in a second, and gave her a squeeze, just to show I appreciated her being such a sport—most girls would have torn me to shreds—and I said, "We haven't passed a cemetery, as far as I know. Does it matter very much?"

"Oh, there'll be others," she said. "I'm not particular."

I didn't know what to make of that. I thought she wanted to get out at the cemetery stopping point because it was her nearest stop for home, like the way you say, "Put me down at Woolworth's" if you live handy. I puzzled over it for a bit, and then I said, "How do you mean, there'll be others? It's not a thing you see often along a bus route."

"I was speaking in general terms," she answered. "Don't bother to talk, I like you silent best."

It wasn't a slap on the face, the way she said it. Fact was, I knew what she meant. Talking's all very pleasant with people like Mr. and Mrs. Thompson, over supper, and you say how the day has gone, and one of you reads a bit out of the paper, and the other says, "Fancy, there now," and so it goes on, in bits and pieces until one of you yawns, and somebody says, "Who's for bed?" Or it's nice enough with a chap like the boss, having a cuppa mid-morning, or about three when there's nothing doing, "I tell you what I think, those blokes in the government are making a mess of things, no better than the last lot," and then we'll be interrupted with someone coming to fill up with petrol. And I like talking to my old Mum when I go and see her, which I don't do often enough, and she tells me how she spanked my bottom when I was a kid, and I sit on the kitchen table like I did then, and she bakes rock cakes and gives me peel, saying, "You always were one for peel." That's talk, that's conversation.

But I didn't want to talk to my girl. I just wanted to keep my arm round her the way I was doing, and rest my chin against her head, and that's what she meant when she said she liked me silent. I liked it too.

One last thing bothered me a bit, and that was whether I

could kiss her before the bus stopped and we were turned out
at the terminus. I mean, putting an arm round a girl is one
thing, and kissing her is another. It takes a little time as a rule
to warm up. You start off with a long evening ahead of you,
and by the time you've been to a picture or a concert, and then
had something to eat and to drink, well, you've got yourselves
acquainted, and it's the usual thing to end up with a bit of kissing and a cuddle, the girls expect it. Truth to tell, I was never
much of a one for kissing. There was a girl I walked out with
back home, before I went into the army, and she was quite a
good sort, I liked her. But her teeth were a bit prominent, and
even if you shut your eyes and tried to forget who it was you
were kissing, well, you knew it was her, and there was nothing
to it. Good old Doris from next door. But the opposite kind are
even worse, the ones that grab you and nearly eat you. You
come across plenty of them, when you're in uniform. They're
much too eager, and they muss you about, and you get the
feeling they can't wait for a chap to get busy about them. I
don't mind saying it used to make me sick. Put me dead off,
and that's a fact. I suppose I was born fussy. I don't know.

But now, this evening in the bus, it was all quite different. I
don't know what it was about the girl—the sleepy eyes, and
the copper hair, and somehow not seeming to care if I was
there yet liking me at the same time; I hadn't found anything
like this before. So I said to myself, "Now, shall I risk it, or
shall I wait?" and I knew, from the way the driver was going
and the conductor was whistling below and saying "good-
night" to the people getting off, that the final stop couldn't be
far away; and my heart began to thump under my coat, and
my neck grew hot below the collar—darn silly, only a kiss,
you know, she couldn't kill me—and then... It was like diving
off a springboard. I thought, "Here goes," and I bent down,
and turned her face to me, and lifted her chin with my hand,
and kissed her good and proper.

Well, if I was poetical, I'd say what happened then was a
revelation. But I'm not poetical, and I can only say that she
kissed me back, and it lasted a long time, and it wasn't a bit
like Doris.

Then the bus stopped with a jerk, and the conductor called out in a singsong voice, "All out, please." Frankly, I could have wrung his neck.

She gave me a kick on the ankle. "Come on, move," she said, and I stumbled from my seat and racketed down the stairs, she following behind, and there we were, standing in a street. It was beginning to rain too, not badly but just enough to make you notice and want to turn up the collar of your coat, and we were right at the end of a great wide street, with deserted unlighted shops on either side, the end of the world it looked to me, and sure enough there was a hill over to the left, and at the bottom of the hill a cemetery. I could see the railings and the white tombstones behind, and it stretched a long way, nearly half way up the hill. There were acres of it.

"God darn it," I said, "is this the place you meant?"

"Could be," she said, looking over her shoulder vaguely, and then she took my arm. "What about a cup of coffee first?" she said.

First…? I wondered if she meant before the long trudge home, or was this home? It didn't really matter. It wasn't much after eleven. And I could do with a cup of coffee, and a sandwich too. There was a stall across the road, and they hadn't shut up shop.

We walked over to it, and the driver was there too, and the conductor, and the Air Force fellow who had been up in front on the top deck. They were ordering cups of tea and sandwiches, and we had the same, only coffee. They cut them tasty at the stalls, the sandwiches, I've noticed it before, nothing stingy about it, good slices of ham between thick white bread, and the coffee is piping hot, full cups too, good value, and I thought to myself, "Six bob will see this lot all right."

I noticed my girl looking at the Air Force chap, sort of thoughtful-like, as though she might have seen him before, and he looked at her too. I couldn't blame him for that. I didn't mind either; when you're out with a girl it gives you a kind of pride if other chaps notice her. And you couldn't miss this one. Not my girl.

Then she turned her back on him, deliberate, and leant with

her elbows on the stall, sipping her hot coffee, and I stood beside her doing the same. We weren't stuck up or anything, we were pleasant and polite enough, saying good evening all round, but anyone could tell that we were together, the girl and I, we were on our own. I liked that. Funny, it did something to me inside, gave me a protective feeling. For all they knew we might have been a married couple on our way home.

They were chaffing a bit, the other three and the chap serving the sandwiches and tea, but we didn't join in.

"You want to watch out, in that uniform," said the conductor to the Air Force fellow, "or you'll end up like those others. It's late too, to be out on your own."

They all started laughing. I didn't quite see the point, but I supposed it was a joke.

"I've been awake a long time," said the Air Force fellow. "I know a bad lot when I see one."

"That's what the others said, I shouldn't wonder," remarked the driver, "and we know what happened to them. Makes you shudder. But why pick on the Air Force, that's what I want to know?"

"It's the colour of our uniform," said the fellow. "You can spot it in the dark."

They went on laughing in that way. I lighted up a cigarette, but my girl wouldn't have one.

"I blame the war for all that's gone wrong with the women," said the coffee-stall bloke, wiping a cup and hanging it up behind. "Turned a lot of them balmy, in my opinion. They don't know the difference between right or wrong."

"'Tisn't that, it's sport that's the trouble," said the conductor. "Develops their muscles and that, what weren't never meant to be developed. Take my two youngsters, f'r instance. The girl can knock the boy down any time, she's a proper little bully. Makes you think."

"That's right," agreed the driver, "equality of the sexes, they call it, don't they? It's the vote that did it. We ought never to have given them the vote."

"Garn," said the Air Force chap, "giving them the vote didn't turn the women balmy. They've always been the same, under the skin. The people out East know how to treat 'em. They keep 'em shut up, out there. That's the answer. Then you don't get any trouble."

"I don't know what my old woman would say if I tried to shut her up," said the driver. And they all started laughing again.

My girl plucked at my sleeve and I saw she had finished her coffee. She motioned with her head towards the street.

"Want to go home?" I said.

Silly. I somehow wanted the others to believe we were going home. She didn't answer. She just went striding off, her hands in the pockets of her mac. I said good-night and followed her, but not before I noticed the Air Force fellow staring after her over his cup of tea.

She walked off along the street, and it was still raining, dreary somehow, made you want to be sitting over a fire some-where snug, and when she had crossed the street, and had come to the railings outside the cemetery she stopped, and looked up at me, and smiled.

"What now?" I said.

"Tombstones are flat," she said, "sometimes."

"What if they are?" I asked, bewildered-like.

"You can lie down on them," she said.

She turned and strolled along, looking at the railings, and then she came to one that was bent wide, and the next beside it broken, and she glanced up at me and smiled again.

"It's always the same," she said. "You're bound to find a gap if you look long enough."

She was through that gap in the railings as quick as a knife through butter. You could have knocked me flat.

"Here, hold on," I said, "I'm not as small as you."

But she was off and away, wandering among the graves. I got through the gap, puffing and blowing a bit, and then I looked around, and bless me if she wasn't lying on a long flat gravestone, with her arms under her head and her eyes closed.

Well, I wasn't expecting anything. I mean, it had been in my mind to see her home and that. Date her up for the next evening. Of course, seeing as it was late, we could have stopped a bit when we came to the doorway of her place. She needn't have gone in right away. But lying there on the gravestone wasn't hardly natural.

I sat down, and took her hand.

"You'll get wet lying there," I said. Feeble, but I didn't know what else to say.

"I'm used to that," she said.

She opened her eyes and looked at me. There was a street light not far away, outside the railings, so it wasn't all that dark, and anyway in spite of the rain the night wasn't pitch black, more murky somehow. I wish I knew how to tell about her eyes, but I'm not one for fancy talk. You know how a luminous watch shines in the dark. I've got one myself. When you wake up in the night, there it is on your wrist, like a friend. Somehow my girl's eyes shone like that, but they were lovely too. And they weren't lazy cat's eyes any more. They were loving and gentle, and they were sad, too, all at the same time.

"Used to lying in the rain?" I said.

"Brought up to it," she answered. "They gave us a name in the shelters. The dead-end kids, they used to call us, in the war days."

"Weren't you never evacuated?" I asked.

"Not me," she said. "I never could stop any place. I always came back."

"Parents living?"

"No. Both of them killed by the bomb that smashed my home." She didn't speak tragic-like. Just ordinary.

"Bad luck," I said.

She didn't answer that one. And I sat there, holding her hand, wanting to take her home.

"You been on your job some time, at the picture-house?" I asked.

"About three weeks," she said. "I don't stop anywhere long. I'll be moving on again soon."

"Why's that?"

"Restless," she said.

She put up her hands suddenly and took my face and held it. It was gentle the way she did it, not as you'd think.

"You've got a good kind face. I like it," she said to me.

It was queer. The way she said it made me feel daft and soft, not sort of excited like I had been in the bus, and I thought to myself, well, maybe this is it, I've found a girl at last I really want. But not for an evening, casual. For going steady.

"Got a bloke?" I asked.

"No," she said.

"I mean, regular."

"No, never."

It was a funny line of talk to be having in a cemetery, and she lying there like some figure carved on the old tombstone.

"I haven't got a girl either," I said. "Never think about it, the way other chaps do. Faddy, I guess. And then I'm keen on my job. Work in a garage, mechanic you know, repairs, anything that's going. Good pay. I've saved a bit, besides what I send my old Mum. I live in digs. Nice people, Mr. and Mrs. Thompson, and my boss at the garage is a nice chap too. I've never been lonely, and I'm not lonely now. But since I've seen you, it's made me think. You know, it's not going to be the same any more."

She never interrupted once, and somehow it was like speaking my thoughts aloud.

"Going home to the Thompsons is all very pleasant and nice," I said, "and you couldn't wish for kinder people. Good grub too, and we chat a bit after supper, and listen to the wireless. But d'you know, what I want now is different. I want to come along and fetch you from the cinema, when the programme's over, and you'd be standing there by the curtains, seeing the people out, and you'd give me a bit of a wink to show me you'd be going through to change your clothes and I could wait for you. And then you'd come out into the street, like you did tonight, but you wouldn't go off on your own, you'd take my arm, and if you didn't want to wear your coat I'd carry it for you, or a parcel maybe, or whatever you had. Then we'd go off to the Corner House or some place for supper, handy. We'd have a table reserved—they'd know us, the waitresses and them; they'd keep back something special, just for us."

I could picture it too, clear as anything. The table with the ticket on "Reserved." The waitress nodding at us, "Got curried eggs tonight." And we going through to get our trays, and my girl acting like she didn't know me, and me laughing to myself.

"D'you see what I mean?" I said to her. "It's not just being friends, it's more than that."

I don't know if she heard. She lay there looking up at me, touching my ear and my chin in that funny, gentle way. You'd say she was sorry for me.

"I'd like to buy you things," I said, "flowers sometimes. It's nice to see a girl with a flower tucked in her dress, it looks clean and fresh. And for special occasions, birthdays, Christmas, and that, something you'd seen in a shop window, and wanted, but hadn't liked to go in and ask the price. A brooch, perhaps, or a bracelet, something pretty. And I'd go in and get it when you weren't with me, and it'd cost much more than my week's pay, but I wouldn't mind."

I could see the expression on her face, opening the parcel. And she'd put it on, what I'd bought, and we'd go out together, and she'd be dressed up a bit for the purpose, nothing glaring I don't mean, but something that took the eye. You know, saucy.

"It's not fair to talk about getting married," I said, "not in these days, when everything's uncertain. A fellow doesn't mind the uncertainty, but it's hard on a girl. Cooped up in a couple of rooms maybe, and queueing and rations and all. They like their freedom, and being in a job, and not being tied down, the same as us. But it's nonsense the way they were talking back in the coffee stall just now. About girls not being the same as in old days, and the war to blame. As for the way they treat them out East—I've seen some of it. I suppose that fellow meant to be funny, they're all smart Alicks in the Air Force, but it was a silly line of talk, I thought."

She dropped her hands to her side and closed her eyes. It was getting quite wet there on the tombstone. I was worried for her, though she had her mac of course, but her legs and feet were damp in her thin stockings and shoes.

"You weren't ever in the Air Force, were you?" she said.

Queer. Her voice had gone quite hard. Sharp, and different. Like as if she was anxious about something, scared even.

"Not me," I said, "I served my time with R.E.M.E. Proper lot they were. No swank, no nonsense. You know where you are with them."

"I'm glad," she said. "You're good and kind. I'm glad."

I wondered if she'd known some fellow in the R.A.F. who had let her down. They're a wild crowd, the ones I've come across. And I remembered the way she'd looked at the boy drinking his tea at the stall. Reflective, somehow. As if she was thinking back. I couldn't expect her not to have been around a bit, with her looks, and then brought up to play about the shelters, without parents, like she said. But I didn't want to think of her being hurt by anyone.

"Why, what's wrong with them?" I said. "What's the R.A.F. done to you?"

"They smashed my home," she said.

"That was the Germans, not our fellows."

"It's all the same, they're killers, aren't they?" she said.

I looked down at her, lying on the tombstone, and her voice wasn't hard any more, like when she'd asked me if I'd been in the Air Force, but it was tired, and sad, and oddly lonely, and it did something queer to my stomach, right in the pit of it, so that I wanted to do the darnedest silliest thing and take her home with me, back to where I lived with Mr. and Mrs. Thompson, and say to Mrs. Thompson—she was a kind old soul, she wouldn't mind—"Look, this is my girl. Look after her." Then I'd know she'd be safe, she'd be all right, nobody could do anything to hurt her. That was the thing I was afraid of suddenly, that someone would come along and hurt my girl.

I bent down and put my arms round her and lifted her up close.

"Listen," I said, "it's raining hard. I'm going to take you home. You'll catch your death, lying here on the wet stone."

"No," she said, her hands on my shoulders, "nobody ever sees me home. You're going back where you belong, alone."

"I won't leave you here," I said.

"Yes, that's what I want you to do. If you refuse I shall be angry. You wouldn't want that, would you?"

I stared at her, puzzled. And her face was queer in the

murky old light there, whiter than before, but it was beautiful, Jesus Christ, it was beautiful. That's blasphemy. But I can't say it no other way.

"What do you want me to do?" I asked.

"I want you to go and leave me here, and not look back," she said, "like someone dreaming, sleepwalking, they call it. Go back walking through the rain. It will take you hours. It doesn't matter, you're young and strong and you've got long legs. Go back to your room, wherever it is, and get into bed, and go to sleep, and wake and have your breakfast in the morning, and go off to work, the same as you always do."

"What about you?"

"Never mind about me. Just go."

"Can I call for you at the cinema tomorrow night? Can it be like what I was telling you, you know...going steady?"

She didn't answer. She only smiled. She sat quite still, looking in my face, and then she closed her eyes and threw back her head and said, "Kiss me again, stranger."

I left her, like she said. I didn't look back. I climbed through the railings of the cemetery, out on to the road. No one seemed to be about, and the coffee stall by the bus-stop had closed down, the boards were up.

I started walking the way the bus had brought us. The road was straight, going on for ever. A High Street it must have been. There were shops on either side, and it was right away north-east of London, nowhere I'd ever been before. I was proper lost, but it didn't seem to matter. I felt like a sleepwalker, just as she said.

I kept thinking of her all the time. There was nothing else, only her face in front of me as I walked. They had a word for it in the army, when a girl gets a fellow that way, so he can't see straight or hear right or know what he's doing; and I thought it a lot of cock, or it only happened to drunks, and now I knew it was true and it had happened to me. I wasn't going to worry any more about how she'd get home; she'd told me not to, and she must have lived handy, she'd never have ridden out so far else, though it was funny living such a way from her work. But maybe in time she'd tell me more, bit by bit. I wouldn't drag it from her. I had one thing fixed in my mind, and that was to pick her up the next evening from the picture palace. It was firm and set, and nothing would budge me from that. The hours in between would just be a blank for me until ten p.m. came round.

I went on walking in the rain, and presently a lorry came along and I thumbed a lift, and the driver took me a good part of the way before he had to turn left in the other direction, and so I got down and walked again, and it must have been close on three when I got home.

I would have felt bad, in an ordinary way, knocking up Mr. Thompson to let me in, and it had never happened before either, but I was all lit up inside from loving my girl, and I didn't seem to mind. He came down at last and opened the door. I had to ring several times before he heard, and there he was, grey with sleep, poor old chap, his pyjamas all crumpled from the bed.

"Whatever happened to you?" he said. "We've been worried, the wife and me. We thought you'd been knocked down, run over. We came back here and found the house empty and your supper not touched."

"I went to the pictures," I said.

"The pictures?" He stared up at me, in the passageway. "The pictures stop at ten o'clock."

"I know," I said, "I went walking after that. Sorry. Good-night."

And I climbed up the stairs to my room, leaving the old chap muttering to himself and bolting the door, and I heard Mrs. Thompson calling from her bedroom, "What is it? Is it him? Is he come home?"

I'd put them to trouble and to worry, and I ought to have gone in there and then and apologized, but I couldn't some-how, it wouldn't have come right; so I shut my door and threw off my clothes and got into bed, and it was like as if she was with me still, my girl, in the darkness.

They were a bit quiet at breakfast the next morning, Mr. and Mrs. Thompson. They didn't look at me. Mrs. Thompson gave me my kipper without a word, and he went on looking at his newspaper.

I ate my breakfast, and then I said, "I hope you had a nice evening up at Highgate?" and Mrs. Thompson, with her mouth a bit tight, she said, "Very pleasant, thank you, we were home by ten," and she gave a little sniff and poured Mr. Thompson out another cup of tea.

We went on being quiet, no one saying a word, and then Mrs. Thompson said, "Will you be in to supper this evening?" and I said, "No, I don't think so. I'm meeting a friend," and then I saw the old chap look at me over his spectacles.

"If you're going to be late," he said, "we'd best take the key for you."

Then he went on reading his paper. You could tell they were proper hurt that I didn't tell them anything, or say where I was going.

I went off to work, and we were busy at the garage that day, one job after the other came along, and any other time I wouldn't have minded. I liked a full day and often worked overtime, but today I wanted to get away before the shops closed; I hadn't thought about anything else since the idea came into my head.

It was getting on for half-past four, and the boss came to me and said, "I promised the doctor he'd have his Austin this evening. I said you'd be through with it by seven-thirty. That's O.K., isn't it?"

My heart sank. I'd counted on getting off early, because of what I wanted to do. Then I thought quickly that if the boss let me off now, and I went out to the shop before it closed, and came back again to do the job on the Austin, it would be all right, so I said, "I don't mind working a bit of overtime, but I'd like to slip out now, for half an hour, if you're going to be here. There's something I want to buy before the shops shut."

He told me that suited him, so I took off my overalls and washed and got my coat and I went off to the line of shops down at the bottom of Haverstock Hill. I knew the one I wanted. It was a jeweller's, where Mr. Thompson used to take his clock to be repaired, and it wasn't a place where they sold trash at all, but good stuff, solid silver frames and that, and cutlery.

There were rings, of course, and a few fancy bangles, but I didn't like the look of them. All the girls in the N.A.A.F.I. used to wear bangles with charms on them, quite common it was, and I went on staring in at the window and then I spotted it, right at the back.

It was a brooch. Quite small, not much bigger than your thumbnail, but with a nice blue stone on it and a pin at the back, and it was shaped like a heart. That was what got me, the shape. I stared at it a bit, and there wasn't a ticket to it, which meant it would cost a bit, but I went in and asked to have a look at it. The jeweller got it out of the window for me, and he gave it a bit of a polish and turned it this way and that, and I saw it pinned on my girl, showing up nice on her frock or her jumper, and I knew this was it.

"I'll take it," I said, and then asked him the price.

I swallowed a bit when he told me, but I took out my wallet and counted the notes, and he put the heart in a box wrapped up careful with cotton wool, and made a neat package of it, tied with fancy string. I knew I'd have to get an advance from the boss before I went off work that evening, but he was a good chap and I was certain he'd give it to me.

I stood outside the jeweller's, with the packet for my girl safe in my breast pocket, and I heard the church clock strike a quarter to five. There was time to slip down to the cinema and make sure she understood about the date for the evening, and then I'd beat it fast up the road and get back to the garage, and I'd have the Austin done by the time the doctor wanted it.

When I got to the cinema my heart was beating like a sledgehammer and I could hardly swallow. I kept picturing to myself how she'd look, standing there by the curtains going in, with that velvet jacket and the cap on the back of her head.

There was a bit of a queue outside, and I saw they'd changed the programme. The poster of the western had gone, with the cowboy throwing a knife in the Indian's guts, and they had instead a lot of girls dancing, and some chap prancing in front of them with a walking-stick. It was a musical.

I went in, and didn't go near the box office but looked

straight to the curtains, where she'd be. There was an usherette there all right, but it wasn't her. This was a great tall girl, who looked silly in the clothes, and she was trying to do two things at once—tear off the slips of tickets as the people went past, and hang on to her torch at the same time.

I waited a moment. Perhaps they'd switched over positions and my girl had gone up to the circle. When the last lot had got in through the curtains and there was a pause and she was free, I went up to her and I said, "Excuse me, do you know where I could have a word with the other young lady?"

She looked at me. "What other young lady?"

"The one who was here last night, with copper hair," I said.

She looked at me closer then, suspicious-like.

"She hasn't shown up today," she said. "I'm taking her place."

"Not shown up?"

"No. And it's funny you should ask. You're not the only one. The police was here not long ago. They had a word with the manager, and the commissionaire too, and no one's said anything to me yet, but I think there's been trouble."

My heart beat different then. Not excited, bad. Like when someone's ill, took to hospital, sudden.

"The police?" I said. "What were they here for?"

"I told you, I don't know," she answered, "but it was something to do with her, and the manager went with them to the police station, and he hasn't come back yet. This way, please, circle on the left, stalls to the right."

I just stood there, not knowing what to do. It was like as if the floor had been knocked away from under me.

The tall girl tore another slip off a ticket and then she said to me, over her shoulder, "Was she a friend of yours?"

"Sort of," I said. I didn't know what to say.

"Well, if you ask me, she was queer in the head, and it wouldn't surprise me if she'd done away with herself and they'd found her dead. No, ice-creams served in the interval, after the news reel."

I went out and stood in the street. The queue was growing for the cheaper seats, and there were children too, talking, excited. I brushed past them and started walking up the street, and I felt sick inside, queer. Something had happened to my girl. I knew it now. That was why she had wanted to get rid of me last night, and for me not to see her home. She was going to do herself in, there in the cemetery. That's why she talked funny and looked so white, and now they'd found her, lying there on the gravestone by the railings.

If I hadn't gone away and left her she'd have been all right. If I'd stayed with her just five minutes longer, coaxing her, I'd have got her round to my way of thinking and seen her home, standing no nonsense, and she'd be at the picture palace now, showing the people to their seats.

It might be it wasn't as bad as what I feared. It might be she was found wandering, lost her memory and got picked up by the police and taken off, and then they found out where she worked and that, and now the police wanted to check up with the manager at the cinema to see if it was so. If I went down to the police station and asked them there, maybe they'd tell me what had happened, and I could say she was my girl, we were walking out, and it wouldn't matter if she didn't recognize me even, I'd stick to the story. I couldn't let down my boss, I had to get that job done on the Austin, but afterwards, when I'd finished, I could go down to the police station.

All the heart had gone out of me, and I went back to the garage hardly knowing what I was doing, and for the first time ever the smell of the place turned my stomach, the oil and the grease, and there was a chap roaring up his engine, before backing out his car, and a great cloud of smoke coming from his exhaust, filling the workshop with stink.

I went and got my overalls, and put them on, and fetched the tools, and started on the Austin, and all the time I was wondering what it was that had happened to my girl, if she was down at the police station, lost and lonely, or if she was lying somewhere...dead. I kept seeing her face all the time like it was last night.

It took me an hour and a half, not more, to get the Austin ready for the road, filled up with petrol and all, and I had her facing outwards to the street for the owner to drive out, but was all in by then, dead tired, and the sweat pouring down my face. I had a bit of a wash and put on my coat, and I felt the package in the breast-pocket. I took it out and looked at it, done so neat with the fancy ribbon, and I put it back again, and I hadn't noticed the boss come in—I was standing with my back to the door.

"Did you get what you want?" he said, cheerful-like and smiling.

He was a good chap, never out of temper, and we got along well.

"Yes," I said.

But I didn't want to talk about it. I told him the job was done and the Austin was ready to drive away. I went to the office with him so that he could note down the work done, and the overtime, and he offered me a fag from the packet lying on his desk beside the evening paper.

"I see Lady Luck won the three-thirty," he said. "I'm a couple of quid up this week."

He was entering my work in his ledger, to keep the payroll right.

"Good for you," I said.

"Only backed it for a place, like a clot," he said. "She was twenty-five to one. Still, it's all in the game."

I didn't answer. I'm not one for drinking, but I needed one bad, just then. I mopped my forehead with my handkerchief. I wished he'd get on with the figures, and say good-night, and let me go.

"Another poor devil's had it," he said. "That's the third now in three weeks, ripped right up the guts, same as the others. He died in hospital this morning. Looks like there's a hoodoo on the R.A.F."

"What was it, flying jets?" I asked.

"Jets?" he said. "No, damn it, murder. Sliced up the belly, poor sod. Don't you ever read the papers? It's the third one in three weeks, done identical, all Air Force fellows, and each time they've found 'em near a graveyard or a cemetery. I was saying just now, to that chap who came in for petrol, it's not only men who go off their rockers and turn sex maniacs, but women too. They'll get this one all right though, you see. It says in the paper they've a line on her, and expect an arrest shortly. About time too, before another poor blighter cops it."

He shut up his ledger and stuck his pencil behind his ear.

"Like a drink?" he said. "I've got a bottle of gin in the cupboard."

"No," I said, "no, thanks very much. I've...I've got a date."

"That's right," he said smiling, "enjoy yourself."

I walked down the street and bought an evening paper. It was like what he said about the murder. They had it on the front page. They said it must have happened about two a.m. Young fellow in the Air Force, in north-east London. He had managed to stagger to a call-box and get through to the police, and they found him there on the floor of the box when they arrived.

He made a statement in the ambulance before he died. He said a girl called to him, and he followed her, and he thought it was just a bit of lovemaking—he'd seen her with another fellow drinking coffee at a stall a little while before—and he thought she'd thrown this other fellow over and had taken a fancy to him, and then she got him, he said, right in the guts.

It said in the paper that he had given the police a full description of her, and it said also that the police would be glad if the man who had been seen with the girl earlier in the evening would come forward to help in identification.

I didn't want the paper any more. I threw it away. I walked about the streets till I was tired, and when I guessed Mr. and Mrs. Thompson had gone to bed I went home, and groped for the key they'd left on a piece of string hanging inside the letterbox, and I let myself in and went upstairs to my room.

Mrs. Thompson had turned down the bed and put a Thermos of tea for me, thoughtful-like, and the evening paper, the late edition.

They'd got her. About three o'clock in the afternoon. I didn't read the writing, nor the name nor anything. I sat down on my bed, and took up the paper, and there was my girl staring up at me from the front page.

Then I took the package from my coat and undid it, and threw away the wrapper and the fancy string, and sat there looking down at the little heart I held in my hand.

The Fork in the Graveyard

TRADITIONAL

Imagine yourself sitting round a campfire with a group of friends. The only sounds you hear are the crackling fire, the bullfrogs down in the pond, and the voice of the storyteller. As each person around the fire tells a story, the scariest ones are those that are said to be true. In fact, some may find the story of Peter MacIntyre to be a little too close to home, given that it happened in our very own Prince Edward Island. So edge a little closer to the fire, enjoy the comforting warmth and flickering shadows of the flames, and get set for one of Canada's scariest legends, as recounted here by Julie V. Watson.

T he tale of Peter MacIntyre is as exciting a story of the supernatural as one is likely to find and, as such, is still repeated by the people of Tracadie who puzzle over the episode to this day.

The spirit, or ghost, of a dead man is said to have committed the dastardly deed of murdering our Peter, a Scottish settler, who arrived in the area on the good ship *Alexander* in 1773.

It began on a cold day in late October with a fine mist blowing in from the sea. Seated about the pot-bellied stove in the little country store were a group of farmer folk whose talk had turned from problems of the day to current superstitions. When Peter arrived, room was made for him in the warmth, and conversation continued until one Ben Peters mentioned having seen a light in the old French burying place at Scotch Fort. He described a huge ball of fire, dancing across the graves, and lighting up the whole cemetery.

Peter, the newcomer, scoffed at the idea, boasting that such exaggerations would not keep him from walking through any churchyard, even the Scotch Fort one, on that very night.

There were, he claimed, more devils to fear among his mortal companions than in the resting-place of the dead.

His boasting, of course, was quickly taken up on, and the challenge thrown out to do more than brag by the comfort of the fire.

"It's all very well to put on a brave front when yer in the company of humans," piped a fellow lounger. "But going to a graveyard that's haunted in the dead of night, and alone, is a horse of another colour. Why, man, you must be clear off your beam to even suggest such a thing let alone go through with it. That old cemetery may be full of dead men's bones, but it's also full of dead men's spirits."

Peter took offence at the remarks, shrugging off superstitious talk as nonsense. The ire was up in his companions, who were slighted by his attitude, and quickly a bet was made that Peter should go to the old cemetery and plant a hay-fork in a grave, to prove he had been there. Should he succeed, a pound of tobacco would be his.

Peter accepted the challenge, and with a jaunty air left the cabin, telling them to have his tobacco ready on the morn, for "I don't expect to be detained by the dead," he said, "I've never knowed dead people to harm anyone."

As it was midnight, all filed from the store. Peter in a long black rain slicker was given the hay-fork and bid on his way to Scotch Fort while the others scuttled for the dry warmth of their own beds.

Come dawn, all were seeking Peter, who it seemed had disappeared. His cabin was empty and cold, obviously vacant for some time. More ominous, his livestock was bleating with hunger. With the realization that Peter was not to be found came fear, fear for the fate of a man brazen enough to risk defying the very spirits of the dead at the witching hour on a night that seemed to portray the very depths of Hell itself.

The men armed themselves, justifying their actions by expressing a concern about bears in the vicinity, and set out to solve the mystery.

The cemetery was a small clearing in the heart of the forest, reached by means of a narrow footpath, permitting not more than two persons to walk abreast. Every now and then the search party stopped to peer through the branches of the trees, their voices never above a whisper. Finally they were out of the woods and staring in amazement at the sight that met their eyes.

The handle of a hay-fork showed plainly above a grave situated right in the centre of the graveyard. A large black object was curled up on the ground beside it.

Cautiously the party pressed forward, and as they neared the spot the black object began to take shape. A few more steps and they raised their voices in unison, "Peter! Can't you speak to us?"

There was no answer save the echo of their own voices. MacIntyre's body lay across the grave, his face turned toward them. It was a face frozen in agony, a haunted, fear-crazed face that made the living tremble and wish they'd never seen it.

A hand reached out and grabbed the dead man's collar. The hand pulled hard on the collar but the body wouldn't come loose.

A second hand reached out and grasped the fork. It had been driven into the grave with a powerful thrust and right through the tail of Peter MacIntyre's long black coat.

Silent Snow, Secret Snow

by
CONRAD AIKEN
(1889–1973)

This is a scary story of a different sort, where the horrors are of the mind—in this case, the fragile, beautiful, but none the less haunting imaginative world of a twelve-year-old named Paul. Aiken's accomplishment in probing the mind of someone the outside world would call "mentally ill" is truly remarkable—but our sympathy for Paul cannot prevent a feeling of horror at his helplessness in the face of the gathering storm.

Conrad Aiken was a poet, and his feeling for language is gloriously apparent here, in phrases like "something of cease, and peace, and the long bright curve of space!" This is a tale that manages to be as lovely as it is menacing.

J ust why it should have happened, or why it should have happened just when it did, he could not, of course, possibly have said; nor perhaps would it even have occurred to him to ask. The thing was above all a secret, something to be preciously concealed from Mother and Father; and to that very fact it owed an enormous part of its deliciousness. It was like a peculiarly beautiful trinket to be carried unmentioned in one's trouser-pocket—a rare stamp, an old coin, a few tiny gold links found trodden out of shape on the path in the park, a pebble of carnelian, a sea shell distinguishable from all others by an unusual spot or stripe—and, as if it were any one of these, he carried around with him everywhere a warm and persistent and increasingly beautiful sense of possession. Nor was it only a sense of possession—it was also a sense of protection. It was as if, in some delightful way, his secret gave him a fortress, a wall behind which he could retreat into heavenly seclusion. This was almost the first thing he had noticed about it—apart from the oddness of the thing itself—and it was this that now again, for the fiftieth time, occurred to him, as he sat in the little schoolroom. It was the half-hour for geography. Miss Buell was revolving with one finger, slowly, a huge terrestrial globe which had been placed on her desk. The green and yellow continents passed and repassed, questions were asked and answered, and now the little girl in front of him, Deirdre, who had a funny little constellation of freckles on the back of her neck, exactly like the Big Dipper, was standing up and telling Miss Buell that the equator was the line that ran round the middle.

Miss Buell's face, which was old and greyish and kindly, with grey stiff curls beside the cheeks, and eyes that swam very brightly, like little minnows, behind thick glasses, wrinkled itself into a complication of amusements.

"Ah! I see. The earth is wearing a belt, or a sash. Or someone drew a line round it!"

"Oh, no—not that—I mean— "

In the general laughter, he did not share, or only a very little. He was thinking about the Arctic and Antarctic regions, which of course, on the globe, were white. Miss Buell was now telling them about the tropics, the jungles, the steamy heat of equatorial swamps, where the birds and butterflies, and even the snakes, were like living jewels. As he listened to these things, he was already, with a pleasant sense of half-effort, putting his secret between himself and the words. Was it really an effort at all? For effort implied something voluntary, and perhaps even something one did not especially want; whereas this was distinctly pleasant, and came almost of its own accord. All he needed to do was to think of that morning, the first one, and then of all the others—

But it was all so absurdly simple! It had amounted to so little. It was nothing, just an idea—and just why it should have become so wonderful, so permanent, was a mystery—a very pleasant one, to be sure, but also, in an amusing way, foolish. However, without ceasing to listen to Miss Buell, who had now moved up to the north temperate zones, he deliberately invited his memory of the first morning. It was only a moment or two after he had waked up—or perhaps the moment itself. But was there, to be exact, an exact moment? Was one awake all at once? Or was it gradual? Anyway, it was after he had stretched a lazy hand up toward the headrail, and yawned, and then relaxed again among his warm covers, all the more grateful on a December morning, that the thing had happened. Suddenly, for no reason, he had thought of the postman, he remembered the postman. Perhaps there was nothing so odd in that. After all, he heard the postman almost every morning in his life—his heavy boots could be heard clumping round the corner at the top of the little cobbled hill-street, and then, progressively nearer, progressively louder, the double knock at each door, the crossings and re-crossings of the street, till finally the clumsy steps came stumbling across to the very door, and the tremendous knock came which shook the house itself.

(Miss Buell was saying, "Vast wheat-growing areas in North America and Siberia."

Deirdre had for the moment placed her left hand across the back of her neck.)

But on this particular morning, the first morning, as he lay there with his eyes closed, he had for some reason *waited* for the postman. He wanted to hear him come round the corner. And that was precisely the joke—he never did. He never came. He never had come—*round the corner*—again. For when at last the steps *were* heard, they had already, he was quite sure, come a little down the hill, to the first house; and even so, the steps were curiously different—they were softer, they had a new secrecy about them, they were muffled and indistinct; and while the rhythm of them was the same, it now said a new thing—it said peace, it said remoteness, it said cold, it said sleep. And he had understood the situation at once— nothing could have seemed simpler—there had been snow in the night, such as all winter he had been longing for; and it was this which had rendered the postman's first footsteps inaudible, and the later ones faint. Of course! How lovely! And even now it must be snowing—it was going to be a snowy day—the long white ragged lines were drifting and sifting across the street, across the faces of the old houses, whispering and hushing, making little triangles of white in the corners between cobblestones, seething a little when the wind blew

them over the ground to a drifted corner; and so it would be
all day, getting deeper and deeper and silenter and silenter.

(Miss Buell was saying, "Land of perpetual snow.")

All this time, of course (while he lay in bed), he had kept
his eyes closed, listening to the nearer progress of the postman, the muffled footsteps thumping and slipping on the
snow-sheathed cobbles; and all the other sounds—the double
knocks, the frosty far-off voice or two, a bell ringing thinly and
softly as if under a sheet of ice—had the same slightly
abstracted quality, as if removed by one degree from actuali-
ty—as if everything in the world had been insulated by snow.
But when at last, pleased, he opened his eyes, and turned
them toward the window, to see for himself this long-desired
and now so clearly imagined miracle—what he saw instead
was brilliant sunlight on a roof; and when, astonished, he
jumped out of bed and stared down into the street, expecting
to see the cobbles obliterated by the snow, he saw nothing but
the bare bright cobbles themselves.

Queer, the effect this extraordinary surprise had had upon
him—all the following morning he had kept with him a sense
as of snow falling about him, a secret screen of new snow
between himself and the world. If he had not dreamed such a
thing—and how could he have dreamed it while awake?—
how else could one explain it? In any case, the delusion had
been so vivid as to affect his entire behaviour. He could not
now remember whether it was on the first or the second
morning—or was it even the third?—that his mother had
drawn attention to some oddness in his manner.

"But my darling"—she had said at the breakfast table—
"what has come over you? You don't seem to be listening...."

And how often that very thing had happened since!

(Miss Buell was now asking if anyone knew the difference
between the North Pole and the Magnetic Pole. Deirdre was
holding up her flickering brown hand, and he could see the
four white dimples that marked the knuckles.)

Perhaps it hadn't been either the second or third morning—
or even the fourth or fifth. How could he be sure? How could
he be sure just when the delicious *progress* had become clear?

Just when it had really *begun*? The intervals weren't very precise.... All he now knew was, that at some point or other—
perhaps the second day, perhaps the sixth—he had noticed
that the presence of the snow was a little more insistent, the
sound of it clearer; and, conversely, the sound of the postman's
footsteps more indistinct. Not only could he not hear the steps
come round the corner, he could not even hear them at the
first house. It was below the first house that he heard them;
and then, a few days later, it was below the second house that
he heard them; and a few days later again, below the third.
Gradually, gradually, the snow was becoming heavier, the
sound of its seething louder, the cobblestones more and more
muffled. When he found, each morning, on going to the window, after the ritual of listening, that the roofs and cobbles
were as bare as ever, it made no difference. This was, after all,
only what he had expected. It was even what pleased him,
what rewarded him: the thing was his own, belonged to no
one else. No one else knew about it, not even his mother and
father. There, outside, were the bare cobbles; and here, inside,
was the snow. Snow growing heavier each day, muffling the
world, hiding the ugly, and deadening increasingly—above
all—the steps of the postman.

"But my darling"—she had said at the luncheon table—
"what has come over you? You don't seem to listen when people speak to you. That's the third time I've asked you to pass
your plate...."

How was one to explain this to Mother? or to Father? There
was, of course, nothing to be done about it: nothing. All one
could do was to laugh embarrassedly, pretend to be a little
ashamed, apologize, and take a sudden and somewhat disin-
genuous interest in what was being done or said. The cat had
stayed out all night. He had a curious swelling on his left
cheek—perhaps somebody had kicked him, or a stone had
struck him. Mrs. Kempton was or was not coming to tea. The
house was going to be housecleaned, or "turned out," on
Wednesday instead of Friday. A new lamp was provided for
his evening work—perhaps it was eyestrain which accounted
for this new and so peculiar vagueness of his—Mother was

looking at him with amusement as she said this, but with something else as well. A new lamp? A new lamp. Yes, Mother, No, Mother, Yes, Mother. School is going very well. The geometry is very easy. The history is very dull. The geography is very interesting—particularly when it takes one to the North Pole. Why the North Pole? Oh, well, it would be fun to be an explorer. Another Peary or Scott or Shackleton. And then abruptly he found his interest in the talk at an end, stared at the pudding on his plate, listened, waited, and began once more—ah, how heavenly, too, the first beginnings—to hear or feel—for could he actually hear it?—the silent snow, the secret snow.

(Miss Buell was telling them about the search for the Northwest Passage, about Hendrik Hudson, the *Half Moon*.)

This had been, indeed, the only distressing feature of the new experience: the fact that it so increasingly had brought him into a kind of mute misunderstanding, or even conflict, with his father and mother. It was as if he were trying to lead a double life. On the one hand, he had to be Paul Hasleman, and keep up the appearance of being that person—dress, wash, and answer intelligently when spoken to—; on the other, he had to explore this new world which had been opened to him. Nor could there be the slightest doubt—not the slightest—that the new world was the profounder and more wonderful of the two. It was irresistible. It was miraculous. Its beauty was simply beyond anything—beyond speech as beyond thought—utterly incommunicable. But how then, between the two worlds, of which he was thus constantly aware, was he to keep a balance? One must get up, one must go to breakfast, one must talk with Mother, go to school, do one's lessons—and, in all this, try not to appear too much of a fool. But if all the while one was also trying to extract the full deliciousness of another and quite separate existence, one which could not easily (if at all) be spoken of—how was one to manage? How was one to explain? Would it be safe to explain? Would it be absurd? Would it merely mean that he would get into some obscure kind of trouble?

These thoughts came and went, came and went, as softly

and secretly as the snow; they were not precisely a disturbance, perhaps they were even a pleasure; he liked to have
them; their presence was something almost palpable, something he could stroke with his hand, without closing his eyes,
and without ceasing to see Miss Buell and the schoolroom and
the globe and the freckles on Deirdre's neck; nevertheless he
did in a sense cease to see, or to see the obvious external
world, and substituted for this vision the vision of snow, the
sound of snow, and the slow, almost soundless, approach of
the postman. Yesterday, it had been only at the sixth house
that the postman had become audible; the snow was much
deeper now, it was falling more swiftly and heavily, the sound
of its seething was more distinct, more soothing, more persistent. And this morning, it had been—as nearly as he could figure—just above the seventh house—perhaps only a step or
two above; at most, he had heard two or three footsteps before
the knock had sounded.... And with each such narrowing of
the sphere, each nearer approach of the limit at which the
postman was first audible, it was odd how sharply was
increased the amount of illusion which had to be carried into
the ordinary business of daily life. Each day it was harder to
get out of bed, to go to the window, to look out at the—as
always—perfectly empty and snowless street. Each day it was
more difficult to go through the perfunctory motions of greeting Mother and Father at breakfast, to reply to their questions,
to put his books together and go to school. And at school,
how extraordinarily hard to conduct with success simultaneously the public life and the life that was secret! There were
times when he longed—positively ached—to tell everyone
about it—to burst out with it—only to be checked almost at
once by a far-off feeling as of some faint absurdity which was
inherent in it—but *was* it absurd?—and more importantly by a
sense of mysterious power in his very secrecy. Yes: it must be
kept secret. That, more and more, became clear. At whatever
cost to himself, whatever pain to others—

(Miss Buell looked straight at him, smiling, and said,
"Perhaps we'll ask Paul. I'm sure Paul will come out of his day-
dream long enough to be able to tell us. Won't you, Paul?" He

rose slowly from him chair, resting one hand on the brightly varnished desk, and deliberately stared through the snow toward the blackboard. It was an effort, but it was amusing to make it. "Yes," he said slowly, "it was what we now call the Hudson River. This he thought to be the Northwest Passage. He was disappointed." He sat down again, and as he did so Deirdre half turned in her chair and gave him a shy smile, of approval and admiration.)

At whatever pain to others.

This part of it was very puzzling, very puzzling. Mother was very nice, and so was Father. Yes, that was all true enough. He wanted to be nice to them, to tell them everything—and yet, was it really wrong of him to want to have a secret place of his own?

At bedtime, the night before, Mother had said, "If this goes on, my lad, we'll have to see a doctor, we will! We can't have our boy—" But what was it she had said? "Live in another world"? "Live so far away"? The word "far" had been in it, he was sure, and then Mother had taken up a magazine again and laughed a little, but with an expression which wasn't mirthful. He had felt sorry for her....

The bell rang for dismissal. The sound came to him through long curved parallels of falling snow. He saw Deirdre rise, and had himself risen almost as soon—but not quite as soon—as she.

II

On the walk homeward, which was timeless, it pleased him to see through the accompaniment, or counterpoint, of snow, the items of mere externality on his way. There were many kinds of bricks in the sidewalks, and laid in many kinds of pattern. The garden walls too were various, some of wooden palings, some of plaster, some of stone. Twigs of bushes leaned over the walls; the little hard green winter-buds of lilac, on grey stems, sheathed and fat; other branches very thin and fine and black and desiccated. Dirty sparrows huddled in the bushes, as dull in colour as dead fruit left in leafless trees. A single starling creaked on a weather vane. In the gutter, beside a

drain, was a scrap of torn and dirty newspaper, caught in a little delta of filth; the word ECZEMA appeared in large capitals,
and below it was a letter from Mrs. Amelia D. Cravath, 2100
Pine Street, Fort Worth, Texas, to the effect that after being a
sufferer for years she had been cured by Caley's Ointment. In
the little delta, beside the fan-shaped and deeply runnelled
continent of brown mud, were lost twigs, descended from
their parent trees, dead matches, a rusty horse-chestnut burr, a
small concentration of sparkling gravel on the lip of the sewer,
a fragment of eggshell, a streak of yellow sawdust which had
been wet and was now dry and congealed, a brown pebble,
and a broken feather. Further on was a cement sidewalk, ruled
into geometrical parallelograms, with a brass inlay at one end
commemorating the contractors who had laid it, and, halfway
across, an irregular and random series of dog-tracks, immor-
talized in synthetic stone. He knew these well, and always
stepped on them; to cover the little hollows with his own foot
had always been a queer pleasure; today he did it once more,
but perfunctorily and detachedly, all the while thinking of
something else. That was a dog, a long time ago, who had
made a mistake and walked on the cement while it was still
wet. He had probably wagged his tail, but that hadn't been
recorded. Now, Paul Hasleman, aged twelve, on his way home
from school, crossed the same river, which in the meantime
had frozen into rock. Homeward through the snow, the snow
falling in bright sunshine. Homeward?

Then came the gateway with the two posts surmounted by
egg-shaped stones which had been cunningly balanced on
their ends, as if by Columbus, and mortared in the very act of
balance: a source of perpetual wonder. On the brick wall just
beyond, the letter H had been stencilled, presumably for some
purpose. H? H.

The green hydrant, with a little green-painted chain
attached to the brass screw-cap.

The elm tree, with the great grey wound in the bark, kid-
ney-shaped, into which he always put his hand—to feel the
cold but living wood. The injury, he had been sure, was due to
the gnawings of a tethered horse. But now it deserved only a

passing palm, a merely tolerant eye. There were more important things. Miracles. Beyond the thoughts of trees, mere elms.
Beyond the thoughts of sidewalks, mere stone, mere brick,
mere cement. Beyond the thoughts even of his own shoes,
which trod these sidewalks obediently, bearing a burden—far
above—of elaborate mystery. He watched them. They were not
very well polished; he had neglected them, for a very good
reason: they were one of the many parts of the increasing difficulty of the daily return to daily life, the morning struggle. To
get up, having at last opened one's eyes, to go to the window,
and discover no snow, to wash, to dress, to descent the curving stairs to breakfast—

At whatever pain to others, nevertheless, one must perse-
vere in severance, since the incommunicability of the experience demanded it It was desirable, of course, to be kind to
Mother and Father, especially as they seemed to be worried,
but it was also desirable to be resolute. If they should
decide—as appeared likely—to consult the doctor, Doctor
Howells, and have Paul inspected, his heart listened to
through a kind of dictaphone, his lungs, his stomach—well,
that was all right. He would go through with it. He would give
them answer for question, too—perhaps such answers as they
hadn't expected? No. That would never do. For the secret
world must, at all costs, be preserved.

The bird-house in the apple tree was empty—it was the
wrong time of year for wrens. The little round black door had
lost its pleasure. The wrens were enjoying other houses, other
nests, remoter trees. But this too was a notion which he only
vaguely and grazingly entertained—as if, for the moment, he
merely touched an edge of it; there was something further on,
which was already assuming a sharper importance; something
which already teased at the corners of his eyes, teasing also at
the corner of his mind. It was funny to think that he so wanted this, so awaited it—and yet found himself enjoying this
momentary dalliance with the bird-house, as if for a quite
deliberate postponement and enhancement of the approaching
pleasure. He was aware of his delay, of his smiling and
detached and now almost uncomprehending gaze at the little

bird-house; he knew what he was going to look at next: it was his own little cobbled hill-street, his own house, the little river at the bottom of the hill, the grocer's shop with the cardboard man in the window—and now, thinking of all this, he turned his head, still smiling, and looking quickly right and left through the snow-laden sunlight.

And the mist of snow, as he had foreseen, was still on it—a ghost of snow falling in the bright sunlight, softly and steadily floating and turning and pausing, soundlessly meeting the snow that covered, as with a transparent mirage, the bare bright cobbles. He loved it—he stood still and loved it. Its beauty was paralysing—beyond all words, all experience, all dream. No fairy story he had ever read could be compared with it—none had ever given him this extraordinary combination of ethereal loveliness with a something else, unnameable, which was just faintly and deliciously terrifying. What was this thing? As he thought of it, he looked upward toward his own bedroom window, which was open—and it was as if he looked straight into the room and saw himself lying half awake in his bed. There he was—at this very instant he was still perhaps actually there—more truly there than standing here at the edge of the cobbled hill-street, with one hand lifted to shade his eyes against the snow-sun. Had he indeed ever left his room, in all this time? since that very first morning? Was the whole progress still being enacted there, was it still the same morning, and himself not yet wholly awake? And even now, had the postman not yet come round the corner?...

This idea amused him, and automatically, as he thought of it, he turned his head and looked toward the top of the hill. There was, of course, nothing there—nothing and no one. The street was empty and quiet. And all the more because of its emptiness it occurred to him to count the houses—a thing which, oddly enough, he hadn't before thought of doing. Of course, he had known there weren't many—many, that is, on his own side of the street, which were the ones that figured in the postman's progress—but nevertheless it came to him as something of a shock to find that there were precisely *six*, above his own house—his own house was the seventh.

Six!

Astonished, he looked at his own house—looked at the
door, on which was the number thirteen—and then realized
that the whole thing was exactly and logically and absurdly
what he ought to have known. Just the same, the realization
gave him abruptly, and even a little frighteningly, a sense of
hurry. He was being hurried—he was being rushed. For—he
knit his brow—he couldn't be mistaken—it was just above the
seventh house, his *own* house, that the postman had first been
audible this very morning. But in that case—in that case—did
it mean that tomorrow he would hear nothing? The knock he
had heard must have been the knock of their own door. Did it
mean—and this was an idea which gave him a really extraordinary feeling of surprise—that he would never hear the postman again?—that tomorrow morning the postman would
already have passed the house, in a snow by then so deep as to
render his footsteps completely inaudible? That he would have
made his approach down the snow-filled street so soundlessly,
so secretly, that he, Paul Hasleman, there lying in bed, would
not have waked in time, or, waking, would have heard nothing?

But how could that be? Unless even the knocker should be
muffled in the snow—frozen tight, perhaps?... But in that
case—

A vague feeling of disappointment came over him; a vague
sadness, as if he felt himself deprived of something which he
had long looked forward to, something much prized. After all
this, all this beautiful progress, the slow delicious advance of
the postman through the silent and secret snow, the knock
creeping closer each day, and the footsteps nearer, the audible
compass of the world thus daily narrowed, narrowed, narrowed, as the snow soothingly and beautifully encroached and
deepened, after all this, was he to be defrauded of the one
thing he had so wanted—to be able to count, as it were, the
last two or three solemn footsteps, as they finally approached
his own door? Was it all going to happen, at the end, so suddenly? or indeed, had it already happened? with no slow and
subtle gradations of menace, in which he could luxuriate?

He gazed upward again, toward his own window which flashed in the sun; and this time almost with a feeling that it would be better if he *were* still in bed, in that room; for in that case this must still be the first morning, and there would be six more mornings to come—or, for that matter, seven or eight or nine—how could he be sure?—or even more.

III

After supper, the inquisition began. He stood before the doctor, under the lamp, and submitted silently to the usual thumpings and tappings.

"Now will you please say 'Ah!'?"

"Ah!"

"Now again please, if you don't mind."

"Ah."

"Say it slowly, and hold it if you can—"

"Ah-h-h-h-h-h—"

"Good."

How silly all this was. As if it had anything to do with his throat! Or his heart, or lungs!

Relaxing his mouth, of which the corners, after all this absurd stretching, felt uncomfortable, he avoided the doctor's eyes, and started toward the fireplace, past his mother's feet (in grey slippers) which projected from the green chair, and his father's feet (in brown slippers) which stood neatly side by side on the hearth-rug.

"Hm. There is certainly nothing wrong there…"

He felt the doctor's eyes fixed upon him, and, as if merely to be polite, returned the look, but with a feeling of justifiable evasiveness.

"Now, young man, tell me—do you feel all right?"

"Yes, sir, quite all right."

"No headaches? No dizziness?"

"No, I don't think so."

"Let me see. Let's get a book, if you don't mind—yes, thank you, that will do splendidly—and now, Paul, if you'll just read it, holding it as you would normally hold it—"

He took the book and read:

"And another praise have I to tell for this city our mother, the gift of a great god, a glory of the land most high; the might or horses, the might of young horses, the might of the sea.... For thou, son of Cronus, our lord Poseidon, hath throned herein this pride, since in these roads first thou didst show forth the curb that cures the rage of steeds. And the shapely oar, apt to men's hands, hath a wondrous speed on the brine, following the hundred-footed Nereids.... O land that art praised above all lands, now is it for thee to make those bright praises seen in deeds."

He stopped, tentatively, and lowered the heavy book.

"No—as I thought—there is certainly no superficial sign of eye strain."

Silence thronged the room, and he was aware of the focused scrutiny of the three people who confronted him....

"We could have his eyes examined—but I believe it is something else."

"What could it be?" That was his father's voice.

"It's only this curious absent-mindedness—" This was his mother's voice.

In the presence of the doctor, they both seemed irritatingly apologetic.

"I believe it is something else. Now, Paul—I would like very much to ask you a question or two. You will answer them, won't you—you know I'm an old, old friend of yours, eh? That's right!..."

His back was thumped twice by the doctor's fat fist—then the doctor was grinning at him with false amiability, while with one fingernail he was scratching the top button of his waistcoat. Beyond the doctor's shoulder was the fire, the fingers of flame making light prestidigitation against the sooty fireback, the soft sound of their random flutter the only sound.

"I would like to know—is there anything that worries you?"

The doctor was again smiling, his eyelids low against the little black pupils, in each of which was a tiny white bead of light. Why answer him? Why answer him at all? "At whatever pain to others"—but it was all a nuisance, this necessity for

resistance, this necessity for attention: it was as if one had been
stood up on a brilliantly lighted stage, under a great round
blaze of spotlight; as if one were merely a trained seal, or a per-
forming dog, or a fish, dipped out of an aquarium and held up
by the tail. It would serve them right if he were merely to bark
or growl. And meanwhile, to miss these last few precious
hours, these hours of which each minute was more beautiful
than the last, more menacing—! He still looked, as if from a
great distance, at the beads of light in the doctor's eyes, at the
fixed false smile, and then, beyond, once more at his mother's
slippers, his father's slippers, the soft flutter of the fire. Even
here, even amongst these hostile presences, and in this
arranged light, he could see the snow, he could hear it—it was
in the corners of the room, where the shadow was deepest,
under the sofa, behind the half-opened door which led to the
dining-room. It was gentler here, softer, its seethe the quietest
of whispers, as if, in deference to a drawing-room, it had quite
deliberately put on its "manners"; it kept itself out of sight,
obliterated itself, but distinctly with an air of saying, "Ah, but
just wait! Wait till we are alone together! Then I will begin to
tell you something new! Something white! something cold!
something sleepy! something of cease, and peace, and the long
bright curve of space! Tell them to go away. Banish them.
Refuse to speak. Leave them, go upstairs to your room, turn
out the light and get into bed—I will go with you, I will be
waiting for you, I will tell you a better story than Little Kay of
the Skates, or The Snow Ghost—I will surround your bed, I
will close the windows, pile a deep drift against the door, so
that none will ever again be able to enter. Speak to them!..." It
seemed as if the little hissing voice came from a slow white spiral of falling flakes in the corner by the front window—but he
could not be sure. He felt himself smiling, then, and said to the
doctor, but without looking at him, looking beyond him still—

"Oh, no, I think not—"

"But are you sure, my boy?"

His father's voice came softly and coldly then—the familiar
voice of silken warning....

"You needn't answer at once, Paul—remember we're trying

to help you—think it over and be quite sure, won't you?"

He felt himself smiling again, at the notion of being quite sure. What a joke! As if he weren't so sure that reassurance was no longer necessary, and all this cross-examination a ridiculous farce, a grotesque parody! What could they know about it? These gross intelligences, these humdrum minds so bound to the usual, the ordinary? Impossible to tell them about it! Why, even now, even now, with the proof so abundant, so formidable, so imminent, so appallingly present here in this very room, could they believe it?—could even his mother believe it? No—it was only too plain that if anything were said about it, the merest hint given, they would be incredulous—they would laugh—they would say "Absurd!"— think things about him which weren't true....

"Why no, I'm not worried—why should I be?"

He looked then straight at the doctor's low-lidded eyes, looked from one of them to the other, from one bead of light to the other, and gave a little laugh.

The doctor seemed to be disconcerted by this. He drew back in his chair, resting a fat white hand on either knee. The smile faded slowly from his face.

"Well, Paul!" he said, and paused gravely, "I'm afraid you don't take this quite seriously enough. I think you perhaps don't quite realize—don't quite realize—" He took a deep quick breath and turned, as if helplessly, at a loss for words, to the others. But Mother and Father were both silent—no help was forthcoming.

"You must surely know, be aware, that you have not been quite yourself, of late? Don't you know that?..."

It was amusing to watch the doctor's renewed attempt at a smile, a queer disorganized look, as of confidential embarrassment.

"I feel all right, sir," he said, and again gave the little laugh.

"And we're trying to help you." The doctor's tone sharpened.

"Yes, sir, I know. But why? I'm all right. I'm just *thinking*, that's all."

His mother made a quick movement forward, resting a hand on the back of the doctor's chair.

"Thinking?" she said. "But my dear, about what?"

This was a direct challenge—and would have to be directly met. But before he met it, he looked again into the corner by the door, as if for reassurance. He smiled again at what he saw, at what he heard. The little spiral was still there, still softly whirling, like the ghost of a white kitten chasing the ghost of a white tail, and making as it did so the faintest of whispers. It was all right! If only he could remain firm, everything was going to be all right.

"Oh, about anything, about nothing—*you* know the way you do!"

"You mean—day-dreaming?"

"Oh, no—thinking!"

"But thinking about *what*?"

"Anything."

He laughed a third time—but this time, happening to glance upward toward his mother's face, he was appalled at the effect his laughter seemed to have upon her. Her mouth had opened in an expression of horror.... This was too bad! Unfortunate! He had known it would cause pain, of course— but he hadn't expected it to be quite so bad as this. Perhaps— perhaps if he just gave them a tiny gleaming hint—?

"About the snow," he said.

"What on earth?" This was his father's voice. The brown slippers came a step nearer on the hearth-rug.

"But my dear, what do you mean?" This was his mother's voice.

The doctor merely stared.

"Just *snow*, that's all. I like to think about it."

"Tell us about it, my boy."

"But that's all it is. There's nothing to tell. *You* know what snow is?"

This he said almost angrily, for he felt that they were trying to corner him. He turned sideways so as no longer to face the doctor, and the better to see the inch of blackness between the window-sill and the lowered curtain—the cold inch of beckoning and delicious night. At once he felt better, more assured.

"Mother—can I go to bed, now, please? I've got a headache."

"But I thought you said—"

"It's just come. It's all these questions—! Can I, Mother?"

"You can go as soon as the doctor has finished."

"Don't you think this thing ought to be gone into thoroughly, and *now*?" This was Father's voice. The brown slippers again came a step nearer, the voice was the well-known "punishment" voice, resonant and cruel.

"Oh, what's the use, Norman—"

Quite suddenly, everyone was silent. And without precisely facing them, nevertheless he was aware that all three of them were watching him with an extraordinary intensity—staring hard at him—as if he had done something monstrous, or was himself some kind of monster. He could hear the soft irregular flutter of the flames; the cluck-click-cluck-click of the clock; far and faint, two sudden spurts of laughter from the kitchen, as quickly cut off as begun; a murmur of water in the pipes; and then, the silence seemed to deepen, to spread out, to become world-long and world-wide, to become timeless and shapeless, and to centre inevitably and rightly, with a slow and sleepy but enormous concentration of all power, on the beginning of a new sound. What this new sound was going to be, he knew perfectly well. It might begin with a hiss, but it would end with a roar—there was no time to lose—he must escape. It mustn't happen here—

Without another word, he turned and ran up the stairs.

IV

Not a moment too soon. The darkness was coming in long white waves. A prolonged sibilance filled the night—a great seamless seethe of wild influence went abruptly across it—a cold low humming shook the windows. He shut the door and flung off his clothes in the dark. The bare black floor was like a little raft tossed in waves of snow, almost overwhelmed, washed under whitely, up again, smothered in curled billows of feather. The snow was laughing; it spoke from all sides at once; it pressed closer to him as he ran and jumped exulting into his bed.

"Listen to us!" it said. "Listen! We have come to tell you the story we told you about. You remember? Lie down. Shut your eyes, now—you will no longer see much—in this white darkness who could see, or want to see? We will take the place of everything.... Listen—"

A beautiful varying dance of snow began at the front of the room, came forward and then retreated, flattened out toward the floor, then rose fountain-like to the ceiling, swayed, recruited itself from a new stream of flakes which poured laughing in through the humming window, advanced again, lifted long white arms. It said peace, it said remoteness, it said cold—it said—

But then a gash of horrible light fell brutally across the room from the opening door—the snow drew back hissing—something alien had come into the room—something hostile. This thing rushed at him, clutched at him, shook him—and he was not merely horrified, he was filled with such a loathing as he had never known. What was this? this cruel disturbance? this act of anger and hate? It was as if he had to reach up a hand toward another world for any understanding of it—an effort of which he was only barely capable. But of that other world he still remembered just enough to know the exorcising words. They tore themselves from his other life suddenly—

"Mother! Mother! Go away! I hate you!"

And with that effort, everything was solved, everything became all right: the seamless hiss advanced once more, the long white wavering lines rose and fell like enormous whispering sea-waves, the whisper becoming louder, the laughter more numerous.

"Listen!" it said. "We'll tell you the last, the most beautiful and secret story—shut your eyes—it is a very small story—a story that gets smaller and smaller—it comes inward instead of opening like a flower—it is a flower becoming a seed—a little cold seed—do you hear? We are leaning closer to you—"

The hiss was now becoming a roar—the whole world was a vast moving screen of snow—but even now it said peace, it said remoteness, it said cold, it said sleep.

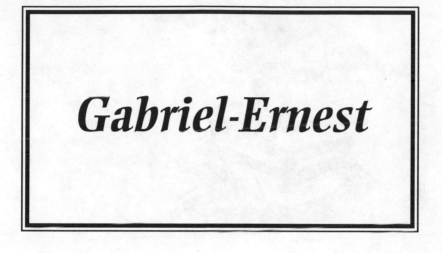

Gabriel-Ernest

by
SAKI
(H.H. Munro, 1870–1916)

Saki surely ranks alongside O. Henry as one of the great geniuses of the short story. He has the knack of grabbing his readers with his opening few sentences and holding them spellbound till the end, at which point he tends to produce an ironic twist. In "Gabriel-Ernest," we are in the quintessential Saki country of pre-World War I England. It is a carefree time of country-house weekends, eccentric aristocrats and serene summer days, where everyone seems to have a maiden aunt or two. But Saki likes to provide a fly in the ointment: enter Gabriel-Ernest, werewolf...

"There is a wild beast in your woods," said the artist Cunningham, as he was being driven to the station. It was the only remark he had made during the drive, but as Van Cheele had talked incessantly his companion's silence had not been noticeable.

"A stray fox or two and some resident weasels. Nothing more formidable," said Van Cheele. The artist said nothing.

"What did you mean about a wild beast?" said Van Cheele later, when they were on the platform.

"Nothing. My imagination. Here is the train," said Cunningham.

That afternoon Van Cheele went for one of his frequent rambles through his woodland property. He had a stuffed bittern in his study, and knew the names of quite a number of wild flowers, so his aunt had possibly some justification in describing him as a great naturalist. At any rate, he was a great walker. It was his custom to take mental notes of everything he saw during his walks, not so much for the purpose of assisting contemporary science as to provide topics for conversation afterwards. When the bluebells began to show themselves in flower he made a point of informing everyone of the fact; the season of the year might have warned his hearers of the likelihood of

such an occurrence, but at least they felt that he was being
absolutely frank with them.

What Van Cheele saw on this particular afternoon was,
however, something far removed from his ordinary range of
experience. On a shelf of smooth stone overhanging a deep
pool in the hollow of an oak coppice a boy of about sixteen lay
asprawl, drying his wet brown limbs luxuriously in the sun.
His wet hair, parted by a recent dive, lay close to his head, and
his light-brown eyes, so light that there was an almost tigerish
gleam in them, were turned towards Van Cheele with a certain
lazy watchfulness. It was an unexpected apparition, and Van
Cheele found himself engaged in the novel process of thinking
before he spoke. Where on earth could this wild-looking boy
hail from? The miller's wife had lost a child some two months
ago, supposed to have been swept away by the mill-race, but
that had been a mere baby, not a half-grown lad.

"What are you doing there?" he demanded.

"Obviously, sunning myself," replied the boy.

"Where do you live?"

"Here, in these woods."

"You can't live in the woods," said Van Cheele.

"They are very nice woods," said the boy, with a touch of
patronage in his voice.

"But where do you sleep at night?"

"I don't sleep at night; that's my busiest time."

Van Cheele began to have an irritated feeling that he was
grappling with a problem that was eluding him.

"What do you feed on?" he asked.

"Flesh," said the boy, and he pronounced the word with
slow relish, as though he were tasting it.

"Flesh! What flesh?"

"Since it interests you, rabbits, wild-fowl, hares, poultry,
lambs in their season, children when I can get any; they're
usually too well locked in at night, when I do most of my
hunting. It's quite two months since I tasted child-flesh."

Ignoring the chaffing nature of the last remark, Van Cheele
tried to draw the boy on the subject of possible poaching
operations.

"You're talking rather through your hat when you speak of feeding on hares." (Considering the nature of the boy's toilet, the simile was hardly an apt one.) "Our hillside hares aren't easily caught."

"At night I hunt on four feet," was the somewhat cryptic response.

"I suppose you mean that you hunt with a dog?" hazarded Van Cheele.

The boy rolled slowly over on to his back, and laughed a weird low laugh, that was pleasantly like a chuckle and disagreeably like a snarl.

"I don't fancy any dog would be very anxious for my company, especially at night."

Van Cheele began to feel that there was something positively uncanny about the strange-eyed, strange-tongued youngster.

"I can't have you staying in these woods," he declared authoritatively.

"I fancy you'd rather have me here than in your house," said the boy.

The prospect of this wild, nude animal in Van Cheele's primly ordered house was certainly an alarming one.

"If you don't go, I shall have to make you," said Van Cheele.

The boy turned like a flash, plunged into the pool, and in a moment had flung his wet and glistening body half-way up the bank where Van Cheele was standing. In an otter the movement would not have been remarkable; in a boy Van Cheele found it sufficiently startling. His foot slipped as he made an involuntary backward movement, and he found himself almost prostrate on the slippery weed-grown bank, with those tigerish yellow eyes not very far from his own. Almost instinctively he half-raised his hand to his throat. The boy laughed again, a laugh in which the snarl had nearly driven out the chuckle, and then, with another of his astonishing lightning movements, plunged out of view into a yielding tangle of weed and fern.

"What an extraordinary wild animal!" said Van Cheele as he picked himself up. And then he recalled Cunningham's remark, "There is a wild beast in your woods."

Walking slowly homeward, Van Cheele began to turn over

in his mind various local occurrences which might be trace-able to the existence of this astonishing young savage.

Something had been thinning the game in the woods lately, poultry had been missing from the farms, hares were growing unaccountably scarcer, and complaints had reached him of lambs being carried off bodily from the hills. Was it possible that this wild boy was really hunting the countryside in com-pany with some clever poacher dog? He had spoken of hunting "four-footed" by night, but then, again, he had hinted strangely at no dog caring to come near him, "especially at night." It was certainly puzzling. And then, as Van Cheele ran his mind over the various depredations that had been committed during the last month or two, he came suddenly to a dead stop, alike in his walk and his speculations. The child missing from the mill two months ago—the accepted theory was that it had tumbled into the mill-race and been swept away; but the mother had always declared she had heard a shriek on the hill side of the house, in the opposite direction from the water. It was unthink-able, of course, but he wished that the boy had not made that uncanny remark about child-flesh eaten two months ago. Such dreadful things should not be said even in fun.

Van Cheele, contrary to his usual wont, did not feel dis-posed to be communicative about his discovery in the wood. His position as a parish councillor and justice of the peace seemed somehow compromised by the fact that he was har-bouring a personality of such doubtful repute on his property; there was even a possibility that a heavy bill of damages for raided lambs and poultry might be laid at his door. At dinner that night he was quite unusually silent.

"Where's your voice gone to?" said his aunt. "One would think you had seen a wolf."

Van Cheele, who was not familiar with the old saying, thought the remark rather foolish; if he *had* seen a wolf on his property his tongue would have been extraordinarily busy with the subject.

At breakfast next morning Van Cheele was conscious that his feeling of uneasiness regarding yesterday's episode had not wholly disappeared, and he resolved to go by train to the neighbouring cathedral town, hunt up Cunningham, and learn from him what he had really seen that had prompted the remark about a wild beast in the woods. With this resolution taken, his usual cheerfulness partially returned, and he hummed a bright little melody as he sauntered to the morning-room for his customary cigarette. As he entered the room the melody made way abruptly for a pious invocation. Gracefully asprawl on the ottoman, in an attitude of almost exaggerated repose, was the boy of the woods. He was drier than when Van Cheele had last seen him, but no other alteration was noticeable in his toilet.

"How dare you come here?" asked Van Cheele furiously.

"You told me I was not to stay in the woods," said the boy calmly.

"But not to come here. Supposing my aunt should see you!"

And with a view to minimizing that catastrophe Van Cheele hastily obscured as much of his unwelcome guest as possible under the folds of a *Morning Post*. At that moment his aunt entered the room.

"This is a poor boy who has lost his way—and lost his memory. He doesn't know who he is or where he comes from," explained Van Cheele desperately, glancing apprehensively at the waif's face to see whether he was going to add inconvenient candour to his other savage propensities.

Miss Van Cheele was enormously interested.

"Perhaps his underlinen is marked," she suggested.

"He seems to have lost most of that, too," said Van Cheele, making frantic little grabs at the *Morning Post* to keep it in its place.

A naked, homeless child appealed to Miss Van Cheele as warmly as a stray kitten or derelict puppy would have done.

"We must do all we can for him," she decided, and in a very short time a messenger, dispatched to the rectory, where a page-boy was kept, had returned with a suit of pantry clothes, and the necessary accessories of shirt, shoes, collar, etc. Clothed, clean and groomed, the boy lost none of his uncanniness in Van Cheele's eyes, but his aunt found him sweet.

"We must call him something till we know who he really

is," she said. "Gabriel-Ernest, I think; those are nice suitable names."

Van Cheele agreed, but he privately doubted whether they were being drafted on to a nice suitable child. His misgivings were not diminished by the fact that his staid and elderly spaniel had bolted out of the house at the first incoming of the boy, and now obstinately remained shivering and yapping at the farther end of the orchard, while the canary, usually as vocally industrious as Van Cheele himself, had put itself on an allowance of frightened cheeps. More than ever he was resolved to consult Cunningham without loss of time.

As he drove off to the station his aunt was arranging that Gabriel-Ernest should help her to entertain the infant members of her Sunday-school class at tea that afternoon.

Cunningham was not at first disposed to be communicative.

"My mother died of some brain trouble," he explained, "so you will understand why I am averse to dwelling on anything of an impossibly fantastic nature that I may see or think that I have seen."

"But what *did* you see?" persisted Van Cheele.

"What I thought I saw was something so extraordinary that no really sane man could dignify it with the credit of having actually happened. I was standing, the last evening I was with you, half-hidden in the hedgegrowth by the orchard gate, watching the dying glow of the sunset. Suddenly I became aware of a naked boy, a bather from some neighbouring pool, I took him to be, who was standing out on the bare hillside also watching the sunset. His pose was so suggestive of some wild faun of Pagan myth that I instantly wanted to engage him as a model, and in another moment I think I should have hailed him. But just then the sun dipped out of view, and all the orange and pink slid out of the landscape, leaving it cold and grey. And at the same moment an astounding thing happened—the boy vanished too!"

"What! Vanished away into nothing?" asked Van Cheele excitedly.

"No; that is the dreadful part of it," answered the artist; "on the open hillside where the boy had been standing a second ago, stood a large wolf, blackish in colour, with gleaming fangs and cruel, yellow eyes. You may think—"

But Van Cheele did not stop for anything as futile as thought. Already he was tearing at top speed towards the station. He dismissed the idea of a telegram. "Gabriel-Ernest is a werewolf" was a hopelessly inadequate effort at conveying the situation, and his aunt would think it was a code message to which he had omitted to give her the key. His one hope was that he might reach home before sundown. The cab which he chartered at the other end of the railway journey bore him with what seemed exasperating slowness along the country roads, which were pink and mauve with the flush of the sinking sun. His aunt was putting away some unfinished jams and cake when he arrived.

"Where is Gabriel-Ernest?" he almost screamed.

"He is taking the little Toop child home," said his aunt. "It was getting so late, I thought it wasn't safe to let it go back alone. What a lovely sunset, isn't it?"

But Van Cheele, although not oblivious of the glow in the western sky, did not stay to discuss its beauties. At a speed for which he was scarcely geared he raced along the narrow lane that led to the home of the Toops. On one side ran the swift current of the mill-stream, on the other rose the stretch of bare hillside. A dwindling rim of red sun showed still on the sky-line, and the next turning must bring him in view of the ill-assorted couple he was pursuing. Then the colour went suddenly out of things, and a grey light settled itself with a quick shiver over the landscape. Van Cheele heard a shrill wail of fear, and stopped running.

Nothing was ever seen again of the Toop child or Gabriel-Ernest, but the latter's discarded garments were found lying in the road, so it was assumed that the child had fallen into the water, and that the boy had stripped and jumped in, in a vain endeavour to save it. Van Cheele and some workmen who were near by at the time testified to having heard a child scream loudly just near the spot where the clothes were found. Mrs. Toop, who had eleven other children, was decently resigned to her bereavement, but Miss Van Cheele sincerely mourned her lost foundling. It was on her initiative that a memorial brass was put up in the parish church to "Gabriel-Ernest, an unknown boy, who bravely sacrificed his life for another."

Van Cheele gave way to his aunt in most things, but he flatly refused to subscribe to the Gabriel-Ernest memorial.

The Trial for Murder

by
CHARLES DICKENS
(1812–1870)

This tale originally appeared as one of a series of stories with the title "Doctor Marigold's Prescriptions." Subtitled "To Be Taken with a Grain of Salt," it was the sixth of the good doctor's prescriptions. However you take it, immersing yourself in this particular medicine will no doubt have the effect of holding you in suspense and relieving you of your daily cares, as it whisks you to a haunted courtroom in the long-ago days of Queen Victoria.

I have always noticed a prevalent want of courage, even among persons of superior intelligence and culture, as to imparting their own psychological experiences when those have been of a strange sort. Almost all men are afraid that what they could relate in such wise would find no parallel or response in a listener's internal life, and might be suspected or laughed at. A truthful traveller, who should have seen some extraordinary creature in the likeness of a sea-serpent, would have no fear of mentioning it; but the same traveller, having had some singular presentiment, impulse, vagary of thought, vision (so-called), dream, or other remarkable mental impression, would hesitate considerably before he would own to it. To this reticence I attribute much of the obscurity in which such subjects are involved. We do not habitually communicate our experiences of these subjective things as we do our experiences of objective creation. The consequence is, that the general stock of experience in this regard appears exceptional, and really is so, in respect of being miserably imperfect.

In what I am going to relate, I have no intention of setting up, opposing, or supporting, any theory whatever. I know the history of the bookseller in Berlin. I have studied the case of the wife of a late Astronomer Royal as related by Sir David Brewster, and I have followed the minutest details of a much more remarkable case of spectral illusion occurring within my private circle of friends. It may be necessary to state as to this last, that the sufferer (a lady) was in no degree, however distant, related to me. A mistaken assumption on that head might suggest an explanation of a part of my own case—but only a part—which would be wholly without foundation. It cannot be referred to my inheritance of any developed peculiarity, nor had I ever before any at all similar experience, nor have I ever had any at all similar experience since.

It does not signify how many years ago, or how few, a certain murder was committed in England, which attracted great attention. We hear more than enough of murderers as they rise in succession to their atrocious eminence, and I would bury the memory of this particular brute, if I could, as his body was buried, in Newgate Jail. I purposely abstain from giving any direct clue to the criminal's individuality.

When the murder was first discovered, no suspicion fell— or I ought rather to say, for I cannot be too precise in my facts, it was nowhere publicly hinted than any suspicion fell—on the man who was afterwards brought to trial. As no reference was at that time made to him in the newspapers, it is obviously impossible that any description of him can at that time have been given in the newspapers. It is essential that this fact be remembered.

Unfolding at breakfast my morning paper, containing the account of that first discovery, I found it to be deeply interesting, and I read it with close attention. I read it twice, if not three times. The discovery had been made in a bedroom, and, when I laid down the paper, I was aware of a flash—rush, flow—I do not know what to call it, no word I can find is satisfactorily descriptive, in which I seemed to see that bedroom passing through my room, like a picture impossibly painted on a running river. Though almost instantaneous in its passing, it was perfectly clear; so clear that I distinctly, and with a sense of relief, observed the absence of the dead body from the bed.

It was in no romantic place that I had this curious sensation, but in chambers in Piccadilly, very near to the corner of St. James's Street. It was entirely new to me. I was in my easy-chair at the moment, and the sensation was accompanied with a peculiar shiver which started the chair from its position. (But it is to be noted that the chair ran easily on castors.) I went to one of the windows (there are two in the room, and the room is on the second floor) to refresh my eyes with the moving objects down in Piccadilly. It was a bright autumn morning, and the street was sparkling and cheerful. The wind was high. As I looked out, it brought down from the park a quantity of fallen leaves, which a gust took, and whirled into a spiral pillar. As the pillar fell and the leaves dispersed, I saw two men on the opposite side of the way, going from west to east. They were one behind the other. The foremost man often looked back over his shoulder. The second man followed him, at a distance of some thirty paces, with his right hand menacingly raised. First, the singularity and steadiness of this threatening gesture in so public a thoroughfare attracted my attention; and next, the more remarkable circumstance that nobody heeded it. Both men threaded their way among the other passengers with a smoothness hardly consistent even with the action of walking on a pavement; and no single creature, that I could see, gave them place, touched them, or looked after them. In passing before my windows, they both stared up at me. I saw their two faces very distinctly, and I knew that I could recognize them anywhere. Not that I had consciously noticed anything very remarkable in either face, except that the man who went first had an unusually lowering appearance, and that the face of the man who followed him was of the colour of impure wax.

I am a bachelor, and my valet and his wife constitute my whole establishment. My occupation is in a certain branch bank, and I wish that my duties as head of a department were as light as they are popularly supposed to be. They kept me in town that autumn, when I stood in need of change. I was not ill, but I was not well. My reader is to make the most that can be reasonably made of my feeling jaded, having a depressing sense upon me of a monotonous life, and being "slightly dyspeptic." I am assured by my renowned doctor that my real state of health at that time justifies no stronger description, and I quote his own from his written answer to my request for it.

As the circumstances of the murder, gradually unravelling, took stronger and stronger possession of the public mind, I kept them away from mine by knowing as little about them as was possible in the midst of the universal excitement. But I knew that a verdict of wilful murder had been found against the suspected murderer, and that he had been committed to Newgate for trial. I also knew that his trial had been postponed over one Sessions of the Central Criminal Court, on the ground of general prejudice and want of time for the preparation of the defence. I may further have known, but I believe I did not, when, or about when, the Sessions to which his trial stood postponed would come on.

My sitting-room, bedroom, and dressing-room, are all on one floor. With the last there is no communication but through the bedroom. True, there is a door in it, once communicating with the staircase; but a part of the fitting of my bath has been—and had then been for some years—fixed across it. At the same period, and as a part of the same arrangement, the door had been nailed up and canvassed over.

I was standing in my bedroom late one night, giving some directions to my servant before he went to bed. My face was towards the only available door of communication with the dressing-room, and it was closed. My servant's back was towards that door. While I was speaking to him, I saw it open, and a man look in, who very earnestly and mysteriously beckoned to me. That was the man who had gone second of the two along Piccadilly, and whose face was of the colour of impure wax.

The figure, having beckoned, drew back, and closed the door. With no longer pause than was made by my crossing the bedroom, I opened the dressing-room door, and looked in. I had a lighted candle already in my hand. I felt no inward expectation of seeing the figure in the dressing-room, and I did not see it there.

Conscious that my servant stood amazed, I turned round to
him, and said, "Derrick, could you believe that in my cool
senses I fancied I saw a—"

As I there laid my hand upon his breast, with a sudden start
he trembled violently, and said, "O Lord, yes, sir! A dead man
beckoning!"

Now I do not believe that this John Derrick, my trusty and
attached servant for more than twenty years, had any impression whatever of having seen any such figure, until I touched
him. The change in him was so startling, when I touched him,
that I fully believe he derived his impression in some occult
manner from me at that instant.

I bade John Derrick bring some brandy, and I gave him a
dram, and was glad to take one myself. Of what had preceded
that night's phenomenon, I told him not a single word.
Reflecting on it, I was absolutely certain that I had never seen
that face before, except on the one occasion in Piccadilly.
Comparing its expression when beckoning at the door with its
expression when it had stared up at me as I stood at my window, I came to the conclusion that on the first occasion it had
sought to fasten itself upon my memory, and that on the second
occasion it had made sure of being immediately remembered.

I was not very comfortable that night, though I felt a certainty difficult to explain, that the figure would not return. At
daylight I fell into a heavy sleep, from which I was awakened
by John Derrick's coming to my bedside with a paper in his
hand.

This paper, it appeared, had been the subject of an alterca-
tion at the door between its bearer and my servant. It was a
summons to me to serve upon a jury at the forthcoming
Sessions at the Central Criminal Court at the Old Bailey. I had
never before been summoned on such a jury, as John Derrick
well knew. He believed—I am not certain at this hour whether
with reason or otherwise—that the class of jurors were cus-
tomarily chosen on a lower qualification than mine, and he
had at first refused to accept the summons. The man who
served it had taken the matter very coolly. He had said that my
attendance or non-attendance was nothing to him; there the

summons was; and I should deal with it at my own peril, and not at his.

For a day or two I was undecided whether to respond to this call, or take no notice of it. I was not conscious of the slightest mysterious bias, influence, or attraction, one way or other. Of that I am as strictly sure as of every other statement that I make here. Ultimately I decided, as a break in the monotony of my life, that I would go.

The appointed morning was a raw morning in the month of November. There was a dense brown fog in Piccadilly, and it became positively black and in the last degree oppressive east of Temple Bar. I found the passages and staircases of the court-house flaringly lighted with gas, and the court itself similarly illuminated. I *think* that, until I was conducted by officers into the old court and saw its crowded state, I did not know that the murderer was to be tried that day. I *think* that, until I was so helped into the old court with considerable difficulty, I did not know into which of the two courts sitting my summons would take me. But this must not be received as a positive assertion, for I am not completely satisfied in my mind on either point.

I took my seat in the place appropriated to jurors in wait-ing, and I looked about the court as well as I could through the cloud of fog and breath that was heavy in it. I noticed the black vapour hanging like a murky curtain outside the great windows, and I noticed the stifled sound of wheels on the straw or tan that was littered in the street; also, the hum of the people gathered there, which a shrill whistle, or a louder song or hail than the rest, occasionally pierced. Soon afterwards the judges, two in number, entered, and took their seats. The buzz in the court was awfully hushed. The direction was given to put the murderer to the bar. He appeared there. And in that same instant I recognized in him the first of the two men who had gone down Piccadilly.

If my name had been called then, I doubt if I could have answered it audibly. But it was called about sixth or eighth in the panel, and I was by that time able to say, "Here!" Now, observe. As I stepped into the box, the prisoner, who had been looking on attentively, but with no sign of concern, became violently agitated, and beckoned to his attorney. The prisoner's wish to challenge me was so manifest, that it occasioned a pause, during which the attorney, with his hand upon the dock, whispered with his client, and shook his head. I afterwards had it from that gentleman, that the prisoner's first affrighted words to him were, "At all hazards, challenge that man!" But that, as he would give no reason for it, and admitted that he had not even known my name until he heard it called and I appeared, it was not done.

Both on the ground already explained, that I wish to avoid reviving the unwholesome memory of that murderer, and also because a detailed account of his long trial is by no means indispensable to my narrative, I shall confine myself closely to such incidents in the ten days and nights during which we, the jury, were kept together, as directly bear on my own curious personal experience. It is in that, and not in the murderer, that I seek to interest my reader. It is to that, and not to a page of the Newgate Calendar, that I beg attention.

I was chosen foreman of the jury. On the second morning of the trial, after evidence had been taken for two hours (I heard the church clocks strike), happening to cast my eyes over my brother jurymen, I found an inexplicable difficulty in counting them. I counted them several times, yet always with the same difficulty. In short, I made them one too many.

I touched the brother juryman whose place was next me, and I whispered to him, "Oblige me by counting us."

He looked surprised by the request, but turned his head and counted. "Why," says he, suddenly, "we are Thirt—; but no, it's not possible. No. We are twelve."

According to my counting that day, we were always right in detail, but in the gross we were always one too many. There was no appearance—no figure—to account for it; but I had now an inward foreshadowing of the figure that was surely coming.

The jury were housed at the London Tavern. We all slept in one large room on separate tables, and we were constantly in the charge and under the eye of the officer sworn to hold us in safe-keeping. I see no reason for suppressing the real name of that officer. He was intelligent, highly polite, and obliging, and (I was glad to hear) much respected in the City. He had an agreeable presence, good eyes, enviable black whiskers, and a fine sonorous voice. His name was Mr. Harker.

When we turned into our twelve beds at night, Mr. Harker's bed was drawn across the door. On the night of the second day, not being disposed to lie down, and seeing Mr. Harker sitting on his bed, I went and sat beside him, and offered him a pinch of snuff. As Mr. Harker's hand touched mine in taking it from my box, a peculiar shiver crossed him, and he said, "Who is this?"

Following Mr. Harker's eyes, and looking along the room, I saw again the figure I expected—the second of the two men who had gone down Piccadilly. I rose, and advanced a few steps; then stopped, and looked round at Mr. Harker. He was quite unconcerned, laughed, and said in a pleasant way, "I thought for a moment we had a thirteenth juryman, without a bed. But I see it is the moonlight."

Making no revelation to Mr. Harker, but inviting him to take a walk with me to the end of the room, I watched what the figure did. It stood for a few moments by the bedside of each of my eleven brother jurymen, close to the pillow. It always went to the right-hand side of the bed, and always passed out crossing the foot of the next bed. It seemed, from the action of the head, merely to look down pensively at each recumbent figure. It took no notice of me, or of my bed, which was that nearest to Mr. Harker's. It seemed to go out where the moonlight came in, through a high window, as by an aerial flight of stairs.

Next morning, at breakfast, it appeared that everybody present had dreamed of the murdered man last night, except myself and Mr. Harker.

I now felt as convinced that the second man who had gone down Piccadilly was the murdered man (so to speak), as if it had been borne into my comprehension by his immediate testimony. But even this took place, and in a manner for which I was not at all prepared.

On the fifth day of the trial, when the case for the prosecution was drawing to a close, a miniature of the murdered man, missing from his bedroom upon the discovery of the deed, and afterwards found in a hiding-place where the murderer had been seen digging, was put in evidence. Having been identified by the witness under examination, it was handed up to the bench, and thence handed down to be inspected by the jury. As an officer in a black gown was making his way with it across to me, the figure of the second man who had gone down Piccadilly impetuously started from the crowd, caught the miniature from the officer, and gave it to me with his own hands, at the same time saying, in a low and hollow tone— before I saw the miniature, which was in a locket—"I was younger then, and my face was not then drained of blood." It also came between me and the brother juryman to whom I would have given the miniature, and between him and the brother juryman to whom he would have given it, and so passed it on through the whole of our number, and back into my possession. Not one of them, however, detected this.

At table, and generally when we were shut up together in Mr. Harker's custody, we had from the first naturally discussed the day's proceedings a good deal. On that fifth day, the case for the prosecution being closed, and we having that side of the question in a completed shape before us, our discussion was more animated and serious. Among our number was a vestryman—the densest idiot I have ever seen at large—who met the plainest evidence with the most preposterous objections, and who was sided with by two flabby parochial parasites; all the three impanelled from a district so delivered over to fever that they ought to have been upon their own trial for five hundred murders. When these mischievous blockheads were at their loudest, which was towards midnight, while some of us were already preparing for bed, I again saw the murdered man. He stood grimly behind them, beckoning to me. On my going towards them, and striking into the conversation, he immediately retired. This was the beginning of a separate series of appearances, confined to that long room in which *we* were confined. Whenever a knot of my brother jurymen laid their heads together, I saw the head of the murdered man among theirs. Whenever their comparison of notes was going against him, he would solemnly and irresistibly beckon to me.

It will be borne in mind that down to the production of the miniature, on the fifth day of the trial, I had never seen the appearance in court. Three changes occurred now that we entered on the case for the defence. Two of them I will mention together, first. The figure was now in court continually, and it never there addressed itself to me, but always to the person who was speaking at the time. For instance: the throat of the murdered man had been cut straight across. In the opening speech for the defence, it was suggested that the deceased might have cut his own throat. At that very moment, the figure, with its throat in the dreadful condition referred to (this it had concealed before), stood at the speaker's elbow, motioning across and across its windpipe, now with the right hand, now with the left, vigorously suggesting to the speaker himself the impossibility of such a wound having been self-inflicted by either hand. For another instance: a witness to character, a woman, deposed to the prisoner's being the most amiable of mankind. The figure in that instant stood on the floor before her, looking her full in the face, and pointing out the prisoner's evil countenance with an extended arm and an outstretched finger.

The third change now to be added impressed me strongly as the most marked and striking of all. I do not theorize upon it; I accurately state it, and there leave it. Although the appearance was not itself perceived by those whom it addressed, its coming close to such persons was invariably attended by some trepidation or disturbance on their part. It seemed to me as if it were prevented, by laws to which I was not amenable, from fully revealing itself to others, and yet as if it could invisibly, dumbly, and darkly overshadow their minds. When the leading counsel for the defence suggested that hypothesis of suicide, and the figure stood at the learned gentleman's elbow, frightfully sawing at its severed throat, it is undeniable that the counsel faltered in his speech, lost for a few seconds the thread of his ingenious discourse, wiped his forehead with his handkerchief, and

turned extremely pale. When the witness to character was confronted by the appearance, her eyes most certainly did follow
the direction of its pointed finger, and rest in great hesitation
and trouble upon the prisoner's face. Two additional illustra-
tions will suffice. On the eighth day of the trial, after the pause
which was every day made early in the afternoon for a few
minutes' rest and refreshment, I came back into court with the
rest of the jury some little time before the return of the judges.
Standing up in the box and looking about me, I thought the
figure was not there, until, chancing to raise my eyes to the
gallery, I saw it bending forward, and leaning over a very
decent woman, as if to assure itself whether the judges had
resumed their seats or not. Immediately afterwards that
woman screamed, fainted, and was carried out. So with the
venerable, sagacious, and patient judge who conducted the
trial. When the case was over, and he settled himself and his
papers to sum up, the murdered man, entering by the judges'
door, advanced to his Lordship's desk, and looked eagerly over
his shoulder at the pages of his notes which he was turning. A
change came over his Lordship's face; his hand stopped; the
peculiar shiver, that I knew so well, passed over him; he faltered, "Excuse me, gentlemen, for a few moments. I am somewhat oppressed by the vitiated air"; and did not recover until
he had drunk a glass of water.

Through all the monotony of six of those interminable ten
days—the same judges and others on the bench, the same
murderer in the dock, the same lawyers at the table, the same
tones of question and answer rising to the roof of the court,
the same scratching of the judge's pen, the same ushers going
in and out, the same lights kindled at the same hour when
there had been any natural light of day, the same foggy curtain
outside the great windows when it was foggy, the same rain
pattering and dripping when it was rainy, the same footmarks
and turnkeys and prisoner day after day on the same sawdust,
the same keys locking and unlocking the same heavy doors—
through all the wearisome monotony which made me feel as if
I had been foreman of the jury for a vast period of time, and
Piccadilly had flourished coevally with Babylon, the murdered

man never lost one trace of his distinctness in my eyes, nor was he at any moment less distinct than anybody else. I must not omit, as a matter of fact, that I never once saw the appearance which I call by the name of the murdered man look at the murderer. Again and again I wondered, "Why does he not?" But he never did.

Nor did he look at me, after the production of the miniature, until the last closing minutes of the trial arrived. We retired to consider, at seven minutes before ten at night. The idiotic vestryman and his two parochial parasites gave us so much trouble that we twice returned into court to beg to have certain extracts from the judge's notes reread. Nine of us had not the smallest doubt about those passages, neither, I believe, had anyone in the court; the dunderheaded triumvirate, however, having no idea but obstruction, disputed them for that very reason. At length we prevailed, and finally the jury returned into court at ten minutes past twelve.

The murdered man at that time stood directly opposite the jury-box, on the other side of the court. As I took my place, his eyes rested on me with great attention; he seemed satisfied, and slowly shook a great grey veil, which he carried on his arm for the first time, over his head and whole form. As I gave in our verdict, "Guilty," the veil collapsed, all was gone, and his place was empty.

The murderer, being asked by the judge, according to usage, whether he had anything to say before sentence of death should be passed upon him, indistinctly muttered something which was described in the leading newspapers of the following day as "a few rambling, incoherent, and half-audible words, in which he was understood to complain that he had not had a fair trial, because the foreman of the jury was prepossessed against him." The remarkable declaration that he really made was this: "My Lord, I knew I was a doomed man, when the foreman of my jury came into the box. My Lord, I knew he would never let me off, because before I was taken, he somehow got to my bedside in the night, woke me, and put a rope round my neck."

The Snail-Watcher

by
PATRICIA HIGHSMITH
(1921–   )

The acclaimed British novelist Graham Greene once wrote that the reader enters the world of Patricia Highsmith "with a sense of personal danger, with the head half turned over the shoulder...." How true. Miss Highsmith is not concerned with the supernatural, which can so easily be dismissed, but rather with the fears and concerns of "real life"—which, in her writing, often emerges as more bizarre, tense and spine-chilling than anything we could imagine. So, armed with the knowledge that we're entering a land where the real is stranger than the supernatural, we turn to the story of Mr. Knoppert and his unusual obsession....

When Mr. Peter Knoppert began to make a hobby of snail-watching, he had no idea that his handful of specimens would become hundreds in no time. Only two months after the original snails were carried up to the Knoppert study, some thirty glass tanks and bowls, all teeming with snails, lined the walls, rested on the desk and window-sills, and were beginning even to cover the floor. Mrs. Knoppert disapproved strongly, and would no longer enter the room. It smelled, she said, and besides she had once stepped on a snail by accident, a horrible sensation she would never forget. But the more his wife and friends deplored his unusual and vaguely repellent pastime, the more pleasure Mr. Knoppert seemed to find in it.

"I never cared for nature before in my life," Mr. Knoppert often remarked—he was a partner in a brokerage firm, a man who had devoted all his life to the science of finance—"but snails have opened my eyes to the beauty of the animal world."

If his friends commented that snails were not really animals, and their slimy habitats hardly the best example of the beauty of nature, Mr. Knoppert would tell them with a superior smile that they simply didn't know all that he knew about snails.

And it was true. Mr. Knoppert had witnessed an exhibition that was not described, certainly not adequately described, in any encyclopedia or zoology book that he had been able to find. Mr. Knoppert had wandered into the kitchen one evening for a bite of something before dinner, and had happened to notice that a couple of snails in the china bowl on the draining-board were behaving very oddly. Standing more or less on their tails, they were weaving before each other for all the world like a pair of snakes hypnotized by a flute player. A moment later, their faces came together in a kiss of voluptuous intensity. Mr. Knoppert bent closer and studied them from all angles. Something else was happening: a protuberance like an ear was appearing on the right side of the head of both snails. His instinct told him that he was watching a sexual activity of some sort.

The cook came in and said something to him, but Mr. Knoppert silenced her with an impatient wave of his hand. He couldn't take his eyes from the enchanted little creatures in the bowl.

When the ear-like excrescences were precisely together rim to rim, a whitish rod like another small tentacle shot out from one ear and arched over toward the ear of the other snail. Mr. Knoppert's first surmise was dashed when a tentacle sallied from the other snail, too. Most peculiar, he thought. The two tentacles withdrew, then came forth again, and as if they had found some invisible mark, remained fixed in either snail. Mr. Knoppert peered intently closer. So did the cook.

"Did you ever see anything like this?" Mr. Knoppert asked.

"No. They must be fighting," the cook said indifferently and went away. That was a sample of the ignorance on the subject of snails that he was later to discover everywhere.

Mr. Knoppert continued to observe the pair of snails off and on for more than an hour, until first the ears, then the rods, withdrew, and the snails themselves relaxed their attitudes and paid no further attention to each other. But by that time, a different pair of snails had begun a flirtation, and were slowly rearing themselves to get into a position for kissing. Mr. Knoppert told the cook that the snails were not to be served that evening. He took the bowl of them up to his study. And snails were never again served in the Knoppert household.

That night, he searched his encyclopedias and a few general science books he happened to possess, but there was absolutely nothing on snails' breeding habits, though the oyster's dull reproductive cycle was described in detail. Perhaps it hadn't been a mating he had seen after all, Mr. Knoppert decided after a day or two. His wife Edna told him either to eat the snails or get rid of them—it was at this time that she stepped upon a snail that had crawled out on to the floor—and Mr. Knoppert might have, if he hadn't come across a sentence in Darwin's *Origin of Species* on a page given to gastropoda. The sentence was in French, a language Mr. Knoppert did not know, but the word *sensualité* made him tense like a blood-hound that has suddenly found the scent. He was in the public library at that time, and laboriously he translated the sentence with the aid of a French–English dictionary. It was a statement of less than a hundred words, saying that snails manifested a sensuality in their mating that was not to be found elsewhere in the animal kingdom. That was all. It was from the notebooks of Henri Fabre. Obviously Darwin had decided not to translate it for the average reader, but to leave it in its original language for the scholarly few who really cared. Mr. Knoppert considered himself one of the scholarly few now, and his round, pink face beamed with self-esteem.

He had learned that his snails were the freshwater type that laid their eggs in sand or earth, so he put moist earth and a little saucer of water into a big wash-bowl and transferred his snails into it. Then he waited for something to happen. Not even another mating happened. He picked up the snails one by one and looked at them, without seeing anything suggestive of pregnancy. But one snail he couldn't pick up. The shell might have been glued to the earth. Mr. Knoppert suspected the snail had buried its head in the ground to die. Two more days went by, and on the morning of the third, Mr. Knoppert found a spot of crumbly earth where the snail had been. Curious, he investigated the crumbles with a match stem, and to his delight discovered a pit full of shiny new eggs. Snail eggs! He hadn't been wrong. Mr. Knoppert called his wife and the cook to look at them. The eggs looked very much like big caviar, only they were white instead of black or red.

"Well, naturally they have to breed some way," was his wife's comment. Mr. Knoppert couldn't understand her lack of interest. He had to go and look at the eggs every hour that he was at home. He looked at them every morning to see if any change had taken place, and the eggs were his last thought every night before he went to bed. Moreover, another snail was now digging a pit. And another pair of snails was mating! The first batch of eggs turned a greyish colour, and minuscule spirals of shells became discernible on one side of each egg. Mr. Knoppert's anticipation rose to a higher pitch. At last a morning arrived—the eighteenth after laying, according to Mr. Knoppert's careful count—when he looked down into the egg pit and saw the first tiny moving head, the first stubby little antennae uncertainly exploring the nest. Mr. Knoppert was as happy as the father of a new child. Every one of the seventy or more eggs in the pit came miraculously to life. He had seen the entire reproductive cycle evolve to a successful conclusion. And the fact that no one, at least no one that he knew of, was acquainted with a fraction of what he knew, lent his knowledge a thrill of discovery, the piquancy of the esoteric. Mr. Knoppert made notes on successive matings and egg hatchings. He narrated snail biology to fascinated, more often shocked, friends and guests, until his wife squirmed with embarrassment.

"But where is it going to stop, Peter? If they keep on reproducing at this rate, they'll take over the house!" his wife told him after fifteen or twenty pits had hatched.

"There's no stopping nature," he replied good-humouredly. "They've only taken over the study. There's plenty of room there."

So more and more glass tanks and bowls were moved in. Mr. Knoppert went to the market and chose several of the more lively-looking snails, and also a pair he found mating, unobserved by the rest of the world. More and more egg pits appeared in the dirt floors of the tanks, and out of each pit crept finally from seventy to ninety baby snails, transparent as

dewdrops, gliding up rather than down the strips of fresh lettuce that Mr. Knoppert was quick to give all the pits as edible
ladders for the climb. Mating went on so often that he no
longer bothered to watch them. A mating could last twenty-
four hours. But the thrill of seeing the white caviar become
shells and start to move—that never diminished however
often he witnessed it.

His colleagues in the brokerage office noticed a new zest for
life in Peter Knoppert. He became more daring in his moves,
more brilliant in his calculations, became in fact a little vicious
in his schemes, but he brought money in for his company. By
unanimous vote, his basic salary was raised from forty to sixty
thousand dollars per year. When anyone congratulated him on
his achievements, Mr. Knoppert gave all the credit to his snails
and the beneficial relaxation he derived from watching them.

He spent all his evenings with his snails in the room that
was no longer a study but a kind of aquarium. He loved to
strew the tanks with fresh lettuce and pieces of boiled potato
and beet, then turn on the sprinkler system that he had
installed in the tanks to simulate natural rainfall. Then all the
snails would liven up and begin eating, mating, or merely gliding through the shallow water with obvious pleasure. Mr.
Knoppert often let a snail crawl on to his forefinger—he fancied his snails enjoyed this human contact—and he would
feed it a piece of lettuce by hand, would observe the snail from
all sides, finding as much aesthetic satisfaction as another man
might from contemplating a Japanese print.

By now, Mr. Knoppert did not allow anyone to set foot in
his study. Too many snails had the habit of crawling around
on the floor, of going to sleep glued to chair bottoms, and to
the backs of books on the shelves. Snails spent much of their
time sleeping, especially the older snails. But there were
enough less indolent snails who preferred love-making. Mr.
Knoppert estimated that about a dozen pairs of snails must be
kissing all the time. And certainly there was a multitude of
baby and adolescent snails. They were impossible to count.
But Mr. Knoppert did count the snails sleeping and creeping
on the ceiling alone, and arrived at something between eleven

and twelve hundred. The tanks, the bowls, the underside of his desk and the bookshelves must surely have held fifty times that number. Mr. Knoppert meant to scrape the snails off the ceiling one day soon. Some of them had been up there for weeks, and he was afraid they were not taking in enough nourishment. But of late he had been a little too busy, and too much in need of the tranquillity that he got simply from sitting in the study in his favourite chair.

During the month of June he was so busy he often worked late into the evening at his office. Reports were piling in at the end of the fiscal year. He made calculations, spotted a half-dozen possibilities of gain, and reserved the most daring, the least obvious moves for his private operations. By this time next year, he thought, he should be three or four times as well off as now. He saw his bank account multiplying as easily and rapidly as his snails. He told his wife this, and she was overjoyed. She even forgave him the ruination of the study, and the stale, fishy smell that was spreading throughout the whole upstairs.

"Still, I do wish you'd take a look just to see if anything's happening, Peter," she said to him rather anxiously one morning. "A tank might have overturned or something, and I wouldn't want the rug to be spoilt. You haven't been in the study for nearly a week, have you?"

Mr. Knoppert hadn't been in for nearly two weeks. He didn't tell his wife that the rug was pretty much gone already. "I'll go up tonight," he said.

But it was three more days before he found time. He went in one evening just before bedtime and was surprised to find the floor quite covered with snails, with three or four layers of snails. He had difficulty closing the door without mashing any. The dense clusters of snails in the corners made the room look positively round, as if he stood inside some huge, conglomerate stone. Mr. Knoppert cracked his knuckles and gazed around him in astonishment. They had not only covered every surface, but thousands of snails hung down into the room from the chandelier in a grotesque clump.

Mr. Knoppert felt for the back of a chair to steady himself. He felt only a lot of shells under his hand. He had to smile a little: there were snails in the chair seat, piled up on one another, like a lumpy cushion. He really must do something about the ceiling, and immediately. He took an umbrella from the corner, brushed some of the snails off it, and cleared a place on his desk to stand. The umbrella point tore the wallpaper, and then the weight of the snails pulled down a long strip that hung almost to the floor. Mr. Knoppert felt suddenly frustrated and angry. The sprinklers would make them move. He pulled the lever.

The sprinklers came on in all the tanks, and the seething activity of the entire room increased at once. Mr. Knoppert slid his feet along the floor, through tumbling snails' shells that made a sound like pebbles on a beach, and directed a couple of the sprinklers at the ceiling. This was a mistake, he saw at once. The softened paper began to tear, and he dodged one slowly falling mass only to be hit by a swinging festoon of snails, really hit quite a stunning blow on the side of the head. He went down on one knee, dazed. He should open a window, he thought, the air was stifling. And there were snails crawling over his shoes and up his trouser legs. He shook his feet irritably. He was just going to the door, intending to call for one of the servants to help him, when the chandelier fell on him. Mr. Knoppert sat down heavily on the floor. He saw now that he couldn't possibly get a window open, because the snails were fastened thick and deep over the window-sills. For a moment, he felt he couldn't get up, felt as if he were suffocating. It was not only the musty smell of the room, but everywhere he looked long wallpaper strips covered with snails blocked his vision as if he were in a prison.

"Edna!" he called, and was amazed at the muffled, ineffectual sound of his voice. The room might have been soundproof.

He crawled to the door, heedless of the sea of snails he crushed under hands and knees. He could not get the door open. There were so many snails on it, crossing and recrossing the crack of the door on all sides, they actually resisted his strength.

"Edna!" A snail crawled into his mouth. He spat it out in disgust. Mr. Knoppert tried to brush the snails off his arms.

But for every hundred he dislodged, four hundred seemed to slide upon him and fasten to him again, as if they deliberately sought him out as the only comparatively snail-free surface in the room. There were snails crawling over his eyes. Then just as he staggered to his feet, something else hit him—Mr. Knoppert couldn't even see what. He was fainting! At any rate, he was on the floor. His arms felt like leaden weights as he tried to reach his nostrils, his eyes, to free them from the sealing, murderous snail bodies.

"Help!" He swallowed a snail. Choking, he widened his mouth for air and felt a snail crawl over his lips on to his tongue. He was in hell! He could feel them gliding over his legs like a glutinous river, pinning his legs to the floor. "Ugh!" Mr. Knoppert's breath came in feeble gasps. His vision grew black, a horrible, undulating black. He could not breathe at all, because he could not reach his nostrils, could not move his hands. Then through the slit of one eye, he saw directly in front of him, only inches away, what had been, he knew, the rubber plant that stood in its pot near the door. A pair of snails were quietly making love in it. And right beside them, tiny snails as pure as dewdrops were emerging from a pit like an infinite army into their widening world.

Thou Shalt Not Suffer a Witch...

by
DOROTHY K. HAYNES
(1918–1987)

According to folklore, the guilt of a suspected witch could be firmly established by tying her arms and legs together and tossing her into deep water. If she was a witch, she would float, in which case she could be retrieved from the surface of the water and burned at the stake in time-honoured fashion. If she wasn't a witch, she would sink and drown. Talk about a catch-22.

This witch story has an unusual quality due to its Scottish setting and the fact that the main character is a child. It has something to say about the extremism that geographical isolation can bring, and the dangers of untrammelled superstition.

T he child sat alone in her bedroom, weaving the
fringe of the counterpane in and out of her fingers.
It was a horrible room, the most neglected one of
the house. The grate was narrow and rusty, cluttered
up with dust and hair combings, and the floorboards creaked
at every step. When the wind blew, the door rattled and
banged, but the window was sealed tight, webbed, fly-spotted,
a haven for everything black and creeping.

In and out went her fingers, the fringe pulled tight between
nail and knuckle. Outside, the larches tossed and flurried,
brilliant green under a blue sky. Sometimes the sun would go
in, and rain would hit the window like a handful of nails
thrown at the glass; then the world would lighten suddenly,
the clouds would drift past in silver and white, and the larches
would once more toss in the sunshine.

"Jinnot! Jinnot!" called a voice from the yard. "Where've you
got to, Jinnot?"

She did not answer. The voice went farther away, still calling. Jinnot sat on the bed, hearing nothing but the voice
which had tormented her all week.

"You'll do it, Jinnot, eh? Eh, Jinnot? An' I'll give you a sixpence to spend. We've always got on well, Jinnot. You like me better than her. She never gave you ribbons for your hair, did she? She never bought you sweeties in the village? It's not much to ask of you, Jinnot, just to say she looked at you, an' it happened. It's not as if it was telling lies. It has happened before; it has, eh, Jinnot?"

She dragged herself over to the mirror, the cracked sheet of glass with the fawn fly-spots. The door on her left hand, the window on her right, neither a way of escape. Her face looked back at her, yellow in the reflected sunlight. Her hair was the colour of hay, her heavy eyes had no shine in them. Large teeth, wide mouth, the whole face was square and dull. She went back to the bed, and her fingers picked again at the fringe.

Had it happened before? Why could she not remember properly? Perhaps it was because they were all so kind to her after it happened, trying to wipe it out of her memory. "You just came over faint, lassie. Just a wee sickness, like. Och, you don't need to cry, you'll be fine in a minute. Here's Minty to see to you..."

But Minty would not see to her this time.

The voice went on and on in her head, wheedling, in one ear and out of the other.

"Me and Jack will get married, see, Jinnot? And when we're married, you can come to our house whenever you like. You can come in, and I'll bake some scones for you, Jinnot, and sometimes we'll let you sleep in our wee upstairs room. You'll do it, Jinnot, will you not? For Jack as well as for me. You like Jack. Mind he mended your Dolly for you? And you'd like to see us married thegither, would you not?

"He'd never be happy married to her, Jinnot. You're a big girl now, you'll see that for yourself. She's good enough in her way, see, but she's not the right kind for him. She sits and sews and works all day, but she's never a bit of fun with him, never a word to say. But he's never been used to anyone better, see, Jinnot, and he'll not look at anybody else while she's there. It's for his own good, Jinnot, and for her sake as well. They'd never be happy married.

"And, Jinnot, you're not going to do her any harm. Someday you'll get married yourself, Jinnot, and you'll know. So it's just kindness...and she is like that, like what I said. Mebbe she's been the cause of the trouble you had before, you never know. So you'll do it, Jinnot, eh? You'll do it?"

She did not want to. The door rattled in the wind, and the sun shone through the dirt and the raindrops on the window. Why did she want to stay here, with the narrow bed, the choked grate, the mirror reflecting the flaked plaster of the opposite wall? The dust blew along the floor, and the chimney and the keyhole howled together. "Jinnot! Jinnot!" went the voice again. She paid no attention. Pulling back the blankets, she climbed fully dressed into the bed, her square, suety face like a mask laid on the pillows. "Jinnot! Jinnot!" went the voice, calling, coaxing through the height of the wind. She whimpered, and curled herself under the bedclothes, hiding from the daylight and the question that dinned at her even in the dark. "You'll do it, Jinnot, eh? Will you? Eh, Jinnot?"

Next day, the weather had settled. A quiet, spent sun shone on the farm, the tumbledown dykes and the shabby thatch. Everything was still as a painting, the smoke suspended blue in the air, the ducks so quiet on the pond that the larches doubled themselves in the water. Jinnot stood at the door of the byre, watching Jack Hyslop at work. His brush went swish swish, swirling the muck along to the door. He was a handsome lad. No matter how dirty his work, he always looked clean. His boots were bright every morning, and his black hair glistened as he turned his head. He whistled as his broom spattered dung and dirty water, and Jinnot turned her face away. The strong, hot smell from the byre made something grip her stomach with a strong, relentless fist.

Now Minty came out of the kitchen, across the yard with a basin of pigswill. With her arm raised, pouring out the slops, she looked at the byre door for a long minute. To the child, the world seemed to stop in space. The byreman's broom was poised in motion, his arms flexed for a forward push; his whistle went on on the same note, high and shrill; and Minty was a statue of mute condemnation, with the dish spilling its contents in a halted stream.

A moment later, Jinnot found that Jack Hyslop was holding her head on his knee. Minty had run up, her apron clutched in both hands. Beatrice, the dairymaid, was watching too, bending over her. There was a smell of the dairy on her clothes, a slight smell of sourness, of milk just on the turn, and her hair waved dark under her cap. "There now," she said. "All right, dearie, all right! What made you go off like that, now?"

The child's face sweated all over, her lips shivered as the air blew cold on her skin. All she wanted now was to run away, but she could not get up to her feet. "What was it, Jinnot?" said the voice, going on and on, cruel, kind, which was it? "Tell me, Jinnot. Tell me."

She could not answer. Her tongue seemed to swell and press back on her throat, so that she vomited. Afterwards, lying in bed, she remembered it all, the sense of relief when she had thrown up all she had eaten, the empty languor of the sleep which followed. Beatrice had put her to bed, and petted her and told her she was a good girl. "It was easy done, eh, Jinnot? You'd have thought it was real." She gave a high, uneasy laugh. "Aye, you're a good wee thing, Jinnot. All the same, you fair frichted me at the beginning!"

She was glad to be left alone. After her sleep, strangely cold, she huddled her knees to her shoulders and tried to understand. Sometime, in a few months or a few years, it did not seem to matter, Minty and Jack Hyslop were to be married. Minty was kind. Since Jinnot's mother had died, she had been nurse and foster mother, attending to clothes and food and evening prayers. She had no time to do more. Her scoldings were frequent, but never unjust. Jinnot had loved her till Beatrice came to the dairy, handsome, gay and always ready with bribes.

"You're a nice wee girl, Jinnot. Look—will you do something for Jack and me—just a wee thing? You've done it before; I know you have. Sometime, when Minty's there..."

And so she had done it, for the sake of sixpence, and the desire to be rid of the persistent pleading; but where she had

meant to pretend to fall in a fit at Minty's glance, just to pretend, she had really lost her senses, merely thinking about it.
She was afraid now of what she had done...was it true then,
about Minty, that the way she looked at you was enough to
bring down a curse?

It could not be true. Minty was kind, and would make a
good wife. Beatrice was the bad one, with her frightening
whispers—and yet, it wasn't really badness; it was wisdom.
She knew all the terrible things that children would not
understand.

Jinnot got up and put on her clothes. Down in the kitchen,
there was firelight, and the steam of the evening meal. Her
father was eating heartily, his broad shoulders stooped over his
plate. "All right again, lassie?" he asked, snuggling her to him
with one arm. She nodded, her face still a little peaked with
weakness. At the other side of the room, Minty was busy at the
fireside, but she did not turn her head. Jinnot clung closer to
her father.

All the air seemed to be filled with whispers.

From nowhere at all, the news spread that Jinnot was
bewitched. She knew it herself. She was fascinated by the
romance of her own affliction, but she was frightened as well.
Sometimes she would have days with large blanks which
memory could not fill. Where had she been? What had she
done? And the times when the world seemed to shrivel to the
size of a pinhead, with people moving like grains of sand, tiny,
but much, much clearer, the farther away they seemed—who
was behind it all? When had it started?

In time, however, the trouble seemed to right itself. But
now, Jack Hyslop courted Beatrice instead of Minty. Once, following them, Jinnot saw them kiss behind a hayrick. They
embraced passionately, arms clutching, bodies pressed together. It had never been like that with Minty, no laughter, no
sighs. Their kisses had been mere respectful tokens, the concession to their betrothal.

Minty said nothing, but her sleek hair straggled, her once
serene eyes glared under their straight brows. She began to be

abrupt with the child. "Out the road!" she would snap. "How is it a bairn's aye at your elbow?" Jinnot longed for the friendliness of the young dairymaid. But Beatrice wanted no third party to share her leisure, and Jinnot was more lonely than ever before.

Why had she no friends? She had never had young company, never played games with someone of her own age. Her pastimes were lonely imaginings, the dark pretence of a brain burdened with a dull body. She made a desperate bid to recover her audience. Eyes shut, her breathing hoarse and ragged, she let herself fall to the ground, and lay there until footsteps came running, and kind hands worked to revive her.

So now she was reinstated, her father once more mindful of her, and the household aware of her importance, a sick person in the house. The voices went on whispering around her, "Sshh! It's wee Jinnot again. Fell away in a dead faint. Poor lassie, she'll need to be seen to...Jinnot—Jinnot...wee Jinnot..."

But this time, there was a difference. They waited till she waked, and then questioned her. Her father was there, blocking out the light from the window, and the doctor sat by the bedside, obviously displeased with his task. Who was to blame? Who was there when it happened? She knew what they wanted her to say; she knew herself what to tell them. "Who was it?" pressed her father. "This has been going on too long." "Who was it?" said the doctor. "There's queer tales going around, you know, Jinnot!" "You know who it was," said the voice in her mind. "You'll do it, Jinnot, eh?"

"I—I don't know," she sighed, her eyes drooping, her mouth hot and dry. "I...only..." She put her hand to her head, and sighed. She could almost believe she was really ill, she felt so tired and strange.

After that, the rumours started agan. The voice came back to Jinnot, the urgent and convincing warning—"She is like that, like what I said..." For her own peace of mind, she wanted to know, but there was no one she could ask. She could not trust her own judgement.

It was months before she found out, and the days had

lengthened to a queer tarnished summer, full of stale yellow heat. The larches had burned out long ago, and their branches drooped in dull fringes over the pond. The fields were tangled with buttercups and tall moon daisies, but the flowers dried and shrivelled as soon as they blossomed. All the brooks were silent; and the nettles by the hedges had a curled, thirsty look. Jinnot kept away from the duckpond these days. With the water so low, the floating weeds and mud gave off a bad, stagnant smell.

Over the flowers, the bees hovered, coming and going endlessly, to and from the hives. One day, a large bumble, blundering home, tangled itself in the girl's collar, and stung her neck. She screamed out, running into the house, squealing that she had swallowed the insect, and that something with a sting was flying round in her stomach, torturing her most cruelly. They sent for the doctor, and grouped round her with advice. Later, they found the bee, dead, in the lace which had trapped it; but before that, she vomited up half her inside, with what was unmistakably yellow bees' bodies, and a quantity of waxy stuff all mixed up with wings and frail, crooked legs.

She looked at the watchers, and knew that the time had come. "It was Minty Fraser!" she wailed. "It was her! She *looked* at me!" She screamed, and hid her face as the sickness once more attacked her in heaving waves.

They went to the house, and found Minty on her knees, washing over the hearthstone. One of the farm-men hauled her to her feet, and held her wrists together. "Witch! Witch! Witch!" shouted the crowd at the door.

"What— What—"

"Come on, witch! Out to the crowd!"

"No! No, I never—"

"Leave her a minute," roared Jack Hyslop. "Mebbe she— give her a chance to speak!" His mouth twitched a little. At one time, he was thinking, he had been betrothed to Minty, before Beatrice told him... He faltered at the thought of Beatrice. "Well, don't be rough till you're sure," he finished lamely, turning away and leaving the business to the others.

Those who sympathized with witches, he remembered, were apt to share their fate.

The women were not so blate. "Witch! Witch!" they shrilled. "Burn the witch! Our bairns are no' safe when folks like her is let to live!"

She was on the doorstep now, her cap torn off, her eye bleeding, her dress ripped away at the shoulder. Jinnot's father, pushing through the mob, raised his hand for the sake of order. "Look, men! Listen, there! This is my house; there'll be no violence done on the threshold."

"Hang her! Burn her! A rope, there!"

"No hanging till you make sure. Swim her first. If the devil floats—"

"Jinnot! Here's Jinnot!"

The girl came through a lane in the throng, Beatrice holding her hand, clasping her round the waist. She did not want to see Minty, but her legs forced her on. The she looked up. A witch...she saw the blood on her face, the torn clothes, the look of horror and terrible hurt. That was Minty, who cooked her meals and looked after her and did the work of a mother. She opened her mouth and screamed, till the foam dripped over her chin.

Her father's face was as white as her own spittle. "Take the beast away," he said, "and if she floats, for God's sake get rid of her as quick as you can!"

It was horrible. They all louped at her, clutching and tearing and howling as they plucked at her and trussed her for ducking. She was down on the ground, her clothes flung indecently over her head, her legs kicking as she tried to escape. "It wasna me!" she skirled. "It wasna me! I'm no' a witch! Aaah!" The long scream cut the air like a blade. Someone had wrenched her leg and snapped the bone at the ankle, but her body still went flailing about in the dust, like a kitten held under a blanket.

They had her trussed now, wrists crossed, legs crossed, her body arched between them. She was dragged to the pond, blood from her cuts and grazes smearing the clothes of those who handled her. Her hair hung over her face and her broken foot scraped the ground. "No! No!" she screamed. "Ah, God…!" and once, "Jinnot! Tell them it wasna me—"

A blow over the mouth silenced her, and she spat a tooth out with a mouthful of blood. She shrieked as they swung and hurtled her through the air. There was a heavy splash, and drops of green, slimy water spattered the watching faces. If Minty was a witch, she would float; and then they would haul her out and hang her, or burn her away, limb by limb.

She sank; the pond was shallow, but below the surface, green weed and clinging mud drew her down in a deadly clutch. The crowd on the bank watched her, fascinated. It was only when her yammering mouth was filled and silenced that they realized what had happened, and took slow steps to help her. By that time, it was too late.

What must it be like to be a witch? The idea seeped into her mind like ink, and all her thoughts were tinged with the black poison. She knew the dreadful aftermath; long after, her mind would be haunted by the sight she had seen. In her own nostrils, she felt the choke and snuffle of the pond slime; but what must it feel like, the knowledge of strange power, the difference from other people, the danger? Her imagination played with the thrilling pain of it, right down to the last agony.

She asked Beatrice about it. Beatrice was married now, with a baby coming, and Jinnot sat with her in the waning afternoons, talking with her, woman to woman.

"I didn't like to see them set on her like yon. She never done me any harm. If it hadn't been for me—"

"Are you sure, Jinnot? Are you sure? Mind the bees, Jinnot, an' yon time at the barn door? What about them?"

"I—I don't know."

"Well, I'm telling you. She was a witch, that one, if anybody was."

"Well, mebbe she couldn't help it."

"No, they can't help the power. It just comes on them. Sometimes they don't want it, but it comes, just the same. It's hard, but you know what the Bible says: 'Thou shalt not suffer a witch…'"

She had a vision of Minty, quiet, busy, struggling with a force she did not want to house in her body. Beside this, her own fits and vomitings seemed small things. She could forgive knowing that. "How...how do they first know they're witches?" she asked.

"Mercy, I don't know! What questions you ask, Jinnot! How would I know, eh? I daresay they find out soon enough."

So that was it; they knew themselves. Her mind dabbled and meddled uncomfortably with signs and hints. She wanted to curse Beatrice for putting the idea into her head; she would not believe it; but once there, the thought would not be removed. What if she was a witch? "I'm not," she said to herself. "I'm too young," she said; but there was no conviction in it. Long before she had been bewitched, she had known there was something different about her. Now it all fell into place. No wonder the village children would not call and play with her. No wonder her father was just rather than affectionate, shielding her only because she was his daughter. And no wonder Beatrice was so eager to keep in with her, with the incessant "Eh, Jinnot?" always on her lips.

Well, then, she was a witch. As well to know it sooner as later, to accept the bothers with the benefits, the troubles and trances with the new-found sense of power. She had never wanted to kill or curse, never in her most unhappy moments, but now, given the means, would it not be as well to try? Did her power strengthen by being kept, or did it spring up fresh from some infernal reservoir? She did not know. She was a very new witch, uncertain of what was demanded of her. Week after week passed, and she was still no farther forward.

She continued her visits to Beatrice, though the thought of it all made her grue. It angered her to see the girl sitting stout and placid at the fireside, unhaunted, unafraid. "You'll come and see the baby when it's born, eh, Jinnot?" she would say. "Do you like babies? Do you?" Nothing mattered to her now, it seemed, but the baby. In the dark winter nights, Jinnot made a resolve to kill her. But for Beatrice, she might never have discovered this terrible fact about herself. Beatrice was to blame for everything, but a witch has means of revenge, and one witch may avenge another.

She had no idea how to cast a spell, and there was no one to help her. What had Minty done? She remembered the moment at the byre-door, the upraised arm, and the long, long look. It would be easy. Bide her time, and Beatrice would die when the spring came.

She sat up in the attic, twining her fingers in the fringe of the bedcover, in and out, under and over. Beatrice was in labour. It had been whispered in the kitchen, spreading from mouth to mouth. Now, Jinnot sat on the bed, watching the larches grow black in the dusk. She was not aware of cold, or dirt, or darkness. All her senses were fastened on the window of Beatrice's cottage, where a light burned, and women gathered round the bed. She fixed her will, sometimes almost praying in her effort to influence fate. "Kill her! Kill her! Let her die!" Was she talking to God, or to the devil? The thoughts stared and screamed in her mind. She wanted Beatrice to suffer every agony, every pain, and wrench, to bear Minty's pain, and her own into the bargain. All night she sat, willing pain and death, and suffering it all in her own body. Her face was grey as the ceiling, her flesh sweated with a sour smell. Outside, an owl shrieked, and she wondered for a moment if it was Beatrice.

Suddenly, she knew it was all over. The strain passed out of her body, the lids relaxed over her eyes, her body seemed to melt and sprawl over the bed. When she woke, it was morning, and the maids were beaming with good news. "Did you hear?" they said. "Beatrice has a lovely wee boy! She's fair away wi' herself!"

Jinnot said nothing. She stopped her mouth and her disappointment with porridge. It did not cross her mind that perhaps, after all, she was no witch. All she thought was that the spell had not worked, and Beatrice was still alive. She left the table, and hurried over to the cottage. The door was ajar, the fire bright in the hearth, and Beatrice was awake in bed, smiling, the colour already flushed back into her cheeks.

"He's a bonny baby, Jinnot. He's lovely, eh? Eh, Jinnot?"

She crept reluctantly to the cradle. Why, he was no size at

all, so crumpled, so new, a wee sliver of flesh in a bundle of white wool. She stared for a long time, half sorry for what she had to do. The baby was snuffling a little, its hands and feet twitching under the wrappings. He was so young, he would not have his mother's power to resist a witch.

She glared at him for a long minute, her eyes fixed, her lips firm over her big teeth. His face, no bigger than a lemon, turned black, and a drool of foam slavered from the mouth. When the twitching stopped, and the eyes finally uncrossed themselves, she walked out, and left the door again on the latch. She had not spoken one word.

It seemed a long time before they came for her, a long time of fuss and running about while she sat on the bed, shivering in the draught from the door. When she crossed to the window, her fingers probing the webs and pressing the guts from the plumpest insects, she saw them arguing and gesticulating in a black knot. Jack Hyslop was there, his polished hair ruffled, his face red. The women were shaking their heads, and Hyslop's voice rose clear in the pale air.

"Well, that's what she said. The wee thing had been dead for an hour. An' it was that bitch Jinnot came in an' glowered at it."

"Och, man, it's a sick woman's fancy! A wee mite that age can easy take convulsions."

"It wasna convulsions. My wife said Jinnot was in and out with a face like thunder. She was aye askin' about witches too, you can ask Beatrice if you like."

"Well, she was in yon business o' Minty Fraser. Ye cannie blame her, a young lassie like that...mind, we sympathize about the bairn, Jacky, but—"

They went on placating him, mindful of the fact that Jinnot was the farmer's daughter. It would not do to accuse *her*; but one of the women went into the cottage, and came out wiping her eyes. "My, it would make anybody greet. The wee lamb's lying there like a flower, that quiet! It's been a fair shock to the mother, poor soul. She gey faur through..."

They muttered, then, and drifted towards the house. Jinnot left the window, and sat again on the bed. She was not afraid, only resigned, and horribly tired of it all.

When they burst into her room, clumping over the bare boards, her father was with them. They allowed him to ask the questions. Was he angry with them, or with her? She could not guess.

"Jinnot," he said sternly, "what's this? What's all this?"

She stared at him.

"What's all this? Do you know what they're saying about you? They say you killed Beatrice Hyslop's bairn. Is that true, Jinnot?"

She did not answer. Her father held up his hand as the men began to growl.

"Come now, Jinnot, enough of this sulking! It's for your own good to answer, and clear yourself. Mind of what happened to Minty Fraser! Did you do anything to the baby?"

"I never touched it. I just looked at it."

"Just looked?"

"Yes."

A rough cry burst from Jack Hyslop. "Is that not what Minty Fraser said? Was that not enough from her?"

"Hyslop, hold your tongue, or you lose your job."

"Well, by God, I lose it then! There's been more trouble on this bloody farm—"

"Aye! Leave this to us!"

"We'll question the wench. If she's no witch, she's nothing to fear."

The women had come in now, crowding up in angry curiosity. The farmer was pushed back against the wall. "One word, and you'll swim along with her," he was warned, and he knew them well enough to believe them. They gathered round Jinnot, barking questions at her, and snatching at the answers. Every time she paused to fidget with the fringe, they lammed her across the knuckles till her hands were swollen and blue.

"Tell the truth now; are you a witch?"

"No. No, I'm not!"

"Why did you kill the baby this morning?"

"I—I never. I can't kill folk. I—"

"You hear that? She can't kill folk! Have you ever tried?"

She cowered back from them, the faces leering at her like

ugly pictures. She would tell the truth, as her father said, and be done with all this dreamlike horror. "Leave me alone!" she said. "Leave me, and I'll tell!"

"Hurry then. Out with it! Have you ever tried to kill anybody?"

"Yes. I tried, and—and I couldn't. It was her, she started telling me I was bewitched—"

"Who?"

"Beatrice—Mistress Hyslop."

"My God!" said Jack and her father, starting forward together.

"Hold on, there! Let her speak."

"She said I was bewitched, an' I thought I was. I don't know if it was right...it was all queer, and I didn't know...and then, when she said about witches, she put it in my head, and it came over me I might be one. I *had* to find out—"

"There you are. She's admitting it!"

"No!" She began to shout as they laid hold of her, screaming in fright and temper till her throat bled. "No! *Leave* me alone! I never; I tried, and I couldn't do it! I couldn't, I tell you! She *wouldn't* die. She'd have died if I'd been a witch, wouldn't she? She's a witch herself; I don't care, Jack Hyslop, she is! It was her fault Minty Fraser—oh God, no! NO!"

She could not resist the rope round her, the crossing of her limbs, the tight pull of cord on wrists and ankles. When she knew it was hopeless, she dared not resist remembering Minty's broken leg, her cuts and blood and bruises, the tooth spinning out in red spittle. She was not afraid of death, but she was mortally afraid of pain. Now, if she went quietly, there would only be the drag to the pond, the muckle splash, and the slow silt and suffocation in slime...

She had no voice left to cry out when they threw her. Her throat filled with water, her nose filled, and her ears. She was tied too tightly to struggle. Down, down she went, till her head sang, and her brain nearly burst; but the pond was full with spring rains, and her body was full-fleshed and buoyant. Suddenly, the cries of the crowd burst upon her again, and she realized that she was floating. Someone jabbed at her, and pushed her under again with a long pole, but she bobbed up

again a foot away, her mouth gulping, her eyes bulging under
her dripping hair. The mob on the bank howled louder.

"See, see! She's floating!"

"Witch! Burn her! Fish her out and hang her!"

"There's proof now. What are you waiting for? Out with her.
See, the besom'll *no'* sink!"

So now they fished her out, untied her, and bound her
again in a different fashion, hands by her side, feet together.
She was too done to protest, or to wonder what they would
do. She kept her eyes shut as they tied her to a stake, and she
ignored the tickle of dead brushwood being piled round her
feet and body. She could hardly realize that she was still alive,
and she was neither glad nor sorry.

They were gentle with her now, sparing her senses for the
last pain. At first, she hardly bothered when the smoke nipped
her eyes and her nostrils; she hardly heard the first snap of the
thin twigs. It was only when the flames lapped her feet and
legs that she raised her head and tried to break free. As the
wood became red-hot, and the flames mounted to bite her
body, she screamed and writhed and bit her tongue to mince-
meat. When they could not see her body through the fire, the
screams still went on.

The crowd drifted away when she lost consciousness. There
was no more fun to be had; or perhaps, it wasn't such fun after
all. The men went back to the fields, but they could not settle
to work. Jinnot's father was gnawing his knuckles in the attic,
and they did not know what would happen when he came
down. Beatrice tossed in a muttering, feverish sleep; and beside
the pond, a few veins and bones still sizzled and popped in the
embers.

The Tomb
of Sarah

by
F.G. LORING
(1869–1951)

An ancient church in the wild and rugged West Country of England...a mouldering tomb carrying instructions not to disturb the occupant...a huge dog with glowing green eyes that terrorizes the countryside at night... These are the ingredients for a classic vampire tale, related with a kind of wide-eyed wonder that reminds me of Dr. Watson's enthusiastic enjoyment of Holmes's escapades.

My father was the head of a celebrated firm of church restorers and decorators about sixty years ago. He took a keen interest in his work, and made an especial study of any old legends or family histories that came under his observation. He was necessarily very well read and thoroughly well posted in all questions of folklore and medieval legend. As he kept a careful record of every case he investigated the manuscripts he left at his death have a special interest. From amongst them I have selected the following, as being a particularly weird and extraordinary experience. In presenting it to the public I feel it is superfluous to apologize for its supernatural character.

My Father's Diary

1841—*June 17th.* Received a commission from my old friend Peter Grant to enlarge and restore the chancel of his church at Hagarstone, in the wilds of the West Country.

July 5th. Went down to Hagarstone with my head man, Somers. A very long and tiring journey.

July 7th. Got the work well started. The old church is one of special interest to the antiquarian, and I shall endeavour while restoring it to alter the existing arrangements as little as possible. One large tomb, however, must be moved bodily ten feet at least to the southward. Curiously enough, there is a somewhat forbidding inscription upon it in Latin, and I am sorry that this particular tomb should have to be moved. It stands amongst the graves of the Kenyons, an old family which has been extinct in these parts for centuries. The inscription on it runs thus:

SARAH.

1630.

For the sake of the dead and the welfare
of the living, let this sepulchre remain
untouched and its occupant undisturbed till
the coming of Christ.
In the name of the Father, the Son, and
the Holy Ghost.

July 8th. Took counsel with Grant concerning the "Sarah Tomb." We are both very loath to disturb it, but the ground has sunk so beneath it that the safety of the church is in danger; thus we have no choice. However, the work shall be done as reverently as possible under our own direction.

Grant says there is a legend in the neighbourhood that it is the tomb of the last of the Kenyons, the evil Countess Sarah, who was murdered in 1630. She lived quite alone in the old castle, whose ruins still stand three miles from here on the road to Bristol. Her reputation was an evil one even for those days. She was a witch or were-woman, the only companion of her solitude being a familiar in the shape of a huge Asiatic wolf. This creature was reputed to seize upon children, or failing these, sheep and other small animals, and convey them to the castle, where the Countess used to suck their blood. It was popularly supposed that she could never be killed. This, however, proved a fallacy, since she was strangled one day by a mad peasant woman who had lost two children, she declaring that they had both been seized and carried off by the

Countess's familiar. This is a very interesting story, since it points to a local superstition very similar to that of the Vampire, existing in Slavonic and Hungarian Europe.

The tomb is built of black marble, surmounted by an enormous slab of the same material. On the slab is a magnificent group of figures. A young and handsome woman reclines upon a couch; round her neck is a piece of rope, the end of which she holds in her hand. At her side is a gigantic dog with bared fangs and lolling tongue. The face of the reclining figure is a cruel one: the corners of the mouth are curiously lifted, showing the sharp points of long canine or dog teeth. The whole group, though magnificently executed, leaves a most unpleasant sensation.

It we move the tomb it will have to be done in two pieces, the covering slab first and then the tomb proper. We have decided to remove the covering slab tomorrow.

***July 9th.*—6 p.m.** A very strange day.

By noon everything was ready for lifting off the covering stone, and after the men's dinner we started the jacks and pulleys. The slab lifted easily enough, though it fitted closely into its seat and was further secured by some sort of mortar or putty, which must have kept the interior perfectly airtight.

None of us were prepared for the horrible rush of foul, mouldy air that escaped as the cover lifted clear of its seating. And the contents that gradually came into view were more startling still. There lay the fully dressed body of a woman, wizened and shrunk and ghastly pale as if from starvation. Round her neck was a loose cord, and, judging by the scars still visible, the story of death by strangulation was true enough.

The most horrible part, however, was the extraordinary freshness of the body. Except for the appearance of starvation, life might have been only just extinct. The flesh was soft and white, the eyes were wide open and seemed to stare at us with a fearful understanding in them. The body itself lay on mould, without any pretence to coffin or shell.

For several moments we gazed with horrible curiosity, and then it became too much for my workmen, who implored us to replace the covering slab. That, of course, we would not do; but I set the carpenters to work at once to make a temporary cover while we moved the tomb to its new position. This is a long job, and will take two or three days at least.

July 9th.—9 p.m. Just at sunset we were startled by the howling of, seemingly, every dog in the village. It lasted for ten minutes or a quarter of an hour, and then ceased as suddenly as it began. This, and a curious mist that has risen round the church, makes me feel rather anxious about the "Sarah Tomb." According to the best established traditions of the Vampire-haunted countries, the disturbance of dogs or wolves at sunset is supposed to indicate the presence of one of these fiends, and local fog is always considered to be a certain sign. The Vampire has the power of producing it for the purpose of concealing its movements near its hiding-place at any time.

I dare not mention or even hint my fears to the Rector, for he is, not unnaturally perhaps, a rank disbeliever in many things that I know, from experience, are not only possible but even probable. I must work this out alone at first, and get his aid without his knowing in what direction he is helping me. I shall now watch till midnight at least.

10.15 p.m. As I feared and half expected. Just before ten there was another outburst of the hideous howling. It was commenced most distinctly by a particularly horrible and blood-curdling wail from the vicinity of the churchyard. The chorus lasted only a few minutes, however, and at the end of it I saw a large dark shape, like a huge dog, emerge from the fog and lope away at a rapid canter towards the open country. Assuming this to be what I fear, I shall see it return soon after midnight.

12.30 p.m. I was right. Almost as midnight struck I saw the beast returning. It stopped at the spot where the fog seemed to commence, and lifting up its head, gave tongue to that particularly horrible long-drawn wail that I had noticed as preceding the outburst earlier in the evening.

Tomorrow I shall tell the Rector what I have seen; and if, as I expect, we hear of some neighbouring sheepfold having

been raided, I shall get him to watch with me for this noctur-
nal marauder. I shall also examine the "Sarah Tomb" for
something which he may notice without any previous hint
from me.

July 10th. I found the workmen this morning much disturbed
in mind about the howling of the dogs. "We doan't like it,
zur," one of them said to me—"we doan't like it; there was
summat abroad last night that was unholy." They were still
more uncomfortable when the news came round that a large
dog had made a raid upon a flock of sheep, scattering them far
and wide, and leaving three of them dead with torn throats in
the field.

When I told the Rector of what I had seen and what was
being said in the village, he immediately decided that we must
try and catch or at least identify the beast I had seen. "Of
course," said he, "it is some dog lately imported into the
neighbourhood, for I know of nothing about here nearly as
large as the animal you describe, though its size may be due to
the deceptive moonlight."

This afternoon I asked the Rector, as a favour, to assist me
in lifting the temporary cover that was on the tomb, giving as
an excuse the reason that I wished to obtain a portion of the
curious mortar with which it had been sealed. After a slight
demur he consented, and we raised the lid. If the sight that
met our eyes gave me a shock, at least it appalled Grant.

"Great God!" he exclaimed; "the woman is alive!"

And so it seemed for a moment. The corpse had lost much
of its starved appearance and looked hideously fresh and alive.
It was still wrinkled and shrunken, but the lips were firm, and
of the rich red hue of health. The eyes, if possible, were more
appalling than ever, though fixed and staring. At one corner of
the mouth I thought I noticed a slight dark-coloured froth, but
I said nothing about it then.

"Take your piece of mortar, Harry," gasped Grant, "and let
us shut the tomb again. God help me! Parson though I am,
such dead faces frighten me!"

Nor was I sorry to hide that terrible face again; but I got my bit of mortar, and I have advanced a step towards the solution of the mystery.

This afternoon the tomb was moved several feet towards it new position, but it will be two or three days yet before we shall be ready to replace the slab.

10.15 p.m. Again the same howling at sunset, the same fog enveloping the church, and at ten o'clock the same great beast slipping silently out into the open country. I must get the Rector's help and watch for its return. But precautions we must take, for if things are as I believe, we take our lives in our hands when we venture out into the night to waylay the— Vampire. Why not admit it at once? For that the beast I have seen is the Vampire of that evil thing in the tomb I can have no reasonable doubt.

Not yet come to its full strength, thank Heaven! after the starvation of nearly two centuries, for at present it can only maraud as wolf apparently. But, in a day or two, when full power returns, that dreadful woman in new strength and beauty will be able to leave her refuge. Then it would not be sheep merely that would satisfy her disgusting lust for blood, but victims that would yield their lifeblood without a murmur to her caressing touch—victims that, dying of her foul embrace, themselves must become Vampires in their turn to prey on others.

Mercifully my knowledge gives me a safeguard; for that little piece of mortar that I rescued today from the tomb contains a portion of the Sacred Host, and who holds it, humbly and firmly believing in its virtue, may pass safely through such an ordeal as I intend to submit myself and the Rector to tonight.

12.30 p.m. Our adventure is over for the present, and we are back safe.

After writing the last entry recorded above, I went off to find Grant and tell him that the marauder was out on the prowl again. "But, Grant," I said, "before we start out tonight I must insist that you will let me prosecute this affair in my own way; you must promise to put yourself completely under my orders, without asking any questions as to the why and wherefore."

After a little demur, and some excusable chaff on his part at the serious view I was taking of what he called a "dog hunt," he gave me his promise. I then told him that we were to watch tonight and try and track the mysterious beast, but not to interfere with it in any way. I think, in spite of his jests, that I impressed him with the fact that there might be, after all, good reason for my precautions.

It was just after eleven when we stepped out into the still night.

Our first move was to try and penetrate the dense fog round the church, but there was something so chilly about it, and a faint smell so disgustingly rank and loathsome, that neither our nerves nor our stomachs were proof against it. Instead, we stationed ourselves in the dark shadow of a yew tree that commanded a good view of the wicket entrance to the churchyard.

At midnight the howling of the dogs began again, and in a few minutes we saw a large grey shape, with green eyes shining like lamps, shamble swiftly down the path towards us.

The Rector started forward, but I laid a firm hand upon his arm and whispered a warning "Remember!" Then we both stood very still and watched as the great beast cantered swiftly by. It was real enough, for we could hear the clicking of its nails on the stone flags. It passed within a few yards of us, and seemed to be nothing more nor less than a great grey wolf, thin and gaunt, with bristling hair and dripping jaws. It stopped where the mist commenced, and turned round. It was truly a horrible sight, and made one's blood run cold. The eyes burnt like fires, the upper lip was snarling and raised, showing the great canine teeth, while round the mouth clung and dripped a dark-coloured froth.

It raised its head and gave tongue to its long wailing howl, which was answered from afar by the village dogs. After standing for a few moments it turned and disappeared into the thickest part of the fog.

Very shortly afterwards the atmosphere began to clear, and within ten minutes the mist was all gone, the dogs in the village were silent, and the night seemed to reassume its normal aspect. We examined the spot where the beast had been standing and found, plainly enough upon the stone flags, dark spots of froth and saliva.

"Well, Rector," I said, "will you admit now, in view of the things you have seen today, in consideration of the legend, the woman in the tomb, the fog, the howling dogs, and, last but not least, the mysterious beast you have seen so close, that there is something not quite normal in it all? Will you put yourself unreservedly in my hands and help me, *whatever I may do*, to first make assurance doubly sure, and finally take the necessary steps for putting an end to this horror of the night?" I saw that the uncanny influence of the night was strong upon him, and wished to impress it as much as possible.

"Needs must," he replied, "when the Devil drives: and in the face of what I have seen I must believe that some unholy forces are at work. Yet, how can they work in the sacred precincts of a church? Shall we not call rather upon Heaven to assist us in our need?"

"Grant," I said solemnly, "that we must do, each in his own way. God helps those who help themselves, and by His help and the light of my knowledge we must fight this battle for Him and the poor lost soul within."

We then returned to the rectory and to our rooms, though I have sat up to write this account while the scene is fresh in my mind.

July 11th. Found the workmen again very much disturbed in their minds, and full of a strange dog that had been seen during the night by several people, who had hunted it. Farmer Stotman, who had been watching his sheep (the same flock that had been raided the night before), had surprised it over a fresh carcase and tried to drive it off, but its size and fierceness so alarmed him that he had beaten a hasty retreat for a gun. When he returned the animal was gone, though he found that three more sheep from his flock were dead and torn.

The "Sarah Tomb" was moved today to its new position; but it was a long, heavy business, and there was not time to replace the covering slab. For this I was glad, as in the prosaic light of day the Rector almost disbelieves the events of the night, and is prepared to think everything to have been magnified and distorted by our imagination.

As, however, I could not possibly proceed with my war of extermination against this foul thing without assistance, and as there is nobody else I can rely upon, I appealed to him for one more night—to convince him that it was no delusion, but a ghastly, horrible truth, which must be fought and conquered for our own sakes, as well as that of all those living in the neighbourhood.

"Put yourself in my hands, Rector," I said, "for tonight at least. Let us take those precautions which my study of the subject tells me are the right ones. Tonight you and I must watch in the church; and I feel assured that tomorrow you will be as convinced as I am, and be equally prepared to take those awful steps which I know to be proper, and I must warn you that we shall find a more startling change in the body lying there than you noticed yesterday."

My words came true; for on raising the wooden cover once more the rank stench of a slaughterhouse arose, making us feel positively sick. There lay the Vampire, but how changed from the starved and shrunken corpse we saw two days ago for the first time! The wrinkles had almost disappeared, the flesh was firm and full, the crimson lips grinned horribly over the long pointed teeth, and a distinct smear of blood had trickled down one corner of the mouth. We set our teeth, however, and hardened our hearts. Then we replaced the cover and put what we had collected into a safe place in the vestry. Yet even now Grant could not believe that there was any real or pressing danger concealed in that awful tomb, as he raised strenuous objections to any apparent desecration of the body without further proof. This he shall have tonight. God grant that I am not taking too much on myself! If there is any truth in old legends it would be easy enough to destroy the Vampire now; but Grant will not have it.

I hope for the best of this night's work, but the danger in waiting is very great.

6 p.m. I have prepared everything: the sharp knives, the pointed stake, fresh garlic, and the wild dog-roses. All these I have taken and concealed in the vestry, where we can get at them when our solemn vigil commences.

If either or both of us die with our fearful task undone, let those reading my record see that this is done. I lay it upon them as a solemn obligation. "That the Vampire be pierced through the heart with the stake, then let the Burial Service be read over the poor clay at last released from its doom. Thus shall the Vampire cease to be, and a lost soul rest."

July 12th. All is over. After the most terrible night of watching and horror one Vampire at least will trouble the world no more. But how thankful should we be to a merciful Providence that that awful tomb was not disturbed by anyone not having the knowledge necessary to deal with its dreadful occupant! I write this with no feelings of self-complacency, but simply with a great gratitude for the years of study I have been able to devote to this special subject.

And now to my tale.

Just before sunset last night the Rector and I locked ourselves into the church, and took up our position in the pulpit. It was one of those pulpits, to be found in some churches, which is entered from the vestry, the preacher appearing at a good height through an arched opening in the wall. This gave us a sense of security (which we felt we needed), a good view of the interior, and direct access to the implements which I had concealed in the vestry.

The sun set and the twilight gradually deepened and faded. There was, so far, no sign of the usual fog, nor any howling of the dogs. At nine o'clock the moon rose, and her pale light gradually flooded the aisles, and still no sign of any kind from the "Sarah Tomb." The Rector had asked me several times what we might expect, but I was determined that no words or thought of mine should influence him, and that he should be convinced by his own senses alone.

By half-past ten we were both getting very tired, and I began to think that perhaps after all we should see nothing that night. However, soon after eleven we observed a light mist rising from the "Sarah Tomb." It seemed to scintillate and sparkle as it rose, and curled in a sort of pillar or spiral.

I said nothing, but I heard the Rector give a sort of gasp as he clutched my arm feverishly. "Great Heaven!" he whispered, "it is taking shape."

And, true enough, in a very few moments we saw standing erect by the tomb the ghastly figure of the Countess Sarah!

She looked thin and haggard still, and her face was deadly white; but the crimson lips looked like a hideous gash in the pale cheeks, and her eyes glared like red coals in the gloom of the church.

It was a fearful thing to watch as she stepped unsteadily down the aisle, staggering a little as if from weakness and exhaustion. This was perhaps natural, as her body must have suffered much physically from her long incarceration, in spite of the unholy forces which kept it fresh and well.

We watched her to the door, and wondered what would happen; but it appeared to present no difficulty, for she melted through it and disappeared.

"Now, Grant," I said, "do you believe?"

"Yes," he replied, "I must. Everything is in your hands, and I will obey your commands to the letter, if you can only instruct me how to rid my poor people of this unnameable terror."

"By God's help I will," said I; "but you shall be yet more convinced first, for we have a terrible work to do, and much to answer for in the future, before we leave the church again this morning. And now to work, for in its present weak state the Vampire will not wander far, but may return at any time, and must not find us unprepared."

We stepped down from the pulpit and, taking dog-roses and garlic from the vestry, proceeded to the tomb. I arrived first and, throwing, off the wooden cover, cried, "Look! it is empty!" There was nothing there! Nothing except the impress of the body in the loose damp mould!

I took the flowers and laid them in a circle round the tomb, for legend teaches us that Vampires will not pass over these particular blossoms if they can avoid it.

Then, eight or ten feet away, I made a circle on the stone pavement, large enough for the Rector and myself to stand in, and within the circle I placed the implements that I had brought into the church with me.

"Now," I said, "from this circle, which nothing unholy can step across, you shall see the Vampire face to face, and see her afraid to cross that other circle of garlic and dog-roses to regain her unholy refuge. But on no account step beyond the holy place you stand in, for the Vampire has a fearful strength not her own, and, like a snake, can draw her victim willingly to his own destruction."

Now so far my work was done, and, calling the Rector, we stepped into the Holy Circle to await the Vampire's return.

Nor was this long delayed. Presently a damp, cold odour seemed to pervade the church, which made our hair bristle and flesh to creep. And then, down the aisle with noiseless feet came That which we watched for.

I heard the Rector mutter a prayer, and I held him tightly by the arm, for he was shivering violently.

Long before we could distinguish the features we saw the glowing eyes and the crimson sensual mouth. She went straight to her tomb, but stopped short when she encountered my flowers. She walked right round the tomb seeking a place to enter, and as she walked she saw us. A spasm of diabolical hate and fury passed over her face; but it quickly vanished, and a smile of love, more devilish still, took its place. She stretched out her arms towards us. Then we saw that round her mouth gathered a bloody froth, and from under her lips long pointed teeth gleamed and champed.

She spoke: a soft soothing voice, a voice that carried a spell with it, and affected us both strangely, particularly the Rector. I wished to test as far as possible, without endangering our lives, the Vampire's power.

Her voice had a soporific effect, which I resisted easily enough, but which seemed to throw the Rector into a sort of trance. More than this: it seemed to compel him to her in spite of his efforts to resist.

"Come!" she said—"come! I give sleep and peace—sleep and peace—sleep and peace."

She advanced a little towards us; but not far, for I noted that the Sacred Circle seemed to keep her back like an iron hand.

My companion seemed to become demoralized and spellbound. He tried to step forward and, finding me detain him, whispered, "Harry, let go! I must go! She is calling me! I must! I must! Oh, help me! help me!" And he began to struggle.

It was time to finish.

"Grant!" I cried, in a loud, firm voice, "in the name of all that you hold sacred, have done and play the man!"

He shuddered violently and gasped, "Where am I?" Then he remembered, and clung to me convulsively for a moment.

At this a look of damnable hate changed the smiling face before us, and with a sort of shriek she staggered back.

"Back!" I cried: "back to your unholy tomb! No longer shall you molest the suffering world! Your end is near."

It was fear that now showed itself in her beautiful face (for it was beautiful in spite of its horror) as she shrank back, back and over the circlet of flowers, shivering as she did so. At last, with a low mournful cry, she appeared to melt back again into her tomb.

As she did so the first gleams of the rising sun lit up the world, and I knew all danger was over for the day.

Taking Grant by the arm, I drew him with me out of the circle and led him to the tomb. There lay the Vampire once more, still in her living death as we had a moment before seen her in her devilish life. But in the eyes remained that awful expression of hate, and cringing, appalling fear.

Grant was pulling himself together.

"Now," I said, "will you dare the last terrible act and rid the world for ever of this horror?"

"By God!" he said solemnly, "I will. Tell me what to do."

"Help me to lift her out of her tomb. She can harm us no more," I replied.

With averted faces we set to our terrible task, and laid her out upon the flags.

"Now," I said, "read the Burial Service over the poor body, and then let us give it its release from this living hell that holds it."

Reverently the Rector read the beautiful words, and reverently I made the necessary responses. When it was over I took the stake and, without giving myself time to think, plunged it with all my strength through the heart.

As though really alive, the body for a moment writhed and kicked convulsively, and an awful heart-rending shriek woke the silent church; then all was still.

Then we lifted the poor body back; and, thank God! the consolation that legend tells is never denied to those who have to do such awful work as ours came at last. Over the face stole a great and solemn peace; the lips lost their crimson hue, the prominent sharp teeth sank back into the mouth, and for a moment we saw before us the calm, pale face of a most beautiful woman, who smiled as she slept. A few minutes more, and she faded away to dust before our eyes as we watched. We set to work and cleaned up every trace of our work, and then departed for the rectory. Most thankful were we to step out of the church, with its horrible associations, into the rosy warmth of the summer morning.

With the above end the notes in my father's diary, though a few days later this further entry occurs:

July 15th. Since the 12th everything has been quiet and as usual. We replaced and sealed up the "Sarah Tomb" this morning. The workmen were surprised to find the body had disappeared, but took it to be the natural result of exposing it to the air.

One odd thing came to my ears today. It appears that the child of one of the villagers strayed from home the night of the 11th inst., and was found asleep in a coppice near the church, very pale and quite exhausted. There were two small marks on her throat, which have since disappeared.

What does this mean? I have, however, kept it to myself, as, now that the Vampire is no more, no further danger either to that child or any other is to be apprehended. It is only those who die of the Vampire's embrace that become Vampires at death in their turn.

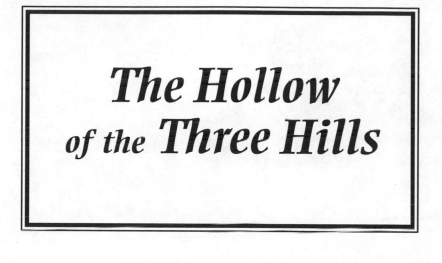

The Hollow
of the *Three Hills*

by
NATHANIEL HAWTHORNE
(1804–1864)

Hawthorne is one of my favourite writers, mostly because his stories really come to life when they are read aloud. In fact, they beg to be read aloud, rather in the manner of a cautionary sermon. Somehow, Hawthorne always manages to slip in a moral message or two.

"The Hollow of the Three Hills" reminds me of Dickens's "A Christmas Carol." In both stories, supernatural forces enable a human being to range over his or her past life, to recognize and repent wrongs committed long ago. But Hawthorne's "withered crone" is missing the benign quality of Dickens's ghosts, displaying an unsettling indifference to the fate of the unhappy woman who seeks her aid. And the disparaging cackle of the old witch echoes in the reader's mind, even as it echoes through the hollows of the hills.

133

I n those strange old times, when fantastic dreams and madmen's reveries were realized among the actual circumstances of life, two persons met together at an appointed hour and place. One was a lady, graceful in form and fair of feature, though pale and troubled, and smitten with an untimely blight in what should have been the fullest bloom of her years; the other was an ancient and meanly-dressed woman, of ill-favoured aspect, and so withered, shrunken, and decrepit, that even the space since she began to decay must have exceeded the ordinary term of human existence. In the spot where they encountered, no mortal could observe them. Three little hills stood near each other, and down in the mist of them sunk a hollow basin, almost mathematically circular, two or three hundred feet in breadth, and of such depth that a stately cedar might but just be visible above the sides. Dwarf pines were numerous upon the hills, and partly fringed the outer verge of the intermediate hollow, within which there was nothing but the brown grass of October, and here and there a tree trunk that had fallen long ago, and lay mouldering with no green successor from its roots. One of these masses of decaying wood, formerly a majestic oak, rested close beside a pool of green and sluggish water at the bottom of the basin. Such scenes as this (so grey tradition tells) were once the resort of the Power of Evil and his plighted subjects; and here, at midnight or on the dim verge of evening, they were said to stand round the mantling pool, disturbing its putrid waters in the performance of an impious baptismal rite. The chill beauty of an autumnal sunset was now gilding the three hill-tops, whence a paler tint stole down their sides into the hollow.

"Here is our pleasant meeting come to pass," said the aged crone, "according as thou hast desired. Say quickly what thou wouldst have of me, for there is but a short hour that we may tarry here."

As the old withered woman spoke, a smile glimmered on her countenance, like lamplight on the wall of a sepulchre. The lady trembled, and cast her eyes upward to the verge of the basin, as if meditating to return with her purpose unaccomplished. But it was not so ordained.

"I am a stranger in this land, as you know," said she at length. "Whence I come it matters not; but I have left those behind me with whom my fate was intimately bound, and from whom I am cut off forever. There is a weight in my bosom that I cannot away with, and I have come hither to inquire of their welfare."

"And who is there by this green pool that can bring thee news from the ends of the earth?" cried the old woman, peering into the lady's face. "Not from my lips mayst thou hear these tidings; yet, be thou bold, and the daylight shall not pass away from yonder hill-top before thy wish be granted."

"I will do your bidding though I die," replied the lady desperately.

The old woman seated herself on the trunk of the fallen tree, threw aside the hood that shrouded her grey locks, and beckoned her companion to draw near.

"Kneel down," she said, "and lay your forehead on my knees."

She hesitated a moment, but the anxiety that had long been kindling burned fiercely up within her. As she knelt down, the border of her garment was dipped into the pool; she laid her forehead on the old woman's knees, and the latter drew a cloak about the lady's face, so that she was in darkness. Then she heard the muttered words of prayer, in the midst of which she started, and would have arisen.

"Let me flee—let me flee and hide myself, that they may not look upon me!" she cried. But, with returning recollection, she hushed herself, and was still as death.

For it seemed as if other voices—familiar in infancy, and unforgotten through many wanderings, and in all the vicissitudes of her heart and fortune—were mingling with the accents of the prayer. At first the words were faint and indistinct, not rendered so by distance, but rather resembling the dim pages of a book which we strive to read by an imperfect and gradually brightening light. In such a manner, as the prayer proceeded, did those voices strengthen upon the ear; till at length the petition ended, and the conversation of an aged man, and of a woman broken and decayed like himself, became distinctly audible to the lady as she knelt. But those strangers appeared not to stand in the hollow depth between the three hills. Their voices were encompassed and re-echoed by the walls of a chamber, the windows of which were rattling in the breeze; the regular vibration of a clock, the crackling of a fire, and the tinkling of the embers as they fell among the ashes, rendered the scene almost as vivid as if painted to the eye. By a melancholy hearth sat these two old people, the man calmly despondent, the woman querulous and tearful, and their words were all of sorrow. They spoke of a daughter, a wanderer they knew not where, bearing dishonour along with her, and leaving shame and affliction to bring their grey heads to the grave. They alluded also to other and more recent woe, but in the midst of their talk their voices seemed to melt into the sound of the wind sweeping mournfully among the autumn leaves; and when the lady lifted her eyes, there was she kneeling in the hollow between three hills.

"A weary and lonesome time yonder old couple have of it," remarked the old woman, smiling in the lady's face.

"And did you also hear them?" exclaimed she, a sense of

intolerable humiliation triumphing over her agony and fear.

"Yea; and we have yet more to hear," replied the old woman. "Wherefore, cover thy face quickly."

Again the withered hag poured forth the monotonous words of a prayer that was not meant to be acceptable in heaven; and soon, in the pauses of her breath, strange murmurings began to thicken, gradually increasing so as to drown and overpower the charm by which they grew. Shrieks pierced through the obscurity of sound, and were succeeded by the singing of sweet female voices, which, in their turn, gave way to a wild roar of laughter, broken suddenly by groanings and sobs, forming altogether a ghastly confusion of terror and mourning and mirth. Chains were rattling, fierce and stern voices uttered threats, and the scourge resounded at their command. All these noises deepened and became substantial to the listener's ear, till she could distinguish every soft and dreamy accent of the love songs that died causelessly into funeral hymns. She shuddered at the unprovoked wrath which blazed up like the spontaneous kindling of flame, and she grew faint at the fearful merriment raging miserably around her. In the midst of this wild scene, where unbound passions jostled each other in a drunken career, there was one solemn voice of a man, and a manly and melodious voice it might once have been. He went to and fro continually, and his feet sounded upon the floor. In each member of that frenzied company, whose own burning thoughts had become their exclusive world, he sought an auditor for the story of his individual wrong, and interpreted their laughter and tears as his reward of scorn or pity. He spoke of woman's perfidy, of a wife who had broken her holiest vows, of a home and heart made desolate. Even as he went on, the shout, the laugh, the shriek, the sob, rose up in unison, till they changed into the hollow, fitful, and uneven sound of the wind, as it fought among the pine-trees on those three lonely hills. The lady looked up, and there was the withered woman smiling in her face.

"Couldst thou have thought there were such merry times in a madhouse?" inquired the latter.

"True, true," said the lady to herself; "there is mirth within its walls, but misery, misery without."

"Wouldst thou hear more?" demanded the old woman.

"There is one other voice I would fain listen to again," replied the lady, faintly.

"Then, lay down thy head speedily upon my knees, that thou mayst get thee hence before the hour be past."

The golden skirts of day were yet lingering upon the hills, but deep shades obscured the hollow and the pool, as if sombre night were rising thence to overspread the world. Again that evil woman began to weave her spell. Long did it proceed unanswered, till the knolling of a bell stole in among the intervals of her words, like a clang that had travelled far over valley and rising ground, and was just ready to die in the air. The lady shook upon her companion's knees as she heard that boding sound. Stronger it grew and sadder, and deepened into the tone of a death bell, knolling dolefully from some ivy-mantled tower, and bearing tidings of mortality and woe to the cottage, to the hall, and to the solitary wayfarer, that all might weep for the doom appointed in turn to them. Then came a measured tread, passing slowly, slowly on, as of mourners with a coffin, their garments trailing on the ground, so that the ear could measure the length of their melancholy array. Before them went the priest, reading the burial service, while the leaves of his book were rustling in the breeze. And though no voice but his was heard to speak aloud, still there were revilings and anathemas, whispered but distinct, from women and from men, breathed against the daughter who had wrung the aged hearts of her parents—the wife who had betrayed the trusting fondness of her husband—the mother who had sinned against natural affection, and left her child to die. The sweeping sound of the funeral train faded away like a thin vapour, and the wind, that just before had seemed to shake the coffin pall, moaned sadly round the verge of the Hollow between three Hills. But when the old woman stirred the kneeling lady, she lifted not her head.

"Here has been a sweet hour's sport!" said the withered crone, chuckling to herself.

The Walker
of the Snow

by
CHARLES DAWSON SHANLY
(1811–1875)

There is something distinctly Canadian about the legend recounted in this nineteenth-century poem by the Irish-born Shanly, who eventually left Canada to settle in New York and then died in Florida. The concept of a ghost who appears to lone walkers in the snowy wilderness will strike a chord with anyone who has ever trudged along through bleak wintry fields, longing for a companion to talk to. But not a companion of this ilk!

peed on, speed on, good Master!
    The camp lies far away;
We must cross the haunted valley
    Before the close of day.

How the snow-blight came upon me
    I will tell you as we go,
The blight of the Shadow Hunter
    Who walks the midnight snow.

To the cold December heaven
    Came the pale moon and the stars
As the yellow sun was sinking
    Behind the purple bars.

The snow was deeply drifted
    Upon the ridges drear
That lay for miles between me
    And the camp for which we steer.

'Twas silent on the hillside,
        And by the sombre wood
No sound of life or motion
        To break the solitude,

Save the wailing of the moose-bird
        With a plaintive note and low,
And the skating of the red leaf
        Upon the frozen snow.

And said I, "Though dark is falling,
        And far the camp must be,
Yet my heart it would be lightsome
        If I had but company."

And then I sang and shouted,
        Keeping measure, as I sped,
To the harp-twang of the snowshoe
        As it sprang beneath my tread.

Nor far into the valley
        Had I dipped upon my way
When a dusky figure joined me
        In a capuchon of grey,

Bending upon the snowshoes
        With a long and limber stride,
And I hailed the dusky stranger
        As we travelled side by side.

But no token of communion
        Gave he by word or look,
And the fear-chill fell upon me
        At the crossing of the brook,

For I saw by the sickly moonlight
        As I followed, bending low,
That the walking of the stranger
        Left no footmarks on the snow.

Then the fear-chill gathered o'er me
        Like a shroud around me cast,
And I sank upon the snowdrift
        Where the Shadow Hunter passed.

And the otter-trappers found me
        Before the break of day,
With my dark hair blanched and whitened
        As the snow in which I lay.

But they spoke not as they raised me,
        For they knew that in the night
I had seen the Shadow Hunter
        And had withered in his blight.

Sancta Maria speed us!
        The sun is falling low—
Before us lies the valley
        Of the Walker of the Snow!

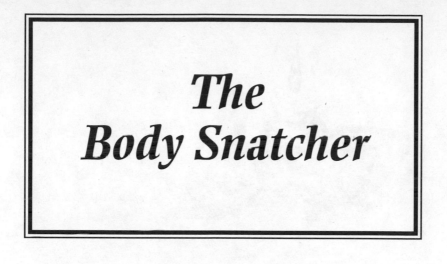

The
Body Snatcher

by

ROBERT LOUIS STEVENSON

(1850–1894)

This is a classic from one of the all-time world champions of horror stories, and as dark a tale as one can imagine. In the evocation of mood—an all-pervasive sense of oppressive evil, damp and cold, danger and creeping terror—Stevenson cannot be outdone. Had he lived a little longer, the author of Dr. Jekyll and Mr. Hyde might now be regarded as the Shakespeare of horror writers.

Some readers may be familiar with this story through a film version. But Stevenson was one of the most accomplished wordsmiths who ever wrote in the English language, and the sheer pleasure to be gained from reading his powerful words is not to be missed. As well, his tale possesses a distinct moral quality that comes through in his narration; this is a portrait of crime and guilt, and of the spread of evil through apathy.

So curl up beside the fire (for this is a particularly chilling tale), and get ready to enjoy the work of a genius.

very night in the year, four of us sat in the small parlour of the George at Debenham—the undertaker,
and the landlord, and Fettes, and myself. Sometimes
there would be more; but blow high, blow low, come
rain or snow or frost, we four would be each planted in his own
particular armchair. Fettes was an old drunken Scotsman, a
man of education obviously, and a man of some property, since
he lived in idleness. He had come to Debenham years ago,
while still young, and by a mere continuance of living had
grown to be an adopted townsman. His blue camlet cloak was a
local antiquity, like the church-spire. His place in the parlour at
the George, his absence from church, his old, crapulous, dis-
reputable vices, were all things of course in Debenham. He had
some vague Radical opinions and some fleeting infidelities,
which he would now and again set forth and emphasize with
tottering slaps upon the table. He drank rum—five glasses reg-
ularly every evening; and for the greater portion of his nightly
visit to the George sat, with his glass in his right hand, in a state
of melancholy alcoholic saturation. We called him the Doctor,
for he was supposed to have some special knowledge of medicine and had been known, upon a pinch, to set a fracture or

reduce a dislocation; but beyond these slight particulars, we had no knowledge of his character and antecedents.

One dark winter night—it had struck nine some time before the landlord joined us—there was a sick man in the George, a great neighbouring proprietor suddenly struck down with apoplexy on his way to Parliament; and the great man's still greater London doctor had been telegraphed to his bedside. It was the first time that such a thing had happened in Debenham, for the railway was but newly open, and we were all proportionately moved by the occurrence.

"He's come," said the landlord, after he had filled and lighted his pipe.

"He?" said I. "Who?—not the doctor?"

"Himself," replied our host.

"What is his name?"

"Dr. Macfarlane," said the landlord.

Fettes was far through his third tumbler, stupidly fuddled, now nodding over, now staring mazily around him; but at the last word he seemed to awaken and repeated the name "Macfarlane" twice, quietly enough the first time, but with sudden emotion at the second.

"Yes," said the landlord, "that's his name, Doctor Wolfe Macfarlane."

Fettes became instantly sober; his eyes awoke, his voice became clear, loud and steady, his language forcible and earnest. We were all startled by the transformation, as if a man had risen from the dead.

"I beg your pardon," he said, "I am afraid I have not been paying much attention to your talk. Who is this Wolfe Macfarlane?" And then, when he had heard the landlord out, "It cannot be, it cannot be," he added; "and yet I would like well to see him face to face."

"Do you know him, Doctor?" asked the undertaker, with a gasp.

"God forbid!" was the reply. "And yet the name is a strange one; it were too much to fancy two. Tell me, landlord, is he old?"

"Well," said the host, "he's not a young man, to be sure, and his hair is white; but he looks younger than you."

"He is older, though; years older. But," with a slap upon the table, "it's the rum you see in my face—rum and sin. This man, perhaps, may have an easy conscience and a good digestion. Conscience! Hear me speak. You would think I was some good, old, decent Christian, would you not? But no, not I; I never canted. Voltaire might have canted if he'd stood in my shoes; but the brains"—with a rattling fillip on his bald head—"the brains were clear and active and I saw and made no deductions."

"If you know this doctor," I ventured to remark, after a somewhat awful pause, "I should gather that you do not share the landlord's good opinion."

Fettes paid no regard to me.

"Yes," he said, with sudden decision, "I must see him face to face."

There was another pause and then a door was closed rather sharply on the first floor and a step was heard upon the stair.

"That's the doctor," cried the landlord. "Look sharp and you can catch him."

It was but two steps from the small parlour to the door of the old George inn; the wide oak staircase landed almost in the street; there was room for a Turkey rug and nothing more between the threshold and the last round of the descent; but this little space was every evening brilliantly lit up, not only by the light upon the stair and the great signal-lamp below the sign, but by the warm radiance of the bar-room window. The George thus brightly advertised itself to passers-by in the cold street. Fettes walked steadily to the spot and we, who were hanging behind, beheld the two men meet, as one of them had phrased it, face to face. Dr. Macfarlane was alert and vigorous. His white hair set off his pale and placid, although energetic, countenance. He was richly dressed in the finest of broadcloth and the whitest of linen, with a great gold watch-chain, and studs and spectacles of the same precious material. He wore a broad-folded tie, white and speckled with lilac, and he carried on his arm a comfortable driving-coat of fur. There was no doubt but he became his years, breathing, as he did, of wealth and consideration; and it was a surprising contrast to see our parlour sot—bald, dirty, pimpled and robed in his old camlet cloak—confront him at the bottom of the stairs.

"Macfarlane!" he said somewhat loudly, more like a herald than a friend.

The great doctor pulled up short on the fourth step, as though the familiarity of the address surprised and somewhat shocked his dignity.

"Toddy Macfarlane!" repeated Fettes.

The London man almost staggered. He stared for the swiftest of seconds at the man before him, glanced behind him with a sort of scare, and then in a startled whisper, "Fettes!" he said, "you!"

"Ay," said the other, "me! Did you think I was dead too? We are not so easy shut of our acquaintance."

"Hush, hush!" exclaimed the doctor. "Hush, hush! this meeting is so unexpected—I can see you are unmanned. I hardly knew you, I confess, at first, but I am overjoyed—overjoyed to have this opportunity. For the present it must be how-d'ye-do and goodbye in one, for my fly is waiting and I must not fail the train; but you shall—let me see—yes—you shall give me your address and you can count on early news of me. We must do something for you, Fettes. I fear you are out at elbows; but we must see to that for auld lang syne, as once we sang at suppers."

"Money!" cried Fettes; "money from you! The money that I had from you is lying where I cast it in the rain."

Dr. Macfarlane had talked himself into some measure of superiority and confidence, but the uncommon energy of this refusal cast him back into his first confusion.

A horrible, ugly look came and went across his almost venerable countenance. "My dear fellow," he said, "be it as you please; my last thought is to offend you. I would intrude on none. I will leave you my address, however—"

"I do not wish it—I do not wish to know the roof that shelters you," interrupted the other. "I heard your name; I feared it might be you; I wished to know if, after all, there were a God; I know now that there is none. Begone!"

He still stood in the middle of the rug, between the stair

and the doorway; and the great London physician, in order to escape, would be forced to step to one side. It was plain that he hesitated before the thought of this humiliation. White as he was, there was a dangerous glitter in his spectacles; but while he still paused uncertain, he became aware that the driver of his fly was peering in from the street at this unusual scene and caught a glimpse at the same time of our little body from the parlour, huddled by the corner of the bar. The presence of so many witnesses decided him at once to flee. He crouched together, brushing on the wainscot, and made a dart like a serpent, striking for the door. But his tribulation was not yet entirely at an end, for even as he was passing Fettes clutched him by the arm and these words came in a whisper, and yet painfully distinct, "Have you seen it again?"

The great rich London doctor cried out aloud with a sharp, throttling cry; he dashed his questioner across the open space, and, with his hands over his head, fled out of the door like a detected thief. Before it had occurred to one of us to make a movement, the fly was already rattling towards the station. The scene was over like a dream, but the dream had left proofs and traces of its passage. Next day the servant found the fine gold spectacles broken on the threshold, and that very night we were all standing breathless by the bar-room window, and Fettes at our side, sober, pale, and resolute in look.

"God protect us, Mr. Fettes!" said the landlord, coming first into possession of his customary senses. "What in the universe is all this? These are strange things you have been saying."

Fettes turned towards us; he looked us each in succession in the face. "See if you can hold your tongues," said he. "That man Macfarlane is not safe to cross; those that have done so already have repented it too late."

And then, without so much as finishing his third glass, far less waiting for the other two, he bade us goodbye and went forth, under the lamp of the hotel, into the black night.

We three turned to our places in the parlour, with the big red fire and four clear candles; and as we recapitulated what had passed the first chill of our surprise soon changed into a glow of curiosity. We sat late; it was the latest session I have known in the old George. Each man, before we parted, had his theory that he was bound to prove; and none of us had any nearer business in this world than to track out the past of our condemned companion, and surprise the secret that he shared with the great London doctor. It was no great boast, but I believe I was a better hand at worming out a story than either of my fellows at the George; and perhaps there is now no other man alive who could narrate to you the following foul and unnatural events.

In his young days Fettes studied medicine in the schools of Edinburgh. He had talent of a kind, the talent that picks up swiftly what it hears and readily retails it for its own. He worked little at home; but he was civil, attentive, and intelligent in the presence of his masters. They soon picked him out as a lad who listened closely and remembered well; nay, strange as it seemed to me when I first heard it, he was in those days well favoured, and pleased by his exterior. There was, at that period, a certain extramural teacher of anatomy, whom I shall here designate by the letter K. His name was subsequently too well known. The man who bore it skulked through the streets of Edinburgh in disguise, while the mob that applauded at the execution of Burke called loudly for the blood of his employer. But Mr. K— was then at the top of his vogue; he enjoyed a popularity due partly to his own talent and address, partly to the incapacity of his rival, the university professor. The students, at least, swore by his name, and Fettes believed himself, and was believed by others, to have laid the foundations of success when he had acquired the favour of this meteorically famous man. Mr. K— was a *bon vivant* as well as an accomplished teacher; he liked a sly allusion no less than a careful preparation. In both capacities Fettes enjoyed and deserved his notice, and by the second year of his attendance he held the half-regular position of second demonstrator or sub-assistant in his class.

In this capacity, the charge of the theatre and lecture room developed in particular upon his shoulders. He had to answer for the cleanliness of the premises and the conduct of the other students, and it was a part of his duty to supply, receive, and divide the various subjects. It was with a view to this last—at that time very delicate—affair that he was lodged by Mr. K— in the same wynd, and at last in the same building, with the dissecting-rooms. Here, after a night of turbulent pleasures, his hand still tottering, his sight still misty and confused, he would be called out of bed in the black hours before the winter dawn by the unclean and desperate interlopers who supplied the table. He would open the door to these men, since infamous throughout the land. He would help them with their tragic burthen, pay them their sordid price, and remain alone, when they were gone, with the unfriendly relics of humanity. From such a scene he would return to snatch another hour or two of slumber, to repair the abuses of the night, and refresh himself for the labours of the day.

Few lads could have been more insensible to the impressions of a life thus passed among the ensigns of mortality. His mind was closed against all general considerations. He was incapable of interest in the fate and fortunes of another, the slave of his own desires and low ambitions. Cold, light and selfish in the last resort, he had that modicum of prudence, miscalled morality, which keeps a man from inconvenient drunkenness or punishable theft. He coveted, besides, a measure of consideration from his masters and his fellow-pupils, and he had no desire to fail conspicuously in the external parts of life. Thus he made it his pleasure to gain some distinction in his studies, and day after day rendered unimpeachable eye-service to his employer, Mr. K—. For his day of work he indemnified himself by nights of roaring, blackguardly enjoyment; and when that balance had been struck, the organ that he called his conscience declared itself content.

The supply of subjects was a continual trouble to him as well as to his master. In that large and busy class, the raw material of the anatomists kept perpetually running out; and the business thus rendered necessary was not only unpleasant in itself, but threatened dangerous consequences to all who were concerned. It was the policy of Mr. K— to ask no questions in his dealings with the trade. "They bring the body, and we pay the price," he used to say, dwelling on the alliteration—"*quid pro quo*." And again, and somewhat profanely, "Ask no questions," he would tell his assistants, "for conscience' sake." There was no understanding that the subjects were provided by the crime of murder. Had that idea been broached to him in words, he would have recoiled in horror; but the lightness of his speech upon so grave a matter was, in itself, an offence against good manners, and a temptation to the men with whom he dealt. Fettes, for instance, had often remarked to himself upon the singular freshness of the bodies. He had been struck again and again by the hangdog, abominable looks of the ruffians who came to him before the dawn; and, putting things together clearly in his private thoughts, he perhaps attributed a meaning too immoral and too categorical to the unguarded counsels of his master. He understood his duty, in short, to have three branches: to take what was brought, to pay the price, and to avert the eye from any evidence of crime.

One November morning this policy of silence was put sharply to the test. He had been awake all night with a racking toothache—pacing his room like a caged beast or throwing himself in fury on his bed—and had fallen at last into that profound, uneasy slumber that so often follows on a night of pain, when he was awakened by the third or fourth angry repetition of the concerted signal. There was a thin, bright moonshine: it was bitter cold, windy, and frosty; the town had not yet awakened, but an indefinable stir already preluded the noise and business of the day. The ghouls had come later than usual, and they seemed more than usually eager to be gone. Fettes, sick with sleep, lighted them upstairs. He heard their grumbling Irish voices through a dream; and as they stripped the sack from their sad merchandise he leaned dozing with his shoulder propped against the wall; he had to shake himself to find the men their money. As he did so his eyes lighted on the dead face. He started; he took two steps nearer, with the candle raised.

"God Almighty!" he cried. "That is Jane Galbraith!"

The men answered nothing, but they shuffled nearer the door.

"I know her, I tell you," he continued. "She was alive and hearty yesterday. It's impossible she can be dead; it's impossible you should have got this body fairly."

"Sure, sir, you're mistaken entirely," asserted one of the men.

But the other looked Fettes darkly in the eyes, and demanded the money on the spot.

It was impossible to misconceive the threat or to exaggerate the danger. The lad's heart failed him. He stammered some excuses, counted out the sum, and saw his hateful visitors depart. No sooner were they gone than he hastened to confirm his doubts. By a dozen unquestionable marks he identified the girl he had jested with the day before. He saw, with horror, marks upon her body that might well betoken violence. A panic seized him, and he took refuge in his room. There he reflected at length over the discovery that he had made; considered soberly the bearing of Mr. K—'s instructions and the danger to himself of interference in so serious a business, and at last, in sore perplexity, determined to wait for the advice of his immediate superior, the class assistant.

This was a young doctor, Wolfe Macfarlane, a high favourite among all the restless students, clever, dissipated, and unscrupulous to the last degree. He had travelled and studied abroad. His manners were agreeable and a little forward. He was an authority on the stage, skilful on the ice or the links with skate or golf club; he dressed with nice audacity, and, to put the finishing touch upon his glory, he kept a gig and a strong trotting-horse. With Fettes he was on terms on intimacy; indeed their relative positions called for some community of life; and when subjects were scarce the pair would drive far into the country in Macfarlane's gig, visit and desecrate some lonely graveyard, and return before dawn with their booty to the door of the dissecting-room.

On that particular morning Macfarlane arrived somewhat earlier than his wont. Fettes heard him, and met him on the stairs, told him his story, and showed him the cause of his alarm. Macfarlane examined the marks on her body.

"Yes," he said with a nod, "it looks fishy."

"Well, what should I do?" asked Fettes.

"Do?" repeated the other. "Do you want to do anything? Least said soonest mended, I should say."

"Someone else might recognize her," objected Fettes. "She

was as well known as the Castle Rock."

"We'll hope not," said Macfarlane, "and if anybody does— well you didn't, don't you see, and there's an end. The fact is, this has been going on too long. Stir up the mud, and you'll get K— into the most unholy trouble; you'll be in a shocking box yourself. So will I, if you come to that. I should like to know how any one of us would look, or what the devil we should have to say for ourselves, in any Christian witness-box. For me, you know there's one thing certain—that, practically speaking, all our subjects have been murdered."

"Macfarlane!" cried Fettes.

"Come now!" sneered the other. "As if you hadn't suspected it yourself!"

"Suspecting is one thing—"

"And proof another. Yes, I know; and I'm as sorry as you are this should have come here," tapping the body with his cane. "The next best thing for me is not to recognize it; and," he added coolly, "I don't. You may, if you please. I don't dictate, but I think a man of the world would do as I do; and I may add, I fancy that is what K— would look for at our hands. The question is, why did he choose us two for his assistants? And I answer, because he didn't want old wives."

This was the tone of all others to affect the mind of a lad like Fettes. He agreed to imitate Macfarlane. The body of the unfortunate girl was duly dissected, and no one remarked or appeared to recognize her.

One afternoon, when his day's work was over, Fettes dropped into a popular tavern and found Macfarlane sitting with a stranger. This was a small man, very pale and dark, with coal-black eyes. The cut of his features gave a promise of intellect and refinement which was but feebly realized in his manners, for he proved, upon a nearer acquaintance, coarse, vulgar, and stupid. He exercised, however, a very remarkable control over Macfarlane; issued orders like the Great Bashaw; became inflamed at the least discussion or delay, and commented rudely on the servility with which he was obeyed. This most offensive person took a fancy to Fettes on the spot, plied him with drinks, and honoured him with unusual confidences on his past career. If a tenth part of what he confessed were true, he was a very loathsome rogue; and the lad's vanity was tickled by the attention of so experienced a man.

"I'm a pretty bad fellow myself," the stranger remarked, "but Macfarlane is the boy—Toddy Macfarlane I call him. Toddy, order your friend another glass." Or it might be, "Toddy, you jump up and shut the door." "Toddy hates me," he said again. "Oh, yes, Toddy, you do!"

"Don't call me that confounded name," growled Macfarlane.

"Hear him! Did you ever see the lads play knife? He would like to do that all over my body," remarked the stranger.

"We medicals have a better way than that," said Fettes. "When we dislike a dead friend of ours, we dissect him."

Macfarlane looked up sharply, as though this jest was scarcely to his mind.

The afternoon passed. Gray, for that was the stranger's name, invited Fettes to join them at dinner, ordered a feast so sumptuous that the tavern was thrown in commotion, and when all was done commanded Macfarlane to settle the bill. It was late before they separated; the man Gray was incapably drunk. Macfarlane, sobered by his fury, chewed the cud of the money he had been forced to squander and the slights he had been obliged to swallow. Fettes, with various liquors singing in his head, returned home with devious footsteps and a mind entirely in abeyance. Next day Macfarlane was absent from the class, and Fettes smiled to himself as he imagined him still squiring the intolerable Gray from tavern to tavern. As soon as the hour of liberty had struck he posted from place to place in quest of his last night's companions. He could find them, however, nowhere; so returned early to his rooms, went early to bed, and slept the sleep of the just.

At four in the morning he was awakened by the well-known signal. Descending to the door, he was filled with astonishment to find Macfarlane with his gig, and in the gig one of those long and ghastly packages with which he was so well acquainted.

"What?" he cried. "Have you been out alone? How did you manage?"

But Macfarlane silenced him roughly, bidding him turn to business. When they had got the body upstairs and laid it on the table, Macfarlane made at first as if he were going away. Then he paused and seemed to hesitate; and then, "You had better look at the face," said he, in tones of some constraint. "You had better," he repeated, as Fettes only stared at him in wonder.

"But where, and how, and when did you come by it?" cried the other.

"Look at the face," was the only answer.

Fettes was staggered; strange doubts assailed him. He looked from the young doctor to the body, and then back again. At last, with a start, he did as he was bidden. He had almost expected the sight that met his eyes, and yet the shock was cruel. To see, fixed in the rigidity of death and naked on that coarse layer of sackcloth, the man whom he had left well-clad and full of meat and sin upon the threshold of a tavern, awoke, even in the thoughtless Fettes, some of the terrors of the conscience. It was a *cras tibi* which re-echoed in his soul, that two whom he had known should have come to lie upon these icy tables. Yet these were only secondary thoughts. His first concern regarded Wolfe. Unprepared for a challenge so momentous, he knew not how to look his comrade in the face. He durst not meet his eye, and he had neither words nor voice at his command.

It was Macfarlane himself who made the first advance. He came up quietly behind and laid his hand gently but firmly on the other's shoulder.

"Richardson," said he, "may have the head."

Now Richardson was a student who had long been anxious for that portion of the human subject to dissect. There was no answer, and the murderer resumed: "Talking of business, you must pay me; your accounts, you see, must tally."

Fettes found a voice, the ghost of his own: "Pay you!" he cried. "Pay you for that?"

"Why, yes, of course you must. By all means and on every possible account, you must," returned the other. "I durst not give it for nothing, you dare not take it for nothing; it would compromise us both. This is another case like Jane Galbraith's.

The more things are wrong the more we must act as if all were right. Where does old K— deep his money—"

"There," answered Fettes hoarsely, pointing to a cupboard in the corner.

"Give me the key, then," said the other, holding out his hand.

There was an instant's hesitation, and the die was cast. Macfarlane could not suppress a nervous twitch, the infinitesimal mark of an immense relief, as he felt the key turn between his fingers. He opened the cupboard, brought out pen and ink and a paper-book that stood in one compartment, and separated from the funds in a drawer a sum suitable to the occasion.

"Now, look here," he said, "there is the payment made—first proof of your good faith: first step to your security. You have now to clinch it by a second. Enter the payment in your book, and then you for your part may defy the devil."

The next few seconds were for Fettes an agony of thought; but in balancing his terrors it was the most immediate that triumphed. Any future difficulty seemed almost welcome if he could avoid a present quarrel with Macfarlane. He set down the candle which he had been carrying all the time, and with a steady hand entered the date, the nature, and the amount of the transaction.

"And now," said Macfarlane, "it's only fair that you should pocket the lucre. I've had my share already. By-the-by, when a man of the world falls into a bit of luck, he has a few shillings extra in his pocket—I'm ashamed to speak of it, but there's a rule of conduct in the case. No treating, no purchase of expensive class-books, no squaring of old debts; borrow, don't lend."

"Macfarlane," began Fettes, still somewhat hoarsely. "I have put my neck in a halter to oblige you."

"To oblige me?" cried Wolfe. "Oh, come! You did, as near as I can see the matter, what you downright had to do in self-defence. Suppose I got into trouble, where would you be? This second little matter flows clearly from the first. Mr. Gray is the continuation of Miss Galbraith. You can't begin and then stop. If you begin, you must keep on beginning; that's the truth. No rest for the wicked."

A horrible sense of blackness and the treachery of fate

seized hold upon the soul of the unhappy student.

"My God!" he cried, "but what have I done? and when did I begin? To be made a class assistant—in the name of reason, where's the harm in that? Service wanted the position; Service might have got it. Would *he* have been where *I* am now?"

"My dear fellow," said Macfarlane, "what a boy you are! What harm *has* come to you? What harm *can* come to you if you hold your tongue? Why, man, do you know what this life is? There are two squads of us—the lions and the lambs. If you're a lamb, you'll come to lie upon these tables like Gray or Jane Galbraith; if you're a lion, you'll live and drive a horse like me, like K—, like all the world with any wit or courage. You're staggered at the first. But look at K—! My dear fellow, you're clever, you have pluck. I like you, and K— likes you. You were born to lead the hunt: and I tell you, on my honour and my experience of life, three days from now you'll laugh at all these scarecrows like a high-school boy at a farce."

And with that Macfarlane took his departure and drove off up the wynd in his gig to get under cover before daylight. Fettes was thus left alone with his regrets. He saw the miserable peril in which he stood involved. He saw, with inexpressible dismay, that there was no limit to his weakness, and that, from concession to concession, he had fallen from the arbiter of Macfarlane's destiny to his paid and helpless accomplice. He would have given the world to have been a little braver at the time, but it did not occur to him that he might still be brave. The secret of Jane Galbraith and the cursed entry in the day-book closed his mouth.

Hours passed; the class began to arrive; the members of the unhappy Gray were dealt out to one and to another, and received without remark. Richardson was made happy with the head; and before the hour of freedom rang Fettes trembled with exultation to perceive how far they had already gone towards safety.

For two days he continued to watch, with increasing joy, the dreadful process of disguise.

On the third day Macfarlane made his appearance. He had been ill, he said; but he made up for lost time by the energy with which he directed the students. To Richardson in particular he extended the most valuable assistance and advice, and that student, encouraged by the praise of the demonstrator, burned high with ambitious hopes, and saw the medal already in his grasp.

Before the week was out Macfarlane's prophecy had been fulfilled. Fettes had outlived his terrors and had forgotten his baseness. He began to plume himself upon his courage, and had so arranged the story in his mind that he could look back on these events with an unhealthy pride. Of his accomplice he saw but little. They met, of course, in the business of the class; they received their orders together from Mr. K—. At times they had a word or two in private, and Macfarlane was from first to last particularly kind and jovial. But it was plain that he avoided any reference to their common secret; and even when Fettes whispered to him that he had cast in his lot with the lions and forsworn the lambs, he only signed to him smilingly to hold his peace.

At length an occasion arose which drew the pair once more into a closer union. Mr. K— was again short of subjects; pupils were eager, and it was a part of this teacher's pretensions to be always well supplied. At the same time there came the news of a burial in the rustic graveyard of Glencorse. Time has little changed the place in question. It stood then, as now, upon the crossroad, out of call of human habitations, and buried fathom deep in the foliage of six cedar trees. The cries of the sheep upon the neighbouring hills, the streamlets upon either hand, one loudly singing among pebbles, the other dripping furtively from pond to pond, the stir of the wind in mountainous old flowering chestnuts, and once in seven days the voice of the bell and the old tunes of the precentor, were the only sounds that disturbed the silence around the rural church. The Resurrection Man—to use a by-name of the period—was not to be deterred by any of the sanctities of customary piety. It was part of his trade to despise and desecrate the scrolls and trumpets of old tombs, the paths worn by the feet of worshippers and mourners, and the offerings and the inscriptions of bereaved affection. To rustic neighbourhoods, where love is more than commonly tenacious, and where some bonds of blood or fellowship unite the entire society of a parish, the body snatcher, far from being repelled by natural respect, was attracted by the ease and safety of the task. To bodies that had been laid in earth, in joyful expectation of a far different awakening, there came that hasty, lamp-lit, terror haunted resurrection of the spade and mattock. The coffin was forced, the cerements torn, and the melancholy relics, clad in sackcloth, after being rattled for hours on moonless byways, were at length exposed to uttermost indignities before a class of gaping boys.

Somewhat as two vultures may swoop upon a dying lamb, Fettes and Macfarlane were to be let loose upon a grave in that green and quiet resting-place. The wife of a farmer, a woman who had lived for sixty years, and been known for nothing but good butter and a godly conversation, was to be rooted from her grave at midnight and carried, dead and naked, to that far-away city that she had always honoured with her Sunday best; the place beside her family was to be empty till the crack of doom; her innocent and almost venerable members to be exposed to that last curiosity of the anatomist.

Late one afternoon the pair set forth, well wrapped in cloaks and furnished with a formidable bottle. It rained without remission—a cold, dense, lashing rain. Now and again there blew a puff of wind, but these sheets of falling water kept it down. Bottle and all, it was a sad and silent drive as far as Penicuik, where they were to spend the evening. They stopped once, to hide their implements in a thick bush not far from the churchyard, and once again at the Fisher's Tryst, to have a toast before the kitchen fire and vary their nips of whisky with a glass of ale. When they reached their journey's end the gig was housed, the horse was fed and comforted, and the two young doctors in a private room sat down to the best dinner and the best wine the house afforded. The lights, the fire, the beating rain upon the window, the cold, incongruous work that lay before them, added zest to their enjoyment of the meal. With every glass their cordiality increased. Soon Macfarlane handed a little pile of gold to his companion.

"A compliment," he said. "Between friends these little

damned accommodations ought to fly like pipe-lights."

Fettes pocketed the money, and applauded the sentiment to the echo. "You are a philosopher," he cried. "I was an ass till I knew you. You and K— between you, by the Lord Harry! but you'll make a man of me."

"Of course we shall," applauded Macfarlane. "A man? I tell you, it required a man to back me up the other morning. There are some big, brawling, forty-year-old cowards who would have turned sick at the look of the damned thing; but not you—you kept your head. I watched you."

"Well, and why not?" Fettes thus vaunted himself. "It was no affair of mine. There was nothing to gain on the one side but disturbance, and on the other I could count on your gratitude, don't you see?" And he slapped his pocket till the gold pieces rang.

Macfarlane somehow felt a certain touch of alarm at these unpleasant words. He may have regretted that he had taught his young companion so successfully, but he had no time to interfere, for the other noisily continued in this boastful strain:

"The great thing is not to be afraid. Now, between you and me, I don't want to hand—that's practical; but for all cant, Macfarlane, I was born with a contempt. Hell, God, Devil, right, wrong, sin, crime, and all the old gallery of curiosities— they may frighten boys, but men of the world, like you and me, despise them. Here's to the memory of Gray!"

It was by this time growing somewhat late. The gig, according to order was brought round to the door with both lamps brightly shining, and the young men had to pay their bill and take the road. They announced that they were bound for Peebles, and drove in that direction till they were clear of the last houses of the town; then, extinguishing the lamps, returned upon their course, and followed a byroad towards Glencorse. There was no sound but that of their own passage, and the incessant, strident pouring of the rain. It was pitch dark; here and there a white gate or a white stone in the wall guided them for a short space across the night; but for the most part it was at a foot pace, and almost groping, that they picked their way through that resonant blackness to their solemn and isolated destination. In the sunken woods that traverse the neighbourhood of the burying-ground the last glimmer failed them, and it became necessary to kindle a match and re-illumine one of the lanterns of the gig. Thus, under the dripping trees, and environed by huge and moving shadows, they reached the scene of their unhallowed labours.

They were both experienced in such affairs, and powerful with the spade; and they had scarce been twenty minutes at their task before they were rewarded by a dull rattle on the coffin lid. At the same moment Macfarlane, having hurt his hand upon a stone, flung it carelessly above his head. The grave, in which they now stood almost to the shoulders, was close to the edge of the plateau of the graveyard; and the gig lamp had been propped, the better to illuminate their labours, against a tree, and on the immediate verge of the steep bank descending to the stream. Chance had taken a sure aim with the stone. Then came a clang of broken glass; night fell upon them; sounds alternately dull and ringing announced the bounding of the lantern down the bank and its occasional collision with the trees. A stone or two, which it had dislodged in its descent, rattled behind it into the profundities of the glen; and then silence, like night, resumed its sway; and they might bend their hearing to its utmost pitch, but naught was to be heard except the rain, now marching to the wind, now steadily falling over miles of open country.

They were so nearly at an end of their abhorred task that they judged it wisest to complete it in the dark. The coffin was exhumed and broken open; the body inserted in the dripping sack and carried between them to the gig; one mounted to keep it in its place, and the other, taking the horse by the mouth, groped along by the wall and bush until they reached the wider road by the Fisher's Tryst. Here was a faint disused radiancy, which they hailed like daylight; by that they pushed the horse to a good pace and began to rattle along merrily in the direction of the town.

They had both been wetted to the skin during their operations, and now, as the gig jumped among the deep ruts, the thing that stood propped between them fell now upon one

and now upon the other. At every repetition of the horrid contact each instinctively repelled it with greater haste; and the
process, natural though it was, began to tell upon the nerves
of the companions. Macfarlane made some ill-favoured jest
about the farmer's wife, but it came hollowly from his lips, and
was allowed to drop in silence. Still their unnatural burthen
bumped from side to side; and now the head would be laid, as
if in confidence, upon their shoulders, and now the drenching
sackcloth would flap icily about their faces. A creeping chill
began to possess the soul of Fettes. He peered at the bundle,
and it seemed somehow larger than at first. All over the countryside, and from every degree of distance, the farm dogs
accompanied their passage with tragic ululations; and it grew
and grew upon his mind that some unnatural miracle had
been achieved, that some nameless change had befallen the
dead body, and that it was in fear of their unholy burthen that
the dogs were howling.

"For God's sake," said he, making a great effort to arrive at
speech, "for God's sake, let's have a light!"

Seemingly Macfarlane was affected in the same direction;
for though he made no reply, he stopped the horse, passed the
reins to his companion, got down, and proceeded to kindle
the remaining lamp. They had by that time got no farther than
the crossroad to Auchendinny. The rain still poured as though
the deluge were returning, and it was no easy matter to make
a light in such a world of wet and darkness. When at last the
flickering blue flame had been transferred to the wick and
began to expand and clarify, and shed a wide circle of misty
brightness round the gig, it became possible for the two young
men to see each other and the thing they had along with
them. The rain had moulded the rough sacking to the outlines
of the body underneath; the head was distinct from the trunk,
the shoulders plainly modelled; something at once spectral
and human riveted their eyes upon the ghastly comrade of
their drive.

For some time Macfarlane stood motionless, holding up the
lamp. A nameless dread was swathed, like a wet sheet, above
the body, and tightened the white skin upon the face of Fettes;

a fear that was meaningless, a horror of what could not be, kept mounting to his brain. Another beat of the watch, and he had spoken. But his comrade forestalled him.

"That is not a woman," said Macfarlane, in a hushed voice.

"It was a woman when we put her in," whispered Fettes.

"Hold that lamp," said the other. "I must see her face."

And as Fettes took the lamp his companion untied the fastenings of the sack and drew down the cover from the head. The light fell very clear upon the dark, well-moulded features and smooth-shaven cheeks of a too familiar countenance, often beheld in dreams of both of these young men. A wild yell rang up into the night; each leaped from his own side into the roadway; the lamp fell, broke, and was extinguished; and the horse, terrified by this unusual commotion, bounded and went off towards Edinburgh at a gallop, bearing along with it, sole occupant of the gig, the body of the dead and long-dissected Gray.

Angeline
or *The Haunted House*

by
EMILE ZOLA
(1840–1902)

Have you ever gazed at a deserted old house and wanted to ask the bricks and mortar to tell their story? When I was a child, there was a high-Victorian house in the town where my grandparents lived, with steeply pitched gables and intricate, decaying woodwork around its eaves. It stood vacant for several years, eventually falling into disrepair, and my friends and I were convinced that it was haunted and would dare one another to go there after dark. Emile Zola's exquisitely romantic story explores the human appetite for drama and horror that is excited by the gaping windows and crumbling masonry of an empty house. Such a craving is as universal as it is natural, though Zola imbues it with a decidedly Gallic flair.

165

1

Almost two years ago now, I found myself riding on my bicycle along a deserted country lane in the region of Orgeval, just north of Poissy, when I was greatly surprised by the sudden appearance, quite close to the road, of a large house. I alighted from my machine in order that I might see it more clearly. It stood there under the grey November sky, as the cold wind swept the fallen leaves, a brick-built house of no especial character in the middle of a vast garden filled with elderly trees. But what made it unusual, what, indeed, endowed it with a wild strangeness which set one's nerves on edge, was the awful state of abandon in which it had been left. And so it was, since one of the iron gates had broken from its hinges, and since a large board announced in paint which had been faded by the rains that the property was for sale, that I entered the garden, yielding to a curiosity which was tinged with apprehension.

The house must have been uninhabited for some thirty or forty years. Through the course of many winters, bricks had worked loose from the cornices and by the window-frames, allowing an invasion of moss and lichens. The walls were lined with cracks, like premature wrinkles, marking what was still a sound enough building but for which no one cared any longer. Below the front door the stone steps, broken by the frosts and guarded by nettles and brambles, seemed to present a threshold to desolation and death. But most of all, the atmosphere of melancholy emanated from those bare, glaucous windows, their curtains gone, their glass smashed by stones from passing children, which permitted a view into the sombre emptiness of the rooms, like the open eyes of a corpse whose soul has been extinguished. Around the house the vast garden was a scene of devastation. What once had been a flower-bed was now scarcely recognizable under the rampant growth of weeds, whole paths had been devoured by voracious plants, the shrubberies had reverted to the character of virgin forests: I was presented with an impression of wild vegetation such as one finds in an abandoned cemetery, and all, that day, under the damp shade of ancient trees whose last leaves were being carried off by the autumn wind crying its sad complaint.

For a long time I stood there surrounded by this wail of despair which seemed to come from all that I saw about me. My heart was heavy with a dull fear, a growing unease, yet I was held by a burning compassion, a need to know and sympathize with all I could feel around me of unhappiness and suffering. Then, having finally made my decision to leave, and having perceived beyond the way, in the fork of two roads, a sort of inn, a poor place where one could buy a drink, I went in, resolved to satisfy my curiosity by encouraging the local people to talk.

The only person I found there was an old woman, who served me a glass of beer with a great deal of complaining. She complained that she found herself here on this forgotten road, where not two cyclists a day would pass. She talked aimlessly, related the story of her life, revealed that she was known as "mère Toussaint," that she had come from Vernon with her man in order to take over the inn, that at first things had not gone too badly, but that since she was widowed everything had gone from bad to worse. Finally, after this flood of words, when I started to ask her about the nearby house, she became suddenly more circumspect, regarding me with a suspicious eye, as if I were attempting to tear from her some awful secret.

"Oh, you mean 'La Sauvagière,' the haunted house, as they call it round here... I know nothing of that, Monsieur. That goes back before my time. I shall have been here just thirty years next Easter, and that all goes back nearly forty years. When we came out here the house was already more or less in the state you see it in now. Summers pass and winters pass and no one sees anything move in there, except for the occasional falling stone."

"But," I asked, "why hasn't it been sold, since it is for sale?"

"Oh, why indeed? How should I know?... They talk about it enough..."

In the end, I must have gained her confidence, whereupon it was clear that she was only too anxious to recount to me what it was that people talked about. First she told me how not one of the girls from the village would dare to venture into the grounds of "La Sauvagière" after dusk, because it was rumoured that some poor soul returned there by night to haunt it. When I expressed surprise that such a story should still be found credible so near to Paris, she shrugged her shoulders, endeavouring at first to appear composed, but before long revealing her unspoken terror.

"But consider the facts, Monsieur. Why has it never been sold? I have seen prospective purchasers come and go, but they always leave more quickly than they arrived, and not one has ever come back a second time. And I can tell you one thing for sure, if any visitor dares to venture inside that house extraordinary things happen: doors slam noisily of their own accord, as if some awful wind were blowing; cries, moans, and the sound of sobbing rise from the cellars; and if anyone dares to stay longer a heart-rending voice starts to call out again and again 'Angeline! Angeline! Angeline!' in such an anguished tone as to chill the very marrow of your bones... What I am telling you are proven facts. No one will deny them."

I assure you that my own emotions were beginning to stir, and a shiver ran down my spine.

"But who is this Angeline?"

"I can see, Monsieur, that you are determined to know the

whole story, though I must tell you again that I really know nothing myself."

Nevertheless, she proceeded eventually to tell me everything. Some forty years previously, in about 1858, just at the time when the victorious Second Empire was holding one celebration after another, Monsieur de G——, who held a post at the Tuileries Palace, lost his wife. He had by her a daughter, some ten years old, called Angeline, indescribably beautiful, and the living image of her mother. Two years later Monsieur de G—— married again, and his second wife was another renowned beauty, the widow of a general. Apparently, following this second marriage a terrible jealousy grew up between Angeline and her stepmother: the one grief-stricken to see her mother already forgotten, her place in the family so quickly usurped by this outsider; the other obsessed to distraction by the idea of having constantly before her this living portrait of a woman she feared she could never cause to be forgotten. "La Sauvagière" belonged to the new Madame de G——, and it was there, so the story went, that one evening, on seeing the father lovingly embrace his daughter, in her jealous rage she struck the little girl such a blow that the wretched child fell to the floor dead, her neck broken. The end of the story was gruesome. The distraught father consented to bury his daughter himself in one of the cellars of the house, in order to save the murderess. The body of the child remained hidden there for years, while the story was put about that she had gone away to an aunt's. Then, one day, the howling of a dog who was found feverishly scratching at the ground caused the crime to be discovered, although the scandal of the discovery was subsequently suppressed by the Tuileries authorities. Now both Monsieur and Madame de G—— were dead, but Angeline still returned every night to answer the call of the pitiful voice which summoned her from that mysterious world beyond the darkness.

"No one will deny what I have told you," concluded the old woman. "It is all as true as I am standing here."

I had listened to her account in awe, struck by its implausibility, yet captivated by the dark and violent singularity of the drama. I had heard of this Monsieur de G——. I think I had

known that he had remarried and that a family tragedy had
overtaken him. Was it then true? What a moving and tragic
story, exposing human passion to the point of exasperated
frenzy, the most awful crime of passion one could ever imagine: a little girl as beautiful as a summer's day, loved and cher-
ished, struck down by her stepmother, and then buried by her
father in the corner of a cellar! What exquisite horror! I wanted to hear more, to talk about it, but I asked myself, to what
end? Why not depart with the flower of popular imagination,
this terrifying tale?

As I remounted my bicycle I cast a last glance in the direction of "La Sauvagière." Night was falling, and the desolate
house looked back at me through the lifeless eyes of its dull,
empty windows, whilst the autumn wind sighed a lament
among the decaying trees.

2

Why should that story have become fixed in my mind until it
became an agonizing obsession? It is one of those intellectual
mysteries which are difficult to account for. In vain I told
myself that such myths are rife in the countryside, that this particular one could have no real interest for me personally.
Despite it all, the dead child haunted my thoughts: sweet, tragic Angeline, summoned every night for forty years by a voice
whimpering among the empty rooms of the abandoned house.

So, for the first two months of the winter, I set about doing
some research. Obviously, if ever such a disappearance, such a
dramatic happening, had been noised abroad, the newspapers
of the time would surely have spoken of it. I searched through
the collections in the National Library without success: there
was not a line which could have been linked with such a story.
Then I questioned people who might have known something
at the time, employees of the Tuileries: none was able to give
me a clear answer—all I obtained was contradictory information. In fact, I had all but abandoned any hope of finding out
the truth, though I was still tormented by the mystery, when,
one morning, fate guided me on to a new track.

Every two or three weeks, out of a feeling of comradeship,

affection and admiration, it was my habit to visit the elderly
poet V—, who died last April, aged seventy. For many years
his legs had been paralysed, and he was restricted to an armchair in his little studio in the rue Assas, the window of which
looked out on to the Luxembourg Gardens. He was coming to
the end of a life of dreaming: he had lived by his imagination,
and created for himself a fabulous palace, where, far from the
real world, he had loved and suffered. Which of us does not
recall his kind, delicate face, his white hair and childish curls,
his pale blue eyes with the youthful innocence? It would be
wrong to say that he never told the truth, but the fact is that
he was for ever inventing, with the result that one never quite
knew where reality ended for him and where illusion began.
He was a charming old man, who had long since ceased to be
part of everyday life, but whose conversation often touched
me deeply as a vague, discreet revelation of the unknown.

Thus I found myself that day chatting with him by the
window in his tiny room, warmed as always by a blazing
fire. Outside, there was the severest of frosts, so that the
Luxembourg Gardens presented a snow white carpet, a vast
horizon of immaculate purity. For some reason, I suddenly
found myself telling him of "La Sauvagière" and the story which
still preoccupied me: the father's remarriage, the stepmother's
evil jealousy of the little girl who was the living portrait of her
mother, the clandestine burial in the cellar. He listened to me
with the same tranquil smile he wore even when he was sad.
There followed a silence; his pale blue eyes gazed into the far
distance, across the white expanses of the Luxembourg
Gardens, and the shadow of a vision, which emanated from
him, seemed to shudder vaguely around him.

"I used to know Monsieur de G— very well," he said slowly.
"I knew his first wife, a divinely beautiful woman; I knew his
second wife also, whose beauty was every bit as dazzling; and
I was passionately in love with them both, although I never
revealed the fact. I also knew Angeline, who was even more
lovely and whom any man would have worshipped on his
knees... But things did not happen quite as you have said."

I became very excited. Was it here, then, the unexpected

truth I had despaired of ever knowing? Was I about to discover everything? At first I was only too ready to believe what he was about to tell me, and I replied, "Oh my dear friend, what a service you will render me! at last my poor head will be eased. Tell me quickly, I must know everything."

But he was not listening to me; he was still gazing distractedly into the distance. When at last he spoke, it was as if in a dream, as if he had created the beings and the things he evoked for me.

"Angeline, by the age of twelve years, already possessed a woman's power to love, with all its capacity to feel joy and pain. It was she who became insanely jealous of her father's new wife, whom she saw daily in his arms. She suffered at the sight of this terrible betrayal on the part of the new couple. It was no longer just her mother they were affronting, it was she herself who was being tortured, it was her heart that was wounded. Every night she heard her mother calling her from the grave; and one night, determined to be reunited with her, no longer able to stand the pain, already dying from an excess of love, this little girl of twelve years thrust a knife into her heart."

I cried out, "Good heavens! Can that really be?"

He went on without hearing me. "Imagine with what terror, what horror, Monsieur and Madame de G— discovered Angeline the next morning in her bed, the knife plunged into her breast right up to the handle! They were due to leave for Italy the following day, and there was nobody left in the house other than an elderly maid who had brought up the child. In their panic that they might be accused of a crime, they had the old maid help them bury the young body; but they in fact buried it in a corner of the conservatory behind the house, at the foot of a giant orange tree. And there it was that it was found when, after the death of both parents, the old maid told her story."

By this time some doubts had begun to enter my mind, and I looked at him anxiously, asking myself whether he was fabricating.

"But," I asked, "do you believe then that Angeline really could return again every night in order to answer the heart-rending cry of the mysterious voice which summons her?"

"Return again, my friend? Ah, but everyone returns again. Why shouldn't the soul of the poor child inhabit again the place in which she has both loved and suffered? If a voice is heard calling after her, then life has not yet begun again for her; but it will do, be assured of that, for everything begins again, love is never lost, nor beauty... Angeline! Angeline! Angeline! One day she will live again in the sun and the flowers."

Decidedly, I was now neither convinced nor comforted. My old friend V—, the child poet, had done nothing but increase my discomposure. It was evident that he was fabricating. Yet, like all seers, perhaps he was able to divine the truth?

"You are sure that everything you have told me is the absolute truth?" I ventured to inquire with a laugh.

"Of course, it is the truth. Is not everything to do with the Infinite the truth?"

I was never to see him again, as shortly afterwards I was obliged to leave Paris. He remains in my mind, however, his pensive gaze lost on the white expanse of the Luxembourg Gardens, so calm in the certainty of his infinite dream, whereas I was still tortured by my desire to establish once and for all that elusive phenomenon, the truth.

3

A year and a half went by. I had been obliged to travel. My life had been affected by many joys and many sorrows on the stormy seas which bear us all away to unknown shores. But again and again I would hear, at a certain hour, first far away, then entering my conscious mind, that desperate cry: "Angeline! Angeline! Angeline!" And it would leave me trembling, full of new doubts, tortured by the need to know. I could not forget, and there is nothing worse for me than the hell of uncertainty.

I cannot say how it came about that one glorious June evening I found myself once more on my bicycle in the deserted lane by "La Sauvagière." Had I consciously wished to see it again? Or was it an instinct which had directed me to turn off the main road and return to these parts? It was close on eight o'clock, but at the end of one of the longest days of the year the sky was still brilliant with a triumphantly setting sun, without a cloud, an infinity of azure and gold. And how sweet and delicate the air was, how fine the scents of the trees and the grass, what a subtle delight the immense peacefulness of the fields!

As on the first occasion when I arrived before "La Sauvagière," astonishment caused me to jump down from my machine. For a moment I hesitated: was this the same place? A fine new gate shone in the light of the setting sun, the garden walls had been restored, and the house, which I would barely perceive behind the trees, seemed to me to have regained the joyful gaiety of youth. Was this then the promised resurrection? Had Angeline returned to life in answer to that distant voice?

I was standing transfixed in the roadway when the sound of a shuffling gait behind me caused me to start. It was "mère Toussaint" bringing home her cow from a neighbouring field.

"So they weren't afraid?" I asked, motioning towards the house.

She recognized me and halted her animal.

"Ah, Monsieur, there are those who would trample on God Himself. The house was bought over a year ago now. It was a painter that did it, the artist B—, and you know what these artists will do."

Whereupon she moved her cow on, adding with a shake of the head, "Well, we shall just have to wait and see what happens."

The painter B—, that delicate, inventive artist who had portrayed so many delightful Parisiennes! I knew him slightly: we had shaken hands at the theatre, in exhibitions, places where one runs into people. Suddenly I was overcome by an irresistible desire to enter, to confess to him, to beg him to tell me what he knew of the truth about this "Sauvagière," whose mystery obsessed me. And without further thought, without care for my dusty cyclist's attire, which custom is beginning to tolerate these days in any case, I wheeled my bicycle over to the mossy trunk of an old tree. At the clear sound of the bell, the lever of which had accidentally struck the gate, there appeared a servant to whom I gave my card and who bade me wait a moment in the garden.

My surprise increased when I looked around me. The facade of the house had been repaired: no more cracks, no dislodged bricks. The steps, garnished with roses, had become once again a threshold of joyous welcome. The living windows were now smiling, telling of the joy within, behind their white lace curtains. As for the garden, it had been cleared of its nettles and brambles, the flower-bed had reappeared like a gigantic scented bouquet, the ancient trees had acquired new youth in their peaceful old age, under the golden rain of the spring sunshine.

When the servant reappeared, he led me into a drawing-room, informing me that his master had gone off to the neighbouring village but would be back before long. I was ready to wait for hours. I passed the time examining the room in which I found myself: it was luxuriously furnished with thick carpets, and cretonne curtains which matched the massive sofa and deep armchairs. These hangings were so extensive that when dusk suddenly arrived it took me by surprise. Before long it was almost completely dark. I do not know how long I had to wait there. I had evidently been forgotten; not even a lamp was brought for me. Seated in the shadows I started to relive the whole tragic story, to lose myself in reverie. Had Angeline been murdered? Had she thrust a knife into her own heart? And I have to admit that in this haunted house, upon which darkness had fallen once again, I felt fear. What initially was not much more than a certain unease, a slight chill, proceeded to grow beyond all proportion into an irrational terror which froze my whole being.

At first it seemed to me that I could hear obscure sounds in the distance. They must be coming from the depths of the cellars: a vague moaning, stifled sobs, heavy, ghostly footsteps. Then whatever it was began to come up from below, to draw closer, until the whole house seemed in the darkness to be filled with a terrible distress. Suddenly the awful cry rang out, "Angeline! Angeline! Angeline!", with such growing force that it seemed to me I felt a cold breath touch my face. One of the drawing-room doors opened noisily; Angeline entered, and crossed the room without seeing me. I recognized her in the dim light which had penetrated with her from the hall outside.

It was indeed the dead child of twelve years, incredibly beauti-ful with her exquisite blonde hair upon her shoulders, dressed in white, the white of the earth from which she returned every night. She passed by in silence, abstracted, and disappeared through another door, while once again the voice called out, this time from further off, "Angeline! Angeline! Angeline!" I was left there standing with sweat on my forehead, in a state of horror which caused every hair of my body to rise in the dreadful wind which emanated from the enigma.

Then, almost immediately, as the servant finally came in with a lamp, I was conscious that the artist B— was there, shaking my hand, and apologizing for having let me wait so long. Without any attempt to preserve my self-respect, I rushed into telling him my story. As I did so, I was still trem-bling. At first he listened to me with no little surprise, and then with great good humour he hastened to reassure me.

"My dear fellow, you were probably unaware of the fact that I am a cousin of the second Madame de G—. The poor woman! To be accused of the murder of that child whom she loved and mourned quite as much as the father! For there is only one part of the story which is true: the poor creature did indeed die here, not by her own hand, for heaven's sake, but of a sudden fever. The shock was so great that her parents, having conceived a horror of this house, never wished to return here. Which explains why it remained uninhabited for as long as they were alive. After their deaths there followed interminable legal procedures, which prevented its sale. I wanted it, having coveted it for many years; and I can assure you that we have never yet seen any ghosts here!"

The chill returned to me as I mumbled. "But I have just seen Angeline, here, only a moment ago... That frightful voice was summoning her, and she passed by here, through this very room..."

He looked at me, alarmed, believing perhaps that I was los-ing my sanity. Then suddenly he laughed, the resounding laugh of a man who is happy.

"That was my daughter you saw just now. Her godfather was, in fact, Monsieur de G—, who gave her the name Angeline as an act of devoted memory. Having no doubt been called by her mother, she must have passed through this room."

Thereupon he opened the door himself and called out again, "Angeline! Angeline! Angeline!"

The child returned, now alive, now vibrant with gaiety. It was she, with her white dress, her exquisite blonde hair upon her shoulders, so beautiful, so radiant with hope, that she was like the spring itself, bearing in the form of a bud the promise of love, the lasting happiness of life.

What a charming ghost was this new child, born again from the one who had died. Death had been conquered. My old friend, the poet V——, had not lied; nothing is ever lost for ever, everything begins again, both beauty and love. Their mothers call them, these little girls of today, these lovers of tomorrow, and they live again under the sun and among the flowers. The house had been haunted by the promise of this reawakening; today the house was once more youthful and happy in the rediscovered joy of eternal life.

The Pedler

by
DUNCAN CAMPBELL SCOTT
(1862–1947)

Duncan Campbell Scott was one of the greatest Canadian poets, but he also wrote a number of evocative short stories, many of them set in a fictional Quebec village called Viger (based on a number of places where he lived as a child). "The Pedler" is one of these, and what makes it so compelling is the ambiguous nature of the main character: is he possessed, is he mad, is he merely eccentric—or is he, perhaps, as one of the characters suggests, the Devil himself? I leave it to you to decide.

He used to come in the early springtime, when, in sunny hollows, banks of coarse snow lie thawing, shrinking with almost inaudible tinklings, when the upper grassbanks are covered thickly with the film left by the melted snow, when the old leaves about the grey trees are wet and sodden, when the pools lie bare and clear, without grasses, very limpid with snow-water, when the swollen streams rush insolently by, when the grosbeaks try the cedar buds shyly, and a colony of little birds take a sunny tree slope, and sing songs there.

He used to come with the awakening of life in the woods, with the strange cohosh, and the dog-tooth violet, piercing the damp leaf which it would wear as a ruff about its neck in blossom time. He used to come up the road from St. Valérie, trudging heavily, bearing his packs. To most of the Viger people he seemed to appear suddenly in the midst of the street, clothed with power, and surrounded by an attentive crowd of boys, and a whirling fringe of dogs, barking and throwing up dust.

I speak of what has become tradition, for the pedler walks no more up the St. Valérie road, bearing those magical baskets of his.

There was something powerful, compelling, about him; his short, heavy figure, his hair-covered, expressionless face, the quick hands in which he seemed to weigh everything that he touched, his voluminous, indescribable clothes, the great umbrella he carried strapped to his back, the green spectacles that hid his eyes, all these commanded attention. But his powers seemed to lie in those inscrutable guards to his eyes. They were such goggles as are commonly used by threshers, and were bound firmly about his face by a leather lace; with their setting of iron they completely covered his eye-sockets, not permitting a glimpse of those eyes that seemed to glare out of their depths. They seemed never to have been removed, but to have grown there, rooted by time in his cheek-bones.

He carried a large wicker-basket covered with oiled cloth, slung to his shoulder by a strap; in one hand he carried a light stick, in the other a large oval bandbox of black shiny cloth. From the initials "J.F.," which appeared in faded white letters on the bandbox, the village people had christened him Jean-François.

Coming into the village, he stopped in the middle of the road, set his bandbox between his feet, and took the oiled cloth from the basket. He never went from house to house, his customers came to him. He stood there and sold, almost without a word, as calm as a sphinx, and as powerful. There was something compelling about him; the people bought things they did not want, but they had to buy. The goods lay before them, the handkerchiefs, the laces, the jewelry, the little sacred pictures, matches in coloured boxes, little cased looking-glasses, combs, mouth-organs, pins, and hairpins; and over all, this figure with the inscrutable eyes. As he took in the money and made change, he uttered the word "Good," continually, "good, good." There was something exciting in the way he pronounced that word, something that goaded the hearers into extravagance.

It happened one day in April, when the weather was doubtful and moody, and storms flew low, scattering cold rain, and after that day Jean-Francois, the pedler, was a shape in memory, a fact no longer. He was blown into the village unwetted by a shower that left the streets untouched, and that went through the northern fields sharply, and lost itself in the far woods. He stopped in front of the post office. The Widow Laroque slammed her door and went upstairs to peep through the curtain; "these pedlers spoiled trade," she said, and hated them in consequence. Soon a crowd collected, and great talk arose, with laughter and some jostling. Everyone tried to see into the basket, those behind stood on tiptoe and asked questions, those in front held the crowd back and tried to look at the goods. The air was full of the staccato of surprise and admiration. The latecomers on the edge of the crowd commenced to jostle, and somebody tossed a handful of dust into the air over the group. "What a wretched wind," cried someone, "it blows all ways."

The dust seemed to irritate the pedler; besides, no one had bought anything. He called out sharply, "Buy—buy." He sold two papers of hairpins, a little brass shrine of La Bonne St. Anne, a coloured handkerchief, a horn comb, and a mouth-organ. While these purchases were going on, Henri Lamoureux was eyeing the little red purses, and fingering a coin in his pocket. The coin was a doubtful one, and he was weighing carefully the chances of passing it. At last he said, carelessly, "How much?" touching the purses. The pedler's answer called out the coin from his pocket; it lay in the man's hand. Henri took the purse and moved hurriedly back. At once the pedler grasped after him, reaching as well as his basket would allow; he caught him by the coat; but Henri's dog darted in, nipped the pedler's leg, and got away, showing his teeth. Lamoureux struggled, the pedler swore; in a moment everyone was jostling to get out of the way, wondering what was the matter. As Henri swung his arm around he swept his hand across the pedler's eyes; the shoestring gave way, and the green goggles fell into the basket. Then a curious change came over the man. He let his enemy go, and stood dazed for a moment; he passed his hand across his eyes, and in that interval of quiet the people saw, where they expected to see flash the two rapacious eyes of their imaginings, only the seared, fleshy seams where those eyes should have been.

That was the vision of a moment, for the pedler, like a fiend in fury, threw up his long arms and cursed in a voice so powerful and sudden that the dismayed crowd shrunk away, clinging to one another and looking over their shoulders at the violent figure. "God have mercy!—Holy St. Anne protect us!— He curses his Baptism!" screamed the women. In a second he was alone; the dog that had assailed him was snarling from under the sidewalk, and the women were in the nearest hous- es. Henri Lamoureux, in the nearest lane, stood pale, with a stone in his hand. It was only for one moment; in the second, the pedler had gathered his things, blind as he was, had turned his back, and was striding up the street; in the third, one of the sudden storms had gathered the dust at the end of the village and came down with it, driving everyone indoors. It shrouded the retreating figure, and a crack of unexpected thunder came like a pistol shot, and then the pelting rain.

Some venturesome souls who looked out when the storm was nearly over declared they saw, large on the hills, the figure of the pedler, walking enraged in the fringes of the storm. One of these was Henri Lamoureux, who, to this day, has never found the little red purse.

"I would have sworn I had it in this hand when he caught me; but I felt it fly away like a bird."

"But what made the man curse everyone so when you just bought that little purse—say that?"

"Well, I know not, do you? Anyway he has my quarter, and he was blind—blind as a stone fence."

"Blind! Not he!" cried the Widow Laroque. "He was the Old Boy himself, I told you—it is always as I say, you see now—it was the old Devil himself."

However that might be, there are yet people in Viger who, when the dust blows, and a sharp storm comes up from the south-east, see the figure of the enraged pedler, large upon the hills, striding violently along the fringes of the storm.

The Master of
Rampling Gate

by
ANNE RICE
(1941–   )

*Crenellated towers, mullioned windows, ivy-covered walls, a
beautiful heroine in swishing gowns, a blind housekeeper who
knows more than she's telling—"The Master of Rampling
Gate" has a Gothic quality that is indisputably compelling. It's
a story that I won't be likely to read on the radio because its
female heroine calls out for a female narrator. But I'm delighted to be able to include it here—especially as it provides an
element of romance in a collection that could so easily be lack-
ing in it.*

Rampling Gate: It was so real to us in those old pictures, rising like a fairy-tale castle out of its own dark wood. A wilderness of gables and chimneys between those two immense towers, grey stone walls mantled in ivy, mullioned windows reflecting the drifting clouds.

But why had Father never gone there? Why had he never taken us? And why on his deathbed, in those grim months after Mother's passing, did he tell my brother, Richard, that Rampling Gate must be torn down stone by stone? Rampling Gate that had always belonged to Ramplings, Rampling Gate which had stood for over four hundred years.

We were in awe of the task that lay before us, and painfully confused. Richard had just finished four years at Oxford. Two whirlwind social seasons in London had proven me something of a shy success. I still preferred scribbling poems and stories in the quiet of my room to dancing the night away, but I'd kept that a good secret, and though we were not spoilt children, we had enjoyed the best of everything our parents could give. But now the carefree years were ended. We had to be careful and wise.

And our hearts ached as, sitting together in Father's book-lined study, we looked at the old pictures of Rampling Gate before the small coal fire. "Destroy it, Richard, as soon as I am gone," Father had said.

"I just don't understand it, Julie," Richard confessed, as he filled the little crystal glass in my hand with sherry. "It's the genuine article, that old place, a real fourteenth-century manor-house in excellent repair. A Mrs. Blessington, born and reared in the village of Rampling, has apparently managed it all these years. She was there when Uncle Baxter died, and he was the last Rampling to live under that roof."

"Do you remember," I asked, "the year that Father took all these pictures down and put them away?"

"I shall never forget that," Richard said. "How could I? It was so peculiar, and so unlike Father, too." He sat back, drawing slowly on his pipe. "There had been that bizarre incident in Victoria Station, when he had seen that young man."

"Yes, exactly," I said, snuggling back into the velvet chair and looking into the tiny dancing flames in the grate. "You remember how upset Father was?"

Yet it was a simple incident. In fact nothing really happened at all. We couldn't have been more than six and eight at the time and we had gone to the station with Father to say farewell to friends. Through the window of a train Father saw a young man who startled and upset him. I could remember the face clearly to this day. Remarkably handsome, with a narrow nose and well-drawn eyebrows, and a mop of lustrous brown hair. The large black eyes had regarded Father with the saddest expression as Father had drawn us back and hurried us away.

"And the argument that night, between Father and Mother," Richard said thoughtfully. "I remember that we listened on the landing and we were so afraid."

"And Father said *he* wasn't content to be master of Rampling Gate any more; *he* had come to London and revealed himself. An unspeakable horror, that is what he called it, that *he* should be so bold."

"Yes, exactly, and when Mother tried to quiet him, when she suggested that he was imagining things, he went into a perfect rage."

"But who could it have been, the master of Rampling Gate, if Father wasn't the master? Uncle Baxter was long dead by then."

"I just don't know what to make of it," Richard murmured. "And there's nothing in Father's papers to explain any of it at all." He examined the most recent of the pictures, a lovely tinted engraving that showed the house perfectly reflected in the azure water of its lake. "But I tell you, the worst part of it, Julie," he said, shaking his head, "is that we've never even seen the house ourselves."

I glanced at him and our eyes met in a moment of confusion that quickly passed to something else. I leant forward:

"He did not say we couldn't go there, did he, Richard?" I demanded. "That we couldn't visit the house before it was destroyed."

"No, of course he didn't!" Richard said. The smile broke over his face easily. "After all, don't we owe it to the others, Julie? Uncle Baxter who spent the last of his fortune restoring the house, even this old Mrs. Blessington that has kept it all these years?"

"And what about the village itself?" I added quickly. "What will it mean to these people to see Rampling Gate destroyed? Of course we must go and see the place ourselves."

"Then it's settled. I'll write to Mrs. Blessington immediately. I'll tell her we're coming and that we cannot say how long we will stay."

"Oh, Richard, that would be too marvellous!" I couldn't keep from hugging him, though it flustered him and he pulled on his pipe just exactly the way Father would have done. "Make it at least a fortnight," I said. "I want so to know the place, especially if..."

But it was too sad to think of Father's admonition. And much more fun to think of the journey itself. I'd pack my manuscripts, for who knew, maybe in that melancholy and exquisite setting I'd find exactly the inspiration I required. It was almost a wicked exhilaration I felt, breaking the gloom that had hung over us since the day that Father was laid to rest.

"It is the right thing to do, isn't it, Richard?" I asked uncertainly, a little disconcerted by how much I wanted to go. There was some illicit pleasure in it, going to Rampling Gate at last.

"'Unspeakable horror.'" I repeated Father's words with a little grimace. What did it all mean? I thought again of the strange, almost exquisite young man I'd glimpsed in that railway carriage, gazing at us all with that wistful expression on his lean face. He had worn a black greatcoat with a red woollen cravat, and I could remember how pale he had been against that dash of red. Like bone china his complexion had been. Strange to remember it so vividly, even to the tilt of his head, and that long luxuriant brown hair. But he had been a blaze against the window. And I realized now that, in those few remarkable moments, he had created for me an ideal of masculine beauty which I had never questioned since. But Father had been so angry in those moments...I felt an unmistakable pang of guilt.

"Of course it's the right thing, Julie," Richard answered. He was at the desk, already writing the letters, and I was at a loss to understand the full measure of my thoughts.

It was late afternoon when the wretched old trap carried us up the gentle slope from the little railway station, and we had at last our first real look at that magnificent house. I think I was holding my breath. The sky had paled to a deep rose hue beyond a bank of softly gilded clouds, and the last rays of the sun struck the uppermost panes of the leaded windows and filled them with solid gold.

"Oh, but it's too majestic," I whispered, "too like a great cathedral, and to think that it belongs to us." Richard gave me the smallest kiss on the cheek. I felt mad suddenly and eager somehow to be laid waste by it, through fear or enchantment I could not say, perhaps a sublime mingling of both.

I wanted with all my heart to jump down and draw near on foot, letting those towers grow larger and larger above me, but our old horse had picked up speed. And the little line of stiff starched servants had broken to come forward, the old withered housekeeper with her arms out, the men to take down the boxes and the trunks.

Richard and I were spirited into the great hall by that tiny, nimble figure of Mrs. Blessington, our footfalls echoing loudly on the marble tile, our eyes dazzled by the dusty shafts of light that fell on the long oak table and its heavily carved chairs, the sombre, heavy tapestries that stirred ever so slightly against the soaring walls.

"It is an enchanted place," I cried, unable to contain myself. "Oh, Richard, we are home!" Mrs. Blessington laughed gaily, her dry hand closing tightly on mine.

Her small blue eyes regarded me with the most curiously vacant expression despite her smile. "Ramplings at Rampling Gate again, I cannot tell you what a joyful day this is for me. And yes, my dear," she said as if reading my mind that very second, "I am and have been for many years, quite blind. But if you spy a thing out of place in this house, you're to tell me at once, for it would be the exception, I assure you, and not the rule." And such warmth emanated from her wrinkled little face that I adored her at once.

We found our bedchambers, the very finest in the house, well aired with snow-white linen and fires blazing cosily to dry out the damp that never left the thick walls. The small diamond pane windows opened on a glorious view of the water and the oaks that enclosed it and the few scattered lights that marked the village beyond.

That night, we laughed like children as we supped at the great oak table, our candles giving only a feeble light. And afterwards, it was a fierce battle of pocket billiards in the game room which had been Uncle Baxter's last renovation, and a little too much brandy, I fear.

It was just before I went to bed that I asked Mrs. Blessington if there had been anyone in this house since Uncle Baxter died. That had been the year 1838, almost fifty years ago, and she was already housekeeper then.

"No, my dear," she said quickly, fluffing the feather pillows. "Your father came that year as you know, but he stayed for no more than a month or two and then went on home."

"There was never a young man after that..." I pushed, but in truth I had little appetite for anything to disturb the happiness I felt. How I loved the Spartan cleanliness of this bedchamber, the stone walls bare of paper or ornament, the high lustre of the walnut-panelled bed.

"A young man?" She gave an easy, almost hearty laugh as with unerring certainty of her surroundings she lifted the poker and stirred the fire. "What a strange thing for you to ask."

I sat silent for a moment looking in the mirror, as I took the last of the pins from my hair. It fell down heavy and warm around my shoulders. It felt good, like a cloak under which I could hide. But she turned as if sensing some uneasiness in me, and drew near.

"Why do you say a young man, Miss?" she asked. Slowly, tentatively, her fingers examined the long tresses that lay over my shoulders. She took the brush from my hands.

I felt perfectly foolish telling her the story, but I managed a simplified version, somehow, our meeting unexpectedly a devilishly handsome young man whom my father in anger had later called the master of Rampling Gate.

"Handsome, was he?" she asked as she brushed out the tangles in my hair gently. It seemed she hung upon every word as I described him again.

"There were no intruders in this house, then, Mrs. Blessington?" I asked. "No mysteries to be solved..."

She gave the sweetest laugh.

"Oh, no, darling, this house is the safest place in the world," she said quickly. "It is a happy house. No intruder would dare to trouble Rampling Gate!"

Nothing, in fact, troubled the serenity of the days that followed. The smoke and noise of London, and our father's dying words, became a dream. What was real were our long walks together through the overgrown gardens, our trips in the little skiff to and fro across the lake. We had tea under the hot glass of the empty conservatory. And early evening found us on our way upstairs with the best of the books from Uncle Baxter's library to read by candlelight in the privacy of our rooms.

And all our discreet inquiries in the village met with more or less the same reply: the villagers loved the house and carried no old or disquieting tales. Repeatedly, in fact, we were told that Rampling was the most contented hamlet in all

England, that no one dared—Mrs. Blessington's very words—
to make trouble here.

"It's our guardian angel, that old house," said the old
woman at the bookshop where Richard stopped for the
London papers. "Was there ever the town of Rampling without
the house called Rampling Gate?"

How were we going to tell them of Father's edict? How were
we going to remind ourselves? But we spoke not one word
about the proposed disaster, and Richard wrote to his firm to
say that we should not be back in London till fall.

He was finding a wealth of classical material in the old volumes that had belonged to Uncle Baxter, and I had set up my
writing in the little study that opened off the library which I
had all to myself.

Never had I known such peace and quiet. It seemed the
atmosphere of Rampling Gate permeated my simplest written
descriptions and wove its way richly into the plots and characters I created. The Monday after our arrival I had finished my
first short story and went off to the village on foot to boldly
post it to editors of *Blackwood's Magazine*.

It was a glorious morning, and I took my time as I came
back on foot.

What had disturbed our father so about this lovely corner
of England, I wondered? What had so darkened his last hours
that he laid upon this spot his curse?

My heart opened to this unearthly stillness, to an undeniable grandeur that caused me utterly to forget myself. There
were times here when I felt I was a disembodied intellect drifting through a fathomless silence, up and down garden paths
and stone corridors that had witnessed too much to take cog-
nizance of one small and fragile young woman who in random
moments actually talked aloud to the suits of armour around
her, to the broken statues in the garden, the fountain cherubs
who had not had water to pour from their conches for years
and years.

But was there in this loveliness some malignant force that
was eluding us still, some untold story to explain all?
Unspeakable horror... In my mind's eye I saw that young man,

and the strangest sensation crept over me, that some enrich-
ment of the picture had taken place in my memory or imagination in the recent past. Perhaps in dream I had re-invented
him, given a ruddy glow to his lips and his cheeks. Perhaps in
my re-creation for Mrs. Blessington, I had allowed him to raise
his hand to that red cravat and had seen the fingers long and
delicate and suggestive of a musician's hand.

It was all very much on my mind when I entered the house
again, soundlessly, and saw Richard in his favourite leather
wing-chair by the fire.

The air was warm coming through the open garden doors,
and yet the blaze was cheerful, made the vast room with its
towering shelves of leather-bound volumes appear inviting
and almost small.

"Sit down," Richard said gravely, scarcely giving me a
glance. "I want to read you something right now." He held a
long narrow ledger in his hands. "This was Uncle Baxter's," he
said, "and at first I thought it was only an account book he
kept during the renovations, but I've found some actual diary
entries made in the last weeks of his life. They're hasty, almost
indecipherable, but I've managed to make them out."

"Well, do read them to me," I said, but I felt a little tug of
fear. I didn't want to know anything terrible about this place.
If we could have remained here for ever...but that was out of
the question, to be sure.

"Now listen to this," Richard said, turning the page carefully. "'Fifth of May, 1838: He is here, I am sure of it. He is come
back again.' And several days later: 'He thinks this is his
house, he does, and he would drink my wine and smoke my
cigars if only he could. He reads my books and my papers and
I will not stand for it. I have given orders that everything is to
be locked.' And finally, the last entry written the morning
before he died: 'Weary, weary, unto death and he is no small
cause of my weariness. Last night I beheld him with my own
eyes. He stood in this very room. He moves and speaks exactly
as a mortal man, and dares tell me his secrets, and he a demon
wretch with the face of a seraph and I a mere mortal, how am
I to bear with him?!'"

"Good Lord," I whispered slowly. I rose from the chair where I had settled, and standing behind him, read the page for myself. It was a scrawl, the writing, the very last notation in the book. I knew that Uncle Baxter's heart had given out. He had not died by violence, but peacefully enough in this very room with his prayer-book in his hand.

"Could it be the very same person Father spoke of that night?" Richard asked.

In spite of the sun pouring through the open doors, I experienced a violent chill. For the first time I felt wary of this house, wary of our boldness in coming here, heedful of our father's words.

"But that was years before, Richard..." I said. "And what could this mean, this talk of a supernatural being! Surely the man was mad! It was no spirit I saw in that railway carriage!"

I sank down into the chair opposite and tried to quiet the beating of my heart.

"Julie," Richard said gently, shutting the ledger. "Mrs. Blessington has lived here contentedly for years. There are six servants asleep every night in the north wing. Surely there is nothing to all of this."

"It isn't very much fun, though, is it?" I said timidly, "not at all like swapping ghost stories the way we used to do, and peopling the dark with imaginary beings, and laughing at friends at school who were afraid."

"All my life," he said, his eyes fixing me steadily, "I've heard tales of spooks and spirits, some imagined, some supposedly true, and almost invariably there is some mention of the house in question feeling haunted, of having an atmosphere to it that fills one with foreboding, some sense of menace or alarm..."

"Yes, I know, and there is no such poisonous atmosphere here at all."

"On the contrary, I've never been more at ease in my life." He shoved his hand into his pocket to extract the inevitable match to light his pipe, which had gone out. "As a matter of fact, Julie, I don't know how in the world I'm going to comply with Father's last wish to tear down this place."

I nodded sympathetically. The very same thing had been on

my mind since we'd arrived. Even now, I felt so comfortable, natural, quite safe.

I was wishing suddenly, irrationally, that he had not found the entries in Uncle Baxter's book.

"I should talk to Mrs. Blessington again!" I said almost crossly. "I mean quite seriously..."

"But I have, Julie," he said. "I asked her about it all this morning when I first made the discovery, and she only laughed. She swears she's never seen anything unusual here, and that there's no one left alive in the village who can tell tales of this place. She said again how glad she was that we'd come home to Rampling Gate. I don't think she has an inkling we mean to destroy the house. Oh, it would destroy her heart if she did."

"Never seen anything unusual?" I asked. "That is what she said? But what strange words for her to use, Richard, when she cannot see at all."

But he had not heard me. He had laid the ledger aside and risen slowly, almost sluggishly, and he was wandering out of the double doors into the little garden and was looking over the high hedge at the oaks that bent their heavy elbowed limbs almost to the surface of the lake. There wasn't a sound at this early hour of the day, save the soft rustle of the leaves in the moving air, the cry now and then of a distant bird.

"Maybe it's gone, Julie," Richard said, over his shoulder, his voice carrying clearly in the quiet, "if it was ever here. Maybe there is nothing any longer to frighten anyone at all. You don't suppose you could endure the winter in this house, do you? I suppose you'd want to be in London again by then." He seemed quite small against the towering trees, the sky broken into small gleaming fragments by the canopy of foliage that gently filtered the light.

Rampling Gate had him. And I understood perfectly, because it also had me. I could very well endure the winter here, no matter how bleak or cold. I never wanted to go home.

And the immediacy of the mystery only dimmed my sense of everything and every place else.

After a long moment, I rose and went out into the garden, and placed my hand gently on Richard's arm.

"I know this much, Julie," he said just as if we had been talking to each other all the while. "I swore to Father that I would do as he asked, and it is tearing me apart. Either way, it will be on my conscience for ever, obliterating this house or going against my own father and the charge he laid down to me with his dying breath."

"We must seek help, Richard. The advice of our lawyers, the advice of Father's clergymen. You must write to them and explain the whole thing. Father was feverish when he gave the order. If we could lay it out before them, they would help us decide."

It was three o'clock when I opened my eyes. But I had been awake for a long time. I had heard the dim chimes of the clock below hour by hour. And I felt not fear lying here along in the dark, but something else. Some vague and relentless agitation, some sense of emptiness and need that caused me finally to rise from my bed. What was required to dissolve this tension, I wondered. I stared at the simplest things in the shadows. The little arras that hung over the fireplace with its slim princes and princesses lost in fading fibre and thread. The portrait of an Elizabethan ancestor gazing with one almond-shaped eye from his small frame.

What was this house, really? Merely a place or a state of mind? What was it doing to my soul? Why didn't the entries in Uncles Baxter's book send us flying back to London? Why had we stayed so late in the great hall together after supper, speaking not a single word?

I felt overwhelmed suddenly, and yet shut out of some great and dazzling secret, and wasn't that the very word that Uncle Baxter had used?

Conscious only of an unbearable restlessness, I pulled on my woollen wrapper, buttoning the lace collar and tying the sash. And putting on my slippers, I went out into the hall.

The moon fell full on the oak stairway, and on the deeply recessed door to Richard's room. On tiptoe I approached and, peering in, saw the bed was empty, the covers completely undisturbed.

So he was off on his own tonight the same as I. Oh, if only he had come to me, asked me to go with him.

I turned and made my way soundlessly down the long stairs.

The great hall gaped like a cavern before me, the moonlight here and there touching upon a pair of crossed swords, or a mounted shield. But far beyond the great hall, in the alcove just outside the library, I saw unmistakably a flickering light. And a breeze moved briskly through the room, carrying with it the sound and the scent of a wood fire.

I shuddered with relief. Richard was there. We could talk. Or perhaps we could go exploring together, guarding our fragile candle flames behind cupped fingers as we went from room to room? A sense of well-being pervaded me and quieted me, and yet the dark distance between us seemed endless, and I was desperate to cross it, hurrying suddenly past the long supper table with its massive candlesticks, and finally into the alcove before the library doors.

Yes, Richard was there. He sat with his eyes closed, dozing against the inside of the leather wing-chair, the breeze from the garden blowing the fragile flames of the candles on the stone mantel and on the table at his side.

I was about to go to him, about to shut the doors, and kiss him gently and ask did he not want to go up to bed, when quite abruptly I saw in the corner of my eye that there was someone else in the room.

In the far left corner at the desk stood another figure, looking down at the clutter of Richard's papers, his pale hands resting on the wood.

I knew that it could not be so. I knew that I must be dreaming, that nothing in this room, least of all this figure, could be real. For it was the same young man I had seen fifteen years ago in the railway carriage and not a single aspect of that taut young face had been changed. There was the very same hair, thick and lustrous and only carelessly combed as it hung to the thick collar of his black coat, and the skin so pale it was almost luminous in the shadows, and those dark eyes looking up suddenly and fixing me with the most curious expression as I almost screamed.

We stared at one another across the dark vista of that room, I stranded in the doorway, he visibly and undeniably shaken that I had caught him unawares. My heart stopped.

And in a split second he moved towards me, closed the gap between us, towering over me, those slender white fingers gently closing on my arms.

"Julie!" he whispered, in a voice so low it seemed my own thoughts speaking to me. But this was no dream. He was real. He was holding to me and the scream had broken loose from me, deafening, uncontrollable and echoing from the four walls.

I saw Richard rising from the chair. I was alone. Clutching to the door-frame, I staggered forward, and then again in a moment of perfect clarity I saw the young intruder, saw him standing in the garden, looking back over his shoulder, and then he was gone.

I could not stop screaming. I could not stop even as Richard held me and pleaded with me, and sat me down in the chair.

And I was still crying when Mrs. Blessington finally came.

She got a glass of cordial for me at once, as Richard begged me once more to tell what I had seen.

"But you know who it was!" I said to Richard almost hysterically. "It was he, the young man from the train. Only he wore a frock-coat years out of fashion and his silk tie was open at his throat. Richard, he was reading your papers, turning them over, reading them in the pitch dark."

"All right," Richard said, gesturing with his hand up for calm. "He was standing at the desk. And there was no light there so you could not see him well."

"Richard, it was he! Don't you understand? He touched me, he held my arms." I looked imploringly to Mrs. Blessington who was shaking her head, her little eyes like blue beads in the light. "He called me Julie," I whispered. "He knows my name!"

I rose, snatching up the candle, and all but pushing Richard out of the way, went to the desk. "Oh, dear God," I said, "don't you see what's happened? It's your letters to Dr. Partridge, and Mrs. Sellers, about tearing down the house!"

Mrs. Blessington gave a little cry and put her hand to her cheek. She looked like a withered child in her nightcap as she collapsed into the straight-backed chair by the door.

"Surely you don't believe it was the same man, Julie, after all these years…"

"But he had not changed, Richard, not in the smallest detail. There is no mistake, Richard, it was he, I tell you, the very same."

"Oh, dear, dear…" Mrs. Blessington whispered, "what will he do if you try to tear it down? What will he do now?"

"What will who do?" Richard asked carefully, narrowing his eyes. He took the candle from me and approached her. I was staring at her, only half realizing what I heard.

"So you know who he is!" I whispered.

"Julie, stop it!" Richard said.

But her face had tightened, gone blank and her eyes had become distant and small.

"You knew he was here!" I insisted. "You must tell us at once!"

With an effort she climbed to her feet. "There is nothing in this house to hurt *you*," she said, "nor any of us." She turned, spurning Richard as he tried to help her, and wandered into the dark hallway alone. "You've no need of me here any longer," she said softly, "and if you should tear down this house built by your forefathers, then you should do it without need of me."

"Oh, but we don't mean to do it, Mrs. Blessington!" I insisted. But she was making her way through the gallery back towards the north wing. "Go after her, Richard. You heard what she said. She knows who he is."

"I've had quite enough of this tonight," Richard said almost angrily. "Both of us should go up to bed. By the light of day we will dissect this entire matter and search this house. Now come."

"But he should be told, shouldn't he?" I demanded.

"Told what? Of whom do you speak!"

"Told that we will not tear down this house!" I said clearly, loudly, listening to the echo of my own voice.

The next day was indeed the most trying since we had come. It took the better part of the morning to convince Mrs.

Blessington that we had no intention of tearing down Rampling Gate. Richard posted his letters and resolved that we should do nothing until help came.

And together we commenced a search of the house. But darkness found us only half finished, having covered the south tower and the south wing, and the main portion of the house itself. There remained still the north tower, in a dreadful state of disrepair, and some rooms beneath the ground which in former times might have served as dungeons and were now sealed off. And there were closets and private stairways everywhere that we had scarce looked into, and at times we lost all track of where precisely we had been.

But it was also quite clear by supper time that Richard was in a state of strain and exasperation, and that he did not believe that I had seen anyone in the study at all.

He was further convinced that Uncle Baxter had been mad before he died, or else his ravings were a code for some mundane happening that had him extraordinarily overwrought.

But I knew what I had seen. And as the day progressed, I became ever more quiet and withdrawn. A silence had fallen between me and Mrs. Blessington. And I understood only too well the anger I'd heard in my father's voice on that long-ago night when we had come home from Victoria Station and my mother had accused him of imagining things.

Yet what obsessed me more than anything else was the gentle countenance of the mysterious man I had glimpsed, the dark, almost innocent eyes that had fixed on me for one moment before I had screamed.

"Strange that Mrs. Blessington is not afraid of him," I said in a low distracted voice, no longer caring if Richard heard me. "And that no one here seems in fear of him at all..." The strangest fancies were coming to me. The careless words of the villagers were running through my head. "You would be wise to do one very important thing before you retire," I said. "Leave out in writing a note to the effect that you do not intend to tear down the house."

"Julie, you have created an impossible dilemma," Richard demanded. "You insist we reassure this apparition that the house will not be destroyed, when in fact you verify the existence of the very creature that drove our father to say what he did."

"Oh, I wish I had never come here!" I burst out suddenly.

"Then we should go, both of us, and decide this matter at home."

"No, that's just it. I could never go without knowing...'his secrets'...'the demon wretch.' I could never go on living without knowing now!"

Anger must be an excellent antidote to fear, for surely something worked to alleviate my natural alarm. I did not undress that night, nor even take off my shoes, but rather sat in that dark hollow bedroom gazing at the small square of diamond-paned window until I heard all of the house fall quiet. Richard's door at last closed. There came those distant echoing booms that meant other bolts had been put in place.

And when the grandfather clock in the great hall chimed the hour of eleven, Rampling Gate was as usual fast asleep.

I listened for my brother's step in the hall. And when I did not hear him stir from his room, I wondered at it, that curiosity would not impel him to come to me, to say that we must go together to discover the truth.

It was just as well. I did not want him to be with me. And I felt a dark exultation as I imagined myself going out of the room and down the stairs as I had the night before. I should wait one more hour, however, to be certain. I should let the night reach its pitch. Twelve, the witching hour. My heart was beating too fast at the thought of it, and dreamily I recollected the face I had seen, the voice that had said my name.

Ah, why did it seem in retrospect so intimate, that we had known each other, spoken together, that it was someone I recognized in the pit of my soul?

"What is your name?" I believe I whispered aloud. And then a spasm of fear startled me. Would I have the courage to go in search of him, to open the door to him? Was I losing my mind? Closing my eyes, I rested my head against the high back of the damask chair.

What was more empty than this rural night? What was more sweet?

I opened my eyes. I had been half dreaming or talking to myself, trying to explain to Father why it was necessary that we comprehend the reason ourselves. And I realized, quite fully realized—I think before I was even awake—that he was standing by the bed.

The door was open. And he was standing there, dressed exactly as he had been the night before, and his dark eyes were riveted on me with that same obvious curiosity, his mouth just a little slack like that of a schoolboy, and he was holding to the bedpost almost idly with his right hand. Why, he was lost in contemplating me. He did not seem to know that I was looking at him.

But when I sat forward, he raised his finger as if to quiet me, and gave a little nod of his head.

"Ah, it is you!" I whispered.

"Yes," he said in the softest, most unobtrusive voice.

But we had been talking to each other, hadn't we, I had been asking him questions, no, telling him things. And I felt suddenly I was losing my equilibrium or slipping back into a dream.

No. Rather I had all but caught the fragment of some dream from the past. That rush of atmosphere that can engulf one at any moment of the day following when something evokes the universe that absorbed one utterly in sleep. I mean I heard our voices for an instant, almost in argument, and I saw Father in his top hat and black overcoat rushing alone through the streets of the West End, peering into one door after another, and then, rising from the marble-top table in the dim smoky music-hall you...your face.

"Yes..."

Go back, Julie! It was Father's voice.

"...to penetrate the soul of it," I insisted, picking up the lost thread. But did my lips move? "To understand what it is that frightened him, enraged him. He said, 'Tear it down!'"

"...you must never, never, can't do that." His face was stricken, like that of a schoolboy about to cry.

"No, absolutely, we don't want to, either of us, you know

it...and you are not a spirit!" I looked at his mud-spattered boots, the faintest smear of dust on that perfect white cheek.

"A spirit?" he asked almost mournfully, almost bitterly. "Would that I were."

Mesmerized I watched him come towards me and the room darkened, and I felt his cool silken hands on my face. I had risen. I was standing before him, and I looked up into his eyes.

I heard my own heartbeat. I heard it as I had the night before, right at the moment I had screamed. Dear God, I was talking to him! He was in my room and I was talking to him! And I was in his arms.

"Real, absolutely real!" I whispered, and a low zinging sensation coursed through me so that I had to steady myself against the bed.

He was peering at me as if trying to comprehend something terribly important to him, and he didn't respond. His lips did have a ruddy look to them, a soft look for all his handsomeness, as if he had never been kissed. And a slight dizziness had come over me, a slight confusion in which I was not at all sure that he was even there.

"Oh, but I am," he said softly. I felt his breath against my cheek, and it was almost sweet. "I am here, and you are with me, Julie..."

"Yes..."

My eyes were closing. Uncle Baxter sat hunched over his desk and I could hear the furious scratch of his pen. "Demon wretch!" he said to the night air coming in the open doors.

"No!" I said. Father turned in the door of the music-hall and cried my name.

"Love me, Julie," came that voice in my ear. I felt his lips against my neck. "Only a little kiss, Julie, no harm..." And the core of my being, that secret place where all desires and all commandments are nurtured, opened to him without a struggle or a sound. I would have fallen if he had not held me. My arms closed about him, my hands slipping into the soft silken mass of his hair.

I was floating, and there was as there had always been at Rampling Gate, an endless peace. It was Rampling Gate I felt around me, it was that timeless and impenetrable soul that had opened itself at last... A power within me of enormous ken... To see as a god sees, and take the depth of things as nimbly as the outward eyes can size and shape pervade... Yes, I whispered aloud, those words from Keats, those words... To cease upon the midnight without pain...

No. In a violent instant we had parted, he drawing back as surely as I.

I went reeling across the bedroom floor and caught hold of the frame of the window, and rested my forehead against the stone wall.

For a long moment I stood with my eyes closed. There was a tingling pain in my throat that was almost pleasurable where his lips had touched me, a delicious throbbing that would not stop.

Then I turned, and I saw all the room clearly, the bed, the fireplace, the chair. And he stood still exactly as I'd left him and there was the most appalling distress in his face.

"What have they done to me?" he whispered. "Have they played the cruelest trick of all?"

"Something of menace, unspeakable menace," I whispered.

"Something ancient, Julie, something that defies understanding, something that can and will go on."

"But why, what are you?" I touched that pulsing pain with the tips of my fingers and, looking down at them, gasped. "And you suffer so, and you are so seemingly innocent, and it is as if you can love!"

His face was rent as if by a violent conflict within. And he turned to go. With my whole will, I stood fast not to follow him, not to beg him to turn back. But he did turn, bewildered, struggling and then bent upon his purpose as he reached for my hand. "Come with me," he said.

He drew me to him ever so gently, and slipping his arm around me guided me to the door.

Through the long upstairs corridor we passed hurriedly, and through a small wooden doorway to a screw stairs that I had never seen before.

I soon realized we were ascending the north tower of the house, the ruined portion of the structure that Richard and I had not investigated before.

Through one tiny window after another I saw the gently rolling landscape moving out from the forest that surrounded us, and the small cluster of dim lights that marked the village of Rampling and the pale streak of white that was the London road.

Up and up we climbed until we had reached the topmost chamber, and this he opened with an iron key. He held back the door for me to enter and I found myself in a spacious room whose high narrow windows contained no glass. A flood of moonlight revealed the most curious mixture of furnishings and objects, the clutter that suggests an attic and a sort of den. There was a writing-table, a great shelf of books, soft leather chairs and scores of old yellowed and curling maps and framed pictures affixed to the walls. Candles were everywhere stuck in the bare stone niches or to the tables and the shelves. Here and there a barrel served as a table, right alongside the finest old Elizabethan chair. Wax had dripped over everything, it seemed, and in the very midst of the clutter lay rumpled copies of the most recent papers, the *Mercure de Paris*, the *London Times*.

There was no place for sleeping in this room.

And when I thought of that, where he must lie when he went to rest, a shudder passed over me and I felt, quite vividly, his lips touching my throat again, and I felt the sudden urge to cry.

But he was holding me in his arms, he was kissing my cheeks and my lips again ever so softly, and then he guided me to a chair. He lighted the candles about us one by one.

I shuddered, my eyes watering slightly in the light. I saw more unusual objects: telescopes and magnifying glasses and a violin in its open case, and a handful of gleaming and exquisitely shaped sea shells. There were jewels lying about, and a black silk top hat and a walking-stick, and a bouquet of withered flowers, dry as straw, and daguerreotypes and tintypes in their little velvet cases, and opened books.

But I was too distracted now by the sight of him in the light, the gloss of his large black eyes, and the gleam of his hair. Not even in the railway station had I seen him so clearly as I did now amid the radiance of the candles. He broke my heart.

And yet he looked at me as though I were the feast for his eyes, and he said my name again and I felt the blood rush to my face. But there seemed a great break suddenly in the passage of time. I had been thinking, yes, what are you, how long have you existed... And I felt dizzy again.

I realized that I had risen and I was standing beside him at the window and he was turning me to look down and the countryside below had unaccountably changed. The lights of Rampling had been subtracted from the darkness that lay like a vapour over the land. A great wood, far older and denser than the forest of Rampling Gate, shrouded the hills, and I was afraid suddenly, as if I were slipping into a maelstrom from which I could never, of my own will, return.

There was that sense of us talking together, talking and talking in low agitated voices and I was saying that I should not give in.

"Bear witness, that is all I ask of you..."

And there was in me some dim certainty that by knowledge alone I should be fatally changed. It was the reading of a forbidden book, the chanting of a forbidden charm.

"No, only what was," he whispered.

And then even the shape of the land itself eluded me. And the very room had lost its substance, as if a soundless wind of terrific force had entered this place and was blowing it apart.

We were riding in a carriage through the night. We had long long ago left the tower, and it was late afternoon and the sky was the colour of blood. And we rode into a forest whose trees were so high and so thick that scarcely any sun at all broke to the soft leaf-strewn ground.

We had no time to linger in this magical place. We had come to the open country, to the small patches of tilled earth that surrounded the ancient village of Knorwood with its gabled roofs and its tiny crooked streets. We saw the walls of the monastery of Knorwood and the little church with the bell chiming Vespers under the lowering sky. A great bustling life resided in Knorwood, a thousand hearts beat in Knorwood, a thousand voices gave forth their common prayer.

But far beyond the village on the rise above the forest stood the rounded tower of a truly ancient castle; and to that ruined castle, no more than a shell of itself any more, as darkness fell in earnest, we rode. Through its empty chambers we roamed, impetuous children, the horse and the road quite forgotten, and to the Lord of the Castle, a gaunt and white-skinned creature standing before the roaring fire of the roofless hall, we came. He turned and fixed us with his narrow and glittering eyes. A dead thing he was, I understood, but he carried within himself a priceless magic. And my young companion, my innocent young man passed by me into the Lord's arms. I saw the kiss. I saw the young man grow pale and struggle to turn away. It was as I had done this very night, beyond this dream, in my own bedchamber; and from the Lord he retreated, clutching to the sharp pain in his throat.

I understood. I knew. But the castle was dissolving as surely as anything in this dream might dissolve, and we were in some damp and close place.

The stench was unbearable to me, it was that most terrible of all stenches, the stench of death. And I heard my steps on the cobblestones and I reached to steady myself against the wall. The tiny square was deserted; the doors and windows gaped open to the vagrant wind. Up one side and down the other of the crooked street I saw the marks on the houses. And I knew what the marks meant. The Black Death had come to the village of Knorwood. The Black Death had laid it waste. And in a moment of suffocating horror I realized that no one, not a single person, was left alive.

But this was not quite right. There was someone walking in fits and starts up the narrow alleyway. Staggering he was, almost falling, as he pushed in one door after another, and at last came to a hot, stinking place where a child screamed on the floor. Mother and Father lay dead in the bed. And a great fat cat of the household, unharmed, played with the screaming infant, whose eyes bulged from its tiny sunken face.

"Stop it," I heard myself gasp. I knew that I was holding my head with both hands. "Stop it, stop it please!" I was screaming and my screams would surely pierce the vision and this small crude little room should collapse around me, and I should rouse the household of Rampling Gate to me, but I did not. The young man turned and stared at me, and in the close stinking room, I could not see his face.

But I knew it was he, my companion, and I could smell his fever and his sickness, and the stink of the dying infant, and see the sleek, gleaming body of the cat as it pawed at the child's outstretched hand.

"Stop it, you've lost control of it!" I screamed surely with all my strength, but the infant screamed louder. "Make it stop!"

"I cannot…" he whispered. "It goes on for ever! It will never stop!"

And with a great piercing shriek I kicked at the cat and sent it flying out of the filthy room, overturning the milk pail as it went, jetting like a witch's familiar over the stones.

Blanched and feverish, the sweat soaking his crude jerkin, my companion took me by the hand. He forced me back out of the house and away from the crying child and into the street.

Death in the parlour, death in the bedroom, death in the cloister, death before the high altar, death in the open fields. It seemed the Judgement of God that a thousand souls had died in the village of Knorwood—I was sobbing, begging to be released—it seemed the very end of Creation itself.

And at last night came down over the dead village and he was alive still, stumbling up the slopes, through the forest, towards that rounded tower where the Lord stood with his hand on the stone frame of the broken window waiting for him to come.

"Don't go!" I begged him. I ran alongside him crying, but he didn't hear. Try as I might, I could not affect these things.

The Lord stood over him smiling almost sadly as he watched him fall, watched the chest heave with its last breaths. Finally the lips moved, calling out for salvation when it was damnation the Lord offered, when it was damnation that the Lord would give.

"Yes, damned then, but living, breathing!" the young man cried, rising in a last spasmodic movement. And the Lord, who had remained still until that instant, bent to drink.

The kiss again, the lethal kiss, the blood drawn out of the

dying body, and then the Lord lifting the heavy head of the young man to take the blood back again from the body of the Lord himself.

I was screaming again, *Do not, do not drink.* He turned and looked at me. His face was now so perfectly the visage of death that I couldn't believe there was animation left in him, yet he asked: What would you do? Would you go back to Knorwood, would you open those doors one after another, would you ring the bell in the empty church, and if you did would the dead rise?

He didn't wait for my answer. And I had none now to give. He had turned again to the Lord who waited for him, locked his innocent mouth to that vein that pulsed with every semblance of life beneath the Lord's cold and translucent flesh. And the blood jetted into the young body, vanquishing in one great burst the fever and the sickness that had racked it, driving it out with the mortal life.

He stood now in the hall of the Lord alone. Immortality was his and the blood thirst he would need to sustain it, and that thirst I could feel with my whole soul. He stared at the broken walls around him, at the fire licking the blackened stones of the giant fireplace, at the night sky over the broken roof, throwing out its endless net of stars.

And each and every thing was transfigured in his vision, and in my vision—the vision he gave now to me—to the exquisite essence of itself. A wordless and eternal voice spoke from the starry veil of heaven, it sang in the wind that rushed through the broken timbers; it sighed in the flames that ate the sooted stones of the hearth.

It was the fathomless rhythm of the universe that played beneath every surface, as the last living creature—that tiny child—fell silent in the village below.

A soft wind sifted and scattered the soil from the newturned furrows in the empty fields. The rain fell from the black and endless sky.

Years and years passed. And all that had been Knorwood melted into the very earth. The forest sent out its silent sentinels, and mighty trunks rose where there had been huts, and houses where there had been monastery walls.

Finally nothing of Knorwood remained: not the little cemetery, not the little church, not even the name of Knorwood
lived still in the world. And it seemed the horror beyond all
horrors that no one any more should know of a thousand
souls who had lived and died in that small and insignificant
village, that not anywhere in the great archives in which all
history is recorded should a mention of that town remain.

Yet one being remained who knew, one being who had witnessed, and stood now looking down upon the very spot
where his mortal life had ended, he who had scrambled up on
his hands and knees from the pit of Hell that had been that
disaster; it was the young man who stood beside me, the master of Rampling Gate.

And all through the walls of his old house were the stones
of the ruined castle, and all through the ceilings and floors the
branches of those ancient trees.

What was solid and majestic here, and safe within the
minds of those who slept tonight in the village of Rampling,
was only the most fragile citadel against horror, the house to
which he clung now.

A great sorrow swept over me. Somewhere in the drift of
images I had relinquished myself, lost all sense of the point in
space from which I saw. And in a great rush of lights and noise
I was enlivened now and made whole as I had been when we
rode together through the forest, only it was into the world of
now, this hour, that we passed. We were flying it seemed
through the rural darkness along the railway towards the
London where the night-time city burst like an enormous
bubble in a shower of laughter, and motion, and glaring light.
He was walking with me under the gas lamps, his face all but
shimmering with that same dark innocence, that same irresistible warmth. And it seemed we were holding tight to one
another in the very midst of a crowd. And the crowd was a living thing, a writhing thing, and everywhere there came a dark
rich aroma from it, the aroma of fresh blood. Women in white
fur and gentlemen in opera capes swept into the brightly lighted doors of the theatre; the blare of the music-hall inundated

us, then faded away. Only a thin soprano voice was left, singing a high, plaintive song. I was in his arms, and his lips were covering mine, and there came that dull zinging sensation again, that great uncontrollable opening within myself. Thirst, and the promise of satiation measured only by the intensity of that thirst. Up stairs we fled together, into high-ceilinged bedrooms papered in red damask where the loveliest women reclined on brass bedsteads, and the aroma was so strong now I could not bear it, and before me they offered themselves, they opened their arms. "Drink," he whispered, yes, drink. And I felt the warmth filling me, charging me, blurring my vision, until we broke again, free and light and invisible it seemed as we moved over the rooftops and down again through rain-drenched streets. But the rain did not touch us; the falling snow did not chill us; we had within ourselves a great and indissoluble heat. And together in the carriage, we talked to each other in low, exuberant rushes of language; we were lovers; we were constant; we were immortal. We were as enduring as Rampling Gate.

I tried to speak; I tried to end the spell. I felt his arms around me and I knew we were in the tower room together, and some terrible miscalculation had been made.

"Do not leave me," he whispered. "Don't you understand what I am offering you; I have told you everything; and all the rest is but weariness, the fever and the fret, those old words from the poem. Kiss me, Julie, open to me. Against your will I will not take you…" Again I heard my own scream. My hands were on his cool white skin, his lips were gentle yet hungry, his eyes yielding and ever young. Father turned in the rain-drenched London street and cried out: "Julie!" I saw Richard lost in the crowd as if searching for someone, his hat shadowing his dark eyes, his face haggard, old. Old!

I moved away. I was free. And I was crying softly and we were in this strange and cluttered tower room. He stood against the backdrop of the window, against the distant drift of pale clouds. The candlelight glimmered in his eyes. Immense and sad and wise they seemed, and oh, yes, innocent as I have said again and again. "I revealed myself to them," he said. "Yes, I told my secret. In rage or bitterness, I know not which, I made them my dark co-conspirators and always I won. They could not move against me, and neither will you. But they would triumph still. For they torment me now with their fairest flower. Don't turn away from me, Julie. You are mine, Julie, as Rampling Gate is mine. Let me gather the flower to my heart."

Nights of argument. But finally Richard came round. He would sign over to me his share of Rampling Gate, and I should absolutely refuse to allow the place to be torn down. There would be nothing he could do then to obey Father's command. I had given him the legal impediment he needed, and of course I should leave the house to him and his children. It should always be in Rampling hands.

A clever solution, it seemed to me, as Father had not told *me* to destroy the place, and I had no scruples in the matter now at all.

And what remained was for him to take me to the little train station and see me off for London, and not worry about me going home to Mayfair on my own.

"You stay here as long as you wish, and do not worry," I said. I felt more tenderly towards him than I could ever express. "You knew as soon as you set foot in the place that Father was all wrong. Uncle Baxter put it in his mind, undoubtedly, and Mrs. Blessington has always been right. There is nothing to harm there, Richard. Stay, and work or study as you please."

The great black engine was roaring past us, the carriages slowing to a stop. "Must go now, darling, kiss me," I said.

"But what came over you, Julie, what convinced you so quickly..."

"We've been through all, Richard," I said. "What matters is that we are all happy, my dear." And we held each other close.

I waved until I couldn't see him any more. The flickering lamps of the town were lost in the deep lavender light of the early evening, and the dark hulk of Rampling Gate appeared for one uncertain moment like the ghost of itself on the nearby rise.

I sat back and closed my eyes. Then I opened them slowly, savouring this moment for which I had waited too long.

He was smiling, seated there as he had been all along, in the far corner of the leather seat opposite, and now he rose with a swift, almost delicate movement and sat beside me and enfolded me in his arms.

"It's five hours to London," he whispered in my ear.

"I can wait," I said, feeling the thirst like a fever as I held tight to him, feeling his lips against my eyelids and my hair. "I want to hunt the London streets tonight," I confessed, a little shyly, but I saw only approbation in his eyes.

"Beautiful Julie, my Julie…" he whispered.

"You'll love the house in Mayfair," I said.

"Yes…" he said.

"And when Richard finally tires of Rampling Gate, we shall go home."

Blue Beard

by
CHARLES PERRAULT
(1628–1703)

In the process of considering which stories to include in this volume, I reread many of the fairy tales I knew as a child, in search of witches, warlocks, ogres and other scary creatures who might feel at home in such a collection. Personally, I don't recall having had nightmares after reading them—children are no doubt more resilient than adults believe—but I was genuinely amazed at how gory many of the older fairy tales are. "Blue Beard," for instance, is no doubt nowadays considered by many to be unsuitable for small fry. Like all of the best tales of this type, though, it has a simplicity and narrative drive that are irresistible to children and adults alike.

O nce upon a time there was a man who owned splendid town and country houses, gold and silver plate, tapestries and coaches gilt all over. But the poor fellow had a blue beard, and this made him so ugly and frightful that there was not a woman or girl who did not run away at sight of him.

Amongst his neighbours was a lady of high degree who had two surpassingly beautiful daughters. He asked for the hand of one of these in marriage, leaving it to their mother to choose which should be bestowed upon him. Both girls, however, raised objections, and his offer was bandied from one to the other, neither being able to bring herself to accept a man with a blue beard. Another reason for their distaste was the fact that he had already married several wives, and no one knew what had become of them.

In order that they might become better acquainted, Blue Beard invited the two girls, with their mother and three or four of their best friends, to meet a party of young men from the neighbourhood at one of his country houses. Here they spent eight whole days, and throughout their stay there was a constant round of picnics, hunting and fishing expeditions, dances, dinners, and luncheons; and they never slept at all, through spending all the night in playing merry pranks upon each other. In short, everything went so gaily that the younger daughter began to think the master of the house had not so very blue a beard after all, and that he was an exceedingly agreeable man. As soon as the party returned to town their marriage took place.

At the end of a month Blue Beard informed his wife that important business obliged him to make a journey into a distant part of the country, which would occupy at least six weeks. He begged her to amuse herself well during his absence, and suggested that she should invite some of her friends and take them, if she liked, to the country. He was particularly anxious that she should enjoy herself thoroughly.

"Here," he said, "are the keys of the two large storerooms, and here is the one that locks up the gold and silver plate which is not in everyday use. This key belongs to the strongboxes where my gold and silver is kept, this to the caskets containing my jewels; while here you have the master-key which gives admittance to all the apartments. As regards this little key, it is the key of the small room at the end of the long passage on the lower floor. You may open everything, you may go everywhere, but I forbid you to enter this little room. And I forbid you so seriously that if you were indeed to open the door, I should be so angry that I might do anything."

She promised to follow out these instructions exactly, and after embracing her, Blue Beard steps into his coach and is off upon his journey.

Her neighbours and friends did not wait to be invited before coming to call upon the young bride, so great was their eagerness to see the splendours of her house. They had not dared to venture while her husband was there, for his blue beard frightened them. But in less than no time there they were, running in and out of the rooms, the closets, and the wardrobes, each of which was finer than the last. Presently they went upstairs to the storerooms, and there they could not admire enough the profusion and magnificence of the tapestries, beds, sofas, cabinets, tables, and stands. There were mirrors in which they could view themselves from top to toe, some with frames of plate glass, others with frames of silver and gilt lacquer, that were the most superb and beautiful things that had ever been seen. They were loud and persistent in their envy of their friend's good fortune. She, on the other hand, derived little amusement from the sight of all these riches, the reason being that she was impatient to go and inspect the little room on the lower floor.

So overcome with curiosity was she that, without reflecting upon the discourtesy of leaving her guests, she ran down a private staircase, so precipitately that twice or thrice she nearly broke her neck, and so reached the door of the little room. There she paused for a while, thinking of the prohibition which her husband had made, and reflecting that harm might come to her as a result of disobedience. But the temptation was so great that she could not conquer it. Taking the little key, with a trembling hand she opened the door of the room.

At first she saw nothing, for the windows were closed, but after a few moments she perceived dimly that the floor was entirely covered with clotted blood, and that in this were reflected the bodies of several women that hung along the walls. These were all the wives of Blue Beard, whose throats he had cut, one after another.

She thought to die of terror, and the key of the room, which she had just withdrawn from the lock, fell from her hand.

When she had somewhat regained her senses, she picked up the key, closed the door, and went up to her chamber to compose herself a little. But this she could not do, for her nerves were too shaken. Noticing that the key of the little room was stained with blood, she wiped it two or three times. But the blood did not go. She washed it well, and even rubbed it with sand and grit. Always the blood remained. For the key was bewitched, and there was no means of cleaning it completely. When the blood was removed from one side, it reappeared on the other.

Blue Beard returned from his journey that very evening. He had received some letters on the way, he said, from which he learned that the business upon which he had set forth had just been concluded to his satisfaction. His wife did everything she could to make it appear that she was delighted by his speedy return.

On the morrow he demanded the keys. She gave them to him, but with so trembling a hand that he guessed at once what had happened.

"How comes it," he said to her, "that the key of the little room is not with the others?"

"I must have left it upstairs upon my table," she said.

"Do not fail to bring it to me presently," said Blue Beard.

After several delays the key had to be brought. Blue Beard examined it and addressed his wife.

"Why is there blood on this key?"

"I do not know at all," replied the poor woman, paler than death.

"You do not know at all?" exclaimed Blue Beard; "I know well enough. You wanted to enter the little room! Well, madam, enter it you shall—you shall go and take your place among the ladies you have seen there."

She threw herself at her husband's feet, asking his pardon with tears, and with all the signs of a true repentance for her disobedience. She would have softened a rock, in her beauty and distress, but Blue Beard had a heart harder than any stone.

"You must die, madam," he said; "and at once."

"Since I must die," she replied, gazing at him with eyes that were wet with tears, "give me a little time to say my prayers."

"I give you one quarter of an hour," replied Blue Beard, "but not a moment longer."

When the poor girl was alone, she called her sister to her and said:

"Sister Anne"—for that was her name—"go up, I implore you, to the top of the tower, and see if my brothers are not approaching. They promised that they would come and visit me today. If you see them, make signs to them to hasten."

Sister Anne went up to the top of the tower, and the poor unhappy girl cried out to her from time to time.

"Anne, Sister Anne, do you see nothing coming?"

And Sister Anne replied:

"I see nought but dust in the sun and the green grass growing."

Presently Blue Beard, grasping a great cutlass, cried out at the top of his voice:

"Come down quickly, or I shall come upstairs myself."

"Oh please, one moment more," called out his wife.

And at the same moment she cried in a whisper:

"Anne, Sister Anne, do you see nothing coming?"

"I see nought but dust in the sun and the green grass growing."

"Come down at once, I say," shouted Blue Beard, "or I will come upstairs myself."

"I am coming," replied his wife.

Then she called:

"Anne, Sister Anne, do you see nothing coming?"

"I see," replied Sister Anne, "a great cloud of dust which comes this way."

"Is it my brothers?"

"Alas, sister, no; it is but a flock of sheep."

"Do you refuse to come down?" roared Blue Beard.

"One little moment more," exclaimed his wife.

Once more she cried:

"Anne, Sister Anne, do you see nothing coming?"

"I see," replied her sister, "two horsemen who come this way, but they are as yet a long way off.... Heaven be praised," she exclaimed a moment later, "they are my brothers.... I am signalling to them all I can to hasten."

Blue Beard let forth so mighty a shout that the whole house shook. The poor wife went down and cast herself at his feet, all dishevelled and in tears.

"That avails you nothing," said Blue Beard; "you must die."

Seizing her by the hair with one hand, and with the other brandishing the cutlass aloft, he made as if to cut off her head.

The poor woman, turning towards him and fixing a dying gaze upon him, begged for a brief moment in which to collect her thoughts.

"No! no!" he cried; "commend your soul to Heaven." And raising his arm—

At this very moment there came so loud a knocking at the gate that Blue Beard stopped short. The gate was opened, and two horsemen dashed in, who drew their swords and rode straight at Blue Beard. The latter recognized them as the brothers of his wife—one of them a dragoon, and the other a musketeer—and fled instantly in an effort to escape. But the two brothers were so close upon him that they caught him ere he could gain the first flight of steps. They plunged their swords through his body and left him dead. The poor woman was nearly as dead as her husband, and had not the strength to rise and embrace her brothers.

It was found that Blue Beard had no heirs, and the consequently his wife became mistress of all his wealth. She devoted a portion to arranging a marriage between her Sister Anne and a young gentleman with whom the latter had been for some time in love, while another portion purchased a captain's commission for each of her brothers. The rest formed a dowry for her own marriage with a very worthy man, who banished from her mind all memory of the evil days she had spent with Blue Beard.

The Terror of Blue John Gap

by

SIR ARTHUR CONAN DOYLE

(1859–1930)

Conan Doyle is, of course, best known for the Sherlock Holmes series, known and loved the world over. But he also wrote many short stories with a supernatural bent. "The Terror of Blue John Gap" is one of these—an exercise in terror that deserves to be much better known than it is. Like the Sasquatch or the Loch Ness monster, the creature that terrorizes the Derbyshire countryside is a hold-over from prehistoric times—a scientific oddity whose elusiveness makes this fine tale all the more spine-chilling.

T he following narrative was found among the papers of Dr. James Hardcastle, who died of phthisis on February 4th, 1908, at 36, Upper Coventry Flats, South Kensington. Those who knew him best, while refusing to express an opinion upon this particular statement, are unanimous in asserting that he was a man of a sober and scientific turn of mind, absolutely devoid of imagination, and most unlikely to invent any abnormal series of events. The paper was contained in an envelope, which was docketed, "A Short Account of the Circumstances which Occurred near Miss Allerton's Farm in Northwest Derbyshire in the Spring of Last Year." The envelope was sealed, and on the other side was written in pencil:

Dear Seaton—It may interest, and perhaps pain, you to know that the incredulity with which you met my story has prevented me from ever opening my mouth upon the subject again. I leave this record after my death, and perhaps strangers may be found to have more confidence in me than my friend.

Inquiry has failed to elicit who this Seaton may have been. I may add that the visit of the deceased to Allerton's Farm, and the general nature of the alarm there, apart from his particular explanation, have been absolutely established. With this fore-word I append his account exactly as he left it. It is in the form of a diary, some entries in which have been expanded, while a few have been erased.

April 17th.—Already I feel the benefit of this wonderful upland air. The farm of the Allertons lies fourteen hundred and twenty feet above sea-level, so it may well be a bracing cli-mate. Beyond the usual morning cough I have very little dis-comfort, and, what with the fresh milk and the home-grown mutton, I have every chance of putting on weight. I think Saunderson will be pleased.

The two Miss Allertons are charmingly quaint and kind, two dear little hard-working old maids, who are ready to lav-ish all the heart which might have gone out to husband and to children upon an invalid stranger. Truly, the old maid is a most useful person, one of the reserve forces of the community. They talk of the superfluous woman, but what would the poor superfluous man do without her kindly presence? By the way, in their simplicity they very quickly let out the reason why Saunderson recommended their farm. The Professor rose from the ranks himself, and I believe that in his youth he was not above scaring cows in those very fields.

It is a most lonely spot, and the walks are picturesque in the extreme. The farm consists of grazing land lying at the bottom of an irregular valley. On each side are the fantastic limestone hills, formed of rock so soft that you can break it away with your hands. All this country is hollow. Could you strike it with some gigantic hammer it would boom like a drum, or possibly cave in altogether and expose some huge subterranean sea. A great sea there must surely be, for on all sides the streams run into the mountain itself, never to reappear. There are gaps everywhere amid the rocks, and when you pass through them you find yourself in great caverns, which wind down into the bowels of the earth. I have a small bicycle lamp, and it is a perpetual joy to me to carry it into these weird solitudes, and to see the wonderful silver and black effects when I throw its light upon the stalactites which drape the lofty roofs. Shut off the lamp, and you are in the blackest darkness. Turn it on, and it is a scene from the Arabian Nights.

But there is one of these strange openings in the earth which has special interest, for it is the handiwork, not of Nature, but of Man. I had never heard of Blue John when I came to these parts. It is the name given to a peculiar mineral of a beautiful purplish shade, which is only found at one or two places in the world. It is so rare that an ordinary vase of Blue John would be valued at a great price. The Romans, with that extraordinary instinct of theirs, discovered that it was to be found in this valley, and sank a horizontal shaft deep into the mountain side. The opening of their mine has been called Blue John Gap, a clean-cut arch in the rock, the mouth all overgrown with bushes. It is a goodly passage which the Roman miners have cut, and it intersects some of the great water-worn caves, so that if you enter Blue John Gap you would do well to mark your steps and to have a good store of candles, or you may never make your way back to the daylight again. I have not yet gone deeply into it, but this very day I stood at the mouth of the arched tunnel, and peering down into the black recessed beyond I vowed that when my health returned I would devote some holiday to exploring those mysterious depths and finding out for myself how far the Romans had penetrated into the Derbyshire hills.

Strange how superstitious these countrymen are! I should have thought better of young Armitage, for he is a man of some education and character, and a very fine fellow for his station in life. I was standing at the Blue John Gap when he came across the field to me.

"Well, doctor," said he, "you're not afraid, anyhow."

"Afraid!" I answered. "Afraid of what?"

"Of it," said he, with a jerk of his thumb toward the black vault; "of the Terror that lives in the Blue John Cave."

How absurdly easy it is for a legend to arise in a lonely countryside! I examined him as to the reasons for his weird belief. It seems that from time to time sheep have been missing from the fields, carried bodily away, according to Armitage. That they could have wandered away of their own accord and disappeared among the mountains was an explanation to which he would not listen. On one occasion a pool of blood had been found, and some tufts of wool. That also, I pointed out, could be explained in a perfectly natural way. Further, the nights upon which sheep disappeared were invariably very dark, cloudy nights, with no moon. This I met with the obvious retort that those were the nights which a commonplace sheep stealer would naturally choose for his work. On one occasion a gap had been made in a wall, and some of the stones scattered for a considerable distance. Human agency again, in my opinion. Finally, Armitage clinched all his arguments by telling me that he had actually heard the Creature—indeed, that anyone could hear it who remained long enough at the Gap. It was a distant roaring of an immense volume. I could not but smile at this, knowing, as I do, the strange reverberations which come out of an underground water system running amid the chasms of a limestone formation. My incredulity annoyed Armitage, so that he turned and left me with some abruptness.

And now comes the queer point about the whole business. I was still standing near the mouth of the cave, turning over in my mind the various statements of Armitage and reflecting how readily they could be explained away, when suddenly, from the depth of the tunnel beside me, there issued a most extraordinary sound. How shall I describe it? First of all, it seemed to be a great distance away, far down in the bowels of the earth. Secondly, in spite of this suggestion of distance, it was very loud. Lastly, it was not a boom, nor a crash, such as one would associate with falling water or tumbling rock; but it was a high whine, tremulous and vibrating, almost like the whinnying of a horse. It was certainly a most remarkable experience, and one which for a moment, I must admit, gave a new significance to Armitage's words. I waited by the Blue John Gap for half an hour or more, but there was no return of the sound, so at last I wandered back to the farmhouse, rather mystified by what had occurred. Decidedly, I shall explore that cavern when my strength is restored. Of course, Armitage's explanation is too absurd for discussion, and yet that sound was certainly very strange. It still rings in my ears as I write.

April 20th.—In the last three days I have made several expeditions to the Blue John Gap, and have even penetrated some short distance, but my bicycle lantern is so small and weak that I dare not trust myself very far. I shall do the thing more systematically. I have heard no sound at all, and could almost believe that I had been the victim of some hallucination, suggested, perhaps, by Armitage's conversation. Of course, the whole idea is absurd, and yet I must confess that those bushes at the entrance of the cave do present an appearance as if some heavy creature had forced its way through them. I begin to be keenly interested. I have said nothing to the Miss Allertons, for they are quite superstitious enough already, but I have bought some candles, and mean to investigate for myself.

I observed this morning that among the numerous tufts of sheep's wool which lay among the bushes near the cavern there was one which was smeared with blood. Of course, my reason tells me that if sheep wander into such rocky places they are likely to injure themselves, and yet somehow that splash of crimson gave me a sudden shock, and for a moment I found myself shrinking back in horror from the old Roman arch. A fetid breath seemed to ooze from the black depths into which I peered. Could it indeed be possible that some nameless thing, some dreadful presence, was lurking down yonder? I should have been incapable of such feelings in the days of my strength, but one grows more nervous and fanciful when one's health is shaken.

For the moment I weakened in my resolution, and was ready to leave the secret of the old mine, if one exists, forever unsolved. But tonight my interest has returned and my nerves grown more steady. Tomorrow I trust that I shall have gone more deeply into this matter.

April 22nd.—Let me try and set down as accurately as I can my extraordinary experience of yesterday. I started in the afternoon,

and made my way to the Blue John Gap. I confess that my misgivings returned as I gazed into its depths, and I wished that I
had brought a companion to share my exploration. Finally, with
a return of resolution, I lit my candle, pushed my way through
the briers, and descended into the rocky shaft.

It went down at an acute angle for some fifty feet, the floor
being covered with broken stone. Thence there extended a
long, straight passage cut in the solid rock. I am no geologist,
but the lining of this corridor was certainly of some harder
material than limestone, for there were points where I could
actually see the tool marks which the old miners had left in
their excavation, as fresh as if they had been done yesterday.
Down this strange, old-world corridor I stumbled, my feeble
flame throwing a dim circle of light around me, which made
the shadows beyond the more threatening and obscure. Finally,
I came to a spot where the Roman tunnel opened into a water-
worn cavern—a huge hall, hung with long white icicles of lime
deposit. From this central chamber I could dimly perceive that
a number of passages worn by the subterranean streams wound
away into the depths of the earth. I was standing there wondering whether I had better return, or whether I dare venture farther into this dangerous labyrinth, when my eyes fell upon
something at my feet which strongly arrested my attention.

The greater part of the floor of the cavern was covered with
boulders of rock or with hard incrustations of lime; but at this
particular point there had been a drip from the distant roof,
which had left a patch of soft mud. In the very centre of this
there was a huge mark—an ill-defined blotch, deep, broad,
and irregular, as if a great boulder had fallen upon it. No loose
stone lay near, however, nor was there anything to account for
the impression. It was far too large to be caused by any possible animal, and, besides, there was only the one, and the patch
of mud was of such a size that no reasonable stride could have
covered it. As I rose from the examination of that singular
mark and then looked round into the black shadows which
hemmed me in, I must confess that I felt for a moment a most
unpleasant sinking of my heart, and that, do what I would, the
candle trembled in my outstretched hand.

I soon recovered my nerve, however, when I reflected how absurd it was to associate so huge and shapeless a mark with the track of any known animal. Even an elephant could not have produced it. I determined, therefore, that I would not be scared by vague and senseless fears from carrying out my exploration. Before proceeding I took good note of a curious rock formation in the wall by which I could recognize the entrance of the Roman tunnel. The precaution was very necessary, for the great cave, so far as I could see it, was intersected by passages. Having made sure of my position, and reassured myself by examining my spare candles and my matches, I advanced slowly over the rocky and uneven surface of the cavern.

And now I come to the point where I met with such sudden and desperate disaster. A stream, some twenty feet broad, ran across my path, and I walked for some little distance along the bank to find a spot where I could cross dry-shod. Finally, I came to a place where a single flat boulder lay near the centre, which I could reach in a stride. As it chanced, however, the rock had been cut away and made top-heavy by the rush of the stream, so that it tilted over as I landed on it, and shot me into the ice-cold water. My candle went out, and I found myself floundering about in an utter and absolute darkness.

I staggered to my feet again, more amused than alarmed by my adventure. The candle had fallen from my hand, and was lost in the stream; but I had two others in my pocket, so that it was of no importance. I got one of them ready, and drew out my box of matches to light it. Only then did I realize my position. The box had been soaked in my fall into the river. It was impossible to strike the matches.

A cold hand seemed to close round my heart as I realized my position. The darkness was opaque and horrible. It was so utter that one put one's hand up to one's face as if to press off something solid. I stood still, and by an effort I steadied myself. I tried to reconstruct in my mind a map of the floor of the cavern as I had last seen it. Alas! the bearings which had impressed themselves upon my mind were high on the wall, and not to be found by touch. Still, I remembered in a general way how the sides were situated, and I hoped that by groping my way along them I would at last come to the opening of the Roman tunnel. Moving very slowly, and continually striking against the rocks, I set out on this desperate quest.

But I very soon realized how impossible it was. In that black, velvety darkness one lost all one's bearings in an instant. Before I had made a dozen paces I was utterly bewildered as to my whereabouts. The rippling of the stream, which was the one sound audible, showed me where it lay, but the moment that I left its bank I was utterly lost. The idea of finding my way back in absolute darkness through that limestone labyrinth was clearly an impossible one.

I sat down upon a boulder and reflected upon my unfortunate plight. I had not told anyone that I proposed to come to the Blue John mine, and it was unlikely that a search party would come after me. Therefore, I must trust to my own resources to get clear of the danger. There was only one hope, and that was the matches might dry. When I fell into the river only half of me had got thoroughly wet. My left shoulder had remained above the water. I took the box of matches, therefore, and put it in my left armpit. The moist air of the cavern might possibly be counteracted by the heat of my body, but even so I knew that I could not hope to get a light for many hours. Meanwhile there was nothing for it but to wait.

By good luck I had slipped several biscuits into my pocket before I had left the farmhouse. These I now devoured, and washed them down with a draught from that wretched stream which had been the cause of all my misfortunes. Then I felt about for a comfortable seat among the rocks, and, having discovered a place where I could get a support for my back, I stretched out my legs and settled myself down to wait. I was wretchedly damp and cold, but I tried to cheer myself with the reflection that modern science prescribed open windows and walks in all weather for my disease. Gradually, lulled by the absolute darkness, I sank into an uneasy slumber.

How long this lasted I cannot say. It may have been for one hour, it may have been for several. Suddenly I sat up on my rock couch, with every nerve thrilling and every sense acutely on the alert. Beyond all doubt I had heard a sound—some sound very distinct from the gurgling of the waters. It had passed, but the reverberation of it still lingered in my ear. Was it a search party? They would most certainly have shouted, and vague as this sound was which had wakened me, it was very distinct from the human voice. I sat palpitating and hardly daring to breathe. There it was again! And again! Now it had become continuous. It was a tread—yes, surely it was the tread of some living creature. But what a tread it was! It gave one the impression of enormous weight carried upon spongelike feet, which gave forth a muffled but ear-filling sound. The darkness was as complete as ever, but the tread was regular and decisive. And it was coming beyond all question in my direction.

My skin grew cold, and my hair stood on end as I listened to that steady and ponderous footfall. There was some creature there, and surely, by the speed of its advance, it was one who could see in the dark. I crouched low on my rock and tried to blend myself into it. The steps grew nearer still, then stopped, and presently I was aware of a loud lapping gurgling. The creature was drinking at the stream. Then again there was silence, broken by a succession of long sniffs and snorts, of tremendous volume and energy. Had it caught the scent of me? My own nostrils were filled by a low fetid odour, mephitic and abominable. Then I heard the steps again. They were on my side of the stream now. The stones rattled within a few yards of where I lay. Hardly daring to breathe, I crouched upon my rock. Then the steps drew away. I heard the splash as it returned across the river, and the sound died away in the distance in the direction from which it had come.

For a long time I lay upon the rock, too much horrified to move. I thought of the sound which I had heard coming from the depths of the cave, of Armitage's fears, of the strange impression in the mud, and now came this final and absolute proof that there was indeed come inconceivable monster, something utterly un-English and dreadful, which lurked in the hollow of the mountain. Of its nature or form I could frame no conception, save that it was both light-footed and gigantic. The combat between my reason, which told me that such things could not be, and my senses, which told me that they were, raged within me as I lay. Finally, I was almost ready to persuade myself that this experience had been part of some evil dream, and that my abnormal condition might have conjured up an hallucination. But there remained one final experience which removed the last possibility of doubt from my mind.

I had taken my matches from my armpit and felt them. They seemed perfectly hard and dry. Stooping down into a crevice of the rocks, I tried one of them. To my delight it took fire at once. I lit the candle, and, with a terrified backward glance into the obscure depths of the cavern, I hurried in the direction of the Roman passage. As I did so I passed the patch of mud on which I had seen the huge imprint. Now I stood astonished before it, for there were three similar imprints upon its surface, enormous in size, irregular in outline, of a depth which indicated the ponderous weight which had left them. Then a great terror surged over me. Stooping and shading my candle with my hand, I ran in a frenzy of fear to the rocky archway, hastened down it, and never stopped until, with weary feet and panting lungs, I rushed up the final slope of stones, broke through the tangle of briers, and flung myself exhausted upon the soft grass under the peaceful light of the stars. It was three in the morning when I reached the farmhouse, and today I am all unstrung and quivering after my terrific adventure. As yet I have told no one. I must move warily in the matter. What would the poor lonely women, or the uneducated yokels here, think of it if I were to tell them my experience? Let me go to someone who can understand and advise.

April 25th.—I was laid up in bed for two days after my incredible adventure in the cavern. I use the adjective with a very definite meaning, for I have had an experience since which has shocked me almost as much as the other. I have said that I was looking round for someone who could advise me. There is a Dr. Mark Johnson who practises some few miles away, to whom I had a note of recommendation from Professor Saunderson. To him I drove, when I was strong enough to get about, and I recounted to him my whole strange experience. He listened intently, and then carefully examined me, paying special attention to my reflexes and to the pupils of my eyes. When he had finished he refused to discuss my adventure, saying that it was entirely beyond him, but he gave me the card of a Mr. Picton at Castleton, with the advice that I should instantly go to him and tell him the story exactly as I had done it to himself. He was, according to my adviser, the very man who was pre-eminently suited to help me. I went on to the station, therefore, and made my way to the little town, which is some ten miles away. Mr. Picton appeared to be a man of importance, as his brass plate was displayed upon the door of a considerable building on the outskirts of the town. I was about to ring the bell, when some misgiving came into my mind, and, crossing to a neighbouring shop, I asked the man behind the counter if he could tell me anything of Mr. Picton. "Why," said he, "he is the best mad doctor in Derbyshire, and yonder is his asylum." You can imagine that it was not long before I had shaken the dust of Castleton from my feet and returned to the farm, cursing all unimaginative pedants who cannot conceive that there may be things in creation which have never yet chanced to come across their mole's vision. After all, now that I am cooler, I can afford to admit that I have been no more sympathetic to Armitage than Dr. Johnson has been to me.

April 27th.—When I was a student I had the reputation of being a man of courage and enterprise. I remember that when there was a ghost-hunt at Coltbridge it was I who sat up in the haunted house. Is it advancing years (after all, I am only thirty-five), or is it this physical malady which has caused degeneration? Certainly my heart quails when I think of that horrible cavern in the hill, and the certainty that it has some monstrous occupant. What shall I do? There is not an hour in the day that I do not debate the question. If I say nothing, then the mystery remains unsolved. If I do say anything, then I have the alternative of mad alarm over the whole countryside, or of absolute incredulity which may end in consigning me to an asylum. On the whole, I think that my best course is to wait, and to prepare for some expedition which shall be more deliberate and better thought-out than the last. As a first step I have

been to Castleton and obtained a few essentials—a large acety-
lene lantern for one thing, and a good double-barrelled sporting rifle for another. The latter I have hired, but I have bought
a dozen heavy game cartridges, which would bring down a
rhinoceros. Now I am ready for my troglodyte friend. Give me
better health and a little spate of energy, and I shall try conclu-
sions with him yet. But who and what is he? Ah! there is the
question which stands between me and my sleep. How many
theories do I form, only to discard each in turn! It is all so
utterly unthinkable. And yet the cry, the footmark, the tread in
the cavern—no reasoning can get past these. I think of the
old-world legends of dragons and of monsters. Were they, perhaps, not such fairy tales as we have thought? Can it be that
there is some fact which underlies them, and am I, of all mor-
tals, the one who is chosen to expose it?

May 3rd.—For several days I have been laid up by the
vagaries of an English spring, and during those days there
have been developments, the true and sinister meaning of
which no one can appreciate save myself. I may say that we
have had cloudy and moonless nights of late, which according
to my information were the seasons upon which sheep disappeared. Well, sheep *have* disappeared. Two of Miss Allerton's,
one of old Pearson's of the Cat Walk, and one of Mrs.
Moulton's. Four in all, during three nights. No trace is left of
them at all, and the countryside is buzzing with rumours of
Gypsies and of sheep stealers.

But there is something more serious than that. Young
Armitage has disappeared also. He left his moorland cottage
early on Wednesday night, and has never been heard of since.
He was an unattached man, so there is less sensation than
would otherwise be the case. The popular explanation is that
he owes money, and has found a situation in some other part
of the country, whence he will presently write for his belong-
ings. But I have grave misgivings. Is it not much more likely
that the recent tragedy of the sheep has caused him to take
some steps which may have ended in his own destruction? He
may, for example, have lain in wait for the creature, and been

carried off by it into the recesses of the mountains. What an inconceivable fate for a civilized Englishman of the twentieth century! And yet I feel that it is possible and even probable. But in that case, how far am I answerable both for his death and for any other mishap which may occur? Surely with the knowledge I already possess it must be my duty to see that something is done, or if necessary to do it myself. It must be the latter, for this morning I went down to the local police station and told my story. The inspector entered it all in a large book and bowed me out with commendable gravity, but I heard a burst of laughter before I had got down his garden path. No doubt he was recounting my adventure to his family.

June 10th.—I am writing this, propped up in bed, six weeks after my last entry in this journal. I have gone through a terrible shock both to mind and body, arising from such an experience as has seldom befallen a human being before. But I have attained my end. The danger from the Terror which dwells in the Blue John Gap has passed, never to return. This much at least I, a broken invalid, have done for the common good. Let me now recount what occurred, as clearly as I may.

The night of Friday, May 3rd, was dark and cloudy—the very night for the monster to walk. About eleven o'clock I went from the farmhouse with my lantern and my rifle, having first left a note upon the table of my bedroom in which I said that if I were missing search should be made for me in the direction of the Gap. I made my way to the mouth of the Roman shaft, and, having perched myself among the rocks close to the opening, I shut off my lantern and waited patiently with my loaded rifle ready to my hand.

It was a melancholy vigil. All down the winding valley I could see the scattered lights of the farmhouses, and the church clock of Chapel-le-Dale tolling the hours came faintly to my ears. These tokens of my fellow-men served only to make my own position seem the more lonely, and to call for a greater effort to overcome the terror which tempted me continually to get back to the farm, and abandon forever this dangerous quest. And yet there lies deep in every man a rooted self-respect which makes it hard for him to turn back from that which he has once undertaken. This feeling of personal pride was my salvation now, and it was that alone which held me fast when every instinct of my nature was dragging me away. I am glad now that I had the strength. In spite of all that it has cost me, my manhood is at least above reproach.

Twelve o'clock struck in the distant church, then one, then two. It was the darkest hour of the night. The clouds were drifting low, and there was not a star in the sky. An owl was hooting somewhere among the rocks, but no other sound, save the gentle sough of the wind, came to my ears. And then suddenly I heard it! From far away down the tunnel came those muffled steps, so soft and yet so ponderous. I heard also the rattle of stones as they gave way under that giant tread. They drew nearer. They were close upon me. I heard the crashing of the bushes round the entrance, and then dimly through the darkness I was conscious of the loom of some enormous shape, some monstrous inchoate creature, passing swiftly and very silently out from the tunnel. I was paralysed with fear and amazement. Long as I had waited, now that it had actually come I was unprepared for the shock. I lay motionless and breathless, whilst the great dark mass whisked by me and was swallowed up in the night.

But now I nerved myself for its return. No sound came from the sleeping countryside to tell of the horror which was loose. In no way could I judge how far off it was, what it was doing, or when it might be back. But not a second time should my nerve fail me, not a second time should it pass unchallenged. I swore it between my clenched teeth as I laid my cocked rifle across the rock.

And yet it nearly happened. There was no warning of approach now as the creature passed over the grass. Suddenly, like a dark, drifting shadow, the huge bulk loomed up once more before me, making for the entrance of the cave. Again came that paralysis of volition, which held my crooked fore-finger impotent upon the trigger. But with a desperate effort I shook it off. Even as the brushwood rustled, and the monstrous beast blended with the shadow of the Gap, I fired at the retreating form. In the blaze of the gun I caught a glimpse of a great shaggy mass, something with rough and bristling hair of a withered grey colour, fading away to white in its lower parts, the huge body supported upon short, thick, curving legs. I had just that glance, and then I heard the rattle of the stones as the creature tore down into its burrow. In an instant, with a triumphant revulsion of feeling, I had cast my fears to the wind, and uncovering my powerful lantern, with my rifle in my hand, I sprang down from my rock and rushed after the monster down the old Roman shaft.

My splendid lamp cast a brilliant flood of vivid light in front of me, very different from the yellow glimmer which had aided me down this same passage only twelve days before. As I ran I saw the great beast lurching along before me, its huge bulk filling up the whole space from wall to wall. Its hair looked like coarse faded oakum, and hung down in long, dense masses which swayed as it moved. It was like an enormous unclipped sheep in its fleece, but in size it was far larger than the largest elephant, and its breadth seemed to be nearly as great as its height. It fills me with amazement now to think that I should have dared to follow such a horror into the bowels of the earth, but when one's blood is up, and when one's quarry seems to be flying, the old primeval hunting spirit awakes and prudence is cast to the wind. Rifle in hand, I ran at the top of my speed upon the trail of the monster.

I had seen the creature was swift. Now I was to find out to my cost that it was also very cunning. I had imagined that it was in panic flight, and that I had only to pursue it. The idea that it might turn upon me never entered my excited brain. I have already explained that the passage down which I was racing opened into a great central cave. Into this I rushed, fearful lest I should lose all trace of the beast. But he had turned upon his own traces, and in a moment we were face to face.

That picture, seen in the brilliant white light of the lantern, is etched forever upon my brain. He had reared up on his hind legs as a bear would do, and stood above me, enormous, menacing—such a creature as no nightmare had ever brought to my imagination. I have said that he reared like a bear, and there was something bearlike—if one could conceive a bear which was tenfold the bulk of any bear seen upon earth—in his whole pose and attitude, in his great crooked forelegs with their ivory-white claws, in his rugged skin, and in his red, gaping mouth, fringed with monstrous fangs. Only in one point did he differ from the bear, or from any other creature which walks the earth, and even at that supreme moment a shudder of horror passed over me as I observed that the eyes which glistened in the glow of the lantern were huge, projecting bulbs, white and sightless. For a moment his great paws swung over my head. The next he fell forward upon me, I and my broken lantern crashed to the earth, and I remember no more.

When I came to myself I was back in the farmhouse of the Allertons. Two days had passed since my terrible adventure in the Blue John Gap. It seems that I had lain all night in the cave insensible from concussion of the brain, with my left arm and two ribs badly fractured. In the morning my note had been found, a search party of a dozen farmers assembled, and I had been tracked down and carried back to my bedroom, where I had lain in high delirium ever since. There was, it seems, no sign of the creature, and no bloodstain which would show that my bullet had found him as he passed. Save for my own plight and the marks upon the mud, there was nothing to prove that what I said was true.

Six weeks have now elapsed, and I am able to sit out once more in the sunshine. Just opposite me is the steep hillside, grey with shaly rock, and yonder on its flank is the dark cleft which marks the opening of the Blue John Gap. But it is no longer a source of terror. Never again through that ill-omened tunnel shall any strange shape flit out into the world of men. The educated and the scientific, the Dr. Johnsons and the like, may smile at my narrative, but the poorer folk of the countryside had never a doubt as to its truth. On the day after my recovering consciousness they assembled in their hundreds round the Blue John Gap. As the *Castleton Courier* said:

It was useless for our correspondent, or for any of the

adventurous gentlemen who had come from Matlock, Buxton, and other parts, to offer to descend, to explore the cave to the end, and to finally test the extraordinary narrative of Dr. James Hardcastle. The country people had taken the matter into their own hands, and from an early hour of the morning they had worked hard in stopping up the entrance of the tunnel. There is a sharp slope where the shaft begins, and great boulders, rolled along by many willing hands, were thrust down it until the Gap was absolutely sealed. So ends the episode which has caused such excitement throughout the country. Local opinion is fiercely divided upon the subject. On the one hand are those who point to Dr. Hardcastle's impaired health, and to the possibility of cerebral lesions of tubercular origin giving rise to strange hallucinations. Some *idée fixe*, according to these gentlemen, caused the doctor to wander down the tunnel, and a fall among the rocks was sufficient to account for his injuries. On the other hand, a legend of a strange creature in the Gap has existed for some months back, and the farmers look upon Dr. Hardcastle's narrative and his personal injuries as a final corroboration. So the matter stands, and so the matter will continue to stand, for no definite solution seems to us to be now possible. It transcends human wit to give any scientific explanation which could cover the alleged facts.

Perhaps before the *Courier* published these words they would have been wise to send their representative to me. I have thought the matter out, as no one else has had occasion to do, and it is possible that I might have removed some of the more obvious difficulties of the narrative and brought it one degree nearer to scientific acceptance. Let me then write down the only explanation which seems to me to elucidate what I know to my cost to have been a series of facts. My theory may seem to be wildly improbable, but at least no one can venture to say that it is impossible.

My view is—and it was formed, as is shown by my diary, before my personal adventure—that in this part of England there is a vast subterranean lake or sea, which is fed by the great number of streams which pass down through the limestone. Where there is a large collection of water there must also be some evaporation, mists or rain, and a possibility of vegetation. This in turn suggests that there may be animal life, arising, as the vegetable life would also do, from those seeds and types which had been introduced at an early period of the world's history, when communication with the outer air was more easy. This place had then developed a fauna and flora of its own, including such monsters as the one which I had seen, which may well have been the old cave bear, enormously enlarged and modified by its new environment. For countless aeons the internal and the external creation had kept apart, growing steadily away from each other. Then there had come some rift in the depths of the mountain which had enabled one creature to wander up and, by means of the Roman tunnel, to reach the open air. Like all subterranean life, it had lost the power of sight, but this had no doubt been compensated for by Nature in other directions. Certainly it had some means of finding its way about, and of hunting down the sheep upon the hillside. As to its choice of dark nights, it is part of my theory that light was painful to those great white eyeballs, and that it was only a pitch-black world which it could tolerate. Perhaps, indeed, it was the glare of my lantern which saved my life at that awful moment when we were face to face. So I read the riddle. I leave these facts behind me, and if you can explain them, do so; or if you choose to doubt them, do so. Neither your belief nor your incredulity can alter them, nor affect one whose task is nearly over.

So ended the strange narrative of Dr. James Hardcastle.

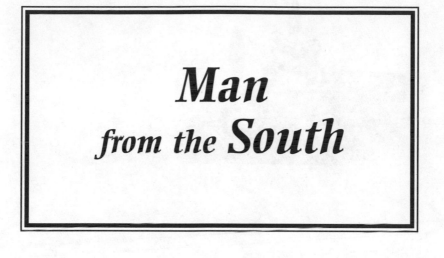

Man
from the South

by
ROALD DAHL
(1916–1990)

It was difficult to pick out a Roald Dahl story for this collection because he wrote so many wonderful ones. He is undoubtedly one of the finest of postwar short-story writers. The thing I love about "Man from the South" is the manner in which the tension is controlled, rising steadily but almost imperceptibly from the most everyday of beginnings.

While most scary stories feature ghosts, vampires, werewolves, witches or monsters, others are every bit as scary without any of these ingredients. "Man from the South" is one of the latter.

243

I t was getting on towards six o'clock so I thought I'd buy myself a beer and go out and sit in a deck-chair by the swimming-pool and have a little evening sun.

I went to the bar and got the beer and carried it outside and wandered down the garden towards the pool.

It was a fine garden with lawns and beds of azaleas and tall coconut palms, and the wind was blowing strongly through the tops of the palm trees, making the leaves hiss and crackle as though they were on fire. I could see the clusters of big brown nuts hanging down underneath the leaves.

There were plenty of deck-chairs around the swimming-pool and there were white tables and huge brightly coloured umbrellas and sunburned men and women sitting around in bathing-suits. In the pool itself there were three or four girls and about a dozen boys, all splashing about and making a lot of noise and throwing a large rubber ball at one another.

I stood watching them. The girls were English girls from the hotel. The boys I didn't know about, but they sounded American, and I thought they were probably naval cadets who'd come ashore from the U.S. naval training vessel which had arrived in harbour that morning.

I went over and sat down under a yellow umbrella where there were four empty seats, and I poured my beer and settled back comfortably with a cigarette.

It was very pleasant sitting there in the sunshine with beer and cigarette. It was pleasant to sit and watch the bathers splashing about in the green water.

The American sailors were getting on nicely with the English girls. They'd reached the stage where they were diving under the water and tipping them up by their legs.

Just then I noticed a small, oldish man walking briskly around the edge of the pool. He was immaculately dressed in a white suit and he walked very quickly with little bouncing strides, pushing himself high up on to his toes with each step. He had on a large creamy Panama hat, and he came bouncing along the side of the pool, looking at the people and the chairs.

He stopped beside me and smiled, showing two rows of very small, uneven teeth, slightly tarnished. I smiled back.

"Excuse plees, but may I sit here?"

"Certainly," I said. "Go ahead."

He bobbed around to the back of the chair and inspected it for safety, then he sat down and crossed his legs. His white buckskin shoes had little holes punched all over them for ventilation.

"A fine evening," he said. "They are all evenings fine here in Jamaica." I couldn't tell if the accent were Italian or Spanish, but I felt fairly sure he was some sort of a South American. And old too, when you saw him close. Probably around sixty-eight or seventy.

"Yes," I said. "It is wonderful here, isn't it."

"And who, might I ask, are all dese? Dese is no hotel people." He was pointing at the bathers in the pool.

"I think they're American sailors," I told him. "They're Americans who are learning to be sailors."

"Of course dey are Americans. Who else in de world is going to make as much noise as dat? You are not American no?"

"No," I said. "I am not."

Suddenly one of the American cadets was standing in front of us. He was dripping wet from the pool and one of the

English girls was standing there with him.

"Are these chairs taken?" he said.

"No," I answered.

"Mind if I sit down?"

"Go ahead."

"Thanks," he said. He had a towel in his hand and when he sat down he unrolled it and produced a pack of cigarettes and a lighter. He offered the cigarettes to the girl and she refused; then he offered them to me and I took one. The little man said, "Tank you, no, but I tink I have a cigar." He pulled out a crocodile case and got himself a cigar, then he produced a knife which had a small scissors in it and he snipped the end off the cigar.

"Here, let me give you a light." The American boy held up his lighter.

"Dat will not work in dis wind."

"Sure it'll work. It always works."

The little man removed his unlighted cigar from his mouth, cocked his head on one side and looked at the boy.

"*All*-ways?" he said slowly.

"Sure, it never fails. Not with me anyway."

The little man's head was still cocked over on one side and he was still watching the boy. "Well, well. So you say dis famous lighter it never fails. Iss dat you say?"

"Sure," the boy said. "That's right." He was about nineteen or twenty with a long freckled face and a rather sharp birdlike nose. His chest was not very sunburned and there were freckles there too, and a few wisps of pale-reddish hair. He was holding the lighter in his right hand, ready to flip the wheel. "It never fails," he said, smiling now because he was purposely exaggerating his little boast. "I promise you it never fails."

"One momint, pleess." The hand that held the cigar came up high, palm outward, as though it were stopping traffic. "Now juss one momint." He had a curiously soft, toneless voice and he kept looking at the boy all the time.

"Shall we not perhaps make a little bet on dat?" He smiled at the boy. "Shall we not make a little bet on whether your lighter lights?"

"Sure, I'll bet," the boy said. "Why not?"

"You like to bet?"

"Sure, I'll always bet."

The man paused and examined his cigar, and I must say I didn't much like the way he was behaving. It seemed he was already trying to make something out of this, and to embarrass the boy, and at the same time I had the feeling he was relishing a private little secret of his own.

He looked up again at the boy and said slowly, "I like to bet, too. Why we don't have a good bet on dis ting? A good big bet."

"Now wait a minute," the boy said. "I can't do that. But I'll bet you a quarter. I'll even bet you a dollar, or whatever it is over here—some shillings, I guess."

The little man waved his hand again. "Listen to me. Now we have some fun. We make a bet. Den we go up to my room here in de hotel where iss no wind and I bet you you cannot light dis famous lighter of yours ten times running without missing once."

"I'll bet I can," the boy said.

"All right. Good. We make a bet, yes?"

"Sure. I'll bet you a buck."

"No, no. I make you a very good bet. I am rich man and I am sporting man also. Listen to me. Outside de hotel iss my car. Iss very fine car. American car from your country. Cadillac—"

"Hey, now. Wait a minute." The boy leaned back in his deck-chair and he laughed. "I can't put up that sort of property. This is crazy."

"Not crazy at all. You strike lighter successfully ten times running and Cadillac is yours. You like to have dis Cadillac, yes?"

"Sure, I'd like to have a Cadillac." The boy was still grinning.

"All right. Fine. We make a bet and I put up my Cadillac."

"And what do I put up?"

The little man carefully removed the red band from his still unlighted cigar. "I never ask you, my friend, to bet something you cannot afford. You understand?"

"Then what do I bet?"

"I make it very easy for you, yes?"

"Okay. You make it easy."

"Some small ting you can afford to give away, and if you did happen to lose it you would not feel too bad. Right?"

"Such as what?"

"Such as, perhaps, de little finger of your left hand."

"My *what*?" The boy stopped grinning.

"Yes. Why not? You win, you take de car. You looss, I take de finger."

"I don't get it. How d'you mean, you take the finger?"

"I chop it off."

"Jumping jeepers! That's a crazy bet. I think I'll just make it a dollar."

The little man leaned back, spread out his hands palms upwards and gave a tiny contemptuous shrug of his shoulders. "Well, well, well," he said. "I do not understand. You say it lights but you will not bet. Den we forget it, yes?"

The boy sat quite still, staring at the bathers in the pool. Then he remembered suddenly he hadn't lighted his cigarette. He put it between his lips, cupped his hands around the lighter and flipped the wheel. The wick lighted and burned with a small, steady, yellow flame and the way he held his hands the wind didn't get to it at all.

"Could I have a light, too?" I said.

"Gee, I'm sorry. I forgot you didn't have one."

I held out my hand for the lighter, but he stood up and came over to do it for me.

"Thank you," I said, and he returned to his seat.

"You having a good time?" I asked.

"Fine," he answered. "It's pretty nice here."

There was a silence then, and I could see that the little man had succeeded in disturbing the boy with his absurd proposal. He was sitting there very still, and it was obvious that a small tension was beginning to build up inside him. Then he started shifting about in his seat, and rubbing his chest, and stroking the back of his neck, and finally he placed both hands on his knees and began tap-tapping with his fingers against the kneecaps. Soon he was tapping with one of his feet as well.

"Now just let me check up on this bet of yours," he said at last. "You say we go up to your room and if I make this lighter light ten times running I win a Cadillac. If it misses just once then I forfeit the little finger of my left hand. Is that right?"

"Certainly. Dat is de bet. But I tink you are afraid."

"What do we do if I lose? Do I have to hold my finger out while you chop it off?"

"Oh, no! Dat would be no good. And you might be tempted to refuse to hold it out. What I should do I should tie one of your hands to de table before we started and I should stand dere with a knife ready to go *chop* de momint your lighter missed."

"What year is the Cadillac?" the boy asked.

"Excuse. I not understand."

"What year—how old is the Cadillac?"

"Ah! How old? Yes. It is last year. Quite new car. But I see you are not betting man. Americans never are."

The boy paused for just a moment and he glanced first at the English girl, then at me. "Yes," he said sharply. "I'll bet you."

"Good!" The little man clapped his hands together quietly, once. "Fine," he said. "We do it now. And you, sir," he turned to me, "you would perhaps be good enough to, what you call it, to—to referee." He had pale, almost colourless eyes with tiny bright black pupils.

"Well," I said. "I think it's a crazy bet. I don't think I like it very much."

"Nor do I," said the English girl. It was the first time she'd spoken. "I think it's a stupid, ridiculous bet."

"Are you serious about cutting off this boy's finger if he loses?"

"Certainly I am. Also about giving him Cadillac if he win. Come now. We go up to my room."

He stood up. "You like to put on some clothes first?" he said.

"No," the boy answered. "I'll come like this." Then he turned to me. "I'd consider it a favour if you'd come along and referee."

"All right," I said. "I'll come along, but I don't like the bet."

"You come too," he said to the girl. "You come and watch."

The little man led the way back through the garden to the hotel. He was animated now, and excited, and that seemed to make him bounce up higher than ever on his toes as he walked along.

"I live in annexe," he said. "You like to see car first? Iss just here."

He took us to where we could see the front driveway of the hotel and he stopped and pointed to a sleek pale-green Cadillac parked close by.

"Dere she iss. De green one. You like?"

"Say, that's a nice car," the boy said.

"All right. Now we go up and see if you can win her."

We followed him into the annexe and up one flight of stairs. He unlocked his door and we all trooped into what was a large pleasant double bedroom. There was a woman's dressing-gown lying across the bottom of one of the beds.

"First," he said, "we 'ave a little Martini."

The drinks were on a small table in the far corner, all ready to be mixed, and there was a shaker and ice and plenty of glasses. He began to make the Martini, but meanwhile he'd rung the bell and now there was a knock on the door and a coloured maid came in.

"Ah!" he said, putting down the bottle of gin, taking a wallet from his pocket and pulling out a pound note. "You will do something for me now, pleess." He gave the maid the pound.

"You keep dat," he said. "And now we are going to play a little game in here and I want you to go off and find for me two—no tree tings. I want some nails; I want a hammer, and I want a chopping-knife, a butcher's chopping-knife which you can borrow from de kitchen. You can get, yes?"

"A *chopping-knife*!" The maid opened her eyes wide and clasped her hands in front of her. "You mean a *real* chopping-knife?"

"Yes, yes, of course. Come on now, pleess. You can find dose tings surely for me."

"Yes, sir, I'll try, sir. Surely I'll try to get them." And she went.

The little man handed round the Martinis. We stood there and sipped them, the boy with the long freckled face and the pointed nose, bare-bodied except for a pair of faded brown bathing-shorts; the English girl, a large-boned fair-haired girl wearing a pale blue bathing-suit, who watched the boy over the top of her glass all the time; the little man with the colourless eyes standing there in his immaculate white suit drinking his Martini and looking at the girl in her pale blue bathing-dress. I didn't know what to make of it all. The man seemed serious about the bet and he seemed serious about the business of cutting off the finger. But hell, what if the boy lost? Then we'd have to rush him to the hospital in the Cadillac that he hadn't won. That would be a fine thing. Now wouldn't that be a really fine thing? It would be a damn silly unnecessary thing so far as I could see.

"Don't you think this is rather a silly bet?" I said.

"I think it's a fine bet," the boy answered. He had already downed one large Martini.

"I think it's a stupid, ridiculous bet," the girl said. "What'll happen if you lose?"

"It won't matter. Come to think of it, I can't remember ever in my life having had any use for the little finger on my left hand. Here he is." The boy took hold of the finger. "Here he is and he hasn't ever done a thing for me yet. So why shouldn't I bet him? I think it's a fine bet."

The little man smiled and picked up the shaker and refilled our glasses.

"Before we begin," he said, "I will present to de—to de referee de key of de car." He produced a car key from his pocket and gave it to me. "De papers," he said, "de owning papers and insurance are in de pocket of de car."

Then the coloured maid came in again. In one hand she carried a small chopper, the kind used by butchers for chopping meat bones, and in the other a hammer and a bag of nails.

"Good! You get dem all. Tank you, tank you. Now you can go." He waited until the maid had closed the door, then he put the implements on one of the beds and said, "Now we prepare ourselves, yes?" And to the boy, "Help me, pleess, with dis table. We carry it out a little."

It was the usual kind of hotel writing-desk, just a plain rectangular table about four feet by three with a blotting-pad, ink, pens and paper. They carried it out into the room away from the wall, and removed the writing things.

"And now," he said, "a chair." He picked up a chair and placed it beside the table. He was very brisk and very animated, like a person organizing games at a children's party. "And now de nails. I must put in de nails." He fetched the nails and he began to hammer them into the top of the table.

We stood there, the boy, the girl, and I, holding Martinis in our hands, watching the little man at work. We watched him hammer two nails into the table, about six inches apart. He didn't hammer them right home; he allowed a small part of each one to stick up. Then he tested them for firmness with his fingers.

Anyone would think the son of a bitch had done this before, I told myself. He never hesitates. Table, nails, hammer, kitchen chopper. He knows exactly what he needs and how to arrange it.

"And now," he said, "all we want is some string." He found some string. "All right, at last we are ready. Will you pleess to sit here at de table?" he said to the boy.

The boy put his glass away and sat down.

"Now place de left hand between dese two nails. De nails are only so I can tie your hand in place. All right, good. Now I tie your hand secure to de table—so."

He wound the string around the boy's wrist, then several times around the wide part of the hand, then he fastened it tight to the nails. He made a good job of it and when he'd finished there wasn't any question about the boy being able to draw his hand away. But he could move his fingers.

"Now pleess, clench de fist, all except for de little finger. You must leave de little finger sticking out, lying on de table."

"*Ex*-cellent! *Ex*-cellent! Now we are ready. Wid your right hand you manipulate de lighter. But one momint pleess."

He skipped over to the bed and picked up the chopper. He came back and stood beside the table with the chopper in his hand.

"We are all ready?" he said. "Mister referee, you must say to begin."

The English girl was standing there in her pale blue bathing-costume right behind the boy's chair. She was just standing there, not saying anything. The boy was sitting quite still, holding the lighter in his right hand, looking at the chopper. The little man was looking at me.

"Are you ready?" I asked the boy.

"I'm ready."

"And you?" to the little man.

"Quite ready," he said and he lifted the chopper up in the air and held it there about two feet above the boy's finger, ready to chop. The boy watched it, but he didn't flinch and his mouth didn't move at all. He merely raised his eyebrows and frowned.

"All right," I said. "Go ahead."

The boy said, "Will you please count aloud the number of times I light it."

"Yes," I said. "I'll do that."

With his thumb he raised the top of the lighter, and again with the thumb he gave the wheel a sharp flick. The flint sparked and the wick caught fire and burned with a small yellow flame.

"One!" I called.

He flicked the wheel very strongly and once more there was a small flame burning on the wick.

"Two!"

No one else said anything. The boy kept his eyes on the lighter. The little man held the chopper up in the air and he too was watching the lighter.

"Three!"

"Four!"

"Five!"

"Six!"

"Seven!" Obviously it was one of those lighters that worked. The flint gave a big spark and the wick was the right length. I watched the thumb snapping the top down on to the flame. Then a pause. Then the thumb raising the top once more. This was an all-thumb operation. The thumb did everything. I took a breath, ready to say eight. The thumb flicked the wheel. The flint sparked. The little flame appeared.

"Eight!" I said, and as I said it the door opened. We all turned and we saw a woman standing in the doorway, a small, black-haired woman, rather old, who stood there for about two seconds then rushed forward shouting, "Carlos! Carlos!" She grabbed his wrist, took the chopper from him, threw it on the bed, took hold of the little man by the lapels of his white suite and began shaking him very vigorously, talking to him fast and loud and fiercely all the time in some Spanish-sounding language. She shook him so fast you couldn't see him any more. He became a faint, misty, quickly moving outline, like the spokes of a turning wheel.

Then she slowed down and the little man came into view again and she hauled him across the room and pushed him backwards on to one of the beds. He sat on the edge of it blinking his eyes and testing his head to see if it would still turn on his neck.

"I am so sorry," the woman said. "I'm terribly sorry that this should happen." She spoke almost perfect English.

"It is too bad," she went on. "I suppose it is really my fault. For ten minutes I leave him alone to go and have my hair washed and I come back and he is at it again." She looked sorry and deeply concerned.

The boy was untying his hand from the table. The English girl and I stood there and said nothing.

"He is a menace," the woman said. "Down where we live at home he has taken altogether forty-seven fingers from different people, and he has lost eleven cars. In the end they threatened to have him put away somewhere. That's why I brought him up here."

"We were only having a little bet," mumbled the little man from the bed.

"I suppose he bet you a car," the woman said.

"Yes," the boy answered. "A Cadillac."

"He has no car. It's mine. And that makes it worse," she said, "that he should bet you when he has nothing to bet with. I am ashamed and very sorry about it all." She seemed an awfully nice woman.

"Well," I said, "then here's the key of your car." I put it on the table.

"We were only having a little bet," mumbled the little man.

"He hasn't anything left to bet with," the woman said. "He hasn't a thing in the world. Not a thing. As a matter of fact I myself won it all from him a long while ago. It took time, a lot of time, and it was hard work, but I won it all in the end." She looked up at the boy and she smiled, a slow sad smile, and she came over and put out a hand to take the key from the table.

I can see it now, that hand of hers; it had only one finger on it, and a thumb.

The Girl
at the Gate

by
LUCY MAUD MONTGOMERY
(1874–1942)

Real old-fashioned Canadian ghost stories are rather thin on the ground. Whether it's because we find enough true-life horror in our experience of winter or because we don't think of our country as romantic enough to be peopled by spirits, we simply have not produced a large body of ghost literature. Luckily, however, the same author who gave the world Anne of Green Gables also bequeathed us a handful of marvellous ghost tales. Curiously enough, "The Girl at the Gate" manages at one and the same time to be genuinely spooky and to inhabit a world that is unmistakably that of Anne—which goes to show that ghosts can be as charming and sentimental as they are terrifying.

257

Something very strange happened the night old Mr. Lawrence died. I have never been able to explain it and I have never spoken of it except to one person and she said that I dreamed it. I did not dream it... I saw and heard, waking.

We had not expected Mr. Lawrence to die then. He did not seem very ill...not nearly so ill as he had been during his previous attack. When we heard of his illness I went over to Woodlands to see him, for I had always been a great favourite with him. The big house was quiet, the servants going about their work as usual, without any appearance of excitement. I was told that I could not see Mr. Lawrence for a little while, as the doctor was with him. Mrs. Yeats, the housekeeper, said the attack was not serious and asked me to wait in the blue parlour, but I preferred to sit down on the steps of the big, arched front door. It was an evening in June. Woodlands was very lovely; to my right was the garden, and before me was a little valley abrim with the sunset. In places under the big trees it was quite dark even then.

There was something unusually still in the evening...a stillness as of waiting. It set me thinking of the last time Mr.

Lawrence had been ill...nearly a year ago in August. One night during his convalescence I had watched by him to relieve the nurse. He had been sleepless and talkative, telling me many things about his life. Finally he told me of Margaret.

I knew a little about her...that she had been his sweetheart and had died very young. Mr. Lawrence had remained true to her memory ever since, but I had never heard him speak of her before.

"She was very beautiful," he said dreamily, "and she was only eighteen when she died, Jeanette. She had wonderful pale-golden hair and dark-brown eyes. I have a little ivory miniature of her. When I die it is to be given to you, Jeanette. I have waited a long while for her. You know she promised she would come."

I did not understand his meaning and kept silence, thinking that he might be wandering a little in his mind.

"She promised she would come and she will keep her word," he went on. "I was with her when she died. I held her in my arms. She said to me, 'Herbert, I promise that I will be true to you forever, through as many years of lonely heaven as I must know before you come. And when your time is at hand I will come to make your deathbed easy as you have made mine. I will come, Herbert.' She solemnly promised, Jeanette. We made a death-tryst of it. And I know she will come."

He had fallen asleep then and after his recovery he had not alluded to the matter again. I had forgotten it, but I recalled it now as I sat on the steps among the geraniums that June evening. I liked to think of Margaret...the lovely girl who had died so long ago, taking her lover's heart with her to the grave. She had been a sister of my grandfather, and people told me that I resembled her slightly. Perhaps that was why old Mr. Lawrence had always made such a pet of me.

Presently the doctor came out and nodded to me cheerily. I asked him how Mr. Lawrence was.

"Better...better," he said briskly. "He will be all right tomorrow. The attack was very slight. Yes, of course you may go in. Don't stay longer than half an hour."

Mrs. Stewart, Mr. Lawrence's sister, was in the sickroom

when I went in. She took advantage of my presence to lie down on the sofa a little while, for she had been up all the preceding night. Mr. Lawrence turned his fine old silver head on the pillow and smiled a greeting. He was a very handsome old man; neither age nor illness had marred his finely modelled face or impaired the flash of his keen, steel-blue eyes. He seemed quite well and talked naturally and easily of many commonplace things.

At the end of the doctor's half-hour I rose to go. Mrs. Stewart had fallen asleep and he would not let me wake her, saying he needed nothing and felt like sleeping himself. I promised to come up again on the morrow and went out.

It was dark in the hall, where no lamp had been lighted, but outside on the lawn the moonlight was bright as day. It was the clearest, whitest night I ever saw. I turned aside into the garden, meaning to cross it, and take the short way over the west meadow home. There was a long walk of rose-bushes leading across the garden to a little gate on the further side...the way Mr. Lawrence had been wont to take long ago when he went over the fields to woo Margaret. I went along it, enjoying the night. The bushes were white with roses, and the ground under my feet was all snowed over with their petals. The air was still and breezeless; again I felt that sensation of waiting...of expectancy. As I came up to the little gate I saw a young girl standing on the other side of it. She stood in the full moonlight and I saw her distinctly.

She was tall and slight and her head was bare. I saw that her hair was a pale gold, shining somewhat strangely about her head as if catching the moonbeams. Her face was very lovely and her eyes large and dark. She was dressed in something white and softly shimmering, and in her hand she held a white rose...a very large and perfect one. Even at the time I found myself wondering where she could have picked it. It was not a Woodlands rose. All the Woodlands roses were smaller and less double.

She was a stranger to me, yet I felt that I had seen her or someone very like her before. Possibly she was one of Mr. Lawrence's many nieces who might have come up to Woodlands upon hearing of his illness.

As I opened the gate I felt an odd chill of positive fear. Then she smiled as if I had spoken my thought.

"Do not be frightened," she said. "There is no reason you should be frightened. I have only come to keep a tryst."

The words reminded me of something, but I could not recall what it was. The strange fear that was on me deepened. I could not speak.

She came through the gateway and stood for a moment at my side.

"It is strange that you should have seen me," she said, "but now behold how strong and beautiful a thing is faithful love— strong enough to conquer death. We who have loved truly love always—and this makes our heaven."

She walked on after she had spoken, down the long rose path. I watched her until she reached the house and went up the steps. In truth I thought the girl was someone not quite in her right mind. When I reached home I did not speak of the matter to anyone, not even to inquire who the girl might possibly be. There seemed to be something in that strange meeting that demanded my silence.

The next morning word came that old Mr. Lawrence was dead. When I hurried down to Woodlands I found all in confusion, but Mrs. Yeats took me into the blue parlour and told me what little there was to tell.

"He must have died soon after you left him, Miss Jeanette," she sobbed, "for Mrs. Stewart wakened at ten o'clock and he was gone. He lay there, smiling, with such a strange look on his face as if he had just seen something that made him wonderfully happy. I never saw such a look on a dead face before."

"Who is here besides Mrs. Stewart?" I asked.

"Nobody," said Mrs. Yeats. "We have sent word to all his friends but they have not had time to arrive here yet."

"I met a young girl in the garden last night," I said slowly. "She came into the house. I did not know her but I thought she must be a relative of Mr. Lawrence's."

Mrs. Yeats shook her head.

"No. It must have been somebody from the village,

although I didn't know of anyone calling after you went away."

I said nothing more to her about it.

After the funeral Mrs. Stewart gave me Margaret's miniature. I had never seen it or any picture of Margaret before. The face was very lovely—also strangely like my own, although I am not beautiful. It was the face of the young girl I had met at the gate!

The Boarded Window

by
<small>AMBROSE BIERCE</small>
(1842–1914)

This story is like one of those Russian wooden dolls: you open it up and there's a smaller doll inside, more finely painted than the first; you open that, and a yet smaller, more finely detailed doll is revealed, more exquisite than all the preceding ones. "The Boarded Window" starts in the author's brightly lit and transparent present and then moves further and further into the murky and mysterious past. And like a Russian doll, it delights and surprises as it reveals new layers, right to the horrific end.

I n 1830, only a few miles away from what is now the great city of Cincinnati, lay an immense and almost unbroken forest. The whole region was sparsely settled by people of the frontier—restless souls who no sooner had hewn fairly habitable homes out of the wilderness and attained to that degree of prosperity which today we should call indigence than, impelled by some mysterious impulse of their nature, they abandoned all and pushed farther westward, to encounter new perils and privations in the effort to regain the meagre comforts which they had voluntarily renounced. Many of them had already forsaken that region for the remoter settlements, but among those remaining was one who had been of those first arriving. He lived alone in a house of logs surrounded on all sides by the great forest, of whose gloom and silence he seemed a part, for no one had ever known him to smile nor speak a needless word. His simple wants were supplied by the sale or barter of skins of wild animals in the river town, for not a thing did he grow upon the land which, if needful, he might have claimed by right of undisturbed possession. There were evidence of "improvement"—a few acres of ground immediately about the house had once been cleared of its trees, the decayed stumps of which were half concealed by the new growth that had been suffered to repair the ravage wrought by the axe. Apparently the man's zeal for agriculture had burned with a failing flame, expiring in penitential ashes.

The little log house, with its chimney of sticks, its roof of warping clapboards weighted with traversing poles and its "chinking" of clay, had a single door and, directly opposite, a window. The latter, however, was boarded up—nobody could remember a time when it was not. And none knew why it was so closed; certainly not because of the occupant's dislike of light and air, for on those rare occasions when a hunter had passed that lonely spot the recluse had commonly been seen sunning himself on his doorstep if heaven had provided sunshine for his need. I fancy there are few persons living today who ever knew the secret of that window, but I am one, as you shall see.

The man's name was said to be Murlock. He was apparently seventy years old, actually about fifty. Something besides years had had a hand in his aging. His hair and long, full beard were white, his grey, lustreless eyes sunken, his face singularly seamed with wrinkles which appeared to belong to two intersecting systems. In figure he was tall and spare, with a stoop of the shoulders—a burden bearer. I never saw him; these particulars I learned from my grandfather, from whom also I got the man's story when I was a lad. He had known him when living near by in that early day.

One day Murlock was found in his cabin, dead. It was not a time and place for coroners and newspapers, and I suppose it was agreed that he had died from natural causes or I should have been told, and should remember. I know only that with what was probably a sense of the fitness of things the body was buried near the cabin, alongside the grave of his wife, who had preceded him by so many years that local tradition had retained hardly a hint of her existence. That closes the final chapter of this true story—excepting, indeed, the circumstances that many years afterwards, in company with an equally intrepid spirit, I penetrated to the place and ventured near enough to the ruined cabin to throw a stone against it, and ran away to avoid the ghost which every well-informed boy thereabout knew haunted the spot. But there is an earlier chapter—that supplied by my grandfather.

When Murlock built his cabin and began laying sturdily about with his axe to hew out a farm—the rifle, meanwhile, his means of support—he was young, strong and full of hope. In that eastern country whence he came he had married, as was the fashion, a young woman in all ways worthy of his honest devotion, who shared the dangers and privations of his lot with a willing spirit and light heart. There is no known record of her name; of her charms of mind and person tradition is silent and the doubter is at liberty to entertain his doubt; but God forbid that I should share it! Of their affection and happiness there is abundant assurance in every added day of the man's widowed life; for what but the magnetism of a blessed memory could have chained that venturesome spirit to a lot like that?

One day Murlock returned from gunning in a distant part of the forest to find his wife prostrate with fever, and delirious. There was no physician within miles, no neighbour; nor was she in a condition to be left, to summon help. So he set about the task of nursing her back to health, but at the end of the third day she fell into unconsciousness and so passed away, apparently, with never a gleam of returning reason.

From what we know of a nature like his we may venture to sketch in some of the details of the outline drawn by my grandfather. When convinced that she was dead, Murlock had sense enough to remember that the dead must be prepared for burial. In performance of this sacred duty he blundered now and again, did certain things incorrectly, and others which he did correctly were done over and over. His occasional failures to accomplish some simple and ordinary act filled him with astonishment, like that of a drunken man who wonders at the suspension of familiar natural laws. He was surprised, too, that he did not weep—surprised and a little ashamed; surely it is unkind not to weep for the dead. "Tomorrow," he said aloud, "I shall have to make the coffin and dig the grave; and then I shall miss her, when she is no longer in sight; but now—she is dead, of course, but it is all right—it *must* be all right, somehow. Things cannot be so bad as they seem."

He stood over the body in the fading light, adjusting the hair and putting the finishing touches to the simple toilet, doing all mechanically, with soulless care. And still through his consciousness ran an undersense of conviction that all was right—that he should have her again as before, and everything explained. He had had no experience in grief; his capacity had not been enlarged by use. His heart could not contain it all, nor his imagination rightly conceive it. He did not know he was so hard struck; that knowledge would come later, and never go. Grief is an artist of powers as various as the instruments upon which he plays his dirges for the dead, evoking from some the sharpest, shrillest notes, from others the low, grave chords that throb recurrent like the slow beating of a distant drum. Some natures it startles; some it stupefies. To one it comes like the stroke of an arrow, stinging all the sensibilities to a keener life; to another as the blow of a bludgeon which, in crushing, benumbs. We may conceive Murlock to have been that way affected, for (and here we are upon surer ground than that of conjecture) no sooner had he finished his pious work than, sinking into a chair by the side of the table upon which the body lay, and noting how white the profile showed in the deepening gloom, he laid his arms upon the table's edge, and dropped his face into them, tearless yet and unutterably weary. At that moment came in through the open window a long, wailing sound like the cry of a lost child in the far deeps of the darkening wood! But the man did not move. Again, and nearer than before, sounded that unearthly cry upon his failing sense. Perhaps it was a wild beast; perhaps it was a dream. For Murlock was asleep.

Some hours later, as it afterwards appeared, this unfaithful watcher awoke, and lifting his head from his arms intently listened—he knew not why. There in the black darkness by the side of the dead, recalling all without a shock, he strained his eyes to see—he knew not what. His senses were all alert, his breath was suspended, his blood had stilled its tides as if to assist the silence. Who—what had waked him, and where was it?

Suddenly the table shook beneath his arms, and at the same moment he heard, or fancied that he heard, a light, soft step—another—sounds as of bare feet upon the floor!

He was terrified beyond the power to cry out or move. Perforce he waited—waited there in the darkness through seeming centuries of such dread as one may know, yet live to tell. He tried vainly to speak the dead woman's name, vainly to stretch forth his hand across the table to learn if she were there. His throat was powerless, his arms and hands were like lead. Then occurred something most frightful. Some heavy body seemed hurled against the table with an impetus that pushed it against his breast so sharply as nearly to overthrow him, and at the same instant he heard and felt the fall of something upon the floor with so violent a thump that the whole house was shaken by the impact. A scuffling ensued, and a confusion of sounds impossible to describe. Murlock had risen to his feet. Fear had by excess forfeited control of his faculties. He flung his hands upon the table. Nothing was there!

There is a point at which terror may turn to madness; and madness incites to action. With no definite intent, from no motive but the wayward impulse of a madman, Murlock sprang to the wall, with a little groping seized his loaded rifle, and without aim discharged it. By the flash which lit up the room with a vivid illumination, he saw an enormous panther dragging the dead woman towards the window, its teeth fixed in her throat! Then there were darkness blacker than before, and silence; and when he returned to consciousness the sun was high and the wood vocal with songs of birds.

The body lay near the window, where the beast had left it when frightened away by the flash and report of the rifle. The clothing was deranged, the long hair in disorder, the limbs lay anyhow. From the throat, dreadfully lacerated, had issued a pool of blood not yet entirely coagulated. The ribbon with which he had bound the wrists was broken; the hands were tightly clenched. Between the teeth was a fragment of the animal's ear.

Confession

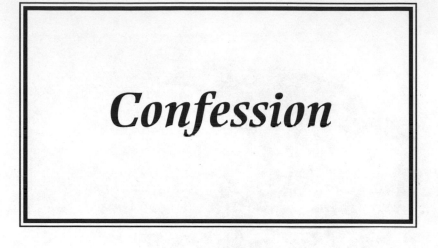

by
ALGERNON BLACKWOOD
(1869–1951)

The English writer Algernon Blackwood, a lifelong Buddhist with a passionate interest in psychic phenomena, led a varied and adventurous life. As well as being a writer, he worked as an actor and storyteller on BBC radio and television.

Blackwood lived in Ontario for several years in the 1890s (some of that time as a prospector for gold), and the main character in this story is a Canadian ex-soldier in London for treatment of shell-shock. There is about the whole story a dreamlike atmosphere, a sense of dislocation that mirrors the soldier's state of mind. And of course the dense fog serves to cast over all the events an elusiveness, as if one can't be certain of having really seen or experienced anything. It is an unsettling story, and it comes as near as any I know to evoking the irrational world of nightmares. It is both a terrific horror story and a powerful portrait of a shattered mind.

269

The fog swirled slowly round him, driven by a heavy movement of its own, for of course there was no wind. It hung in poisonous thick coils and loops; it rose and sank; no light penetrated it directly from street lamp or motorcar, though here and there some big shop window shed a glimmering patch upon its ever-shifting curtain.

O'Reilly's eyes ached and smarted with the incessant effort to see a foot beyond his face. The optic nerve grew tired, and sight, accordingly, less accurate. He coughed as he shuffled forward cautiously through the choking gloom. Only the stifled rumble of crawling traffic persuaded him he was in a crowded city at all—this, and the vague outlines of groping figures, hugely magnified, emerging suddenly and disappearing again, as they fumbled along inch by inch towards uncertain destinations.

The figures, however, were human beings; they were real. That much he knew. He heard their muffled voices, now close, now distant, strangely smothered always. He also heard the tapping of innumerable sticks, feeling for iron railings or the curb. These phantom outlines represented living people. He was not alone.

It was the dread of finding himself *quite* alone that haunted him, for he was still unable to cross an open space without assistance. He had the physical strength, it was the mind that failed him. Midway the panic terror might descend upon him, he would shake all over, his will dissolve, he would shriek for help, run wildly—into the traffic probably—or, as they called it in his North Ontario home, "throw a fit" in the street before advancing wheels. He was not yet entirely cured, although under ordinary conditions he was safe enough, as Dr. Henry had assured him.

When he left Regent's Park by Tube an hour ago the air was clear, the November sun shone brightly, the pale blue sky was cloudless, and the assumption that he could manage the journey across London Town alone was justified. The following day he was to leave for Brighton for the week of final convalescence: this little preliminary test of his powers on a bright November afternoon was all to the good. Doctor Henry furnished minute instructions. "You change at Piccadilly Circus—without leaving the underground station, mind—and get out at South Kensington. You know the address of your V.A.D. friend. Have your cup of tea with her, then come back the same way to Regent's Park. Come back before dark—say six o'clock at latest. It's better." He had described exactly what turns to take after leaving the station, so many to the right, so many to the left; it was a little confusing, but the distance was short. "You can always ask. You can't possibly go wrong."

The unexpected fog, however, now blurred these instructions in a confused jumble in his mind. The failure of outer sight reacted upon memory. The V.A.D. besides had warned him that her address was "not easy to find the first time. The house lies in a backwater. But with your 'backwoods' instincts you'll probably manage it better than any Londoner!" She, too, had not calculated upon the fog.

When O'Reilly came up the stairs at South Kensington Station, he emerged into such murky darkness that he thought he was still underground. An impenetrable world lay round him. Only a raw bite in the damp atmosphere told him he stood beneath an open sky. For some little time he stood and stared—a Canadian soldier, his home among clear brilliant spaces, now face to face for the first time in his life with that thing he had so often read about—a bad London fog. With keenest interest and surprise he "enjoyed" the novel spectacle for perhaps ten minutes, watching the people arrive and vanish, and wondering why the station lights stopped dead the instant they touched the street—then, with a sense of adventure—it cost an effort—he left the covered building and plunged into the opaque sea beyond.

Repeating to himself the directions he had received—first to the right, second to the left, once more to the left, and so forth—he checked each turn, assuring himself it was impossible to go wrong. He made correct if slow progress, until someone blundered into him with an abrupt and startling question: "Is this right, do you know, for South Kensington Station?"

It was the suddenness that startled him; one moment there was no one, the next they were face to face, another, and the stranger had vanished into the gloom with a courteous word of grateful thanks. But the little shock of interruption had put memory out of gear. Had he already turned twice to the right, or had he not? O'Reilly realized sharply he had forgotten his memorized instructions. He stood still, making strenuous efforts at recovery, but each effort left him more uncertain than before. Five minutes later he was lost as hopelessly as any townsman who leaves his tent in the backwoods without blazing the trees to ensure finding his way back again. Even the sense of direction, so strong in him among his native forests, was completely gone. There were no stars, there was no wind, no smell, no sound of running water. There was nothing anywhere to guide him, nothing but occasional dim outlines, groping, shuffling, emerging and disappearing in the eddying fog, but rarely coming within actual speaking, much less touching, distance. He was lost utterly; more, he was alone.

Yet not *quite* alone—the thing he dreaded most. There were figures still in his immediate neighbourhood. They emerged, vanished, reappeared, dissolved. No, he was not quite alone. He saw these thickenings of the fog, he heard their voices, the tapping of their cautious sticks, their shuffling feet as well.

They were real. They moved, it seemed, about him in a circle, never coming very close.

"But they're real," he said to himself aloud, betraying the weak point in his armour. "They're human beings right enough. I'm positive of that."

He had never argued with Dr. Henry—he wanted to get well; he had obeyed implicitly, believing everything the doctor told him—up to a point. But he had always had his own idea about these "figures," because, among them, were often enough his own pals from the Somme, Gallipoli, the Mespot horror, too. And he ought to know his own pals when he saw them! At the same time he knew quite well he had been "shocked," his being dislocated, half dissolved as it were, his system pushed into some lopsided condition that meant inaccurate registration. True. He grasped that perfectly. But, in that shock and dislocation, had he not possibly picked up another gear? Were there not gaps and broken edges, pieces that no longer dovetailed, fitted as usual, interstices, in a word? Yes, that was the word—interstices. Cracks, so to speak, between his perception of the outside world and his inner interpretation of these? Between memory and recognition? Between the various states of consciousness that usually dovetailed so neatly that the joints were normally imperceptible?

His state, he well knew, was abnormal, but were his symptoms on that account unreal? Could not these "interstices" be used by—others? When he saw his "figures," he used to ask himself: "Are not these the real ones, and the others—the human beings—unreal?"

This question now revived in him with a new intensity. Were these figures in the fog real or unreal? The man who had asked the way to the station, was he not, after all, a shadow merely?

By the use of his cane and foot and what of sight was left to him he knew that he was on an island. A lamppost stood up solid and straight beside him, shedding its faint patch of glimmering light. Yet there were railings, however, that puzzled him, for his stick hit the metal rods distinctly in a series. And there should be no railings round an island. Yet he had most certainly crossed a dreadful open space to get where he was.

His confusion and bewilderment increased with dangerous rapidity. Panic was not far away.

He was no longer on an omnibus route. A rare taxi crawled past occasionally, a whitish patch at the window indicating an anxious human face; now and again came a van or cart, the driver holding a lantern as he led the stumbling horse. These comforted him, rare though they were. But it was the figures that drew his attention most. He was quite sure they were real. They were human beings like himself.

For all that, he decided he might as well be positive on the point. He tried one accordingly—a big man who rose suddenly before him out of the very earth.

"Can you give me the trail to Morley Place?" he asked.

But his question was drowned by the other's simultaneous inquiry in a voice much louder than his own.

"I say, is this right for the Tube station, d'you know? I'm utterly lost. I want South Ken."

And by the time O'Reilly had pointed the direction whence he himself had just come, the man was gone again, obliterated, swallowed up, not so much as his footsteps audible, almost as if—it seemed again—he never had been there at all.

This left an acute unpleasantness in him, a sense of bewilderment greater than before. He waited five minutes, not daring to move a step, then tried another figure, a woman this time, who, luckily, knew the immediate neighbourhood intimately. She gave him elaborate instructions in the kindest possible way, then vanished with incredible swiftness and ease into the sea of gloom beyond. The instantaneous way she vanished was disheartening, upsetting: it was so uncannily abrupt and sudden. Yet she comforted him. Morley Place, according to her version, was not two hundred yards from where he stood. He felt his way forward, step by step, using his cane, crossing a giddy open space, kicking the curb with each boot alternately, coughing and choking all the time as he did so.

"They were real, I guess, anyway," he said aloud. "They were both real enough all right. And it may lift a bit soon!" He was making a great effort to hold himself in hand. He was already fighting, that is. He realized this perfectly. The only point was—the reality of the figures. "It may lift now any minute," he repeated louder. In spite of the cold, his skin was sweating profusely.

But, of course, it did not lift. The figures, too, became fewer. No carts were audible. He had followed the woman's directions carefully, but now found himself in some byway, evidently, where pedestrians at the best of times were rare. There was dull silence all about him. His foot lost the curb, his cane swept the empty air, striking nothing solid, and panic rose upon him with its shuddering, icy grip. He was alone, he knew himself alone, worse still—he was in another open space.

It took him fifteen minutes to cross that open space, most of the way upon his hands and knees, oblivious of the icy slime that stained his trousers, froze his fingers, intent only upon feeling solid support against his back and spine again. It was an endless period. The moment of collapse was close, the shriek already rising in his throat, the shaking of the whole body uncontrollable, when—his outstretched fingers struck a friendly curb, and he saw a glimmering patch of diffused radiance overhead. With a great, quick effort he stood upright, and an instant later his stick rattled along an area railing. He leaned against it, breathless, panting, his heart beating painfully while the street lamp gave him the further comfort of its feeble gleam, the actual flame, however, invisible. He looked this way and that; the pavement was deserted. He was engulfed in the dark silence of the fog.

But Morley Place, he knew, must be very close by now. He thought of the friendly little V.A.D. he had known in France, of a warm bright fire, a cup of tea and a cigarette. One more effort, he reflected, and all these would be his. He pluckily groped his way forward again, crawling slowly by the area railings. If things got really bad again, he would ring a bell and ask for help, much as he shrank from the idea. Provided he had no more open spaces to cross, provided he saw no more figures emerging and vanishing like creatures born of the fog and dwelling within it as within their native element—it was the figures he now dreaded more than anything else, more than even the loneliness—provided the panic sense—

A faint darkening of the fog beneath the next lamp caught his eye and made him start. He stopped. It was not a figure this time, it was the shadow of the pole grotesquely magnified. No, it moved. It moved towards him. A flame of fire followed by ice flowed through him. It was a figure—close against his face. It was a woman.

The doctor's advice came suddenly back to him, the counsel that had cured him of a hundred phantoms.

"Do not ignore them. Treat them as real. Speak and go with them. You will soon prove their unreality then. And they will leave you…"

He made a brave, tremendous effort. He was shaking. One hand clutched the damp and icy area railing.

"Lost your way like myself, haven't you, ma'am?" he said in a voice that trembled. "Do you know where we are at all? Morley Place I'm looking for—"

He stopped dead. The woman moved nearer and for the first time he saw her face clearly. Its ghastly pallor, the bright, frightened eyes that stared with a kind of dazed bewilderment into his own, the beauty, above all, arrested his speech midway. The woman was young, her tall figure wrapped in a dark fur coat.

"Can I help you?" he asked impulsively, forgetting his own terror for the moment. He was more than startled. Her air of distress and pain stirred a peculiar anguish in him. For a moment she made no answer, thrusting her white face closer as if examining him, so close, indeed, that he controlled with difficulty his instinct to shrink back a little.

"Where am I?" she asked at length, searching his eyes intently. "I'm lost—I've lost myself. I can't find my way back." Her voice was low, a curious wailing in it that touched his pity oddly. He felt his own distress merging in one that was greater.

"Same here," he replied more confidently. "I'm terrified of being alone, too. I've had shell-shock, you know. Let's go together. We'll find a way together—"

"Who are you?" the woman murmured, still staring at him with her big bright eyes, their distress, however, no whit lessened. She gazed at him as though aware suddenly of his presence.

He told her briefly. "And I'm going to tea with a V.A.D. friend in Morley Place. What's your address? Do you know the name of the street?"

She appeared not to hear him, or not to understand exactly; it was as if she was not listening again.

"I came out so suddenly, so unexpectedly," he heard the low voice with pain in every syllable; "I can't find my way home again. Just when I was expecting him too—" She looked about her with a distraught expression that made O'Reilly long to carry her in his arms to safety then and there. "He may be there now—waiting for me at this very moment—and I can't get back." And so sad was her voice that only by an effort did O'Reilly prevent himself putting out his hand to touch her. More and more he forgot himself in his desire to help her. Her beauty, the wonder of her strange bright eyes in the pallid face, made an immense appeal. He became calmer. This woman was real enough. He asked again the address, the street and number, the distance she thought it was. "Have you any idea of the direction, ma'am, any idea at all? We'll go together and—"

She suddenly cut him short. She turned her head as if to listen, so that he saw her profile a moment, the outline of the slender neck, a glimpse of jewels just below the fur.

"Hark! I hear him calling! I remember...!" And she was gone from his side into the swirling fog.

Without an instant's hesitation O'Reilly followed her, not only because he wished to help, but because he dared not be left alone. The presence of this strange, lost woman comforted him; he must not lose sight of her, whatever happened. He had to run, she went so rapidly, ever just in front, moving with confidence and certainty, turning right and left, crossing the street, but never stopping, never hesitating, her companion always at her heels in breathless haste, and with a growing terror that he might lose her any minute. The way she found her direction through the dense fog was marvellous enough, but O'Reilly's only thought was to keep her in sight, lest his own panic redescend upon him with its inevitable collapse in the dark and lonely street. It was a wild and panting pursuit, and he kept her in view with difficulty, a dim fleeting outline always a few yards ahead of him. She did not once turn her head, she uttered no sound, no cry; she hurried forward with unfaltering instinct. Nor did the chase occur to him once as singular; she was his safety, and that was all he realized.

One thing, however, he remembered afterwards, though at the actual time he no more than registered the detail, paying no attention to it—a definite perfume she left upon the atmosphere, one, moreover, that he knew, although he could not find its name as he ran. It was associated vaguely, for him, with something unpleasant, something disagreeable. He connected it with misery and pain. It gave him a feeling of uneasiness. More than that he did not notice at the moment, nor could he remember—he certainly did not try—where he had known this particular scent before.

Then suddenly the woman stopped, opened a gate and passed into a small private garden—so suddenly that O'Reilly, close upon her heels, only just avoided tumbling into her. "You've found it?" he cried. "May I come in a moment with you? Perhaps you'll let me telephone to the doctor?"

She turned instantly. Her face, close against his own, was livid.

"Doctor!" she repeated in an awful whisper. The word meant terror to her. O'Reilly stood amazed. For a second or two neither of them moved. The woman seemed petrified.

"Dr. Henry, you know," he stammered, finding his tongue again. "I'm in his care. He's in Harley Street."

Her face cleared as suddenly as it had darkened, though the original expression of bewilderment and pain still hung in her great eyes. But the terror left them, as though she suddenly forgot some association that had revived it.

"My home," she murmured. "My home is somewhere here. I'm near it. I must get back—in time—for him. I must. He's coming to me." And with these extraordinary words she turned, walked up the narrow path, and stood upon the porch of a two-storey house before her companion had recovered from his astonishment sufficiently to move or utter a syllable in reply. The front door, he saw, was ajar. It had been left open.

For five seconds, perhaps for ten, he hesitated; it was the

fear that the door would close and shut him out that brought the decision to his will and muscles. He ran up the steps and followed the woman into a dark hall where she had already preceded him, and amid whose blackness she now had finally vanished. He closed the door, not knowing exactly why he did so, and knew at once by an instinctive feeling that the house he now found himself in with this unknown woman was empty and unoccupied. In a house, however, he felt safe. It was the open streets that were his danger. He stood waiting, listening a moment before he spoke; and he heard the woman moving down the passage from door to door, repeating to herself in her low voice of unhappy wailing some words he could not understand:

"Where is it? Oh, where is it? I must get back..."

O'Reilly then found himself abruptly stricken with dumbness, as though, with these strange words, a haunting terror came up and breathed against him in the darkness.

"Is she after all a figure?" ran in letters of fire across his numbed brain. "Is she unreal—or real?"

Seeking relief in action of some kind he put out a hand automatically, feeling along the wall for an electric switch, and though he found it by some miraculous chance, no answering glow responded to the click.

And the woman's voice from the darkness: "Ah! Ah! At last I've found it. I'm home again—at last...!" He heard a door open and close upstairs. He was on the ground floor now—alone. Complete silence followed.

In the conflict of various emotions—fear for himself lest his panic should return, fear for the woman who had led him into this empty house and now deserted him upon some mysterious errand of her own that made him think of madness—in this conflict that held him a moment spellbound, there was a yet bigger ingredient demanding instant explanation, but an explanation that he could not find. Was the woman real or was she unreal? Was she a human being or a "figure"? The horror of doubt obsessed him with an acute uneasiness that betrayed itself in a return of that unwelcome inner trembling he knew was dangerous.

What saved him from a *crise* that must have had most dangerous results for his mind and nervous system generally, seems to have been the outstanding fact that he felt more for the woman than for himself. His sympathy and pity had been deeply moved; her voice, her beauty, her anguish and bewilderment, all uncommon, inexplicable, mysterious, formed together a claim that drove self into the background. Added to this was the detail that she had left him, gone to another floor without a word, and now, behind a closed door in a room upstairs, found herself face to face at last with the unknown object of her frantic search—with "it," whatever "it" might be. Real or unreal, figure or human being, the overmastering impulse of his being was that he must go to her.

It was this clear impulse that gave him decision and energy to do what he then did. He struck a match, he found a stump of candle, he made his way by means of this flickering light along the passage and up the carpetless stairs. He moved cautiously, stealthily, though not knowing why he did so. The house, he now saw, was indeed untenanted; dust-sheets covered the piled-up furniture; he glimpsed, through doors ajar, pictures screened upon the walls, brackets draped to look like hooded heads. He went on slowly, steadily, moving on tiptoe as though conscious of being watched, noting the well of darkness in the hall below, the grotesque shadows that his movements cast on walls and ceiling. The silence was unpleasant, yet, remembering that the woman was "expecting" someone, he did not wish it broken. He reached the landing and stood still. Closed doors on both sides of a corridor met his sight, as he shaded the candle to examine the scene. Behind which of these doors, he asked himself, was the woman, figure or human being, now alone with "it"?

There was nothing to guide him, but an instinct that he must not delay sent him forward again upon his search. He tried a door on the right—an empty room, with the furniture hidden by dust-sheets, and the mattress rolled up on the bed. He tried a second door, leaving the first one open behind him, and it was, similarly, an empty bedroom. Coming out into the corridor again he stood a moment waiting, then called aloud in a low voice that yet woke echoes unpleasantly in the hall below: "Where are you? I want to help—which room are you in?"

There was no answer; he was almost glad he heard no sound, for he knew quite well that he was waiting really for another sound—the steps of him who was "expected." And the idea of meeting with this unknown third sent a shudder through him, as though related to an interview he dreaded with his whole heart, and must at all costs avoid. Waiting another moment or two, he noted that his candlestump was burning low, then crossed the landing with a feeling, at once of hesitation and determination, towards a door opposite to him. He opened it; he did not halt on the threshold. Holding the candle at arm's length, he went boldly in.

And instantly his nostrils told him he was right at last, for a whiff of the strange perfume, though this time much stronger than before, greeted him, sending a new quiver along his nerves. He knew now why it was associated with unpleasant-ness, with pain, with misery, for he recognized it—the odour of a hospital. In this room a powerful anaesthetic had been used—and recently.

Simultaneously with smell, sight brought its message too. On the large double bed behind the door on his right lay, to his amazement, the woman in the dark fur coat. He saw the jewels on the slender neck; but the eyes he did not see, for they were closed—closed too, he grasped at once, in death. The body lay stretched at full length, quite motionless. He approached. A dark thin streak that came from the parted lips and passed downwards over the chin, losing itself then in the fur collar, was a trickle of blood. It was hardly dry. It glistened.

Strange it was perhaps that, while imaginary fears had the power to paralyse him, mind and body, this sight of something real had the effect of restoring confidence. The sight of blood and death, amid conditions often ghastly and even monstrous, was no new thing to him. He went up quietly, and with steady hand he felt the woman's cheek, the warmth of recent life still in its softness. The final cold had not yet mastered this empty form whose beauty, in its perfect stillness, had taken on the new strange sweetness of an unearthly bloom. Pallid, silent, untenanted, it lay before him, lit by the flicker of his guttering candle. He lifted the fur coat to feel for the unbeating heart. A couple of hours ago at most, he judged, this heart was working busily, the breath came through those parted lips, the eyes were shining in full beauty. His hand encountered a hard knob—the head of a long steel hatpin driven through the heart up to its hilt.

He knew then which was the figure—which was the real and which the unreal. He knew also what had been meant by "it."

But before he could think or reflect what action he must take, before he could straighten himself even from his bent position over the body on the bed, there sounded through the empty house below the loud clang of the front door being closed. And instantly rushed over him that other fear he had so long forgotten—fear for himself. The panic of his own shaken nerves descended with irresistible onslaught. He turned, extinguishing the candle in the violent trembling of his hand, and tore headlong from the room.

The following ten minutes seemed a nightmare in which he was not master of himself and knew not exactly what he did. All he realized was that steps already sounded on the stairs, coming quickly nearer. The flicker of an electric torch played on the banisters, whose shadows ran swiftly sideways along the wall as the hand that held the light ascended. He thought in a frenzied second of police, of his presence in the house, of the murdered woman. It was a sinister combination. Whatever happened, he must escape without being so much as even seen. His heart raced madly. He darted across the landing into the room opposite, whose door he had luckily left open. And by some incredible chance, apparently, he was neither seen nor heard by the man who, a moment later, reached the landing, entered the room where the body of the woman lay, and closed the door carefully behind him.

Shaking, scarcely daring to breathe lest his breath be audible, O'Reilly, in the grip of his own personal terror, remnant of his uncured shock of war, had no thought of what duty might demand or not demand of him. He thought only of himself.

He realized one clear issue—that he must get out of the house without being heard or seen. Who the newcomer was he did not know, beyond an uncanny assurance that it was *not* he whom the woman had "expected," but the murderer himself, and that it was the murderer, in his turn, who was expecting this third person. In that room with death at his elbow, a death he had himself brought about but an hour or two ago, the murderer now hid in waiting for his second victim. And the door was closed.

Yet any minute it might open again, cutting off retreat.

O'Reilly crept out, stole across the landing, reached the head of the stairs, and began, with the utmost caution, the perilous descent. Each time the bare boards creaked beneath his weight, no matter how stealthily this weight was adjusted, his heart missed a beat. He tested each step before he pressed upon it, distributing as much of his weight as he dared upon the banisters. It was a little more than halfway down that, to his horror, his foot caught in a projecting carpet tack; he slipped on the polished wood, and only saved himself from falling headlong by a wild clutch at the railing, making an uproar that seemed to him like the explosion of a hand-grenade in the forgotten trenches. His nerves gave way then, and panic seized him. In the silence that followed the resounding echoes he heard the bedroom door opening on the floor above.

Concealment was now useless. It was impossible, too. He took the last flight of stairs in a series of leaps, four steps at a time, reached the hall, flew across it, and opened the front door, just as his pursuer, electric torch in hand, covered half the stairs behind him. Slamming the door, he plunged headlong into the welcome, all-obscuring fog outside.

The fog had now no terrors for him, he welcomed its concealing mantle; nor did it matter in which direction he ran so long as he put distance between him and the house of death. The pursuer had, of course, not followed him into the street. He crossed open spaces without a tremor. He ran in a circle nevertheless, though without being aware he did so. No people were about, no single groping shadow passed him, no boom of traffic reached his ears, when he paused for breath at length against an area railing. Then for the first time he made the discovery that he had no hat. He remembered now. In examining the body, partly out of respect, partly perhaps unconsciously, he had taken it off and laid it—on the very bed.

It was there, a tell-tale bit of damning evidence, in the house of death. And a series of probable consequences flashed through his mind like lightning. It was a new hat fortunately; more fortunate still, he had not yet written name or initials in it; but the maker's mark was there for all to read, and the police would go immediately to the shop where he had bought it only two days before. Would the shop-people remember his appearance? Would his visit, the date, the conversation be recalled? He thought it was unlikely; he resembled dozens of men; he had no outstanding peculiarity. He tried to think, but his mind was confused and troubled, his heart was beating dreadfully, he felt desperately ill. He sought vainly for some story to account for his being out in the fog and far from home without a hat. No single idea presented itself. He clung to the icy railings, hardly able to keep upright, collapse very near— when suddenly a figure emerged from the fog, paused a moment to stare at him, put out a hand and caught him, and then spoke.

"You're ill, my dear sir," said a man's kindly voice. "Can I be of any assistance? Come, let me help you." He had seen at once that it was not a case of drunkenness. "Come, take my arm, won't you? I'm a physician. Luckily, too, you are just out-side my very house. Come in." And he half dragged, half pushed O'Reilly, now bordering on collapse, up the steps and opened the door with his latchkey.

"Felt ill suddenly—lost in the fog...terrified, but be all right soon, thanks awfully—" the Canadian stammered his grati-tude, already feeling better. He sank into a chair in the hall, while the other put down a paper parcel he had been carrying, and led him presently into a comfortable room; a fire burned brightly; the electric lamps were pleasantly shaded; a decanter of whisky and a siphon stood on a small table beside a big armchair; and before O'Reilly could find another word to say the other had poured him out a glass and bade him sip it slowly, without troubling to talk till he felt better.

"That will revive you. Better drink it slowly. You should never have been out a night like this. If you've far to go, better let me put you up—"

"Very kind, very kind, indeed," mumbled O'Reilly, recovering rapidly in the comfort of a presence he already liked and felt even drawn to.

"No trouble at all," returned the doctor. "I've been at the front, you know. I can see what your trouble is—shell-shock, I'll be bound."

The Canadian, much impressed by the other's quick diagnosis, noted also his tact and kindness. He had made no reference to the absence of a hat, for instance.

"Quite true," he said. "I'm with Dr. Henry, in Harley Street," and he added a few words about his case. The whisky worked its effect, he revived more and more, feeling better every minute. The other handed him a cigarette; they began to talk about his symptoms and recovery; confidence returned in a measure, though he still felt badly frightened. The doctor's manner and personality did much to help, for there was strength and gentleness in the face, though the features showed unusual determination, softened occasionally by a sudden hint as of suffering in the bright, compelling eyes. It was the face, thought O'Reilly, of a man who had seen much and probably been through hell, but of a man who was simple, good, sincere. Yet not a man to trifle with; behind his gentleness lay something very stern. This effect of character and personality woke the other's respect in addition to his gratitude. His sympathy was stirred.

"You encourage me to make another guess," the man was saying, after a successful reading of the impromptu patient's state, "that you have had, namely, a severe shock quite recently, and"—he hesitated for the merest fraction of a second—"that it would be a relief to you," he went on, the skilful suggestion in the voice unnoticed by his companion, "it would be wise as well, if you could unburden yourself to—someone—who would understand." He looked at O'Reilly with a kindly and very pleasant smile. "Am I not right, perhaps?" he asked in his gentle tone.

"Someone who would understand," repeated the Canadian. "That's my trouble exactly. You've hit it. It's all so incredible."

The other smiled. "The more incredible," he suggested, "the greater your need for expression. Suppression, as you may know, is dangerous in cases like this. You think you have hidden it, but it bides its time and comes up later, causing a lot of trouble. Confession, you know—" he emphasized the word— "confession is good for the soul!"

"You're dead right," agreed the other.

"Now, if you can, bring yourself to tell it to someone who will listen and believe—to myself, for instance. I am a doctor, familiar with such things. I shall regard all you say as a professional confidence, of course; and, as we are strangers, my belief or disbelief is of no particular consequence. I may tell you in advance of your story, however—I think I can promise it—that I shall believe all you have to say."

O'Reilly told his story without more ado, for the suggestion of the skilled physician had found easy soil to work in. During the recital his host's eyes never once left his own. He moved no single muscle of his body. His interest seemed intense.

"A bit tall, isn't it?" said the Canadian, when his tale was finished. "And the question is—" he continued with a threat of volubility which the other checked instantly.

"Strange, yes, but incredible, no," the doctor interrupted. "I see no reason to disbelieve a single detail of what you have just told me. Things equally remarkable, equally incredible, happen in all large towns, as I know from personal experience. I could give you instances." He paused a moment, but his companion, staring into his eyes with interest and curiosity, made no comment. "Some years ago, in fact," continued the other, "I knew of a very similar case—strangely similar."

"Really! I should be immensely interested—"

"So similar that it seems almost a coincidence. You may find it hard, in your turn, to credit it." He paused again, while O'Reilly sat forward in his chair to listen. "Yes," pursued the doctor slowly, "I think everyone connected with it is now dead. There is no reason why I should not tell it, for one confidence deserves another, you know. It happened during the Boer War—as long ago as that," he added with emphasis. "It is really a very commonplace story in one way, though very dreadful in another, but a man who has served at the front will understand and—I'm sure—will sympathize."

"I'm sure of that," offered the other readily.

"A colleague of mine, now dead, as I mentioned—a surgeon, with a big practice, married a young and charming girl. They lived happily together for several years. His wealth made her very comfortable. His consulting room, I must tell you, was some distance from his house—just as this might be—so that she was never bothered with any of his cases. Then came the war. Like many others, though much over age, he volunteered. He gave up his lucrative practice and went to South Africa. His income, of course, stopped; the big house was closed; his wife found her life of enjoyment considerably curtailed. This she considered a great hardship, it seems. She felt a bitter grievance against him. Devoid of imagination, without any power of sacrifice, a selfish type, she was yet a beautiful, attractive woman—and young. The inevitable lover came upon the scene to console her. They planned to run away together. He was rich. Japan they thought would suit them. Only, by some ill luck, the husband got wind of it and arrived in London just in the nick of time."

"Well rid of her," put in O'Reilly, "*I* think."

The doctor waited a moment. He sipped a glass. Then his eyes fixed upon his companion's face somewhat sternly.

"Well rid of her, yes," he continued, "only he determined to make that riddance final. He decided to kill her—and her lover. You see, he loved her."

O'Reilly made no comment. In his own country this method with a faithless woman was not unknown. His interest was very concentrated. But he was thinking, too, as he listened, thinking hard.

"He planned the time and place with care," resumed the other in a lower voice, as though he might possibly be overheard. "They met, he knew, in the big house, now closed, the house where he and his young wife had passed such happy years during their prosperity. The plan failed, however, in an important detail—the woman came at the appointed hour, but without her lover. She found death waiting for her—it was a painless death. Then her lover, who was to arrive half an hour later, did not come at all. The door had been left open for him purposely. The house was dark, its rooms shut up, deserted; there was no caretaker even. It was a foggy night—just like this."

"And the other?" asked O'Reilly in a failing voice. "The lover—"

"A man did come in," the doctor went on calmly, "but it was not the lover. It was a stranger."

"A stranger?" the other whispered. "And the surgeon— where was he all the time?"

"Waiting outside to see him enter—concealed in the fog. He saw the man go in. Five minutes later he followed, meaning to complete his vengeance, his act of justice, whatever you like to call it. But the man who had come in was a stranger—he came in by chance—just as you might have done—to shelter from the fog—or—"

O'Reilly, though with a great effort, rose abruptly to his feet. He had an appalling feeling that the man facing him was mad. He had a keen desire to get outside, fog or no fog, to leave this room, to escape from the calm accents of this insistent voice. The effect of the whisky was still in his blood. He felt no lack of confidence. But words came to him with difficulty.

"I think I'd better be pushing off now, doctor," he said clumsily. "But I feel I must thank you very much for all your kindness and help." He turned and looked hard into the keen eyes facing him. "Your friend," he asked in a whisper, "the sur-geon—I hope—I mean, was he ever caught?"

"No," was the grave reply, the doctor standing up in front of him, "he was never caught."

O'Reilly waited a moment before he made another remark. "Well," he said at length, but in a louder tone than before, "I think—I'm glad." He went to the door without shaking hands.

"You have no hat," mentioned the voice behind him. "If

you'll wait a moment I'll get you one of mine. You need not trouble to return it." And the doctor passed him, going into the hall. There was a sound of tearing paper. O'Reilly left the house a moment later with a hat upon his head, but it was not till he reached the Tube station half an hour afterwards that he realized it was his own.

The Cask of *Amontillado*

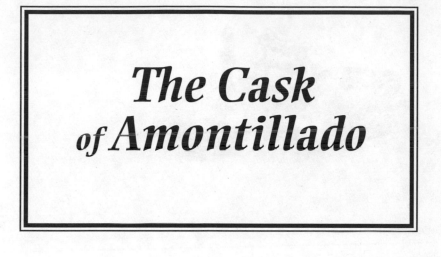

by
 E D G A R   A L L A N   P O E
(1809–1849)

*I cannot conceive of a better way to conclude this collection of
scary stories than in the company of that grand master of the
macabre, Edgar Allan Poe. Everyone who enjoys a good shudder up and down the spine has a favourite Poe story, and this
is mine. To identify more closely with Fortunato, its main
character, you may wish to sip a refreshing glass of amontillado
yourself as you read of the bizarre events occasioned by his
infatuation for that product of sunny Spain. It might also help
to ward off the chill when you enter the catacombs…*

Incidentally (and ironically), the Montresor family motto
Nemo me impune lacessit *translates as "No one provokes
me with impunity," while* In pace requiescat!, *the story's final
words, means "May he rest in peace."*

The thousand injuries of Fortunato I had borne as I best could, but when he ventured upon insult I vowed revenge. You, who so well know the nature of my soul, will not suppose, however, that I gave utterance to a threat. *At length* I would be avenged; this was a point definitely settled—but the very definitiveness with which it was resolved precluded the idea of risk. I must not only punish but punish with impunity. A wrong is unredressed when retribution overtakes its redresser. It is equally unredressed when the avenger fails to make himself felt as such to him who has done the wrong.

It must be understood that neither by word nor deed had I given Fortunato cause to doubt my good will. I continued, as was my wont, to smile in his face, and he did not perceive that my smile *now* was at the thought of his immolation.

He had a weak point—this Fortunato—although in other regards he was a man to be respected and even feared. He prided himself on his connoisseurship in wine. Few Italians have the true virtuoso spirit. For the most part their enthusiasm is adopted to suit the time and opportunity, to practise imposture upon the British and Austrian *millionaires*. In painting and gemmary, Fortunato, like his countrymen, was a quack, but in the matter of old wines he was sincere. In this respect I did not differ from him materially—I was skilful in the Italian vintages myself, and bought largely whenever I could.

It was about dusk, one evening during the supreme madness of the carnival season, that I encountered my friend. He accosted me with excessive warmth, for he had been drinking much. The man wore motley. He had on a tight-fitting partistriped dress, and his head was surmounted by the conical cap and bells. I was so pleased to see him that I thought I should never have done wringing his hand.

I said to him—"My dear Fortunato, you are luckily met. How remarkably well you are looking today. But I have received a pipe of what passes for Amontillado, and I have my doubts."

"How?" said he. "Amontillado? A pipe? Impossible! And in the middle of the carnival!"

"I have my doubts," I replied; "and I was silly enough to pay the full Amontillado price without consulting you in the matter. You were not to be found, and I was fearful of losing a bargain."

"Amontillado!"

"I have my doubts."

"Amontillado!"

"And I must satisfy them."

"Amontillado!"

"As you are engaged, I am on my way to Luchresi. If anyone has a critical turn it is he. He will tell me—"

"Luchresi cannot tell Amontillado from Sherry."

"And yet some fools will have it that his taste is a match for your own."

"Come, let us go."

"Whither?"

"To your vaults."

"My friend, no; I will not impose upon your good nature. I perceive you have an engagement. Luchresi—"

"I have no engagement—come."

"My friend, no. It is not the engagement, but the severe cold with which I perceive you are afflicted. The vaults are insufferably damp. They are encrusted with nitre."

"Let us go, nevertheless. The cold is merely nothing. Amontillado! You have been imposed upon. And as for Luchresi, he cannot distinguish Sherry from Amontillado."

Thus speaking, Fortunato possessed himself of my arm; and putting on a mask of black silk and drawing a *roquelaure* closely about my person, I suffered him to hurry me to my palazzo.

There were no attendants at home; they had absconded to make merry in honour of the time. I had told them that I should not return until the morning, and had given them explicit orders not to stir from the house. These orders were sufficient, I well knew, to insure their immediate disappearance, one and all, as soon as my back was turned.

I took from their sconces two flambeaux, and giving one to Fortunato, bowed him through several suites of rooms to the archway that led into the vaults. I passed down a long and winding staircase, requesting him to be cautious as he followed. We came at length to the foot of the descent, and stood together upon the damp ground of the catacombs of the Montresors.

The gait of my friend was unsteady, and the bells upon his cap jingled as he strode.

"The pipe," he said.

"It is farther on," said I; "but observe the white web-work which gleams from these cavern walls."

He turned towards me, and looked into my eyes with two filmy orbs that distilled the rheum of intoxication.

"Nitre?" he asked, at length.

"Nitre," I replied. "How long have you had that cough?"

"Ugh! ugh! ugh!—ugh! ugh! ugh!—ugh! ugh! ugh!—ugh! ugh! ugh!—ugh! ugh! ugh!"

My poor friend found it impossible to reply for many minutes.

"It is nothing," he said, at last.

"Come," I said, with decision, "we will go back; your health is precious. You are rich, respected, admired, beloved; you are happy, as once I was. You are a man to be missed. For me it is no matter. We will go back; you will be ill, and I cannot be responsible. Besides, there is Luchresi—"

"Enough," he said; "the cough is a mere nothing; it will not kill me. I shall not die of a cough."

"True—true," I replied; "and, indeed, I had no intention of alarming you unnecessarily—but you should use all proper caution. A draught of this Médoc will defend us from the damps."

Here I knocked off the neck of a bottle which I drew from a long row of its fellows that lay upon the mould.

"Drink," I said, presenting him the wine.

He raised it to his lips with a leer. He paused and nodded to me familiarly, while his bells jingled.

"I drink," he said, "to the buried that repose around us."

"And I to your long life."

He again took my arm, and we proceeded.

"These vaults," he said, "are extensive."

"The Montresors," I replied, "were a great and numerous family."

"I forget your arms."

"A huge human foot d'or, in a field azure; the foot crushes a serpent rampant whose fangs are imbedded in the heel."

"And the motto?"

"Nemo me impune lacessit."

"Good!" he said.

The wine sparkled in his eyes and the bells jingled. My own fancy grew warm with the Médoc. We had passed through long walls of piled skeletons, with casks and puncheons intermingling, into the inmost recesses of catacombs. I paused again, and this time I made bold to seize Fortunato by an arm above the elbow.

"The nitre!" I said; "see, it increases. It hangs like moss upon the vaults. We are below the river's bed. The drops of moisture trickle among the bones. Come, we will go back ere it is too late. Your cough—"

"It is nothing," he said; "let us go on. But first, another draught of the Médoc."

I broke and reached him a flagon of De Grâve. He emptied it at a breath. His eyes flashed with a fierce light. He laughed and threw the bottle upwards with a gesticulation I did not understand.

I looked at him in surprise. He repeated the movement—a grotesque one.

"You do not comprehend?" he said.

"Not I," I replied.

"Then you are not of the brotherhood."

"How?"

"You are not of the masons."

"Yes, yes," I said; "yes, yes."

"You? Impossible! A mason?"

"A mason," I replied.

"A sign," he said, "a sign."

"It is this," I answered, producing from beneath the folds of my *roquelaure* a trowel.

"You jest," he exclaimed, recoiling a few paces. "But let us proceed to the Amontillado."

"Be it so," I said, replacing the tool beneath the cloak and again offering my arm. He leaned upon it heavily. We continued our route in search of the Amontillado. We passed through a range of low arches, descended, passed on, and descending again, arrived at a deep crypt, in which the foulness of the air caused our flambeaux rather to glow than flame.

At the most remote end of the crypt there appeared another less spacious. Its walls had been lined with human remains, piled to the vault overhead, in the fashion of the great catacombs of Paris. Three sides of this interior crypt were still ornamented in this manner. From the fourth side the bones had been thrown down, and lay promiscuously upon the earth, forming at one point a mound of some size. Within the wall thus exposed by the displacing of the bones, we perceived a still interior crypt or recess, in depth about four feet, in width three, in height six or seven. It seemed to have been constructed for no especial use within itself, but formed merely the interval between two of the colossal supports of the roof of the catacombs, and was backed by one of their circumscribing walls of solid granite.

It was in vain that Fortunato, uplifting his dull torch, endeavoured to pry into the depth of the recess. Its termination the feeble light did not enable us to see.

"Proceed," I said; "herein is the Amontillado. As for Luchresi—"

"He is an ignoramus," interrupted my friend, as he stepped unsteadily forward, while I followed immediately at his heels. In an instant he had reached the extremity of the niche, and finding his progress arrested by the rock, stood stupidly bewildered. A moment more and I had fettered him to the granite. In its surface were two iron staples, distant from each other about two feet, horizontally. From one of these depended a short chain, from the other a padlock. Throwing the links about his waist, it was but the work of a few seconds to secure it. He was too much astounded to resist. Withdrawing the key I stepped back from the recess.

"Pass your hand," I said, "over the wall; you cannot help feeling the nitre. Indeed, it is *very* damp. Once more let me *implore* you to return. No? Then I must positively leave you. But I must first render you all the little attentions in my power."

"The Amontillado!" ejaculated my friend, not yet recovered from his astonishment.

"True," I replied; "the Amontillado."

As I said these words I busied myself among the pile of bones of which I have before spoken. Throwing them aside, I soon uncovered a quantity of building stone and mortar. With these materials and with the aid of my trowel, I began vigorously to wall up the entrance of the niche.

I had scarcely laid the first tier of the masonry when I discovered that the intoxication of Fortunato had in a great measure worn off. The earliest indication I had of this was a low moaning cry from the depth of the recess. It was *not* the cry of a drunken man. There was then a long and obstinate silence. I laid the second tier, and the third, and the fourth; and then I heard the furious vibrations of the chain. The noise lasted for several minutes, during which, that I might hearken to it with the more satisfaction, I ceased my labours and sat down upon the bones. When at last the clanking subsided, I resumed the trowel, and finished without interruption the fifth, the sixth, and the seventh tier. The wall was now nearly upon a level with my breast. I again paused, and holding the flambeaux over the mason-work, threw a few feeble rays upon the figure within.

A succession of loud and shrill screams, bursting suddenly from the throat of the chained form, seemed to thrust me violently back. For a brief moment I hesitated, I trembled. Unsheathing my rapier, I began to grope with it about the recess; but the thought of an instant reassured me. I placed my hand upon the solid fabric of the catacombs, and felt satisfied. I reapproached the wall; I replied to the yells of him who clamoured. I re-echoed, I aided, I surpassed them in volume and in strength. I did this, and the clamourer grew still.

It was now midnight, and my task was drawing to a close. I had completed the eighth, the ninth, and the tenth tier. I had finished a portion of the last and the eleventh; there remained but a single stone to be fitted and plastered in. I struggled with its weight; I placed it partially in its destined position. But now there came from out the niche a low laugh that erected the hairs upon my head. It was succeeded by a sad voice, which I had difficulty in recognizing as that of the noble Fortunato. The voice said—

"Ha! ha! ha!—he! he! he!—a very good joke, indeed—an excellent jest. We shall have many a rich laugh about it at the palazzo—he! he! he!—over our wine—he! he! he!"

"The Amontillado!" I said.

"He! he! he!—he! he! he!—yes, the Amontillado. But is it not getting late? Will not they be awaiting us at the palazzo, the Lady Fortunato and the rest? Let us be gone."

"Yes," I said, "for the love of God!"

"*For the love of God, Montresor!*"

"Yes," I said, "for the love of God!"

But to these words I hearkened in vain for a reply. I grew impatient. I called aloud—

"Fortunato!"

No answer. I called again—

"Fortunato!"

No answer still. I thrust a torch through the remaining aperture and let it fall within. There came forth in return only a jingling of the bells. My heart grew sick; it was the dampness of the catacombs that made it so. I hastened to make an end of my labour. I forced the last stone into its position; I plastered it up. Against the new masonry I re-erected the old rampart of bones. For the half of a century no mortal has disturbed them. *In pace requiescat!*

COPYRIGHT ACKNOWLEDGMENTS

Conrad Aiken. "Silent Snow, Secret Snow" from *The Collected Short Stories of Conrad Aiken*, copyright © 1960 by Conrad Aiken. All rights reserved. Reprinted by permission of Brandt & Brandt Literary Agents, Inc.

Algernon Blackwood. "Confession" from *The Wolves of God and Other Fey Stories* by Algernon Blackwood and Wilfred Wilson. Copyright © 1921 by E.P. Dutton, renewed. Used by permission of Dutton Signet, a division of Penguin Books USA Inc.

Roald Dahl. "Man from the South" from *Someone Like You* by Roald Dahl (Alfred A. Knopf, 1948), copyright © Roald Dahl, 1948. Reprinted by permission of the Estate of Roald Dahl and the Watkins/Loomis Agency.

Walter de la Mare. "Fear" and "Which?" from *The Complete Poems of Walter de la Mare* (Faber & Faber, 1969). Reprinted by permission of the Literary Trustees of Walter de la Mare, and The Society of Authors as their representative.

Daphne du Maurier. "Kiss Me Again, Stranger" from *The Apple Tree*. Reproduced with permission of Curtis Brown Ltd., London, on behalf of the Estate of Daphne du Maurier. Copyright © Daphne du Maurier, 1952.

William Faulkner. "A Rose for Emily" from *Collected Stories of William Faulkner* by William Faulkner. Copyright © 1930 and renewed 1958 by William Faulkner. Reprinted by permission of Random House, Inc.

"The Fork in the Graveyard" from *Ghost Stories and Legends of Prince Edward Island* by Julie V. Watson (Hounslow Press, 1988), copyright © 1988 by Julie V. Watson.

Dorothy K. Haynes. "Thou Shalt Not Suffer a Witch" from *Thou Shalt Not Suffer a Witch and Other Stories* by Dorothy K. Haynes (Methuen, 1949), copyright © Dorothy K. Haynes, 1949.

Patricia Highsmith. "The Snail-Watcher" from *Eleven*, copyright © 1993 by Diogenes Verlag AG Zurich.

L.M. Montgomery. "The Girl at the Gate" from *Among the Shadows* by L.M. Montgomery. Used by permission of the Canadian Publishers, McClelland & Stewart, Toronto.

Anne Rice. "The Master of Rampling Gate." Copyright © 1983 by Anne O'Brien Rice. Originally published in *Redbook*. Reprinted by permission of the author.

Duncan Campbell Scott. "The Pedler" from *In the Village of Viger and Other Stories* by Duncan Campbell Scott (McClelland & Stewart, 1973). The work of Duncan Campbell Scott is published with the permission of John G. Aylen, Ottawa, Canada.

Emile Zola. "Angeline, or the Haunted House," translated by Clive Smith, from *The Penguin Book of Ghost Stories* edited by J.A. Cuddon (Penguin Books, 1984).

Every effort has been made to contact or trace all copyright holders. The publisher will be glad to make good in future editions any errors or omissions brought to our attention.